# IMPERIUM
# RESTORED

## ALSO BY WALTER JON WILLIAMS

**THE SECOND BOOKS OF THE PRAXIS**

*The Accidental War*
*Fleet Elements*

**THE FIRST BOOKS OF THE PRAXIS: DREAD EMPIRE'S FALL**

*The Praxis*
*The Sundering*
*Conventions of War*
*Investments*
*Impersonations*

**NOVELS**

*Hardwired*
*Knight Moves*
*Voice of the Whirlwind*
*Days of Atonement*
*Aristoi*
*Metropolitan*
*City on Fire*
*Ambassador of Progress*
*Angel Station*
*The Rift*
*Implied Spaces*

**QUILLIFER**

*Quillifer*
*Quillifer the Knight*
*Lord Quillifer*

**MAIJSTRAL**

*The Crown Jewels*
*House of Shards*
*Rock of Ages*

**DAGMAR SHAW THRILLERS**

*This Is Not a Game*
*Deep State*
*The Fourth Wall*
*Diamonds from Tequila*

**HISTORICAL FICTION**

*To Glory Arise*
*Brig of War*
*The Macedonian*
*The Tern Schooner*
*Cat Island*

**COLLECTIONS**

*Facets*
*Frankensteins and Foreign Devils*
*The Green Leopard Plague and Other Stories*
*The Best of Walter Jon Williams*

# IMPERIUM
# RESTORED

## A NOVEL OF THE PRAXIS

## WALTER JON
## WILLIAMS

HARPER Voyager
*An Imprint of HarperCollins Publishers*

IMPERIUM RESTORED. Copyright © 2022 by Walter Jon Williams. All rights reserved. Printed in the United States of America. No part of this book may be used or reproduced in any manner whatsoever without written permission except in the case of brief quotations embodied in critical articles and reviews. For information, address HarperCollins Publishers, 195 Broadway, New York, NY 10007.

HarperCollins books may be purchased for educational, business, or sales promotional use. For information, please email the Special Markets Department at SPsales@harpercollins.com.

Harper Voyager and design are trademarks of HarperCollins Publishers LLC.

FIRST EDITION

Designed by Paula Russell Szafranski

Library of Congress Cataloging-in-Publication Data has been applied for.

ISBN 978-0-06-246705-8

22 23 24 25 26   LSC   10 9 8 7 6 5 4 3 2 1

*For KATHY HEDGES*

*With thanks to Dr. Michael Wester*

*for guiding me through the convex hull*

*of a chaotic dynamical system*

# DRAMATIS PERSONAE

**MARTINEZ FAMILY AND DEPENDENTS**

**MARCUS, LORD MARTINEZ:** Terran, patriarch of Clan Martinez, patron to Laredo, Chee, and Parkhurst.

**LADY MARTINEZ:** Terran, wife to Lord Martinez.

**LORD ROLAND MARTINEZ:** Terran, Lord Martinez's eldest son and heir. Convocate.

**GIRASOLE MARTINEZ:** Terran, Roland's daughter.

**FLEET COMMANDER LORD GARETH MARTINEZ:** Terran, second son of Lord Martinez, awarded the Golden Orb for conduct during the Naxid War.

**LADY TERZA CHEN:** Terran, daughter and heir of Lord Chen, wife of Gareth Martinez.

**GARETH THE YOUNGER ("CHAI-CHAI"):** Terran, son of Gareth Martinez and Terza Chen.

**YALING ("MEI-MEI"):** Terran, daughter of Gareth Martinez and Terza Chen.

**LADY VIPSANIA MARTINEZ:** Terran, daughter of Lord and Lady Martinez, married to Lord Convocate Oda Yoshitoshi and head of Imperial Broadcasting.

**LADY WALPURGA MARTINEZ:** Terran, daughter of Lord and Lady Martinez, widow of PJ Ngeni.

**LADY SEMPRONIA MARTINEZ:** Terran, daughter of Lord and Lady Martinez, estranged from her family. Married to Nikkul Shankaracharya.

**LIEUTENANT LALITA BANERJEE:** Terran female, signals officer on *Los Angeles*.

**AITOR SANTANA:** Terran male, signals officer on *Los Angeles*.

**WEAPONER FIRST CLASS AGUSTIN MPANZA:** Terran male, orderly to Gareth Martinez.

---

## LADY SULA, HER DEPENDENTS AND ASSOCIATES

**SENIOR CAPTAIN CAROLINE, LADY SULA:** Terran, head of Clan Sula, Fleet officer and former head of the Secret Army. Former leader of Action Team 491.

**MASTER CONSTABLE GAVIN MACNAMARA:** Terran, detailed as orderly to Lady Sula, former member of the Secret Army and Action Team 491.

**MASTER ENGINEER SHAWNA SPENCE:** Terran, detailed as orderly to Lady Sula, former member of the Secret Army and Action Team 491.

**MING LIN:** Terran, veteran of the Secret Army, graduate in economics, and Sula's economic adviser.

**DR. SERDAR GUNAYDIN:** Terran male, physician assigned to *Splendid*.

**RICCI (MALE) AND VISWAN (FEMALE):** Sula's signals lieutenants.

---

## THE FLEET

**FLEET COMMANDER LORD PA DO-FAQ:** Lai-own male, commander of the Third Fleet at Felarus, Gareth Martinez's former commander.

**SENIOR FLEET COMMANDER LADY MICHI CHEN:** Terran female, commanding Fourth Fleet at Harzapid. Sister of Lord Chen, aunt to Terza Chen, and Gareth Martinez's commander.

**SANDRA YUEN:** Terran female, one of Michi Chen's aides.

**SENIOR SQUADRON COMMANDER NGUYEN:** Terran, commanding a squadron under Do-faq at Felarus.

**CAPTAIN LORD JEREMY FOOTE:** Terran, commanding light cruiser *Vigilant* and Light Squadron Eight. Veteran of the Naxid War, the First and Second Battles of Magaria, and racing pilot for the Apogee Club.

**LIEUTENANT-CAPTAIN LORD NAAZ VIJANA:** Terran, hero of the Yormak rebellion.

**CAPTAIN LADY ELISSA DALKEITH:** Terran, commanding cruiser *Bombardment of Los Angeles.*

**LIEUTENANT-CAPTAIN ARI ABACHA:** Terran, a friend of Gareth Martinez, and a sporting enthusiast.

**SQUADRON COMMANDER LORD HARVEY CONYNGHAM:** Terran male, commanding battleship *Perfection of the Praxis.*

**LIEUTENANT-CAPTAIN LADY ALANA HAZ:** Terran, former premiere lieutenant on Sula's frigate *Confidence.*

**CAPTAIN LADY CHANDRA PRASAD:** Terran, formerly of Martinez's cruiser *Illustrious.*

**LORD NISHKAD:** Naxid male, senior squadron commander (retired), now businessman on Harzapid.

**CAPTAIN HUI:** Terran female, captain of *Staunch.*

**JUNIOR SQUADRON LEADER KHALIL:** Terran male, commands Heavy Squadron Twenty in the Fourth Fleet.

**FLEET COMMANDER WEI JIAN:** Terran female, commanding defectors from the Second Fleet.

**CAPTAIN YOSHIDA:** Wei Jian's tactical officer.

**LIEUTENANT-CAPTAINS PAIVO AND RANSSU KANGAS:** Terran males, twin sons of the late Fleet Commander Eino Kangas.

**LIEUTENANT-CAPTAIN VONDERHEYDTE:** Terran male, formerly of Martinez's command *Corona.*

**SENIOR CAPTAIN SIZO MAZANKOSI:** Terran female, captain of cruiser *Splendid.*

**LIEUTENANT-CAPTAIN LEPP:** Terran male, captain of frigate *Mentor.*

**LIEUTENANT BENEDICTA KELLY:** Terran female, champion yachtswoman with the Corona Club.

**MARIVIC MANGAHAS:** Terran female, Martinez's chef.

**LADY XIA GAO:** Terran female, second officer on cruiser *Defense*.

**SENIOR SQUADRON COMMANDER RIVVEN:** Daimong male, defector to the Restoration.

**SENIOR CAPTAIN LORD BATUR KHAN-NIYAZ:** Terran male, commanding the Fleet dockyard and ring station on Terra.

**SQUADRON LEADER AN-DAR:** Lai-own male, defector to the Restoration.

**SQUADRON COMMANDER DRAYMESH:** Daimong male, commands Light Squadron Twenty-Two under Do-faq.

**SQUADRON COMMANDER FARHANG:** Terran male, one of Wei Jian's officers.

**CAPTAIN DEVINDAR SURI:** Terran male, civilian commanding *Parkhurst*.

**LIEUTENANT-CAPTAIN BHATTI:** Terran male serving with the Constabulary.

**ELECTRICIAN SECOND CLASS RAJU:** Terran female, on crew of *Los Angeles*.

**WARRANT OFFICER SECOND CLASS FILOMENA JUSKIENE:** Terran female, on crew of *Los Angeles*.

**CONSTABLE FIRST CLASS HADAD:** Terran male, heading police on *Los Angeles*.

**MASTER ELECTRICIAN PARK:** Terran male, head of electrics department on *Los Angeles*.

**RIGGER FIRST CLASS JAPUTRA BLISS:** Terran female, on crew of *Splendid*.

**MASTER ENGINEER TODD BLISS:** Terran male, semi-estranged husband of Japutra Bliss.

**LORD ETHGRO TRIBE:** Daimong, lieutenant-captain on staff at the Commandery.

**KAVASIA:** Terran male, elderly lieutenant brought out of retirement.

## EXPLORATION SERVICE

**SQUADRON COMMANDER (FIRST GRADE) SHUSHANIK SEVERIN ("NIKKI"):** Terran, captain of *Expedition* and puppeteer.

**LIEUTENANT LORD CHUNGSUN CLEGHORNE:** Terran, premiere lieutenant of *Expedition*.

**LIEUTENANT CRESSIDA TOUPAL:** Terran, second lieutenant of *Expedition*.

**PILOT FIRST CLASS LIU:** Terran, on crew of *Expedition*.

**WARRANT OFFICER FALYAZ:** Terran, on crew off *Expedition*.

## PEERS

**MAURICE, LORD CHEN:** Terran. A convocate, member of the Fleet Control Board, and father-in-law of Gareth Martinez.

**LORD SAÏD:** Terran male, head of Clan Saïd, deposed Lord Senior of the Convocation.

**LORD MEHRANG:** Terran, patron to Esley, home planet of the Yormaks.

**LADY KORIDUN:** Torminel, the young head of the Koridun clan.

**LADY DISTCHIN:** Torminel, absentee patron to Spannan.

**LADY GRUUM:** Daimong, former patron to the newly settled world Rol-mar, now Lady Senior of the Convocation.

**LADY TU-HON:** Lai-own, head of the Fleet Control Board in the Zanshaa government.

**LORD MINNO:** Cree, a banker, heading the Treasury.

**LORD ODA YOSHITOSHI:** Terran, heir to Yoshitoshi clan and husband of Vipsania Martinez.

**LORD DURWARD LI:** Terran, former client of the Sulas, now client of the Chens.

**LADY AMITA:** Terran, Lord Durward's first wife.

**LADY MARIETTA LI:** Terran, Lord Durward's second wife, a runaway.

**LORD NGENI:** Terran, member of the Convocation, former patron to the Martinez clan.

**LORD PIERRE NGENI:** Terran, Lord Ngeni's son, member of the Convocation.

**LADY CASSILDA ZYKOV:** Terran, former wife of Roland Martinez and mother of Girasole.

**LORD ZYKOV:** Terran, Lady Cassilda's father.

**LORD ELDEY:** Torminel, a convocate and former governor of Zanshaa.

**LORD HOTTASH:** Torminel male, a convocate.

**LORD TROOM LAMONG:** Daimong, Minister of Right-Mindedness.

**PAR-KAI:** Lai-own female, chair of the Protocol Committee in the Convocation.

## CLIQUEMEN

**NAVEEN PATEL:** Terran male, a member of the Commission.

**JULIEN BAKSHI:** Terran male, a member of the Commission.

**SAGAS:** male Daimong, a member of the Commission.

## LINKBOYS

**HECTOR BRAGA ("LAMEY"):** Terran, sometime gangster from Spannan, lately a lobbyist.

**GREDEL ("EARTHGIRL"):** Terran, a street girl from Spannan.

## OTHERS

**CHESKO:** Daimong, clothes designer in Petty Mount.

**LET-KWAI:** Torminel male, a doorman.

**SIMONE BECKWITH:** Terran female, owner of Stellar Properties on Zanshaa.

**PRINCIPAL THEEL:** Daimong, principal of the Zanshaa College of Economics, a semiautonomous division of Zanshaa University.

# IMPERIUM RESTORED

# CHAPTER 1

The woman called Caroline Sula knelt on the floor, a scrub brush held in both hands as she methodically erased every last trace of blood. The fumes of the cleaning fluid stung her nostrils. She'd scrubbed with a standard household cleaner the previous night, but in the hours since she'd done some research and acquired a liquid that would destroy human DNA. When she was done, there would be no evidence that Lamey had ever been in her Celestial Court apartment.

She'd searched through Fleet stores and found a mirrored pier glass to replace the one into which she'd put two bullets, plus a new carpet that would substitute for that in which she and Gareth Martinez had wrapped Lamey's body. The replacements now waited outside on a motorized cart.

Sula let go of the scrub brush and leaned back to view the floor. The floorboards were compressed dedger fiber sculpted to look like expensive wooden planks of pale gold, and their grain could easily hold trace evidence invisible to the naked eye. She leaned left and right to view the floor from different angles, to make sure she'd covered every bit of it with undiluted cleaning fluid.

As she examined the floor, she reached blindly behind her for the crystal wine goblet she knew was there. She found it, raised it to her lips, and drained it.

Aside from a few experiments as a teenager, Sula had always been a nondrinker. There had been alcoholics in her life when she was young and she wanted very much never to be like them, and the easiest way to do that was not to drink.

But now she was finishing her second bottle since the previous evening and finding that alcohol helped to soften the knowledge that with those two bullets she'd fired into her ex-lover, she'd wrecked her every happiness and every hope. Not because she'd killed Lamey, who after all had threatened and assaulted her, but because she'd done it practically in front of Gareth Martinez, who had walked into her apartment while the pistol was still hot in her hand and the blood pooled beneath Lamey's body.

The fact that he had helped her roll the body in a carpet and hide it in a Fleet storage facility, and given her advice on disposing the evidence, didn't change that he then left, presumably forever.

Despair's talons, blunted slightly by alcohol, clawed at her heart. If only she had managed to assemble an explanation of what had happened . . . but her imagination had failed her, and the truth had seemed unconvincing even to Sula.

*I did it for you.*

While accurate, the claim didn't sound credible.

Sula put the wine down, scrubbed a few places she'd missed, then rose with the brush in her hand and walked toward the dining room. She paused by the dining table, set for two, with the scattered remains of the supper she had planned to share with Martinez. She'd been picking at the food all night as she'd paced and ground her teeth and replayed the evening in her mind, bullet by bullet, drop by bloody drop. *You think Terza won't fight you?* Lamey had snarled. *And when Terza calls her husband to heel, what happens to Earthgirl's dreams then?*

The threat of Terza Chen had been enough to bring Sula's pistol out of its holster.

And Earthgirl's dreams had died anyway.

SULA REPLACED THE carpet and the mirror, then took the old pier glass to a disposal center and left it there. To prevent anyone from wondering why there were two bullet-sized holes in the glass, Sula smashed the mirror with the butt of her gun and left crystal shards strewn across the container floor.

Then she went back to Celestial Court and took a long shower, after which Sula put on her undress uniform and only then noticed that her sleeve display was quietly alerting her to the fact that a message awaited her.

FROM THE OFFICE OF FLEET COMMANDER MARTINEZ.

Well, here it was. She felt an invisible hand close on her throat, and the hand that triggered the display trembled.

The message was in text, and was sent by Lalita Banerjee, one of Martinez's signals techs. Sula read the orders saying that she had been appointed commander of Division Nine of the Fourth Fleet.

"Ah. Hah," she said.

Yesterday there hadn't been a Division Nine. Martinez had wanted her off his ship so badly that he'd created a unit just for her, and done it overnight.

Further investigation showed that Division Nine wasn't much. *Splendid* was an elderly heavy cruiser, though rebuilt in the Naxid

War, and *Mentor* was a fine modern frigate. But the rest of the division was a bewildering and heterogeneous array of civilian vessels, from launches to transports to huge immigration ships. Apparently, Martinez was handing her every stray vessel in the Zarafan system that could be crewed by Terrans.

Once she reread her orders it all made sense. Sula was to take her division in the direction of Laredo, where she would somewhere encounter six light cruisers built by Lord Martinez in his own Laredo dockyard. The cruisers would be crewed by a skeleton force, for Laredo had no facilities for training Fleet personnel and no corps of instructors to do it.

Training would be Sula's job. Since the Fourth Fleet's arrival at Zarafan, thousands of enthusiastic Terran volunteers had offered their services as recruits. About 40 percent were retired veterans of the Fleet, or had at least served a hitch or two; but most had no experience whatever in the military, and had served mainly as a raucous, unruly annoyance while Martinez and his staff tried to round up enough instructors to teach the untrained volunteers their duties.

It would be Sula's task to take the instructors and the recruits with her, and on the way to train them to crew the six light cruisers being sent out from Zanshaa.

The task was, she surmised, impossible—but then it hardly mattered, because the war had already been won at the Second Battle of Shulduc, and Gareth Martinez would, within days, lead the Fourth Fleet to the capital of Zanshaa and the imposition of peace. Sula and her Division Nine would arrive months later, after the celebrations were over and the important decisions had already been made.

But then she really didn't care about that. Let Martinez have the glory. Her war was already lost.

Sula sat at the dining table and looked through her instructions again while she nibbled at a piece of stale bread left on the table overnight. Then she called Shawna Spence on her sleeve display.

"My lady?" Spence answered. She was a straw-haired, pug-nosed engineer a few years older than Sula, and she had been detailed as one of Sula's orderlies since the Naxid War. Spence had played a vital role in the Zanshaa underground and had established a bomb factory that over time had rocked Zanshaa to its foundations.

"I've been appointed to command Division Nine," Sula said. "I'll need you and Macnamara to clean out my quarters on *Los Angeles* and take off all my personal supplies. Make sure to include the chef's pantry."

Spence mastered her surprise—she knew about Sula's relationship with Martinez, and—like Sula, like the whole Fleet—had probably expected that Sula would remain aboard *Bombardment of Los Angeles* as Martinez's tactical officer, and lover, for the rest of the war.

"Yes, my lady," she said. "Where will we be taking your supplies? What ship?"

"I'm not sure yet," Sula said. "I'll be inspecting the ships later today and choose one for my flag. Take the supplies to your quarters, or to mine, until I can give you more information."

"Yes, my lady." Spence hesitated. "My lady, have you heard the news? About the Third Fleet?"

A cold warning finger touched Sula's spine. "No," she said. "What—"

"Do-faq has arrived in the Zanshaa system with the Third Fleet. Apparently, he found some way to kill Nguyen and all his men."

Shock passed through Sula's nerves like the pressure wave of an explosion. When the Accidental War started, Terran ships throughout the empire had abandoned their posts and fled to Harzapid, where Squadron Commander Michi Chen had managed to seize the entire Fourth Fleet and provide a haven for what became the Restoration.

The only Terran ships unable to escape to Harzapid were based at Felarus, home of the Third Fleet. Any route to Harzapid would pass through Zanshaa or Magaria, both of which remained in the hands of enemy forces large enough to annihilate the Terrans. Accordingly Senior Squadron Commander Nguyen had barricaded himself and his crews in their ships and announced that any vessel departing Felarus would be fired on. The result had been a stalemate, with Nguyen badly outnumbered but still in a position to obliterate most of the Third Fleet in vicious point-blank combat with antimatter weapons.

The understanding that Nguyen had paralyzed the Third Fleet had been so widely accepted that no one in the Restoration had thought to question it. But it now appeared that the Third Fleet had managed to break free of Nguyen's blockade and fly to the rescue of the Zanshaa regime. Not counting the Terran ships, the Third Fleet had at least 150 warships, twice the number in Martinez's command.

To make things worse, the Third Fleet was under Fleet Commander Do-faq, a Lai-own who had proved a successful, imaginative leader in the Naxid War, and the opposite of the rigid, hidebound commanders the Zanshaa regime had employed thus far. Do-faq would not be a pushover.

Suddenly, in Sula's revised calculation, those six ships from Laredo began to assume a much greater importance.

She tried to focus her attention on the problem of how to accomplish Division Nine's mission, but her sleepless night got in her way, and she decided the only way to deal with the issue was to visit her command in person.

Which meant a change of uniform, plus a car, a driver, and the Golden Orb.

NORMALLY ONE OF Sula's staff would drive her where she needed to go, but they were busy collecting Sula's belongings from *Los Angeles*, and it would be undignified for a division commander to drive herself, or to use a self-driving vehicle, so Sula was obliged to request a car and driver from the pool.

The driver, a lanky youth with deep brown skin and the traditional round flat cap of the chauffeur, braced to the salute as Sula marched from the sprawling complex that was the Residence of the Lord Commander of the Dockyard. That august personage would be Martinez, who might, Sula thought, be watching from his office window as Sula stepped into view. Not wishing to give Martinez or any other observer a hint of the turmoil that whirled through her mind, she kept her back straight and her chin high as she approached the ovoid automobile, told the driver to stand at ease, and took the back seat.

"Take me to the *Splendid*," she said. The driver had to consult a guide to find where the ship was berthed, and then the car pulled away on its silent electric motors, made a U-turn, and left the Fleet dockyard altogether.

Zarafan had never held a large Fleet base like those of Zanshaa or Harzapid, and so half of the seventy-five warships of the Fourth Fleet were berthed away from the Fleet docks, in civilian areas. *Splendid* was moored nose-in to Zarafan's antimatter-generation ring, amid banners urging workers to *Prioritize Safety!* and *Work for Ultimate Victory!* It was time for the midday meal, and the open spaces were full of dockyard workers, veteran Fleet crouchbacks, and half-disciplined new recruits heading for nearby canteens or gathering in groups to share food brought from home.

The personnel tube leading to *Splendid* was guarded by a pair of constables in their red belts and armbands, and these stared at Sula as she stepped from the car. With her pale gold hair, ivory skin, emerald eyes, and fearsome reputation, she was one of the most recognizable people in the empire, and her very appearance seemed to have tripped several circuits in the constables' heads, so they were a bit tardy in bracing to the salute.

"At ease," she told them as she walked into the docking tube.

The tube was lit by bright white spots every three or four paces along, and the air had a disinfectant tang. She reached for the safety rail as her feet seemed to stumble, and a lance of pain pierced her head. Sula paused, half-raised a hand to her forehead, and then the pain throbbed and faded slightly, like a dangerous character vanishing into an alley, one who might reappear at any instant.

*Was this a hangover?* she wondered. Up till now, her experience of hangovers consisted of feeling superior while other people suffered.

Walking cautiously, she stepped into a small wedge-shaped room in the nose of the ship and encountered another military constable and a cadet, who took one look at her and snapped to a trembling salute, chin lifted to bare her throat to any reprimand Sula might care to inflict with her curved ceremonial knife.

Sula had left her ceremonial throat-cutter back at Celestial Court, but she had armed herself with the empire's highest decoration, the Golden Orb. This was a golden baton topped with a transparent sphere filled with golden liquids of varying densities and shades, colors that swirled inside the sphere like the clouds of a gas giant. Anyone serving in the Fleet or the civil service was obliged to salute the Orb on sight, which meant that in any large crowd there were always people leaping up, like falling dominoes in reverse, to freeze in an attitude of rigid respect until released, either by the holder of the Orb or by a merciful death.

It was best, she'd decided, to make a powerful first impression.

"Stand easy," Sula said. "Where is Captain Mazankosi?"

The cadet's first reply stammered to a halt before it quite started, and she cleared her throat and began again. "The captain is on the surface of the planet, my lady. Visiting friends."

"And the premiere?"

"He's at a meeting at the Office of the Fleet Surgeon, Lady Fleetcom."

"Trying to get a proper doctor for the ship?"

"Yes, Lady Fleetcom. We have only a Pharmacist Second Class at present."

Sula reckoned she ought to be able to find a doctor for *Splendid*, but she'd save that task for later.

"Who is the senior officer aboard?" she asked.

In the end she was given a tour of the ship by the third officer, a warrant officer/first that had been promoted to lieutenant due to the general shortage of trained, competent personnel. Sula knew that *Splendid* had fought well enough at First and Second Shulduc to have survived the deadliest battle in the history of the empire, and so she didn't anticipate finding much wrong. Too, she hadn't heard any complaints about Captain Mazankosi, or any of the other officers, but that didn't mean there weren't things to complain about.

It was immediately apparent that *Splendid* wasn't a taut ship, or at any rate it wasn't taut at present. After Second Shulduc, a triumphant conclusion to the war had been assumed by all and

disciplinary standards had been somewhat relaxed. Before the battle the crouchbacks had been confined to their ships for months,
undergoing constant drills and often enduring high accelerations
for days at a time. The feeling was that the exhausted crews deserved a little rest, a little celebration.

Sula had herself relaxed and celebrated and fallen into bed
with the man who had been her obsession for ten long years. And
for the two months she'd been with Martinez she'd been happy,
an emotion sufficiently unfamiliar to become the subject of suspicion.

She had been right to be suspicious.

The old ship, she found, had in the recent past received a respectful upgrade. Captain Mazankosi—or whoever commanded
prior to Mazankosi—had been fond of light woods accented with
red chesz-wood molding, which gave the ship a bright, varnished
appearance that served as a welcome contrast to the dark panels
and brass fixtures more common in the Fleet. Custom-woven carpets muffled the crew's clomping steps. Sula had to hope it was all
fireproofed as per regulations.

She found the flag officer's quarters being used as storage for
fresh fruits and vegetables, but Sula didn't hold it against whoever
had stacked it there.

Pain throbbed behind Sula's right eye. "Have all this stuff
cleared out," she told the third lieutenant, "and make it suitable for
me by the end of the day. I'll also bring two orderlies, a chef, and
two signals techs, so you'll have to find lodging for them. For now,
take me to Command. I have to send a message."

Command was under the authority of another cadet, this one
looking no more than sixteen. Watching everyone in the room
struggling out of their acceleration cages in order to brace at the

salute had its comic aspect, but Sula took pity on them before they got entirely to their feet and sent them back to their couches.

"Who's on signals?" she asked.

"Here, Lady Fleetcom."

Sula stepped to the shoulder of the warrant officer crewing the signals station. "Send to Captain Mazankosi: '*Splendid* now appointed flagship of newly formed Division Nine. If you don't hurry to the ring, you may miss her departure. Signed, Sula, flag officer, Division Nine.'"

The warrant officer's eyebrow lifted as he sent the message. *Get used to it*, Sula thought. She didn't know if Mazankosi had acquired permission to visit her friends on the surface, but she knew damned well that the captain of a warship shouldn't be so distant from her command, not during a war as perilous as this one.

She contacted Spence, Macnamara, and the others of her staff, and told them to report aboard *Splendid* by the end of the day and to bring all their gear as well as her own. She then sought out the pharmacist second class and got an analgesic for her headache, which she drank with a tall glass of water.

Her headache ebbed as her driver took her back to the Fleet dockyard for a visit to the frigate *Mentor*. She closed her eyes, saw Lamey lying dead in her Celestial Court apartment. The look of horror on Martinez's face as a bouquet of white lu-doi blossoms fell from his hand. Felt the awkward weight of the body as it was rolled in the carpet.

Felt the gaping hole in her chest where her heart had been.

"We've arrived, my lady," the driver said.

Lieutenant-Captain Lepp was aboard *Mentor* and guided her on a brief inspection tour, and it was immediately apparent that the frigate was happy under its captain. The ship and its crew had a buoyant air that spoke of confidence in themselves, their officers, and their ship. The ship had become the center of their world, their home, and they would not hesitate to fight for the ship and one another.

*Mentor* had been part of the Home Fleet before defecting to the Restoration under Senior Squadron Commander Kung, and had survived the deadly battle of Second Shulduc that had killed Kung and so many of his crews. The battle had been bitter seasoning, but the pulpies had come through it very well.

"I suspect we'll be leaving station as soon as practicable," Lepp said. He was a glossy young man with a crooked smile and artfully waved dark hair, and he carried himself with a relaxed sort of assurance designed to set everyone around him at their ease.

"Yes," Sula said. "If *Mentor* needs anything prior to departure, make sure you send parties to get it."

"We've had practice," Lepp said. "When we were here with Squadcom Kung, we looted Zarafan's ring of everything useful before we left."

Sula looked at him with interest. "Division Nine has some very large ships with very large cargo holds," she said. "I think you should consult with their officers to organize some plundering."

"Those ships are full of young recruits with nothing to do." Lepp smiled. "They'd probably enjoy a stretch of plundering."

"I want every missile launcher on the ring carried onto the immigration ships," Sula said. "And the missiles to go with them. Can I count on you to do that?"

Lepp offered a little bow. "I'll do my absolute best, Lady Fleetcom. But first, may I offer you a drink, or something to eat?"

"Thank you, no," she said. "I have other ships to visit."

The first of the giant immigration ships, *Pride of Parkhurst,* was owned by the Martinez family and built to carry thousands of people at a time to the worlds of Chee and Parkhurst, opened since the Naxid War to settlement under Martinez's sponsorship. Sula stood with the ship's captain on a promenade cantilevered above a voluminous concourse and watched masses of recruits swarming over the open space. Some were organized into classes taught by experienced personnel, and some were working in simulators that had been brought onto the ship from Fleet stores, but most just wandered around the area, talking with their friends or sharing bottles. The concourse was noisy and disorganized, and hardly made a suitable teaching environment.

Among the recruits were a few Naxids, conspicuous for their centauroid bodies and distinctive, darting movement. The Naxids wore civilian dress even though they were here in the character of instructors, for they were experienced Fleet crew who had been eased out of the service when their fellow Naxids had rebelled under the Committee for the Salvation of the Praxis. Like most of the Naxids in the empire, these had never been a part of the rebellion but had nevertheless been dismissed from the military and some of the security services as a precaution.

*If they were loyal*, Sula thought, *they would now get a chance to prove it.*

Using her sleeve display, she called former Senior Squadron Commander Nishkad, once a respected officer of the Fleet, now a successful businessman. It was Nishkad who had recruited the Naxids who now served as instructors on *Parkhurst* and other ships, and he had come to Zarafan to discuss higher levels of cooperation with the Restoration hierarchy.

Sula waited for Nishkad's flat head with its graying, worn scales and red-and-black eyes to appear on her sleeve display.

"Greetings, Lord Squadcom," she said.

"It is a pleasure to see you, Lady Fleetcom," Nishkad said. "How may I serve you?"

"We need many more experienced personnel," Sula said. "Can you provide them?"

MARTINEZ HAD ABOUT a thousand orders to issue, and he was grateful for the tedious work, because the monotony dulled the anger, regret, self-reproach, and desolation that stormed through him. *Retreat. Evacuation.* The fleet of the Restoration, on the heels of its greatest victory at Shulduc, was now being forced to flee Zarafan before Do-faq charged into the system with a superior force. While he, who needed Sula in the fight against the enemy, had sent her away because he couldn't abide the thought of ever seeing her again.

He worked from his thronelike chair in the Residence of the Lord Commander of the Dockyard, a palatial complex with handpainted tiles, handsome, handmade furniture, and shining sculpture in the abstract Devis mode. Masses of flowers in tall glossy celadon vases sent their soft aroma whispering through the room. The previous occupant of the office, Lord Trie-var, had been captured by Martinez personally and was now a prisoner, and Martinez wondered who would occupy the office after he left. He thought about wrecking the place before leaving the ring, but decided that the Restoration's energies were better directed elsewhere.

Aitor Santana, one of his communications specialists, looked up from his desk. "Your brother would like to speak with you."

"Put him on my screen."

Roland appeared in the depths of Martinez's desk, his expression harassed. The two brothers strongly resembled each other, with olive skin, dark hair and eyes, and lantern jaws. They also shared the provincial Laredo accent that marked them as standing outside the empire's ruling caste.

"We'll be clearing station in a few hours," Roland said. He was a politician, and had been involved in unsuccessful negotiations to end the war. The time for politicians was at an end, and he would flee to Harzapid as fast as his shuttle could carry him away.

"Have a safe journey," Martinez said automatically.

"Have you seen Hector Braga?" Roland asked. "He's not responding to my calls."

Braga, the political fixer whom Sula called Lamey. Martinez experienced a moment's tactile memory, dragging Braga's body through the side door of the van, then the bang as Braga's lolling head hit the frame.

Martinez shook off the memory and tried to feign an expression of compassion. "Roland," he said. "Have you lost your bagman?"

"I offered him a ride back to Harzapid," Roland said.

"Maybe he doesn't want to go to Harzapid," Martinez said. "Lord Mehrang wants him arrested for misappropriation of funds."

Roland shrugged. "He can come or not. But if he doesn't leave with me, can you arrange for him to get away from Zarafan somehow? I don't want to hand him over to the Legion of Diligence—he knows too much, for one thing."

"Do you really want me to send him on to Laredo? He'll try to pitch his planetary development scheme to our father."

"We can tell our father not to receive him. Father's a busy man."

All of this discussion, Martinez thought, about a man already dead.

"I'll see what can be done," Martinez said. "Anything else?"

"No," said Roland. "Just that I have every confidence that once again you and Lady Sula will manage to give us a glorious victory."

Martinez felt himself wince at Sula's name. "Let's hope," he said.

He returned to his tasks, which involved accelerating repairs of the war-damaged ships, making certain that every ship's magazines were filled with missiles, that each vessel was charged with antimatter, and that the larders were crammed with victuals. Most of the Fourth Fleet had already left the ring and were on their way to Harzapid, and Martinez needed to get the rest away before Do-faq decided to use them for target practice.

"Lord Fleetcom." Aitor Santana again. "Squadron Commander Prasad for you."

Chandra Prasad commanded one of the divisions that had already departed Zarafan's ring, and she was already far enough away for there to be a delay of a few seconds between a transmission and the reception of its reply.

"Gareth," she said. "I have an idea for creating some mischief."

"Directed against the enemy, I hope."

She grinned. "I hope so too."

Martinez and Chandra Prasad had been lovers years ago, when they were both attending a Fleet communications class. The course of the relationship had been stormy, and each had cheated on the other, then blamed the other for the cheating. Chandra's passage through life had remained turbulent, and Martinez was content to have her in another ship, on another trajectory.

For a moment Martinez experienced a realization that ex-lovers flying away from him might be a subtheme in his life.

Chandra passed a hand through her metallic red hair. "Do-faq is bringing his ships toward Zanshaa, correct?" she said. "We have pictures of them entering Zanshaa's system through Wormhole Five with their deceleration torches pointed straight at the camera, correct? And presumably the camera is on Zanshaa's ring?"

"That's a reasonable conclusion," Martinez said.

"So let's accelerate a pack of missiles to relativistic speed, shoot them toward Zanshaa, then put them right on the track from Zanshaa out to Zanshaa Wormhole Five. They'll be on a direct line for Do-faq's force. With luck we can knock some of them out. It looks as if he hasn't bothered to deploy decoys."

Martinez considered this. They had missiles to spare, with the "Fleet Train" of cargo ships bringing a seemingly endless supply from Harzapid.

"It would be better if we could find a way to track Do-faq's ships as the missiles were coming in," he said.

"I'm sure the Zanshaa system is filled with radars and laser range-finders," Chandra said. "And if I were on Zanshaa and a hundred fifty warships were heading my way—even friendly warships—I'd want to know where they were."

Martinez nodded. "Plausible. Can you launch the attack with your division?"

She seemed pleased to be asked. "Certainly. How many missiles should we launch?"

"At least two hundred."

Her grin was blinding. "Very good, Lord Fleetcom." The orange end-stamp filled the screen.

Martinez turned to his work and felt a lance of pain along his spine. He had been bent over his desk for hours, and he'd had no food all day, only cup after cup of coffee. He rose and felt his vertebrae crackle as he straightened and drew his shoulders back. He turned to look out the grand windows of the Lord Commander's office and viewed the courtyard below, the guards checking identification at the gate, the uniformed men and women moving in and out. In the last few hours they seemed to have acquired an air of urgency, moving briskly about their errands. News of Do-faq's arrival in the Zanshaa system had spread quickly among them, and they walked with steely determination.

Martinez walked across the soft carpet of his office, twisting his upper body left and right to loosen his cramping muscles. His stomach rumbled. There were penalties when you skipped dinner in order to hide a corpse. He sent to the kitchens for a couple sandwiches, considered another pot of coffee, then decided he'd already had too much caffeine and asked for Citrine Fling.

His other signals tech, Lalita Banerjee, came through the gilded double doors. She was a plump, gray-haired, grandmotherly woman who had retired as a warrant officer/first with thirty years' service, then rejoined the Fleet at the outbreak of the Accidental War. Martinez had promoted her to lieutenant, which had surprised her greatly but made her the senior officer of his signals section, which he preferred because Santana had scant experience.

"My lord?" Banerjee said. "There is still a roomful of petty officers waiting to see you."

His own misery combined with the press of events had driven from Martinez's mind the fact that he was interviewing for a new orderly. His longtime servant, Khalid Alikhan, had died at Second Shulduc, and since then Martinez had been making do by borrowing Sula's orderly, Gavin Macnamara. Macnamara had barely tolerated him—he was convinced that Martinez would break Sula's heart, and had failed to foresee that it would happen the other way around.

Even if Macnamara wouldn't soon be departing with Sula, the situation was untenable, and Martinez needed a new servant. Alikhan had left a very substantial void, one that would be difficult to fill.

"Are any of them promising?" Martinez asked.

"A couple. And there's another who says he knows you."

"Yes?"

"A Master Rigger Zhou, my lord."

The name struck no chords of memory. Zhou was a common enough name, though, and it was possible Martinez had met the rigger at some point and forgotten.

"I'll start with Zhou, then," he said. "Send him in."

Recognition dawned the moment Zhou slouched into his office, a confiding smile on his face and the *Corona* medal gleaming on his chest. Zhou walked to Martinez's desk and braced, and Martinez let him stand for several seconds before releasing him from attention.

"Master rigger, eh?" he said. "How did that happen?"

Zhou offered what could only be described as a leer. "I was out of the service for a few years," Zhou said, "but I came back when the war started. They were impressed with my skills, my lord—and of course the fact I was with you on *Corona*. So in view of my contribution to victory in the last war I was promoted to master rigger on the spot."

"What ship?"

"*Millicent Thorogood*, Lord Fleetcom." And then, he added, "It's a transport. We brought food supplies from Harzapid."

Martinez wondered how much of the food, fruit particularly, had gone into Zhou's homemade wine. Making illicit wine and liquor—along with running dice games and brawling with civilians and recruits from other ships—were Zhou's bread and butter. When Martinez had been in command of *Corona*, Zhou—along with his pals Ahmet and Knadjian—had been a constant, if predictable, source of turbulence, misbehavior, and sheer indecency.

Whoever had promoted Zhou to master rigger, he thought, had been so desperate for veteran personnel that he was willing to overlook Zhou's record—assuming of course that he'd even *seen* Zhou's record.

There was a knock on the door, and a steward arrived with Martinez's tray of sandwiches. Zhou took one as the steward passed.

"Thank you, Lord Fleetcom," he said. "Very kind."

Martinez let the steward set the plate and his Citrine Fling before him. "I imagine you've made *Thorogood* a little kingdom for yourself," he said. "You want to give that up to become my servant?"

Zhou adopted a pained expression. "Well, the captain's only a cadet, my lord—he's only had a year and a half at the academy before the war started, he's without a commission, and he's never seen active service before now. He doesn't understand the Fleet at all, and there have been a series of . . ." He searched for the word.

"Misunderstandings?" Martinez suggested.

Zhou smiled. "Exactly, my lord."

"Well, I think you should straighten out those misunderstandings before you take any new posting," Martinez said.

Zhou had taken a bite of the sandwich, so there was a moment of chewing before he swallowed and spoke.

"The captain is too young to reason with," he said. "He's pigheaded and refuses to admit he could be mistaken. And this is very good cheese, my lord."

"Enjoy the cheese, Zhou," said Martinez, "and give my regards to your captain."

Chewing again, it took a moment for Zhou to realize he'd been dismissed. He seemed to take it philosophically, with a grimace, a nod, and that confiding smile, and then he braced, turned, and marched away.

Martinez ordered a replacement sandwich from the kitchen. As he finished his call, a message arrived from Chandra Prasad stating that she'd fired 251 missiles in Do-faq's direction.

Of the petty officers waiting in the lobby, Martinez followed

Banerjee's advice concerning who to interview, and eventually narrowed his decision to one of two candidates.

The first was Gunpreet Khand, a stocky woman with pecan-colored skin and white hair cropped short. She had retired at the rank of master machinist, and had returned to the Fleet at the start of the crisis. For the most part she'd been assigned as an instructor to new recruits, and she wanted to get back aboard a warship.

He asked her about her career, her experience. She had spent the last part of the Naxid War aboard the frigate *Courage*, which had been damaged at Second Magaria.

"I would hope to use you as a conduit to the enlisted personnel," Martinez told her. "And likewise, I hope you will be able to let me know if there is anything going on among the enlisted that needs to be brought to my attention."

Khand's gaze sharpened. "You wish me to be a spy?"

Martinez stiffened. "I'm not interested in tales of misbehavior among the recruits," he said. "That's the business of Captain Dalkeith and her officers. I'm more interested in knowing whether the crew is discouraged, is optimistic, is troubled by anything that they don't understand. I wish to know the state of their morale and the state of their apprehensions. I'm commanding the entire fleet, and I need to know that the pulpies are willing to risk their lives for the Restoration."

"Ah," Khand said. "Well, that I can do. But I have never been asked to do such a thing before, and I will have to decide what it is proper for you to know."

"Thank you, Machinist Khand," said Martinez. "I'll be in touch."

Martinez's other candidate was Weaponer First Class Agustin Mpanza, who was still in his twenties. He had caramel skin and wore the waxed, curling mustachios favored by senior male petty officers. Mpanza was a little young for such an affectation, which he wore along with a full, close-cropped beard, possibly in hopes it would make him look older. Beards were contrary to regulations, but since Second Shulduc grooming standards had seemingly been relaxed.

"My mother was from Laredo, my lord," he said. "Her family was named Peralta. My father was in Laredo on a contract, and when he went home she went with him."

Martinez knew any number of Peraltas, though he doubted Mpanza's family were among them. "Are your mother's family still on Laredo?" he asked.

"I think they all emigrated to Chee," Mpanza said. "To Gareth-port in fact, the town named after you."

"It helps when your family does the naming," Martinez said.

"I suppose it does, my lord."

"Do you have experience at being a servant?" Martinez asked. "Serving at table, mixing drinks, looking after someone's uniforms, shoes?"

"I did all those things when I was living with my family," said Mpanza. "Though I wasn't paid for it. And of course I've *seen* how it's done—I've been on assignments where I was able to observe officers being waited on, and so forth."

"But why do *you* want to wait on someone else?"

"It's a chance to do something new," he said. "I've been in the weapons bays for my entire career."

"You won't leave the weapons bays entirely," Martinez said. "Your action station will be in one of the weapon command centers."

Mpanza seemed agreeable. "It's something I've done in two battles now. I can do it again if I need to."

Martinez raised the issue of Mpanza being used as an informal conduit to the enlisted personnel, and he raised no objection.

"Lord Fleetcom, I can give you your first report now, if you like," he said.

Martinez felt surprise. "By all means."

"We are *pissed off*." Mpanza's dark eyes flashed. "We are furious at Do-faq and the Third Fleet for prolonging the war, especially since we'd *already won it*. We've been on shipboard for month after month, and fought the biggest ship battle in history, and we thought we'd earned our leave on Zarafan—and now we're being packed aboard our ships and trying to get out of the system ahead of Do-faq's fleet, and we know that we'll be spending even more months on shipboard with nothing to look forward to but drill after drill after drill."

"I'm not happy about it myself," said Martinez. The ships of the Exploration Service, which spent long periods away from base in their search of habitable worlds, were built for lengthy cruises, but the warships of the Fleet, which spent most of their time in dock, were not. Long months in cramped quarters, often under high accelerations, produced exhaustion and aggravation in equal measure.

"Now," Mpanza said, "we're confident we'll win. We know our jobs, we've won every encounter so far, but we're pissed that we keep having to do this over and over."

"The recruits aren't angry at their officers?" Martinez asked.

"Not as a general rule," said Mpanza. "I mean, *some* officers always manage to get up everyone's nose, but for the most part, my lord, we *like* you. We've seen the way you've put the Fourth Fleet back together with inexperienced crews and junior officers appointed to commands above their level of experience, but you produced a force capable of destroying Lord Tork and his Righteous Fleet for the Suppression of Dissension. So we have great respect for you, my lord, but the truth is we're *tired*."

"And pissed off."

"That, too."

Martinez considered Mpanza's report. If Martinez hadn't been so overwhelmed by events and by the great gaping wound in his heart, none of this would be news: he was feeling tired and exasperated himself, and it wouldn't be hard to extrapolate the mental state of the rest of his command from his own.

"How do we keep them sharp?" he asked. "In focus? Ready to fight?" He had the sense that he was asking the questions as much about himself as about the warships' crews.

"Beating them to death with endless drills would be counterproductive," Mpanza said. "They already know how to fight, and bringing them back to full readiness won't take long."

But without the frequent drills, Martinez thought, the recruits would have a lot of time on their hands, and that might have its own dangers. Idle crew were wont to fill their free time with timeless activities, such as gambling, drinking, fighting, and levels of depravity that staggered the imagination.

"How do we keep them busy?" Martinez asked.

"Their lives are filled with busywork," said Mpanza. "But there's only so many times they can polish the brass fixtures." He spread his hands. "I don't know, Lord Fleetcom," he said. "But we can try everything. Entertainment, contests between the crews of different ships, amateur theatricals . . ." His imagination failed him. "I really couldn't say, my lord."

"Thank you for your candor, Mr. Mpanza," Martinez said.

He knew that Gunpreet Khand had much more experience than Mpanza and would perform the conventional tasks of an orderly very well—he'd find his uniforms laid out ready, the service at meals would be immaculate, and his porcelain and crystal would sparkle—but her reluctance to serve as a channel between Martinez and the recruits counted against her, and so did a perceived lack of imagination. She hadn't understood Martinez's intentions when he broached using her as a conduit and had jumped immediately to the conclusion that he wanted to use her as an informer against members of the crew. In fact, Martinez thought, he may have failed to convince her otherwise.

Mpanza may have been jumped to weaponer/first based on wartime requirements rather than experience, but he seemed alert to the changing situation in the Fleet and offered his ideas freely— far more freely than the formal, circumspect Alikhan would have volunteered, if he had given any opinion whatever. Martinez hoped that he hadn't encouraged Mpanza to openly babble out any idea that occurred to him.

He realized in that moment that he had already decided to accept Mpanza as his orderly. Khand had been quietly shuffled to a different corner of his mind.

"Well, Mpanza," he said, "if you're still willing to be a servant, I'm willing to employ you."

A bright smile crossed Mpanza's features. "Thank you, my lord!"

"Collect your gear and report back to the Residence. Don't unpack, because we'll be going aboard *Los Angeles* tomorrow with the rest of the staff."

"Very good, my lord!"

"And shave off the beard," Martinez said. "A fleetcom's orderly can't wear his disdain for regulations right on his face."

Mpanza accepted the order with a wry smile. "The beard was getting itchy anyway," he said.

MARTINEZ LOOKED AT the video screen in his quarters. His heart lurched uneasily in his chest as his mind roiled with something like horror, something like fascination.

"Chai-chai's last report was good," Terza said. "The teachers were impressed by his vocabulary, and his art teacher also had some complimentary things to say." She smiled. "Chai-chai seems to have inherited your musical ability, and not mine."

Which was a joke, because Terza was a very capable musician, and Martinez's big hands had proven inept at every instrument he'd attempted.

Terza's bulletin had been sent from a universe that no longer existed. When she had recorded the message days ago at Harzapid, the Fourth Fleet had been triumphant and unstoppable and was preparing its final dash to the capital of Zanshaa. But now, with the revelation that Do-faq and 166 warships had gotten to Zanshaa ahead of them, every assumption about the war had been turned to ash.

Terza's message existed in a time bubble in more ways than one. It had been recorded at a moment when Martinez had assumed that he would be spending the rest of his life with Caroline Sula, and that he would have to negotiate an end to his marriage to Terza Chen—an *arranged* marriage, he reminded himself, which he had undertaken very much against his wishes. He then would have needed to separate himself from the powerful Chen family, who had served as his patrons in the Fleet. He would want to place himself in an impregnable position where he no longer needed the Chens, and the best way to do that was to win the war and receive credit for it. After that, with his promotion confirmed and a seat on the Fleet Control Board, he would be the one who gave patronage, not received it.

But that world, where he and Sula could live without consequence in the fury of their mutual passion, had ceased to exist even as a fantasy—Sula had shot it to death with two bullets to the heart, and left it to bleed out in the parlor of her Celestial Court residence. Martinez was not on the verge of winning the war, but instead would be leading his command in hasty and undignified flight.

And now, looking at Terza, lovely and perfectly composed in her black jersey dress, her legs tucked under her as she sat on the sofa in their suite on *Corona*, Martinez wondered how he had managed to so thoroughly find himself alone and stranded amid the wreckage of his hopes.

He had carried a bouquet of fragrant white lu-doi flowers into the Celestial Court apartment the previous night, only to freeze like a terrified animal at the sight awaiting him in the parlor: Hector Braga—Lamey—lay on the carpet, his gaudy gold–and–burnt orange jacket stained with red, his blue eyes staring at the ceiling with what seemed mild puzzlement. The air reeked of propellent, and Martinez's shoes ground broken glass from the mirror that had absorbed the bullets after they'd passed through Lamey's body.

Standing over the body was Caroline Sula, slim in her uniform of viridian green, pistol in her hand, calculation plain in her emerald eyes as she looked down at the body. Her gaze rose to his as the white bouquet tumbled from inert fingers, and she folded her arms, the gun still in plain sight.

"So," she had said, "are you going to help me hide the body?"

She had offered no explanation, she had offered no reasons, she had offered no excuses. Sula had kept to herself whatever had compelled her to murder.

Martinez knew, of course, that she was a hardened street fighter who had led a group of irregulars in the Naxid War and eventually formed an army with which she stormed Zanshaa High City. Some of her connections were dubious, but he'd assumed that the gangsters that formed part of her army were the result of a tactical alliance, not a league of soul mates.

Yet a glance at Sula's hard, calculating eyes told him that everything he thought he knew about Sula was wrong, and he realized in that instant that whatever ruthless being had just manifested behind those green eyes was one that Martinez desired never to see again.

Now, in the privacy of his quarters, he looked at Terza's composed figure and wanted nothing so much as to find his way back to her—yet it was far from clear if that was even possible. His liaison with Sula had begun on a warship, and in those close quarters there was no possibility of keeping it hidden. Probably the whole Fleet knew by now, and surely someone—out of what would be claimed to be compassion for a wronged spouse—would with conceited pleasure tell Terza what was common knowledge in her husband's command.

He closed his eyes and let Terza's image fade to darkness on the backs of his eyelids. Exhaustion oozed through his veins. His head spun with images of flowers and blood.

Martinez decided to delay a response to Terza's message until the next day, when he might have a chance to unsnarl his raveled thoughts and send a message that might somehow, miraculously, repair the fiasco he and Sula had made of his life.

SULA'S COOK HAD very little time to acquaint herself with her small kitchen on *Splendid*, but she had managed well on short notice. She had produced a meal entirely composed of fresh food brought up from the planet below, a fried fillet of fish in a sauce bright with citrus, accompanied by a medley of vegetables.

The fresh food would last only a short time after Division Nine departed Zarafan's ring, so it made sense for Sula to enjoy it while she could, but her appetite was diminished nearly to nothing and she ate half the meal before she pushed it away. She looked at her goblet of water and suddenly a fierce desire rose in her for alcohol, a desire that shot through her veins like fire. She called for a bottle of wine—red, this time, because she wanted to see if she liked it better.

Macnamara brought the bottle in silence. He opened the bottle, then set it on the table to breathe.

Master Constable Gavin Macnamara was tall, with light brown curly hair that formed a halo around his head. He, Shawna Spence, and Sula had comprised Action Team 491 in the Naxid War and had built the Secret Army that had stormed the High City.

Macnamara had never approved of certain of Sula's friends and associates, and though the disapproval was always silent, Sula always sensed its weight. Macnamara's reproach had been at its weightiest where Martinez was concerned, and after a moment of silence, just as Sula was about to tell him he could leave and she could pour her own wine, he spoke.

"I'm very sorry, my lady," he said. "I was afraid that Fleetcom Martinez would do this to you."

Sula barely felt surprise that Macnamara had spoken out after all these years. She felt only an urge to correct the record.

"This isn't Gareth's fault at all," she said. "I was the one who made the five-star fuckup."

*And now let's make another*, she thought, and reached for the bottle.

# CHAPTER 2

Their blazing antimatter torches looking like a shifting constellation of stars, Do-faq's fleet burned toward Zanshaa in a recording that took up most of Severin's office wall.

*Good,* Severin found himself thinking, *more targets.*

He'd been in an unforgiving frame of mind ever since the slaughter at Second Shulduc.

Severin's *Expedition,* flagship of the newly formed Second Light Squadron, had left Zarafan's ring four days earlier with the rest of the squadron and had been gently accelerating at a half-gravity toward Zanshaa until the news about the Third Fleet had reached them, after which they altered course for the wormhole that would take them in the direction of Harzapid and increased acceleration to 1.2 gees.

It was a tawdry, shambolic retreat, but Do-faq could be in the system within days and the Restoration's ships needed to be out of his way.

Shushanik Severin not only had to manage his squadron during the withdrawal but also had to reorganize friendly wormhole relay stations. The relay stations formed the communications web that held the empire together and were crewed with Exploration Service personnel—Severin had served in relay stations himself, before he'd been promoted to the officer class in the last war. Severin had replaced the government stations' crews with crews of his own in every system controlled by Restoration forces. But he'd also prepared an alternate relay system in the event that a star system fell under enemy control, with Exploration Service cutters set adrift in empty space, receiving and broadcasting brief laser transmissions sent through wormholes at unconventional angles well away from the normal course of traffic. Because the laser array generated heat, it would be dangerous for ships to have their laser communications arrays turned on for any length of time, but if communications were restricted to certain set times the danger was minimized. Only a very few cutters had been lost in the campaign that led to Second Shulduc.

Which didn't mean that the enemy wouldn't be more alert this time.

Severin rose from his desk, his thigh muscles taut in the above-normal gravity. He prowled the small room, part of his attention remaining on the screen with its constellation of Do-faq's ships, the rest running through a mental checklist of tasks he needed to finish over the course of the day.

He paused for a moment at the sight of a photograph of a puppet perched impishly and implausibly on the shoulder of a fellow officer. The puppet was modeled on Lady Gruum, the Lady Senior currently presiding over the enemy government. The puppet had starred in a number of short videos that satirized Gruum and her cohorts as ridiculous, greedy, grandiloquent nitwits trying desperately to profit off the war they'd started. Severin had worked on the satires with Lihua, Lady Starkey, captain of the *Explorer*, offspring of the Hua and Starkey clans whose very DNA seems to have been wound about the Exploration Service for centuries. Though she was the result of a matrimonial merger between two high-status

Peer families and Severin was a commoner who had spent much of his career among the enlisted, Starkey and Severin had fallen for each other and planned to marry after the war. While she could expect disapproval from her family, Starkey had pointed out that she was the head of clan Starkey and could do what she wanted.

But Starkey and the crew of her *Explorer* had been turned to atoms at Second Shulduc, and since then Severin hadn't been in the mood for comedic videos. The sorrow and the mourning sluiced through him day and night, a melancholy in his blood that he could ignore only so long as he kept his mind distracted, absorbed either in his work or in preparing some future project.

Severin looked at the photo for a few seconds, sorrow throbbing through him like a heartbeat. His breath rasped in his throat, and he felt tears sting his eyes. And then he thought, *Better get busy*.

Since the battle, Severin had been engaged in an unconventional project. He intended to create a political revolution, overthrow the established order, and replace it with a more responsive, functional, less hidebound state, and furthermore to accomplish this without being executed for crimes against the Praxis. It seemed to him that this was an achievable goal, and he hoped he could complete the work before the empire stumbled into yet another civil war.

But now Do-faq was on his way with a massive fleet, and Severin would have to put his political revolution aside and work out a way to kill Do-faq and his entire command.

Severin knew that he was good at problem-solving. Winning the next battle, he thought, was only a matter of applying his intelligence in the right way.

And then he could get on with toppling the empire's entire political order.

"I'M SURE YOU'VE heard by now," Martinez told the camera, "that Do-faq and the Third Fleet are on their way. We're working very hard at getting our ships off Zarafan and bound for Harzapid, so I apologize if this video is brief."

His chef, Marivic Mangahas, had prepared him a filling breakfast of rice congee with sweet pork and an egg, and that—and a half pot of coffee—had given Martinez enough strength to record his next video message to Terza. He had shifted from his dining table to the office in his quarters, closed the door, told Banerjee to refuse all calls, and in comforting semidarkness began recording.

"We're sending the entire fleet in the direction of Harzapid," he said, "with a few exceptions. Lady Sula has been given her own command, mainly support and training ships, and will be heading for Laredo to provide crews for the cruisers built there. Paivo Kangas will replace her as my tactical officer.

"Please give my love to Chai-chai," he added. "I'd like to see a video from the young genius when his schedule permits."

He hesitated—or perhaps he was feigning hesitation, he seemed not to know. "You know," he said, "watching Chai-chai and Mei-mei grow older only on video reminds me that my relations with my children have always been played out against a background of crisis. Chai-chai was born in wartime, and you were pregnant with Mei-mei when the Chee affair blew up, and now it's wartime again and Mei-mei's off at Laredo and I haven't seen her in a year." He sighed, and again he couldn't tell whether the sigh was a genuine indication of his feelings or a piece of artifice intended to make his performance more convincing.

"Be that as it may," Martinez continued, "I was thinking that once this war is over, we might make another baby, and I could be present for—well—for *all* of its childhood." He shrugged. "Just a thought. A yearning, if you like . . . I thought that in the midst of all the madness it might be pleasant for us to think about our future, after the peace."

He ended the video, ciphered it, and sent it on its way. It was designed to send Terza a number of messages. *Whatever you may have heard,* the message said, *whatever you may believe, Sula is off my ship and far away. And I am planning a very domestic and very comfortable future with you.*

Martinez was all too aware that he was moving pieces on an invisible game board, and all without quite understanding the rules. He was thinking tactically because that was how he'd been thinking since the war began, and though he knew he could not maneuver human beings as if they were squadrons of warships, he also knew that, months away from Terza, he could do little else but set up the pieces and hope.

He told Banerjee that he would resume accepting messages, and she immediately passed on one from his flag captain, Elissa Dalkeith. She spoke in a high-pitched, lisping child's voice that provided a surprising contrast with her gray hair and her middle-aged face.

"Lord Fleetcom," she said, "the inspectors have rated battery one as safe and ready for action. Only cosmetic repairs remain, but we can safely operate in a combat role without them. *Los Angeles* is ready for departure at your earliest convenience."

"I'll be aboard in an hour or two," Martinez said. "Have the ship stand by for immediate departure."

Fragrant steam rose as he poured himself another cup of coffee, after which he called Mpanza on his sleeve display. Mpanza had shaved his beard, though he still wore the curling mustachio. Martinez saw he'd been right that Mpanza had grown the beard to make himself look older, for without it he looked no older than twenty.

"Pack everything," Martinez said, "and prepare transport to get it to the *Los Angeles.*"

"Yes, Lord Fleetcom."

"Mangahas will assist, and you can tell her she's not obliged to leave a clean kitchen behind—let Do-faq do the dishes. I'm going to the Lord Commander's office now, and I'll let you know when I transfer to the port."

"Yes, my lord."

He had given Mpanza and Mangahas a formidable task, for an officer of Martinez's rank didn't travel just with a trunk of clothing and a toiletries case, but with silver wine coolers, with monogrammed porcelain and crystal place settings for formal dinners, with cases of wine and spirits and bags of coffee beans, all of which would have to be packed up and shifted to the flag officer quarters on *Bombardment of Los Angeles*, where it would be tucked away in cupboards, closets, and pantries.

It would be a proper first test for the young man.

Martinez picked up his coffee, buttoned his undress tunic, strapped on his sidearm, and walked the long corridor to the magnificent office of the Lord Commander of the Dockyard. Banerjee and Santana were already at their stations, coping with the flood of communications pouring into the office from the rapidly dispersing Fourth Fleet. Martinez told them to copy onto portable media all the communications data, daily reports, information on stores and repairs, and everything else dating from the Restoration's period on Zarafan, and then zero out all records from the system they were going to leave behind.

"If you can get some dockyard apes to physically destroy the memory cores, so much the better," he said. "After you're done, pack your bags and head for *Los Angeles*."

Another huge task.

When he'd first occupied the Lord Commander's office, he and everyone else had assumed the war was won and had used the facilities available to them. It was all ciphered, of course, but now, with all his assumptions fallen to dust, Martinez didn't want Do-faq deciphering his correspondence or, worse, all the reports concerning the status of his ships.

"Can we get some technical help?" Santana asked.

"All you need," Martinez said. "And hunt down all backups and zero those as well."

He stepped into his office, where the big windows let in light from the boulevard and the big celadon vases had just been filled with fresh-cut flowers. The scent flooded his senses, and for a moment he wasn't smelling flowers, but Sula's Sandama Twilight perfume, and he was swept away in a torrential swirl of sensation that somehow recapitulated his relationship with Sula, from attraction to passion to desolation, then rediscovery and yearning and ardor, joy and contentment, all ending in sudden horror, and all his hopes burning to windblown ash . . .

The force of this passionate memory set him rocking on his feet, and he walked to his desk on legs that seemed reluctant to support him. Instead of sitting he leaned against the large window and gazed out at the courtyard and the boulevard beyond, and he watched all the personnel streaming out of the residence, past the military constabulary on the gate, to their ships and evacuation. His heart beat like a panicked bird against the cage of his ribs.

He was going to have to pull the Fourth Fleet together, he thought, get them ready to meet Do-faq.

But he was going to have to pull himself together first.

ON THE HEADS-UP display in Martinez's helmet, he viewed another message that had arrived from a time bubble now separated from his own, this one from Senior Fleet Commander Michi

Chen, Terza's aunt and his immediate superior. It was Michi who had opened the war by seizing Harzapid and the Fourth Fleet and providing a refuge for Martinez, Sula, and other Terrans in flight from a government determined to blame humankind for the crisis that had precipitated the war.

In the normal course of events Michi would have commanded the Fourth Fleet in battle, but a bomb had blown off one of Michi's legs on Harzapid's ring, and Martinez had been given the fleet until Michi could recover. She had a new leg grafted on now, presumably better than the original.

Her face was drawn, and the sclera of her eyes reflected jaundiced yellow glints. Her hair, worn in bangs across her forehead, was rapidly turning from gray to white. Martinez assumed this wasn't a result of her injury, but overwork. She had been toiling day and night for a year to keep the Restoration together.

Still, she seemed relaxed in her broadcast, and there was an amused smile on her face.

"We've heard from Wei Jian at last," she said. "One of her ships came into range of one of our wormhole stations and asked why the Fourth Fleet hasn't joined her."

At the beginning of the war, Wei Jian had left Magaria with the fifty-five Terran-crewed ships that made up part of the Second Fleet. To avoid action with the superior Home Fleet at Zanshaa, Wei Jian had been forced into a roundabout path to Harzapid, traveling through a series of mostly barren systems. The journey should have taken five or six months, but instead had taken nearly a year.

Michi permitted herself a laugh. "I responded that we had seen no reason to retire toward Jian, because we had engaged Tork and his fleet of over five hundred enemy ships and wiped them out. I explained that you were readying a final attack on Zanshaa, and that if Jian hurried she could be part of the victory parade."

Martinez wasn't as entertained by this as Michi, because he knew the message had originated in the earlier time, mere days ago, when everyone believed the war had been won, and left Wei Jian a faintly comic figure who turned up too late to play her part.

But now Wei Jian was necessary. The Fourth Fleet, which had once comprised more than 250 ships, now numbered 113, of which 19 were repairing battle damage at Harzapid, and a further 16 were a pair of squadrons who had defected to the Restoration after the rest of Tork's Righteous Fleet had been destroyed.

Do-faq had 166, to which could be added the 19 ships Tork had left behind to guard Zanshaa against a sneak attack. Engaging these with the Fourth Fleet as it now stood would be akin to suicide, unless Wei Jian's 55 could be added.

Michi, Martinez concluded, was going to have to send a mortifying message to Wei Jian, and he had to hope that Michi was sufficiently skilled at humiliating herself to be able to bring Jian's squadrons into the war.

He hoped they were all sufficiently humbled enough to get past the mortification and be ready to fight.

Martinez took a series of slow, deliberate breaths as he contemplated whether to respond to Michi's message at all. *Bombardment of Los Angeles* was currently accelerating at two gravities toward the wormhole that would take them toward Harzapid, with the crew lying in their acceleration couches and wearing vac suits. The suits weren't strictly necessary, but Martinez wanted the pulpies to reacquaint themselves with ship discipline and battle conditions after their days of liberty at Zarafan.

Martinez decided that Michi was worthy of his commiseration. "You have my sympathy, Lady Fleetcom," he sent. "I wish you every success in dealing with Squadron Leader Jian. I have no advice to give, as I've never met her, but I hope she proves pliable."

Jian, he knew, had been in charge of ship construction in Seizho during the previous war and had never been in combat. Which meant, he thought, that she was ignorant of the bare facts of combat—and worse, that she didn't even know what she didn't know.

That, he thought, did not bode well.

SULA WOKE SCREAMING from a dream of death and blood. She gasped in air. Stars spun furious circles in her eyes. Her heart hammered like an engine with a broken flywheel, and the thick warm scent of gore clogged her senses.

Sula's sleeping cabin slowly ceased its rotation. She waited until her breath and heartbeat returned to normal, got out of bed, and put on a dressing gown, then went to her kitchen, where she found Shawna Spence filling a tea kettle.

"Sorry I woke you," Sula said.

Spence shrugged. "Would you like tea to keep you awake or tea to put you back to sleep?"

"I don't think I'm going to be doing any more sleeping tonight."

"Right." She opened a cabinet and drew out a container of tea. "Would you like anything to eat?"

"I don't think so." Sula shook her head, and a shaft of pain drove through her skull. She blinked rapidly as her vision seemed to flicker on and off, and put a hand to her temple as the pain eased. "I'm going to go sit down," she said.

She went to her wedge-shaped dining room and sat at the blunt end of the wedge-shaped table. Perhaps, she thought, drinking half a bottle of fortified dessert wine before going to bed hadn't been the wisest course of action, especially as it hadn't stopped the nightmare from creeping into her brain.

The war had triggered a host of toxic memories, and by now her staff was probably used to her shrieks tearing them from sleep at odd hours. Her liaison with Martinez had produced a respite—the nightmares never came when she was lying in Martinez's arms. But now, during the first proper night's sleep she'd had since dropping Lamey at Martinez's feet like a bloody sacrifice, the nightmares had come back to shred her nerves with adamantine claws.

After a few minutes, Spence came into the room carrying a porcelain teapot with a pomegranate-and-tulip pattern, made for Sula on Earth, in Cappadocia. The fragrance of the tea whispered into the air.

"Join me if you want," Sula said. "I can't promise to be good company, though."

"I'll join if I may, thank you." Spence agitated the teapot gently, to help the tea steep, then placed it on the table. She returned to the kitchen for a pair of cups and a squeeze bottle of cane syrup. They sat in silence until the tea had finished steeping, and then Spence poured for them both. Sula reached for the cane syrup and dropped a long, sweet gold serpent into her tea.

The black tea was lychee and had a smooth vanilla taste, still detectable under the sweet syrup. Sula put her cup down and sighed.

"Lots of changes," Spence offered.

"Yes."

"So we're schoolmasters now? Training up hundreds of recruits from nothing?"

Sula studied the pomegranate on her teacup. "Their ships were built at Laredo, and they will meet us between here and there. And once we have crews aboard, we charge off to wherever we're needed, to rescue whoever needs saving."

Spence offered no comment other than a skeptical look. She

sipped her tea, then returned it to the saucer with a decisive click. She frowned, then spoke.

"Gavin says you think it's your fault."

"My fault?"

"Whatever happened in the last two days." Spence leaned forward over her teacup. "Two nights ago, I brought a pair of meals to your quarters so that you and Fleetcom Martinez could dine together, as you'd been doing nearly every night since we arrived in Zarafan. Then, the very next morning, you're no longer the tactical officer, and instead you're headmistress to some kind of ramshackle academy that's supposed to train hundreds of recruits and fight a war at the same time, and you're . . ." She hesitated.

"I'm . . . ?"

"Enjoying libations with dinner," Spence said diplomatically.

Sula sipped her tea and nodded. "That's a fair summary," she said.

"And how is it your fault?" Spence asked. "He's your superior officer—and he's not only married, he's married to a woman so high-powered that he can never afford to leave her. Now his position is basically unchanged, he's still married to a Chen, he's still in command of the Fourth Fleet, and he's still the victor of both battles of Shulduc—and you've lost your post and have been exiled to—" She waved a hand. "To *this*. You're the *victim* here."

Sula sipped her tea and wondered how to respond. Spence was a *servant*, and it wasn't customary for a Peer and officer to confide in a servant. But Spence and Macnamara had been with her for nearly ten years, they had fought side by side to take the High City, and for a very long time they'd been as close as family.

Besides, servants knew practically everything anyway, and in this case, they knew just enough to draw the wrong conclusions.

"What you likely don't know," Sula said, "is that Gareth and I were involved years ago, during the Naxid War. I panicked and ran, and before I could recover, Roland had bought Terza for Gareth. So Terza is sort of my fault."

Spence opened her mouth to protest, and then closed it. Sula went on.

"The other thing you should know is that these last few months, I was in charge. I decided to initiate the affair. I decided its limits and its parameters. When there were lines to be drawn, I drew them." She rubbed the pad of scar tissue on her right thumb. "But I fucked up, I wrecked everything, and it turned out I wasn't in charge because *nobody* was in charge. *Chaos* was in charge. The whirlwind was in charge, and I stepped right in front of it."

Spence blinked. "I don't know how the, the whirlwind could be your fault."

"It wasn't my fault, but it was my fault I didn't see it coming."

"I don't see how you could have—"

"I prefer to keep what's left of my privacy to myself," Sula said sharply. If this conversation continued much further, she might find herself explaining why she'd fired two bullets into Lamey's chest.

The barrier of rank and class had just fallen between them, almost with an audible clang. "Yes, my lady," Spence said promptly.

"Thank you for the tea," Sula said. "I think I'll shower now."

She carried her teacup with her to her bathroom and set the shower at a near-scalding temperature. She let the water pound her shoulders and back and tried to relax the taut muscles that she felt enclosing and confining her like the wrappings of a mummy.

It didn't work.

She toweled herself off, put on her uniform, carried her tea into her office, and began the day's business.

"AND I'LL WANT acceleration couches complying with the Naxid anatomy," Sula said. "One for every Naxid on board."

"Yes, my lady. How many is that?"

Sula hesitated as she looked at Lord Nishkad. "More than five hundred," he said in his papery voice.

"Better make it a thousand," said Sula.

"Yes, Lady Fleetcom. I'll have to find out where they're stored."

"While you're there, take whatever else you think we might need," Sula said. "We won't be back at Zarafan for a long time."

Sula was coordinating her plundering teams from her office on the *Splendid*. Lord Nishkad sat across from her desk curled onto an oval sofa suitable for the centauroid Naxid body. The air still smelled faintly of the groceries that had been stacked here, and the walls of her office were beige and battered.

She and Nishkad were companionably sharing a tisane that filled the air with a sharp herbal scent. The Naxid's black-on-scarlet eyes turned to Sula. "I regret to say, my lady, that I don't know how many volunteers are coming," he said. "Time was too short—I could not organize it properly. I just had to put out the word and hope that we got sufficient volunteers, and I believe we have."

"War never gives us enough time," Sula said, and then smiled. "At least if you're doing it right." She'd known officers who had viewed wartime service with the same degree of urgency as a stroll to their smoking club. Most of them, she thought, were dead now.

"I should like to request transport from Zarafan on one of your vessels," Nishkad said. "I know we have been discreet about our arrangements, but word is certain to leak out, and I would prefer to live my allotted span rather than have the Zanshaa government curtail my existence."

Nishkad had come to Zarafan as a guest on the yacht of Roland

Martinez, but Roland had fled without contacting him, which Sula had to think careless.

"Let me take care of that right away," Sula said. She contacted Ricci, one of her signals techs, and told him to secure the owner's suite on *Pride of Parkhurst* for Lord Nishkad, and if there was any difficulty to refer the matter to Sula.

"Very good, my lady," said Ricci in his pleasing baritone.

"And make sure the furniture is suitable for Naxids," Sula said.

"Of course, Lady Fleetcom."

"That was very good of you, Lady Sula," said Nishkad. Some of his worn black beaded scales flashed red in one of the patterns that Naxids used to communicate among themselves. The signal was probably unintentional, since Sula couldn't read it, but she presumed it reinforced what Nishkad had just said.

"The Restoration owes you a great deal," Sula said. "I only hope that someday your part can be revealed to the public."

She could only imagine the rage that would be unleashed on the Restoration if word came that Naxids were being used to buttress the Fourth Fleet. They weren't crewing warships, but they formed repair gangs, served in the supply ships of the Fleet Train, and were building new ships in the Harzapid yards. Still, as far as the illegitimate Zanshaa government was concerned, all such work was rebellion, and all the Naxids worked under pseudonyms so that they might escape retaliation.

Ricci pinged Sula's signals display, and she answered. "Trouble with the *Parkhurst*?" she asked.

"No, my lady, that's taken care of. Captain Mazankosi has arrived, and wishes to see you."

"Send her in."

Senior Captain Lady Sizo Mazankosi entered in full dress uniform complete with the curved ceremonial knife intended for cutting the throats of disobedient juniors. She was in her early thirties, with brown skin, crisp bright blond hair cut very short, and blue eyes so pale that the irises seemed to fade into the whites, leaving Sula looking into pallid orbs marked only by black pupils.

Mazankosi braced, and Sula viewed her for a few seconds before telling her to stand at ease. "Captain Mazankosi, may I present Senior Squadron Commander Lord Nishkad. Or have you met?"

Mazankosi was surprised to discover a Naxid in Sula's office, but she recovered quickly. "I haven't had that honor, Lady Fleetcom." She turned to Nishkad. "I trust your lordship is well?"

"Tolerably," he said. "Thank you for asking." With a degree of care appropriate for the elderly, he uncoiled his body from the sofa and stood on his four legs. "With your permission, my lady," he said, "I need to move my self, my belongings, and my staff to the *Parkhurst*."

"Of course," Sula said. "Let me know if you have any difficulties."

Nishkad bobbed his flat head. "Thank you, Lady Sula."

Nishkad made his way out, and Sula turned back to Captain Mazankosi. "Have a seat, Captain," she said. "Would you like coffee or tea?"

"Coffee, thank you." Mazankosi seated herself. She was tall, with the muscular development of someone who had spent much of the last year under heavy acceleration.

Sula called for Macnamara to bring coffee for her guest, then turned back to Mazankosi. Those pale eyes, she thought, were a little disturbing.

"You were on the planet's surface, Lady Sizo?" she said.

"Yes. I was hunting." She smiled. "A friend invited me to go down the elevator and shoot a penthrad. I'd never had the opportunity, so I packed up my hunting togs and went."

Sula had a personal and unsportsmanlike relationship with spilled blood and wasn't interested in shooting anything for fun. Still, out of politeness she feigned an interest. "Were you successful?"

"I was. I shot a female with twelve spines." Mazankosi smiled in remembrance. "It will make a fine trophy, but I had to leave it behind when I received your message. I'll have it shipped to me after the war."

Sula decided to get to her point. "I was surprised to find you so far away from your command."

"Well." Mazankosi considered her answer. "Until yesterday *Splendid* was in the Fourth Division, and the division wasn't going to depart the ring until repairs on *Consequence* were completed. I knew I had several days at least, and I hadn't anticipated that a new division would be created and that *Splendid* would be assigned to it."

"The Fourth Division launched earlier today," Sula said. "Repairs will be completed in transit. If *Splendid* hadn't been transferred to the Ninth, you would have been stranded."

Mazankosi straightened in her chair and cleared her throat. "Lady Fleetcom," she said. "I will take care not to be stranded in future."

"I trust you won't," Sula said, her point made. "*Splendid* and *Mentor* will depart the ring within a few hours. The rest of the division will leave as soon as they complete resupply."

"Are we moving on Zanshaa at last?" Mazankosi asked.

*Oh damn*, Sula thought. This was going to be a long explanation.

**LIEUTENANT-CAPTAIN LORD PAIVO** Kangas, like his twin, Ranssu, was a tall blond with broad shoulders and large, big-knuckled hands. Ranssu had been promoted to acting squadron commander following the Battle of Shulduc, and Paivo had commanded a frigate until his last-second appointment as Martinez's tactical officer.

"I'm very honored by this appointment, Lord Fleetcom," Paivo said. "Though I can't imagine it will be easy stepping into Lady Sula's job."

Martinez tried not to wince. "I look forward to our collaboration," he said. "Would you like a glass of wine? Sherry? Something stronger?"

"The last time I enjoyed your hospitality," Paivo said, "I developed a taste for your Laredo whisky."

"Of course." Martinez considered it his happy duty to promote the product of his family-owned distillery throughout the empire.

Martinez sent for a bottle and glasses, then regarded the young officer sitting before him. Like the Martinez clan, the Kangas family were provincial Peers who, though very wealthy, had never mounted the lofty heights inhabited by the High City Peers. The twins' father, Eino Kangas, had commanded the Home Fleet in the last war, and had died in the hour of his victory at Antopone.

"So, Lord Paivo," Martinez said. "Have you worked out how to defeat Do-faq yet?"

Paivo gave him an unsettled look. "I have thought of nothing else."

"I'm happy to tell you that Fleetcom Chen has made contact with Wei Jian and her ships from the Second Fleet," Martinez said. "I'm going to hope that she'll persuade Jian to join us."

Paivo heaved a sigh. "That will make my job easier."

"We'll also have six new cruisers built in Laredo," Martinez said, "assuming they arrive in time." And have crews that can do something with them.

Mpanza arrived with a tray holding a whisky bottle, two glasses, and a small silver pitcher of water. He set out the glasses and reached for the bottle to pour, but Martinez took the bottle himself, poured amber liquid into the glasses, and then added a splash of water to his own. The scent of smoke and peat rose in the room.

"Thank you, Mpanza," Martinez said.

"Mangahas is sending out a cheese platter, my lord," Mpanza said.

Martinez looked at Paivo and raised his eyebrows. "Let's hope we're hungry."

"Cheese and whisky?" Paivo said. "Why not?" He splashed a bit of water into his glass, then picked up the glass and swirled it while he tilted his head to inspect the decor of Martinez's office. Before Michi Chen's coup at Harzapid, the flag officer aboard *Los Angeles* had been a Torminel named Lokan, a martial arts enthusiast. He had decorated his suite with murals of furred Torminels in combat, striking, wrestling each other into knots, and sinking their fangs into one another. Trophies won by Lokan and the elite wrestlers in his command were secured to shelves behind Martinez's chair.

Martinez had once served under a captain who was obsessed by football and had painted his frigate with white stripes against a green background, like a football pitch. But at least that captain hadn't filled his quarters with murals of footballers in action.

Martinez had always intended to replace the wrestlers with something more congenial, but there had always been something more urgent to do. Win the war, for a start.

"You know Do-faq," Paivo said. "What can we expect from him?"

"Nothing good," said Martinez. "He was the first commanding officer to adopt the Method, after the victory at Hone-bar." He had almost said "*my* victory," since he'd been the one who won it, for all that Do-faq had been in command.

"With Tork in charge, Do-faq had to be discreet about advocating the Method," Martinez said. "But now he'll be drilling his crews in the Method every day."

The Method was the tactical system that Martinez and Sula had developed in the previous war, and which had proved successful in every battle in which it was tried, including Fleet Commander Kangas's victory at Antopone. Supreme Commander Tork had considered the Method to be an insult to the perfect tactics decreed by the ancestors and the Shaa Great Masters, and he had forbidden its practice throughout the Fleet. In the end that proved fortunate, for Martinez was able to successfully employ it against Tork and his Righteous Fleet and annihilate them.

But now, with both forces employing the same tactics, the outcome was far less certain.

"We have two advantages," Paivo said, "if we can work out how best to exploit them." He took a sip of the whisky, as if to invigorate himself, and then continued. "First, Do-faq is a Lai-own, and that means his hollow bones can't take heavy accelerations. So if we can maneuver with sufficient, ah, *violence*, we can force him to choose between ruinous accelerations and finding himself at a tactical disadvantage."

Martinez nodded. "And our other advantage?"

"You can thank your brother-in-law Shankaracharya for that," Paivo said. "The sensor suites he's manufactured will allow us to see farther through radiation and fireballs, so once the fireworks start we'll have a better idea of what the enemy is doing than they will have of us. The fog of war will become more transparent."

"But again," Martinez said, "we have to find the best way to employ that knowledge."

"That we do."

Martinez felt the whisky bring a warm shimmer to his limbs. "I've also thought about altering some of the parameters of the Method," he said. "It's a dynamic mathematical formula balancing offensive and defensive power, but both those elements are modified by how well we can perceive the enemy. We'll be seeing them at longer ranges now, and I wonder if that will enable us to alter the other parameters."

"It should. But I'm not sure I'm mathematician enough to dig into the workings of the formula."

For a moment Martinez again felt the loss of Sula, for she was a superb mathematician who had worked out the Method's original formula based on ideas they'd developed together.

"And we'll need a lot of data," Paivo continued, "concerning how well we really *can* see in different circumstances, and that means spooling through records of the last battle and comparing results from the ships with and without the Shankaracharya sensor suites."

"Well," Martinez said hopelessly. "We'll have months."

The door opened and Mpanza came into the room with the cheese platter. The platter was grander than Martinez had expected and featured half a dozen types of cheese, pickles, smoked fish, jams, fruit, and several types of flatbread.

Maybe Martinez needed to invite more staff officers.

"Give Mangahas my thanks," he said.

"I will, Lord Fleetcom."

As Mpanza returned to the kitchen there was a respectful knock on the door to the corridor, and Aitor Santana opened the door a crack and leaned in. He was a powerfully built man from Laredo with thick dark eyebrows and a horseshoe mustache, and he offered the impression that if he ever took up Torminel wrestling, he'd give Lokan's champions a run for their money.

"Beg pardon, Lord Fleetcom," he said. "A message from Lady Sula. I didn't know what answer to give her, so I thought I'd better ask you."

Martinez's heart gave a lurch at the name, and he held out his hand for the envelope, then opened it. Sula reported that *Splendid* and *Mentor* had departed Zarafan's ring, and that the rest of the Ninth Division would follow as soon as they had finished provisioning. She also asked where she and her division, including the six Laredo cruisers, would rendezvous with the rest of the Fourth Fleet.

"Toley," Martinez said. Toley was a crossroads system where two paths to Harzapid converged, and an obvious place for a rendezvous.

"Very good, my lord," said Santana.

"How did you and Banerjee fare with the memory cores?" Martinez asked.

There was a brief flicker behind Santana's eyes as his mind shifted from one track to another. "We decided it was easier to rip the cores out of the servers," he said. "Right now the cores are all in sacks in the flag officer's station until we can work out where to put them."

Martinez considered this. "Are you sure you've got everything?"

Santana grinned. "Digital systems in the Lord Commander's office were centralized in a single room. The backups were in a second server standing right next to the primary—not the safest arrangement from the point of a fire or other disaster, though I'm sure it was convenient for the staff. Any messages going in or out of the building passed through a single gateway, so we took the gateway along with everything else." The grin broadened. "Those servers also control the building, so until they're replaced there won't be any light, heat, cooling, or a working kitchen."

Martinez was impressed. "Well done," he said. "Have some cheese."

"Thank you, my lord."

Santana helped himself to cheese and bread, then braced and left the room. Paivo looked up from his glass of whisky.

"That was interesting," he said.

"Vandalism," Martinez said, "plus a bit of looting." Martinez further considered the matter. "Though is it looting if you're stealing your own data?"

"We're crewing a looted *warship*," Paivo said. "Walking off with some hardware is probably the least of our crimes."

*TOLEY. SULA HAD* expected that answer, though it solved one problem at the expense of creating others.

Under normal conditions, it was a three-month journey from Zarafan to Laredo. For Division Nine to make a rendezvous with the six ships outbound from Laredo, it would have to accelerate for the better part of a month, then decelerate for the same amount of time, while the cruisers from Laredo did more or less the same thing. The end result would be that all the ships would end up in the same space heading more or less in the same direction, albeit at fairly low velocity, and the cruisers' crews could be transferred to their new ships without trouble.

But still the ships would spend half their time decelerating, which would delay their arrival in Toley.

Another option would be for Division Nine to turn toward Harzapid at Colamote, a system adjacent to Zarafan with a wormhole gate that would lead to Toley and thence Harzapid. The cruisers from Laredo could accelerate all the way to Colamote and then catch up with Division Nine on the way to Toley. No one would have to bruise themselves in long decelerations, and Division Nine could practically coast along its route until the Laredo ships caught up with them.

The problem was that the new crews would have very little time to become acquainted with their ships before their arrival at Toley, and that would severely hamper their performance in combat. Simulations could take recruits only so far.

Well . . . she would do the math tomorrow and see which course had the greatest advantage. Right now she was too tired, having spent the day getting *Splendid*, *Mentor*, and some of the smaller supply vessels off Zarafan's ring, while meanwhile supervising the looting of Zarafan's warehouses and armories. Missiles and defensive lasers had to be stored safely, antihydrogen fuel taken aboard, furniture suitable for Naxids installed in their cabins and dining facilities, food supplies suitable for two species crammed into larders . . . thousands of small details that somehow always crept up the chain of command to *her*, the commander who was on another ship, who knew the least about the specific details of the case, but who had to make the decision anyway.

"*Think it out for yourself!*" she wanted to shout, but she knew from experience that they wouldn't. Penalties for making the wrong decision were often severe, and a lifetime's habit of evading important choices wasn't one that could be broken overnight.

Sula looked at her chameleon sleeve display and saw the single word *Toley* glowing against the dark background, and with a command she erased the word, and the display shifted to its normal viridian green.

Her back ached, as did her head. Her eyes felt as if they'd been scoured with sand. Nightmares had broken her sleep for the last three nights, and if she wished to function at all on the morrow she needed a full night's rest.

She sent for a glass of mig brandy—she'd stop with just one, she decided—and then rose from her chair, put her hands on the surface of her desk, and arched her back. She sighed as ligaments released one by one.

Macnamara, his aspect heavy with disapproval, brought her brandy on a tray and placed it before her.

"Thank you," Sula said. "You can go to bed, I don't need anything else."

"Yes, Lady Fleetcom." Macnamara and his disapproval left the beige office together.

Sula bent her back from an arch to a bow, and again ligaments crackled. The sharp scent of the brandy began to infiltrate the room. Sula stood erect, picked up the glass, and took a few paces before letting the cool, smooth crystal touch her lips.

In the end it took two glasses of brandy to get her to bed. She poured the second glass herself, in the pantry.

Her sheets had been scented lightly with bergamot. There was nothing wrong with the bed except that she was alone in it, and that meant not only that Martinez was gone, never to return, but that her only companions were her regrets, her memories, and her nightmares. She wondered who she would dream of tonight: Caro Sula dead in her apartment in Maranic Town; her cousin Goojie bleeding to death in the dining room in Otautahi; her lover Casimir dying of his wounds in the hospital in Zanshaa High City; Lamey staring with blank blue eyes in the apartment on Celestial Court...

She told the bedroom's sound system to play derivoo. Derivoo was a form of musical performance solely practiced by human women, and its subject matter was pure melodrama: death, violence, abandonment, and devastation. Critics of the form complained that it was depressing, or overstated, but Sula thought derivoo told the truth about life, which was that life was fatal.

*Everything dies. Nothing matters.* The conclusions she'd reached after she had made a longed-for trip to Terra and found it shabby and dilapidated and largely ignorant of the history that was piled up everywhere she looked.

For several months, caught up in her life with Martinez, she had forgotten her own maxims, and now she needed to reconnect. She needed the defiant sound of derivoo, the women who sang of the child who died, the love that was never returned, the knife that stopped the heart of a betrayer, or—

Or the lover who walked away and returned to his wife.

At this thought Sula's heart seemed to drop into her boots. But then the first chords of derivoo sounded, and the first angry lyric snarled into the air. Derivoo wasn't only tragedy, she knew, it was *defiance*—these women were not beaten down, they were not apologetic, they stood amid blood and death, defied their destiny, and dared fate to do its worst.

*Everything dies. Nothing matters.* What could fate do that was worse than that?

Sula told the sound system to increase the volume and settled herself in bed.

She supposed that any neighbors might prefer her waking screams to a long night of derivoo, but then she was division commander and they weren't. If rank couldn't get you what you needed, what good was it?

The brandy warming her veins, and surrounded by songs of terror, blood, betrayal, and misery, she slept the night through and rose ready to cry her defiance in the face of fate.

# CHAPTER 3

Morning found Sula's cries of defiance muted. Instead of boldly proclaiming resistance to the blows of fate, she ended up chasing solutions to a storm of problems that had nothing to do with her but that had gotten pushed up the chain of command anyway.

It was frustrating and exhausting, but by the end of the day the full Ninth Division had at last departed from Zarafan's ring and were now engaged in grouping themselves into a formation that would enable them to act more or less in concert if such a thing were ever to prove necessary.

At the last possible minute they had taken aboard a number of passengers—officials and supporters of the Restoration who had worked out that the Fourth Fleet was running for its life, and who now reckoned their chances of surviving the next change of administration were limited. They had arrived with their families, and while Sula wasn't sure what she was going to do with a collection of clerks, bureaucrats, and their children, she decided she couldn't leave them and their families to be massacred by Lady Tu-hon's minions and took them aboard the big immigration ships.

She had been invited to supper that night with Captain Mazankosi and her officers, which took place in a dining room decorated with paintings of living game animals and photographs of Mazankosi standing next to dead animals that she had, apparently, shot. The main course was wild ziege in a sauce flavored with herbs. Some of the lieutenants shared Mazankosi's enthusiasm for blood sports, and talk of stalking and shooting occupied much of the evening and allowed Sula to concentrate on enjoying the wine that was poured with a lavish hand by Mazankosi's steward.

"Do you shoot, Lady Sula?" one lieutenant asked her.

"Yes, but not at game," Sula said.

"You shoot at targets, then? Or do you prefer trap shooting?"

"Most of my targets have been Naxids," Sula said, "though lately I was obliged to kill a company of the Legion of Diligence, and they were all Torminel."

There was a moment of silence, and then Mazankosi rose to the occasion and lifted her glass. "May all your endeavors be crowned by such sublime success, Lady Fleetcom."

"Thank you, Lady Sizo."

A salutary reminder, Sula thought, that this war was not *sport*.

FLEET COMMANDER WEI Jian was a handsome woman with black hair artfully streaked with white and cut short above her ears. She wore a full-dress tunic with two rows of silver buttons and a collar rising to just below her chin. Her gaze was level, her voice mild, her tone implacable.

"I was the superior officer, Squadcom Chen," she said. "I fully expected that you would retire toward me rather than ignore me in order to engage a superior force on your own."

Michi Chen had forwarded the video to Martinez with but a single comment: *See what I'm putting up with now?*

"Under the circumstances," Jian said, "and with your few survivors under threat, I see no reason that I should not order your forces to join me at the earliest opportunity. Most of my forces are stationed in the Tai-ma system, which I have organized into an elaborate booby trap into which we can hope to lure Do-faq."

Martinez bristled at the mention of his "few survivors," which nevertheless outnumbered Jian's command more than two-to-one, and now he frowned at the Torminel wrestlers on the walls of his office while he considered the notion of booby-trapping an entire star system. Tai-ma was a barren system, he knew, full of rocky planets, rocky moons, and rocky asteroids behind which any number of nasty surprises could lurk.

It was not an implausible plan, and nasty surprises could work very well indeed—Martinez had successfully executed any number of traps for Supreme Commander Tork before Second Shulduc—but much depended on how many missiles and other resources Wei Jian had available, and Martinez suspected she didn't have nearly enough.

"From Tai-ma," Jian continued, "positioned between Harzapid and Magaria, we can either wait to engage Do-faq or move toward Magaria, and from there go on to Zanshaa, which we can certainly reach before Do-faq gets his forces turned around."

This, Martinez thought, was an intriguing idea and worth thinking about, though it meant abandoning the Restoration's supporters on Harzapid, Earth, and a score of other planets.

With the video Michi had included her own reply.

"Lady Fleetcom," she said, "I remained at Harzapid for several reasons. The first is that Lord Inspector Ivan Snow ordered all Terran craft to rendezvous at Harzapid, and therefore I have been expecting you here for months. If you received different orders from the rest of us, I was never made aware of this."

Martinez thought there was nothing like opening a message with the suggestion that Wei Jian had been disobeying orders all this time. Michi's polite but unwavering tone mirrored Jian's, and beneath her snowy bangs, her shadowed eyes flared like flint and steel. Her jaundiced complexion, the result of months of overwork, had been concealed with cosmetic.

"Second," Michi said, "I not only seized the hundred and seventy–odd warships of the Fourth Fleet, but I also took the dock-yards, the antimatter-generation ring, the fleet stores, dozens of support vessels, and of course the planet Harzapid itself. We have converted Harzapid into an arsenal that produces an effectively unlimited supply of missiles and antimatter. We are also training recruits and building warships, as are our allies on Earth and else-where, and the first of these will be shaking down within weeks."

Michi offered a gracious nod, like a superior to a promising recruit. "Last," she said, "we have established a working govern-ment and a functioning economy in the areas that we control. To abandon our bases, with all their resources, and leave our friends and supporters in the hands of a murderous clique of deranged and greedy politicians strikes me as highly irresponsible, and not at all the act of a government seeking legitimacy."

Michi affected a judicious nod and clasped her hands on the desk before her. "The idea of coming at Magaria and Zanshaa through the back door had occurred to me, but the problem I see is that taking Zanshaa won't end the war, any more than it ended the war for the Naxids. We'll still have to face the enemy fleet and de-feat it, and it's best to do that from a position of advantage, and with a logistical support train available. Therefore"—the judicious nod again—"I suggest that you bring your forces to Harzapid in order to unite with the Fourth Fleet, defeat Do-faq, and move on to the capital. In the meantime, Fleet Commander Martinez can start sowing booby traps on the route between Zarafan and Harzapid—they proved very effective against Lord Tork in the last campaign."

*Well done*, Martinez sent to Michi afterward, though he had to admit that he had the sense that this dialogue was far from over.

SULA VIEWED THE video with her left eye half-closed, as only her right eye seemed able to focus. A hot cup of coffee, liberally sweetened with cane sugar syrup, stood close to her right hand, its scent sharp in the air. Her lips stung with her last attempt to drink, when she had found the coffee blistering hot.

*Another fine day on the* Splendid, she thought.

"My lady," said Paivo Kangas on the video. "I apologize for this interruption, but I imagine you know that I've been made your successor as tactical officer on *Los Angeles*, a prospect that I find intimidating." He paused, his big hands restless on the desk in front of him. "I would like to ask some questions about the workings of the Method, if I may."

*So Martinez doesn't dare ask me himself*, Sula thought.

Paivo waited a few seconds, as if for a reply, before continuing. "We are trying to determine whether the Shankaracharya sensor suites might allow us to favorably alter the formula in some way. We'll be able to see farther into fireballs and radiation clouds, and that will certainly change our tactics—but will it change the parameters of the Method? As you were primarily responsible for the formula itself, I thought I would ask your opinion." He offered a slight bow. "Again, my lady, I apologize for the interruption." The orange end-stamp filled the wall screen.

Sula cranked open her left eye and contemplated the end-stamp with her blurred vision, then directed her gaze toward the cup of coffee with its pattern of pomegranates and tulips. She picked up the coffee, blew ripples across its surface, then took a tentative sip.

Sweet and bitter crossed her tongue, and the liquid had cooled enough that she managed not to scald herself. She took another sip.

Tea was too weak to deal with her hangover. Only coffee was strong enough to blast her into full consciousness.

It had been another night of brandy and derivoo—after the wine at dinner—and again she had avoided the nightmares that would have robbed her of sleep. But for some reason she had slept badly anyway, tossed all night, and woke tangled in her sheets, with a backache and a head filled with cotton wool.

Shawna Spence entered with a plate and a basket of the sweet pastries Sula favored for breakfast, reached for the silver coffee-pot, realized Sula's cup didn't need topping up, and withdrew.

"Reply: text only," Sula said. "'I will give the matter my full con-sideration. I will also need data of sensor performance at Shulduc.' Message ends: send message."

Sula's reply went to the signals station in Command, where it would be ciphered and sent on its way. She picked up a braided pas-try, broke it, and dipped one end of the braid into a dish of cream butter sent up from Zarafan on one of the last supply shipments.

*Might as well enjoy the butter while it's fresh*, Sula thought, and chewed. Sugar crystals exploded on Sula's tongue, and as if in re-sponse, her vision miraculously cleared.

After two cups of coffee and a pair of pastries, she was able to give thought to Paivo Kangas's request. Without data she could do very little, but she thought she might as well reacquaint herself with her previous work, and so she called up the Structured Math-ematics Display onto the wall screen and pasted the formula into it.

Numbers and symbols leaped into existence before her. She remembered the joy with which she had first beheld this mathe-matical truth, the numbers describing a reality that had existed from the beginning of time, and that had waited all those eons for Sula to find them.

The numbers had been based on data from the First Battle of Magaria, in which the Home Fleet had been nearly wiped out, and the Naxids, though victorious, had lost whole formations. What Magaria had shown was that the tactics traditional in the Fleet were inadequate and had a proclivity for mutual annihilation.

In order to control their formations, commanders tended to group their ships close together, which meant that a lucky missile barrage could wipe them out all at once. When the close formation became too perilous the ships could starburst, each flying in a different direction to escape the threat. This might keep the formation from being engulfed in a single wave of missiles, but at the cost of unit cohesion and the loss of the overlapping fields of defensive fire that helped keep the ships safe.

The Martinez Method—which Sula preferred to call Ghost Tactics, after her onetime underground identity as the White Ghost—allowed a formation to undergo a controlled, dynamic starburst that safely separated the ships while maintaining cohesion and mutually supporting defensive fire.

The formations would not be static, but would undergo constant shifts while the ships moved along the convex hull of a chaotic dynamical system, a type of fractal pattern that would seem locally stochastic to an observer. An enemy would see ships taking what would seem to be unpredictable, random shifts in course and speed, which would make targeting more complicated. Despite being chaotic, the shifting pattern was designed to keep the ships at an ideal distance for overlapping defensive fire.

Sula let the formula roll up the screen, and she absorbed it line by line, letting each statement expand in her mind. She hadn't revisited the formula since she'd first composed it, and the rediscovery was a constant, unfolding delight.

A notice appeared on her sleeve display that another message from Paivo Kangas was pending, so she triggered it.

"Thank you, my lady, for your prompt reply," he said. "I have already sent to the ship captains for data, but there is going to be a lot of it, the whole battle's worth. I'll endeavor to send you only the most useful of the scans, but it may take some time."

Sula considered this, then began a reply. It was only at the last second that she decided to turn the camera on herself and was appalled to discover she was sitting in a dressing gown with tangled hair and the ruins of her breakfast scattered before her. She looked something like a ruined breakfast herself.

She decided to send audio only.

"Lord Paivo," she said, "I think that for this task we might begin by recruiting others. If you can persuade the lord fleetcom to order sensor techs and weapons officers to analyze the scans, we can get this done quickly."

And, she thought, she was late for her first shower of the day, and she should probably put on a uniform once she'd toweled herself off. If a shipboard emergency caught her in her dressing gown, it would hamper her effectiveness and give her a reputation for eccentricity at the same time.

It wasn't that she minded being thought eccentric, because she knew she had been eccentric all her life, but she didn't want to be thought the *wrong kind* of eccentric.

She showered, dried off, then stood before the mirror combing her hair. She looked critically at herself in the mirror, and it occurred to her that she had been wearing Caro Sula's face almost as long as Caro had.

It was Sula's face now. She'd paid for it.

Spence had readied a uniform in Sula's sleeping cabin, and Sula dressed and returned to her desk. Her breakfast had been cleared away, but the silver coffee flask still stood on the desk, next to a clean cup and the cane syrup dispenser.

A brisk knock sounded on her door.

"Enter," she said.

The man who stepped into her office was still in his twenties but walked with the assurance of a man in his prime. He was pale, and he had shaved his head while allowing himself a thick black chevron mustache. Triangular red staff tabs shone on his collar.

"Lady Sula," he said. "I'm Dr. Gunaydin."

He had not bothered to brace in salute, and Sula considered barking at him over it, then decided she didn't have the energy.

"How may I help you, Doctor?" she said.

"I've taken an inventory of the medical supplies available aboard *Splendid*, and I've found we're deficient in several categories, particularly antiradiation meds." He raised his sleeve display. "I can transmit the list to your display, and—"

Sula interrupted him. "I'm not in charge of supplies, Doctor, and you're staff and not even in my chain of command. You should speak to the premiere, or to Captain Mazankosi."

"I've never met the premiere lieutenant or the captain," Gunaydin said. "And while I haven't met you, either, my orders to leave *Judge Kasapa* and report aboard *Splendid* came from you."

"You're needed," Sula said. "The Ninth Division had no physicians. You'll be the sole doctor for the thousands of Terrans under my command, and a group of Naxids too."

"All the more reason to be fully stocked with supplies," Gunaydin said. "And I know the necessary supplies are aboard at least some of our ships, because when I was trying to get necessities out of medical stores on the ring, I found them being looted by recruits from the Ninth Division."

"I don't suppose they mentioned what ship they were from?"

Gunaydin gave a short laugh. "In fact, they refused. After they began threatening me, I searched elsewhere, but found nothing."

Sula nodded. "And now you're doctor to the recruits who threatened you." She considered the problem. "I suppose I *am* the person you should be speaking to, since Captain Mazankosi has no authority to requisition supplies from another ship. Send me your list, and I'll see what I can do."

After Gunaydin left—again without bracing to the salute—Sula sent the list to Ricci and asked him to requisition the supplies. "Tell them we also want an inventory," she said. "Not just of medical supplies, but missile launchers, missiles, antimatter, and any defensive weaponry."

"Yes, Lady Fleetcom." The words, spoken in Ricci's pleasant baritone, acted as a balm to Sula's nerves.

"Thank you," she said, and returned her attention to the Structured Mathematics Display and let the beauty of the equations dwell for a long moment in her mind.

And then she thought, *How would I beat them?*

The equations were a thing of art, but that didn't mean they were perfect in every circumstance. They were based on data from First Magaria, because that was the first and only battle in the Naxid War when the formula was written.

There had been more battles since, so there was more data available now, but was it *better* data? Would it reveal anything new that required her to revise the formula?

She would find out, she supposed, once Paivo began sending her everything they had from Second Shulduc.

But Paivo and Sula weren't the only people thinking about

these matters. Do-faq and his staff had access to the Method, and Do-faq had been an early supporter of Ghost Tactics. They were presumably preparing to fight a battle using the formula, and drilling their squadrons in different scenarios, but might also be doing what she was doing: reexamining it to see if there were tweaks to be made, advantages to be had.

More, the Fourth Fleet, so far as Sula knew, had never drilled one group using Ghost Tactics against another. They had known that Tork's tactics would be out of the old playbook and had based their fleet exercises on that knowledge. Assuming that Do-faq's captains had been drilling Method vs. Method, they would have a much better idea of what to expect in such a battle than anyone in the Fourth Fleet.

Sula would have to create some scenarios for her own warships, particularly once she made her rendezvous with the six from Laredo.

The problem became clear: how could she beat her own Ghost Tactics? Data from Paivo might allow for a few tweaks in the formula, but she doubted any such changes could produce a decisive advantage. One side's chaotic maneuvers would cancel the other's.

Unless, of course, the maneuvers *weren't actually chaotic.* They were theoretically unpredictable, but in reality they were *dictated by a mathematical formula.*

In order to shoot at a warship, you didn't shoot at the space it currently occupied, you shot at the place where the trajectory of the warship and that of the attacking missile would intersect.

Suppose you could get *inside* the formula somehow, so that you could know when and in what direction the enemy warships would change their course. You could fire at the place where you *knew for certain* the enemy would be.

Sula sat up straight at her desk, a soft cry of astonishment on her lips. She looked at her desk and discovered that she'd drunk half a pot of coffee and that sticky syrupy fingerprints marred the desk's surface.

Also, her bladder was about to burst.

When she returned from her visit to the toilet, she got out her stylus and began to make notes.

If the enemy was using Ghost Tactics, and you knew *where every enemy ship was* at a given instant, and you knew their course and trajectory, you *might* be able to predict their next movements. And if you were wrong, even your wrong guesses became data, and you could make another prediction based upon that.

You would start, she thought, by chaining together a series of experiments, each experiment providing a set of inputs that would be used in the following experiment—plus you could do a reverse jump, which would explore a different set of equations with different parameters to allow the exploration of a larger mathematical space.

All results, she thought, could be combined into a single result, a set of trajectories where the most likely results were given greater emphasis than those deemed less plausible.

*This is going to take a hell of a lot of processing power*, she thought, and vanished into the mathematics.

"WELL DONE," MARTINEZ said. "You may secure from general quarters."

His order applied only to his staff in the flag officer's station, since everyone else on *Los Angeles* would have to be released from quarters by Captain Dalkeith. Martinez opened the faceplate of his helmet and inhaled air untainted by the scent of suit seals and disinfectant. His acceleration cage creaked as he shifted to a sitting position.

The Fourth Fleet had just undergone an exercise in which it had been divided into two equal halves, then engaged in combat with both sides using the Martinez Method. Though the margin of victory had been small, Martinez had commanded the winning side, and he felt a modest amount of satisfaction.

Martinez spun his cage to face Paivo Kangas. "Were the captures good?" he asked.

"Nonii," Paivo said. "We produced a lot of data."

This was the fourth exercise intended to provide data for the research that Paivo and Sula had begun, trying to find if the Method's maneuvers were predictable. So far there was no answer—neither side in any of the exercises had successfully predicted anything—but the more data available, the better the chance of a successful prediction. Or so the math suggested, anyway.

The best part was that Martinez didn't have to deal with Sula in person. All that was left to Paivo.

There had been another series of experiments going on in parallel, with live ammunition. Antimatter missiles had been fired into the gaps between formations, to determine how well the sensor suites could see through expanding fireball spheres.

More data for the mathematicians. He could only hope it produced results.

An alert sounded through the ship, followed by Captain Dalkeith's breathy voice informing the crew that the exercise was over and they could leave their action stations.

Martinez unlocked his helmet and drew it off, then pulled off the elastic cap with its electrodes and tossed it in the bowl of his helmet. He ran his fingers through his dark sweat-damp hair.

"Send me the results when you have them," he said.

"Nonii," said Paivo again.

*Nonii* was a word the Kangas twins had brought from their re-

mote but rich home valley of Toimi. It was a word of many mean-
ings: "affirmative," "hello," "all right," "fair enough," "no problem,"
"acceptable," "let's go," "we're ready," and probably a dozen other
possibilities. From Paivo and Ranssu the word had spread to the
whole Fourth Fleet, and everyone from captains to the lowliest recruit had adopted it.

"Nonii," Martinez answered, planted his boots on the deck,
and rose to his feet. *Los Angeles* was accelerating at 0.8 gravities as
it maneuvered into a cruising formation after the disorder of the
mock battle, and he thought he should get out of his vac suit while
the gravity was still light.

Helmet under his arm, Martinez walked to his quarters. His
personal quarters might be ornamented with Torminel wrestlers,
but elsewhere in officers' country the corridors were more conventional, with dark wood paneling accented with brass, then hung
with bland, vaguely allegorical paintings of idealized citizens engaged in idealized activities in idealized settings, urban and rural.
Grain was harvested, buildings were erected, statues were raised
on plinths, people paddled in boats, birds flew overhead in blithe
circles. Everyone and everything was happy under the Praxis.

Except Martinez was not happy under the Praxis, and he was
sick of the corridors with their paintings and paneling, the dinner
parties he was obliged to attend, and the Torminel wrestlers who
blighted the walls of his quarters. He had spent nearly a year on *Los
Angeles*, first drilling its green crew, then leading the Fourth Fleet
against the overwhelming power of Tork and his Righteous Fleet.
It had been ages since he'd set foot on the surface of a planet, felt a
fresh breeze on his cheek or rain pattering his jacket, seen a sunset
or the silver of sunlight on shimmering leaves.

Zarafan's ring with its dockyard was an artificial environment,
with recycled air, but it was large enough for tree-lined boulevards,

parks, restaurants with open-air patios, and freshly grown flowers for his office. Sula's presence had seemed to expand every horizon near to infinity.

Now that he was back on *Los Angeles*, he felt as if he were being fitted for a coffin. Perhaps it was Do-faq doing the fitting, perhaps it was Wei Jian. Maybe he was nailing the coffin together himself, piece by piece.

Mpanza helped him out of his vac suit when he reached his quarters. Martinez showered, put on fresh clothes, and went to his office, where Torminel wrestlers glared at him from the walls and Mpanza was placing the coffee service. Martinez took his seat.

"How are the people doing?" he asked.

"We are frustrated," Mpanza said. "Though we are curious about these tactical experiments and all the data that is being gathered and analyzed. We speculate."

Martinez was amused by the plural pronoun. "At least you—all of you—care," he said.

"Do you wish coffee now, my lord?"

"I'm okay."

Mpanza hesitated, then spoke. "Not all the speculation concerns the exercises," he said.

"Yes?"

"We also wonder about the departure of Lady Sula," he said, almost as if in apology. "You and she formed such a successful partnership that we feel a little uneasy with a new tactical officer."

Martinez felt blood prickle his skin at the mention of Sula's name, and heat flashed behind his eyeballs. He hadn't expected any such question, and he had to take a few breaths before he could compose an answer.

"Lady Sula never wanted a staff position," he said. "She commanded her own squadron before Fleetcom Chen appointed her tactical officer, and now she has a squadron again."

He did not feel obliged to mention their monthslong liaison, which presumably was well-known to Mpanza and everyone else on the ship. If they speculated what had happened to split them up, they were welcome to do it in private.

"I understand, my lord," Mpanza said.

"Lady Sula continues her collaboration with us," Martinez said. "These new exercises are based on her ideas."

"I'm sure we will be comforted to know this," Mpanza said.

Martinez looked up at Mpanza. "Is there any other comfort I can offer all of you?"

Again Mpanza hesitated. "We understand that Fleetcom Jian is in communication with Fleetcom Chen," he said. "We wonder who will command the Fourth Fleet."

Martinez flapped his hands helplessly. "That I cannot tell," he said. He looked sidelong at the silver coffeepot, which had begun to send tendrils of coffee aroma through the air.

"I think I'll have coffee after all," he said.

"Yes, my lord."

After Mpanza left, Martinez sipped coffee while he paged through his messages. He sent answers where appropriate, then saw that messages awaited from both Terza and Michi Chen.

Though he felt a strong desire to view the latest chapter of the battle of wills between Michi and Wei Jian, he dutifully watched Terza's video first. She had recorded her message from a drawing room on the yacht carrier *Corona*, where she and Gareth the Younger had been lodging since *Corona*'s arrival at Harzapid. She wore an ankle-length dark green gown of satiny material, nearly the shade of the Fleet's viridian uniforms, with a necklace of jade beads each carved into the shape of a tougama blossom. Her long black hair had been caught in a large braid pinned in a complicated knot at her nape.

"I'm on my way to a benefit concert," she said. "We'll be performing Arcojag's *Sweet Rivers Suite* for the Health Systems Foundation. Governor Koridun will very kindly introduce us."

Martinez would rather the concert had supported relief for the orphans and other dependents of those the Fourth Fleet had lost at Shulduc, but he understood that the Restoration wouldn't want the money to go exclusively to Terrans. Benefitting Terrans only, as the Restoration never ceased to remind everyone, was not what this war was about.

Terza smiled. "Rehearsals have gone well, so I have hopes that we won't embarrass ourselves. There seems to be quite a tradition of chamber music on Harzapid, so I hope that we can fit in."

Martinez could not imagine Terza not fitting in anywhere she cared to. Her ease in social situations was a product of thousands of years of breeding—as was, perhaps, her aura of slightly unreal perfection, as if she were at the center of a portrait that had been a little overworked by the artist.

"Chai-chai is still in class," she continued. "I know he's composing a message for you. I hope it won't be a blow-by-blow description of his last game of *Barbarians of Terra*, but I fear it might be." She smiled. "I'm sure he would want you to know he used the word *deleterious* in conversation the other day."

Martinez had worked hard to expand his son's vocabulary, and he was gratified that he seemed to have succeeded, even at such a distance.

Terza's dark eyes seemed somehow to deepen as she looked at the camera, and the smile still touched the corners of her lips. "As for your suggestion about awarding ourselves a special gift after the war—well, it was a surprise, but I am not averse. But this should be discussed more thoroughly when we finally meet in person, and we know more about postwar assignments and so forth."

She glanced off camera for a brief moment, then turned back to gaze at Martinez. "I've got to pack up my harp and head to the concert hall," she said. "I'll send another message soon, along with a recording of the concert."

Martinez found himself breathing out a relieved sigh when the orange end-stamp filled the screen. Whatever Terza might have heard about Sula, she seemed to have accepted his message at face value and had pronounced herself "not averse" to having another child.

He seemed to have succeeded in shoring up his marriage. Now if he could only shore up the Fourth Fleet, he would be ready for anything.

The message from Michi Chen had been sent with the command cipher, and he had to use his commander's key to unlock and decipher it. Wei Jian appeared on the screen, expressionless and implacable, the white stripes in her short hair like the markings of a predator beast.

"I have reluctantly ordered my command to move toward Harzapid," Jian said, "though there are several issues yet to be resolved. The first of these is that you seem to have promoted yourself several grades to senior fleet commander, and handed out promotions as well to Lady Sula and to Lord Gareth Martinez and perhaps others I don't know about."

She gave the camera a firm look, and her chin jutted out with more than a hint of defiance. "I remind you that I have always been senior to you, Lady Michi. Before the current conflict you were rated as a squadron commander, whereas I was a senior squadcom, and just before the war's outbreak the Fleet Control Board jumped me two grades to fleet commander. You can scarcely expect me to subordinate myself to someone who has simply announced that she has a higher rank than mine, with no government or other authority to legitimize the promotion."

Wei Jian paused for a moment, as if to let that sink in, and then continued in her imperturbable way.

"When I arrive at Harzapid, I will expect the imaginary promotions to have been forgotten, and that I will remain in uncontested command of the Restoration military for the remainder of the war."

The orange end-stamp filled the screen while Martinez felt a snarl crossing his face. *Imaginary promotions*, he thought. *Uncontested command.* This woman's arrogance was beyond belief.

*Where*, he wondered, *were Sula and her pistol now they were needed?*

As before, Michi had appended her reply to the message. Her impassive face stared darkly into the camera from beneath her crown of white hair, and she still wore the shoulder boards of a senior fleet commander.

"Lady Wei," she said, "I am terribly concerned that you are promoting yourself from the rank of fleetcom to the rank of laughingstock. Kindly allow me to explain.

"First, I'm certain that your promotion to fleetcom was a ruse to draw your squadrons to Magaria so that you and your ships could be boarded and carried by the enemy. Tork and the Fleet Control Board would never have promoted any commander that they intended to arrest unless the promotion was intended only as a lure.

"Second, when I took control of the Fourth Fleet, I found myself in command of over two hundred warships. The military is an ecosystem, and that ecosystem requires that certain niches be filled. I found myself in command not only of a fleet but also of a dockyard, the planet below, and a war. Since I was in command of a fleet, I promoted myself to fleet commander, and I gave other promotions in accordance with the duties the officers in question were ordered to undertake. Officers commanding squadrons were made squadron commanders, officers commanding large elements of the fleet were made fleet commanders, and so forth. Senior Squadron Commander Kung, when he joined us, accepted my arrangements and served under my command."

Martinez had to admire Michi's ability not to smile, at least a little, as she delivered this address. But then her bland expression was broken not only by a slight smile, but a *smug* smile.

"I think events have justified my actions," she said. And then she gave a slight nod, and the self-satisfied smile vanished.

"The Fourth Fleet fought three engagements with the enemy, first at Colamote, and then the two battles at Shulduc. All three of those battles resulted in the annihilation of the enemy. Our crews are battle-hardened, capable, and, more to the point, they are *tested*."

A hint of a smile appeared at the corners of Michi's lips, then vanished. "It isn't your fault, of course, that you've never fought in a single action during your otherwise distinguished career—and yet you insist on putting yourself over experienced officers far more qualified than you to command a fleet in battle . . . and this follows months of your avoiding battle at Tai-ma."

Martinez sensed that Michi was making a substantial effort to keep that smile from once again crossing her features. "It might be said—and it *will* be said, though I will do my best to dampen any such talk—that you were so afraid of combat that you hid in a homemade fort at Tai-ma for months, and only now have emerged to insist on commanding the Fourth Fleet in hopes of victory in the final battle, so that you can take credit for winning the war." Michi shrugged her shoulder boards. "Untrue, naturally, but I cannot prevent my people from drawing uncharitable conclusions about an officer they don't know."

She looked into the camera, her face serene. "I'm pleased to hear that you and your ships are in motion for Harzapid. Once we unite our forces we can win the war together, and the credit for that achievement can safely be left to history."

The end-stamp filled the screen, and Martinez leaned back in his chair and let out a long, reflective breath. He thought that Michi had stated her case rather more tactlessly than was necessary, and that he wouldn't be surprised if Jian reacted with rage or stormed back to Tai-ma in a huff and took her squadrons with her. Michi might end up paying for that brief, smug little smile.

It was bitter, he realized, to admit that Wei Jian's ships were necessary for victory, that he and Michi and Sula, despite all their efforts, their victories, and their valor, did not command forces equal to the task. He wanted to be able to thrash Do-faq himself and lead the fleet that would take the capital. It was what he had planned for months, and what he felt he deserved.

But even for all his desires and goals, winning was paramount. That's what Michi was telling Wei Jian, and it was no easier hearing it himself.

The videos had awakened a restlessness in Martinez, restlessness tinged with anger. He was not accustomed to being an observer of conflict—he was used to plunging into battle, and to winning any battle he chose to plunge into. Sitting on the sidelines while watching a struggle that might determine victory or defeat for the Restoration was not to his taste. Yet Michi Chen would not welcome any intervention on her behalf, and he had no choice but to watch and hope for the best.

What he needed to do, therefore, was to come up with tactics certain to defeat Do-faq no matter *who* was in charge.

"Nonii," he muttered, by which he meant "No problem." Then

he stopped and stared at the grappling Torminels on his walls. He had surprised himself by speaking out loud.

"Nonii," he echoed, and this time he meant "Let's get started."

THE SHIPS OF Division Nine, which had left Zarafan one at a time, as each was supplied or finished repairs, were at last flying more or less together, so Sula invited her captains to dinner. These sorts of events were inevitable: the officers drifted from ship to ship to attend one or another banquet, or the lieutenants would play host to the captain in the wardroom, or the petty officer's mess would invite the squadron commander to dine. Sula was not such a social creature that she could enjoy all this flying back and forth from one dinner to another, and she was inclined to resent it as an imposition.

In Division Nine not all the captains held commissions in the Fleet: some were civilians whose ships had been volunteered or commandeered into the forces of the Restoration, but even these were greeted with the full ceremonial pomp of the Fleet and escorted to Sula's dining room by courteous aides glittering in full-dress uniform.

That was not the end of the pageant, for the meal consisted of nine courses, each presented with ceremony and accompanied by an appropriate wine. *Splendid* probably outdid even the high tables of the immigration ships, where passengers in supreme and first class were treated like royalty under the benign and imperial eye of the captain. Those officers drawn from the smaller cargo vessels seemed overwhelmed.

"Peers, ladies, and gentlemen," Sula said at the end, raising her glass, "I give you the Restoration of the Praxis."

The truth was she didn't give a damn about the Praxis, but she knew her audience, and the toast came back to her echoing and loud in the wedge-shaped room, after which she took a careful sip of wine. She had been cautious about alcohol consumption during the meal, for she had a presentation to make and preferred to be coherent when she did it, so she took a single sip, spice and warmth, before putting the glass down on the far side of her goblet of water.

The meal progressed, and soon coffee and liqueurs made their way around the table, and the conversation became general. Sula took a few moments to review her plans, and then called for attention. She waited for eyes to turn toward her and then spoke.

"Most of you, I think, understand our orders. We are to meet six new-built ships coming from Laredo and crew them with the recruits we'll be training en route. Those ships carrying vital supplies will accompany the warships to Harzapid, and the rest will travel on to Laredo.

"Now what *I* intend to do," she said, as she looked deliberately from one pair of eyes to another, "is to *create more warships* en route, and I hope you will aid me with all your skill and expertise."

Sula watched her audience carefully and saw that the idea struck them first as surprising, then as outlandish. They looked at each other, not in bewilderment, but in something approaching alarm at the possibility that Sula was going to ask them to do something beyond sanity. She waited for the eyes to turn toward her again, then continued.

"I don't know how many of you are familiar with Naxid attempts to convert civilian ships into warships during the last war, but I can assure you that these improvised craft were more successful than not. The Naxids took the largest class of cargo ships—ships bigger than battleships—and stuffed them with rocket launchers. At one point I calculated that each could hold up to six hundred launchers."

Again the eyes of her audience sought one another, this time sending a single question to one another: *Can this possibly be true?*

"I ordered you to scavenge as many missiles and missile launchers from Zarafan's facilities as possible," she said. "And I hope we can work out a way to install them while we're in transit. We won't be able to approach anything like six hundred launchers per ship, but I hope we can engineer a big surprise for Do-faq." She smiled. "Can you imagine what the enemy will think when they see three battleship-sized craft in our formation, and they start hurling missiles out?"

"Lady Sula?" A hand was raised down the table, and Sula recognized Captain Abasi of the immigration ship *Ideal*. He wore a cream-colored tunic flashing with gold and accented with green and scarlet braid, far more imposing than any uniform found in the Fleet.

"Which ships did you have in mind?" he asked.

"Yours, to start with," Sula said. "*Pride of Parkhurst*. And *Lentrec*." Unlike the other two, *Lentrec* was a vast cargo ship, nearly as big as the immigration craft.

"I don't think my company would approve," Abasi said.

"I don't plan to ask their permission," Sula said.

Abasi nodded. "Good," he said, and rubbed his hands briskly together. "I've always wanted to command a battleship."

*Lentrec*'s captain was less eager to command a warship than Abasi, but said that she would contact her company's agent on Zarafan for guidance.

"I advise against it," Sula said. "Zarafan is about to be occupied by the enemy, and we don't want a query of that sort in a place where the enemy might find it. We want the appearance of these new-made warships to be a surprise, not a known contingency the enemy has a chance to plan for." She raised her eyebrows.

"Does your company have agents in any systems controlled by the Restoration?"

"Harzapid and Laredo." Which were about the same distance from Zarafan.

"Contact the agents at Harzapid," Sula said. "They'd probably have more up-to-date information."

*And I will contact Michi Chen*, she thought, *and ask her to exert her influence on the Fleet's behalf.*

"If you are uncomfortable with the notion of commanding a warship," Sula added, "I could put a Fleet officer on board as commander, and you could either serve as executive officer or you could move on with the noncombatants to Laredo."

*Lentrec*'s captain was startled by this suggestion, and it was clear she hadn't thought this far ahead.

"I will be content to do as the agent advises," she said.

"Very good," Sula said. She had hoped for more enthusiasm but would take what she could get.

She turned to Devindar Suri, captain of the *Pride of Parkhurst*. "Captain," she said, "does the project appeal to you?"

*Parkhurst* was owned by the Martinez family, all committed supporters of the Restoration, and she had little doubt that Suri would volunteer both himself and his ship.

"I'm willing to do as your ladyship advises," Suri said. Sula thanked him.

"We've taken a few hundred missile launchers," Sula said, "and we have plenty of missiles, and the Fleet Train can bring us more. Our limitations lie in the plumbing necessary to store missiles and feed them to the launchers, and also in the heavy radiation shielding required around the antimatter warheads."

Because otherwise the radiation from a near miss could destabilize the silicon chips that held the antihydrogen in suspension, and the ship could blow itself up with its own missiles. Which had actually *happened* in the Battle of Naxas, though fortunately to the other side.

"You know your ships better than I do," Sula said. "So what modifications would you make, and where, and how?"

Animated by the wine drunk during dinner, the discussion that followed was lively, and Sula felt herself fortunate that no one had raised the question of whether her scheme was possible at all. The modifications to the Naxid ships had been made in *shipyards*, not improvised on ships already in transit, and not with equipment that had been scavenged from stores at the last minute. Yet the assembled captains, perhaps encouraged by alcohol, seemed willing to contribute to the project.

After an hour they all began to repeat themselves, so Sula brought the meeting to an end. "If you could all send an inventory of relevant supplies on your ships," she said, "we'll have the information necessary to make solid plans."

Her guests were escorted to their waiting shuttles, and Sula filled her wineglass and toasted her own idea.

If Martinez was going to stick her with a heterogeneous mess of a division, she was going to do her best to turn it into a proper fighting force. *And that will be one in the eye for Martinez*, she thought.


"FLEETCOM CHEN AND Fleetcom Jian are having a very spirited discussion about which of them will command our united forces," said Martinez.

"Who's winning?" asked Chandra Prasad.

"It's about even, so far," Martinez said. "Jian is insisting that we all surrender any advance in rank since the beginning of the war, which I'm sure will be of interest to you all."

Shushanik Severin—who at the start of the war had been promoted to squadron commander, first grade, the highest rank in the Exploration Service—considered his position. "Does she plan to put her own commanders over us?" he said.

Martinez looked at him. "She has not confided her plans."

"Do you know," Severin said, "I don't think it really matters."

Martinez was not alone in looking surprised. "How do you mean?"

"If Do-faq is heading as fast as possible for Harzapid," Severin said, "the battle will take place before Jian can intervene. And if Do-faq takes his time . . ." He waved a hand. "Jian will either work out or she won't, and in either case we'll have time to deal with her."

Martinez looked at him. "Deal with her how, Nikki?"

"I would advise subverting her captains," Severin said. "Put it to them that they should prefer to join a winning team rather than take their chances with an inexperienced commander."

Martinez and his guests gave Severin a speculative look. "That's rather bold," said Conyngham, commander of the First Division.

Severin and the other division and squadron commanders were Martinez's guests on *Bombardment of Los Angeles* and were now enjoying Marivic Mangahas's cooking in the dining room with its strange murals of Torminel wrestlers.

"I don't know how many of you know any of Jian's captains," Severin said, "but if you do, you could sound them out."

"I know quite a number," said Ranssu Kangas. "I was brought up in the Fleet, and they were in and out of my father's house all the time."

Ranssu was distinguished from his twin, Paivo, by the two missing fingers of his right hand, and by a shiny skin graft on one cheek, both repairs following a terrorist action on Harzapid's ring. Ranssu had been too eager to take command of his frigate to have the fingers replaced, and the skin graft had also suffered from haste. The graft could be repaired, Severin knew, but it might be too late to replace the fingers.

"My lords," said Senior Squadron Commander Rivven, "I suggest you sound out your own captains to see who they know."

Rivven was one of two nonhumans at the table. He was a Daimong, gray and cadaverous, with a melodic voice and a face permanently fixed in an expression of what seemed to be indignation. A bath and an application of scent had masked the odor of his rotting flesh. He and his fellow commander, a Lai-own named An-dar, had defected to the Restoration in the final moments of the Second Battle of Shulduc, bringing with them sixteen ships and their crews.

"I know several captains in Jian's command," Rivven said. "I will inquire among them, and I consider myself fortunate that I possess the necessary subtlety for this task. I will praise the Fourth Fleet as an unstoppable fighting force with an unparalleled record of victory, and avoid making any direct comparisons between us and Wei Jian. My friends may draw their own conclusions."

That *us*, thought Severin, was a little too much. Rivven had defected only after his side had suffered a decisive loss, and so far neither he nor An-dar had fired a single shot on behalf of the Restoration. Martinez had wanted to make it impossible for Rivven and An-dar to switch sides a second time, and so had given the two a prominent part in a deception scheme that had seized Zarafan's dockyard, hoping their names would be so blackened in the eyes of the Zanshaa government that there was no possibility of their finding a home with the enemy.

Lord Naaz Vijana rolled his eyes. "Though I may lack the required subtlety," he said, "I will do my best to corrupt Jian's captains if I can."

Vijana, who had earned his fighting reputation by bombarding primitive Yormaks from the air, hated all non-Terrans, and was a strong advocate for replacing the caste of Peers with a Terran ruling clique at the end of the war. He particularly despised Rivven as a petty-minded narcissist obsessed with his own status and his own supposed genius.

Not that he was alone in this.

Rivven was blind to Vijana's irony. "You would do well to be cautious," he responded. "Lead them out gently, let them discover their situation for themselves."

Vijana managed to avoid further eye-rolling. "I will follow your example in all things," he said.

"I know only one or two officers in Wei Jian's command," said Chandra Prasad. She shook her head. "But we didn't part on the best of terms. Perhaps I shouldn't contact them."

Severin avoided comment on Chandra's stormy personal life.

"In addition," Chandra said, "I'm still annoyed that we haven't discovered how well I did with my missile strike. Two hundred fifty missiles . . . Do-faq's whole command could have been wiped out, and since intercepted news reports haven't mentioned it, we wouldn't know." She shook her head again, her metallic red hair swaying. "We might be doing exactly the wrong thing. Maybe we should be advancing on Zanshaa instead of retreating."

"I think we're doing the proper thing," Severin said. "If Do-faq and his crews were wiped out, I think Zanshaa would have replied to some of our political proposals, if for no other reason than to drag out negotiations as long as possible. Instead we've heard nothing."

"They've gotten better at censorship," Chandra said. "At the beginning they were letting all sorts of things slip."

"Their leaders were too fond of the sound of their own voices," said Ranssu.

Mpanza and other servants that Martinez had borrowed from Captain Dalkeith began to clear away the plates in preparation for bringing dessert.

"Has Jian's command had an opportunity to view the videos from Lorkin?" Severin asked.

Martinez looked at him with curiosity. "I don't know," he said. "Would there be a benefit to it?"

"The videos show we've been lied to all our lives," Severin said. "If that doesn't inspire people to question authority, I don't know what would."

Lord Jeremy Foote spoke out. "Well, Nikki," he said, "it might cause them to question the *Shaa*. I don't know how it would lead them to reconsider their allegiance to Lady Wei."

Foote came from the most elevated class of Peers, and both his languid manner and affected drawl were intended to demonstrate his superiority over everyone else in the room. Severin might have been offended by Foote's air of familiarity with those he considered his inferiors, but Severin didn't care to waste energy on resentment. If he was going to expend energy, it would be in actions that might produce beneficial results.

"I keep thinking that we could fashion the Lorkin story as propaganda," Severin said. "The Great Masters slaughtered an entire species, then covered it up. That's a *huge* story."

A huge story that he fully intended to make even bigger after the war, as part of his program to shake the foundations of the Praxis, but he thought the story needed to be spread as far as possible now.

Lady Starkey and her ship *Explorer* had discovered the habitable world of Lorkin, along with the remains of Shaa orbital facilities and, on the surface, the lingering radiation of an antimatter bombardment. The Shaa Great Masters had ruled the native

Lorkins for some time before deciding they were worthy of nothing but extermination.

For members of humanity facing their own extermination, the fate of the Lorkins stood as a sinister, unavoidable warning.

The story of Lorkin was also Lady Starkey's memorial. She had discovered the world of the Lorkin, she had led the initial investigation of the wreckage, she had discovered the remnants of the Great Masters' lost, ruined, and radioactive civilization on the planet below. Severin was determined that she receive full credit for her work, and for the questions it had raised.

"I suppose we could send the Lorkin story around to our friends in Jian's command," Martinez said. "It wouldn't do any harm." He gave Severin a look. "We could also send your satirical videos."

"By all means," Severin said.

Mpanza and the other servants entered from the kitchen carrying desserts on trays—perhaps the largest desserts Severin had ever seen, with a broad assortment of toppings sitting on a bowl of shaved ice, with an enormous mound of flan—*purple* flan for some reason—riding atop like a giant scoop of ice cream. The sweet and slightly burned scent of caramelized fruit floated into the room as the assembled officers burst into applause.

*Why* not *purple flan?* Severin wondered, and reached for his spoon.


WEI JIAN'S STONY face gazed implacably from the video screen.

"Lady Michi," she said, "if you are not willing to follow my plainly stated orders, you need not bother to reply to this transmission. If you do not present yourself on video wearing your proper uniform, with your proper rank of squadron commander, and immediately indicate your willingness to place your entire command under my orders, then I will assume that any talk of further collaboration is fruitless. I will turn my ships around and return to Tai-ma, and you may engage the enemy on whatever terms you please."

Martinez winced. Wei Jian understood—had probably understood all along—that she had the winning hand, because she and her command were necessary for any chance at victory. If Jian turned her squadrons around, Michi, Martinez, and the Fourth Fleet would be annihilated—and so would Wei Jian, eventually. Martinez hoped that Michi wouldn't call Jian's bluff, because he was beginning to think Jian's threat was perfectly genuine. She struck him as the sort of officer who would stake her life—and the lives of everyone in her command—on a matter of precedence.

Michi Chen had appended another message, which Martinez deciphered and promptly put on the screen. She didn't look as presentable as she had in her messages to Wei Jian, and she looked at Martinez with weary eyes. Her skin was jaundiced and sallow, and she'd unbuttoned the stiff standing collar of her dress tunic.

"Well, Gareth," she said, "I did my best, but I'm going to have to surrender. Call me 'Squadron Commander' from now on, and I suppose you will be 'Captain Martinez.'" She waved a weary hand. "I'm damned if I'll sit around here to welcome Jian with trumpets and flowers and servility, so I'm awarding myself a squadron and coming out to join you. Nine of the ships you sent back for repairs are ready, so I'll depart within the next day or two, and I'll see you in a few weeks." She laughed. "And I'll forward to Fleet Commander Jian all the correspondence I've been dealing with every day. I've currently reduced my load to twelve hundred messages per day, and it will be my pleasure to let Jian deal with them all."

She clearly was about to end the conversation, but then she hesitated. "Oh—I should mention that I'll recommend to Jian that my officers remain in their current posts, but the All only knows how she'll take that—she'll probably view it as impertinent, and sack you all." Life and anger returned to her weary eyes. "Though if she's completely impossible," she said, "I'll blow her flagship to bits, and deal with the consequences later." A wan smile ghosted across her face. "Ah, I think you should probably erase this message before anyone else finds it. See you soon, Gareth."

Martinez viewed the orange end-stamp with a slowly sinking heart. Michi Chen had been in command of the Fourth Fleet all along, of course, and had missed Second Shulduc only because she'd lost a leg to a terrorist bomb. Yet it now seemed to Martinez that he would be superseded twice, first when Michi and her newly attached leg arrived to command the Fourth Fleet in person, and then again when Wei Jian turned up.

The number of ships under his command were bound to be substantially reduced. And that meant he had to continue his exercises until he developed a system for defeating Do-faq and was able to hand it intact to his successors.

SHAWNA SPENCE PLACED a glass of cold melon soup in front of Sula. A scent of mint and citrus caressed the air. Sula glanced from the Structured Mathematics Display on the wall to view the golden soup in its tall, crystal glass, and then glanced up at Spence.

"Isn't it Macnamara's turn to serve?" she asked.

"Gavin's helping with a dinner in the wardroom," Spence said. "The lieutenants from both warships are dining together."

"Ah," said Sula. She much preferred her melon soup and her math display to another dinner party and was relieved they hadn't invited her. She picked up her spoon.

"I think Gavin might be interested in one of the other orderlies," Spence said.

Sula looked at her in surprise. "Interested? How?"

"She's very attractive," said Spence. "I don't know anything else about her."

"Ah. Hah," Sula said. "I hope it works out for him."

In fact, Macnamara's interest in this woman was a source of relief. His focus had rarely strayed from Sula, and Sula had supposed that he was, to some degree or other, in love with her—she did not care to inquire, nor did she much care to think about it. Macnamara had always been a little possessive, and there had always been the sense that behind his mask of correctness he was making private judgments—judging her conduct, her male friends, and lately her drinking. It was annoying, but then Macnamara had saved her life, he had been stubbornly loyal through all the years since, and any replacement was bound to generate far more annoyance than Macnamara could ever manage.

But now, if Macnamara could turn his focus onto someone else, Sula would be the happier for it.

"Do you know her name?" Sula said.

"Bliss. She's orderly to the second lieutenant."

Sula tasted the melon soup, with its hints of mint and basil and lemon, the flavors enhanced by the effervescence of sparkling wine. "Very nice," she decided.

Spence topped her cup of tea, then withdrew. Sula spooned herself more soup, glanced at the wall display for a moment, then surrendered to impulse and opened her sleeve display to the personnel files, where she searched for the woman named Bliss.

Rigger First Class Japutra Bliss was twenty-six years old, dark-haired, with large brown eyes beneath half-moon eyebrows, a feature that gave her a perpetually surprised expression. She'd spent eight years in the service, all with the Fourth Fleet in Harzapid.

*Married.* The word glowed in the display. Her husband was

Master Engineer Todd Bliss, thirty-four, currently assigned to a cruiser at Harzapid repairing battle damage.

*I wonder if Macnamara knows,* Sula thought, and then felt a touch of self-reproach and closed the display.

She'd just been resenting Macnamara's protectiveness, and here, the first chance she got, she was checking on his new romantic interest. She might as well be stalking him. Or her.

Sula returned to her melon soup and was halfway through when Signaler Ricci knocked on her door and entered without waiting for permission.

"Message from the relay station in Colamote, my lady," he said. His normally tranquil baritone was jagged with alarm. "Three enemy warships have entered the system via the wormhole from Antopone."

"Ah. Hah," Sula said.

Her Division Nine was twenty-odd hours from transiting from Zarafan to Colamote. The three giant transports had not even begun to transform themselves into warships, and the other, smaller vessels were unarmed.

She could alter course to miss the wormhole entirely, spend days in deceleration, then aim for the wormhole that led to Harzapid. But that meant her division would spend additional weeks in the Zarafan system and would be an easy target when Do-faq's fleet came to Zarafan.

Plus the six Laredo cruisers wouldn't get their crews for many extra months, if ever.

No, she decided, she'd have to go to Zarafan ready to fight.

Though if *Splendid* and *Mentor* failed, the entire division would pay the penalty.

# CHAPTER 4

"As I see it, I have no option but to engage," Sula said. "I can't let an enemy force run mad on their way to Laredo, destroying not only six new cruisers but whatever commerce is still operating in that region. I have some ideas concerning how I can keep the enemy on their heels, so at least we'll give a good account of ourselves. End message."

Martinez paused the video message before the orange end-stamp appeared, and looked for a long moment into Sula's blazing emerald eyes. His heart throbbed uneasily against his ribs.

*I can't help her*, he thought.

The Fourth Fleet had left the Zarafan system three days earlier, and the message had been relayed to him via the wormhole stations. He viewed it from his quarters as he was drinking his cocoa and preparing for bed.

Even if he replied, Sula would be in the Colamote system before the message reached her, and possibly she would already be engaged.

Sula's green eyes gazed from the screen without blinking. Martinez had sent her away, and now she was in peril along with her entire command, and it was his fault.

Sula had never commanded an independent force of warships

in battle—she had always served under others. Martinez could only think that they should be facing this together.

The cocoa was turning sour on his tongue. Martinez unfroze Sula's image, and after the orange end-stamp appeared, he said, "Reply to message," and then paused to collect his thoughts.

"I'd say 'Fortune attend you,' but you won't need it," he said finally. "I'll look forward to your report, so I'll know just how badly you thrashed them.

"I will forward your message to Fleet Commander Jian, who seems to be in charge of us all."

He hoped he sounded more sanguine than he felt.

THE THREE ENEMY warships—presumed to be new ships built in the Antopone yards—had the drive signature of heavy cruisers and were decelerating to swing around Colamote's sun, presumably with the intention of then accelerating toward Laredo. Sula assumed they were intended to cut Laredo off from the rest of the Restoration, but along the way they'd run into the six Laredo cruisers coming toward them—ships that had no fighting crews and no missile loads, only civilians enough to manage navigation and the engines. The Antopone warships would destroy them in a few seconds, then sail on to menace Laredo itself.

Sula spent twenty sleepless hours in conference with her captains and put an experienced officer aboard all three of the big transports to make sure they followed Sula's instructions without making amateur mistakes. Sula couldn't spare officers for the smaller transports, but they mattered less in Sula's plan, and Sula would be happy if all they managed was to avoid colliding with other ships.

Eventually she was alone in her office staring at the gray walls.

She could sense the exhaustion pressing in on her, but caffeine and adrenaline was keeping it at bay.

She would probably die very soon now. She had no brave or stirring message to send to the universe outside her command, in part because everyone she liked and cared about was already here, on the ship with her, and would either survive along with her or die in the same annihilating flash that killed her.

Martinez was outside the ship, of course, but she was too tired to sort through her feelings where he was concerned. *Fuck him*, she thought.

But there was one thing she'd left undone, and if she were to die it would be undone forever. She checked her personnel files to find who was in command of the Fleet dockyard on Terra, and then addressed a message to him. She straightened her uniform tunic and brushed her junior fleet commander's shoulder boards.

"To Senior Captain Lord Batur Khan-Niyaz, greetings. This is Junior Fleet Commander Caroline, Lady Sula, commanding the Ninth Division of the Fleet of the Restoration. I'm afraid I'm going to give you a distasteful order—I wish you to locate a Daimong named Lord Peltrot Convil, formerly of the Manado Company on Sulawesi. Once you've found him, I require that you send a party to the planet's surface to put him against a wall and shoot him. Act with all deliberate speed. If anyone questions your actions, refer them to me."

She nodded at the camera. "I assure you that the action is necessary. This is Lady Sula—Long live the Restoration of the Praxis. End message."

Sula didn't bother to review the message lest it give her second thoughts. Instead, she ciphered it herself and put it in the message queue.

*Everything dies*, she thought. *Nothing matters.*

"My lady?" Shawna Spence appeared in the doorway. "Do you require anything?"

"Sleep, mostly," Sula said. "You heard?"

"Oh yes."

Sula gave Spence a searching look. "Any comment?"

Spence hesitated only a brief moment. "He deserves it."

Years ago, when Sula had commanded the dockyard on Terra's ring, Lord Peltrot had grown sufficiently vexed with Sula that he'd sent an assassin to kill her. The assassin had missed Sula but killed her cousin Ermina instead, and had then been shot dead by Macnamara.

The official investigation had failed to connect Lord Peltrot to the crime, but Sula knew better. She had owed Peltrot Convil a death for a long time, and—about to lead an inferior force into combat—it was time she paid that debt.

THE NINTH DIVISION made the transition to Colamote accompanied by a dozen decoys, making the division look to enemy sensors to be twice its actual size. Sula sat in her acceleration cage in the flag officer's station, and wore her viridian dress uniform tunic with its double row of silver buttons, her medals, and the shoulder boards of a junior fleet commander. She kept her eyes on the displays as the black speeding digits counted down the time till the transition.

The transition itself was imperceptible, marked only by the racing digits shifting from black to orange and counting up instead of down, and by the plot going blank for a few moments until the navigation system updated their position. The enemy ships appeared exactly where they were expected to be, three antimatter engine flares bright against the starry background.

The relative positions of the two fleets were unusual. The wormhole to Antopone was on a bearing close to that of the wormhole to Zarafan, but farther away from Colamote's sun. Thus the enemy ships were "behind" the Ninth Division, both aiming for the same point near Colamote's sun so that they could swing onto their course for Laredo. Sooner or later, they were bound to collide.

This also meant that the enemy could not avoid action if Sula chose to begin a fight. Both forces were decelerating, but the enemy had started with higher velocity and were overtaking Sula's ships. All Sula had to do was shift her vessels from her current line of bearing to that of the enemy, and the two forces would inevitably come into close action. If the enemy shifted to another line of bearing, Sula could match them. If they increased their deceleration to forestall combat, Sula could increase her own deceleration by the same amount, and the action would still take place.

It had occurred to Sula not to decelerate at all but to run at full speed for Laredo and hope the enemy wouldn't catch her. But this would betray her weakness, and the transports weren't built to sustain the sorts of accelerations standard in warships. The enemy would overtake the Ninth Division, and the battle would happen anyway.

If combat was inevitable, Sula thought, then it had better be on her terms.

And it had better be *victorious* combat.

Sula's pulse beat high in her throat, and her mouth was dry. She took a quick drink of water from a squeeze bottle, then looked at the camera pickup.

"Transmit to unknown squadron, video and audio both," she told her signals staff. "Send in the clear."

She deliberately relaxed the muscles of her face while she

mulled her message, then adopted a stern, formal expression. "To unknown vessels," she said. "This is Caroline, Lady Sula, commanding the First Battleship Squadron and Division Nine of the Fourth Fleet. Identify yourselves, and if you are hostile to the government of the Restoration, prepare either to surrender or be blasted to atoms. Message ends."

Sula reached for her squeeze bottle again, took another drink, and speculated how the enemy commander might react when the message reached him, in about four minutes. It would follow soon upon the appearance of an armada from the Zarafan wormhole, which would be alarming enough even without a battleship squadron in the mix.

The battleship squadron was problematic, however, as the Restoration was known to have only a single battleship, *Perfection of the Praxis*, which was completing construction at Harzapid when the war broke out. The enemy would have to wonder where the other two came from, and the only possible answer was that they had at some point *defected*—a possibility that would not enhance enemy morale.

Of course, that interpretation depended entirely on whether the enemy was willing to consider that Sula's force contained battleships at all. The three big transports were large enough, but their drive signatures were different from any *Praxis*-class ship. Sula intended to make that less obvious by having her ships aimed straight at the enemy, with the drive plume partly obscured by the body of the ship.

Though if the enemy declined to believe they were faced by battleships, Sula anticipated a way to convince them. But Sula hoped they would be so startled by the appearance of a Restoration flotilla that they wouldn't do any kind of analysis at all. And the best way to keep the enemy from *thinking*, Sula thought, was to behave very aggressively from the very start and keep them so busy reacting that they had inclination to perform any analysis.

"Message to all ships," Sula said. "All ships to alter course to a heading of two hundred forty-six by zero zero one absolute. Increase acceleration to one point five gravities. Execute in three minutes—*mark.*"

Sula was a little concerned that not all the civilian captains would be quite up to managing the maneuver with only three minutes' warning, but all ships responded promptly. *Splendid* cut its engines while it swung to its new heading, and Sula's acceleration cage swung free on its gimbals. In a moment of alarm Sula realized she had forgotten to strap herself in, and she seized the cage supports with both hands just before the engines cut in again, and she dropped back into her seat.

The Ninth Division was now heading to intercept the enemy ships at a greater rate of acceleration, a move calculated to increase the sense of alarm in the enemy.

She wondered if they would react to the word *surrender* or bluster about it first. She had her answer nine minutes after she'd sent her message. A Lai-own appeared on her video display, gazing at her with golden eyes set wide atop his muzzle. He wore a viridian fatigue jumpsuit, which argued that he'd been doing some informal duty when he was suddenly called to Command. The feathery hair on either side of his head was still dark, which meant he was young for commanding an independent force.

"Lady Sula," he said. "I am Senior Captain Sen-thar, commanding the cruiser *Steadfast.* We operate under orders from the Commandery in Zanshaa and must inform you that we shall defend ourselves if attacked. End message."

Sula laughed. "Not exactly a clarion cry of defiance," she said aloud, and was rewarded by a guffaw from Ricci.

"Enemy ships are maneuvering," Viswan said.

Sula turned her attention to the displays and saw the three cruisers shift into a formation contributing to overlapping defensive fire. The maneuver wasn't executed with any great precision, and Sula guessed that the crews were new recruits serving with a very few experienced officers.

She also quietly rejoiced that the enemy was commanded by a Lai-own. The hollow bones of the flightless avians wouldn't support accelerations of more than two and a half gees, which meant that the enemy absolutely could not outmaneuver Division Nine.

She looked up Captain Sen-thar in the database and discovered that he'd participated in the Naxid War as a lieutenant in charge of a supply vessel shuttling between the six planets of the Seizho Reach. He hadn't been anywhere near combat and owed his advancement to arrangements made ahead of time by family friends in the service.

Which made him, sadly, rather typical of a ranking officer in the Fleet.

"Your message has been received," Sula replied, "and I commend your resolution in the face of certain death. Were I you, I'd be wondering about the competence of those in the Commandery who sent you and your brand-new ships and your half-trained crews into this situation. Quite a number of senior officers have been led to question foolish orders in this way, which has resulted in an encouraging number of defections to the Restoration."

She leaned a little closer to the camera, in hopes of developing a degree of intimacy between herself and whoever was listening.

"I would like to remind you that I mentioned the possibility of surrender. You and your crews would be fed, housed, and held in comfort until the conclusion of hostilities. We have no reason to kill you, and after the fighting is over, we hope to work together to reestablish proper government, rebuild the Fleet, and lead the empire out of chaos." She affected to consider the situation.

"Your crews are inexperienced and have no choice but to trust you to make the correct decisions. There seems little point in getting them all killed because of a stupid error in judgment made in the Commandery . . . though if you insist, we will reluctantly oblige." She ventured a smile. "We will be sending you some entertainments that may lighten the mood while you make what will doubtless be the most important decision of your lives. End message."

When the camera light went out, Sula leaned back on her couch and laughed, then thought that perhaps the laughter was a little premature and should perhaps wait for a triumphant resolution of the situation. She was trying to bluff a superior force, and in Senthar she might find someone willing to call that bluff.

In which case, Division Nine might survive only a few more hours. Not only did the enemy have nearly twice her number of missile batteries, but her own warships would be distracted by the necessity of defending the cargo ships, none of which had any defensive armament.

"That was a very good performance, Lady Fleetcom," said Viswan.

"I have my moments," Sula said. "Ricci, have you sent the videos?"

"Doing so now, Lady Fleetcom."

She'd decided to send a selection of Nikki Severin's satiric videos, featuring puppets in the guise of Zanshaa's leaders, gleefully engaging in corruption, bribery, and scapegoating while building their personal fortunes. She wondered if anyone in the enemy force would find them funny.

Sula looked at the displays and calculated that, unless someone changed course or acceleration, the two forces would meet in about sixteen hours. She didn't think Sen-thar would reply immediately, and she decided that as she hadn't really slept in two days, she might try to get some rest in the meantime. She tipped her couch forward, put her feet flat on the floor, and rose. She massed one and a half times her normal weight, but it was perfectly possible to walk under these circumstances if she took care.

"I'm going to my quarters," she said. "Forward any important messages."

She cautiously trudged toward her suite. Though the staff in Command was maintaining a high state of alert, *Splendid* had not yet gone to general quarters, so most of the ship's company was going about their normal business. They braced to attention as she passed, and as she looked into their faces, she saw mingled curiosity and concern, but very little fear. By now they must have gained a good idea of the situation, but they seemed to be trusting her to deal with the matter.

She hoped the trust was warranted.

Still in her uniform, Sula dropped onto her bergamot-scented bed and closed her eyes. Tracks of distant ships painted themselves on the backs of her eyelids. Bright storms like missile strikes bloomed against her retinas. She was aware that somewhere a digit counter was flashing as it ticked up toward the meeting with Sen-thar's ships, and as it counted she could feel her anxiety rising.

She had thought she was prepared, and she'd explained her plan to her subordinates, but it was always possible that she'd missed something. Sula had never before had the sole command of ships in battle; she had always served under Lord Tork, Martinez, or Michi Chen. The thought came to her that, if she made any kind of mistake, she would be responsible for the Restoration's first defeat in combat.

And with that thought, sleep became impossible.

She dragged herself from her bed to her dining table, ate some cheese and cold cuts with flat bread, drank honeyed tea, then plodded again to the flag officer's station.

The bare beige room was silent. Video displays played themselves in silence on the walls. Ricci monitored communications, while Viswan had gone for a meal. Sula dropped onto her couch and pulled the displays down in front of her. Nothing on the plot seemed to have changed, the digit counter flashed ever upward, and the room was so quiet she could hear the sigh of air through the ventilators. The displays blurred before her eyes . . .

"Good shot," said Captain Mazankosi. She stood beneath a black, tangled tree with her rifle tucked under her arm, the sun gleaming on her bright hair. The scent of propellent tainted the air. A spotted beast was stretched out on the ground before her, its fangs bared in death and two bloody wounds visible on its chest.

"Very close range," Sula said. "Couldn't miss, really."

"Look," said Mazankosi. "The creeper creeps."

A thorny vine was writhing like a snake across the mossy ground, twisting and flopping its way toward the dead animal.

"It's looking for the blood," Mazankosi said. She prodded the vine with the barrel of her rifle, and the vine wound around the barrel and Mazankosi drew the barrel upward, bringing the vine with it. Mazankosi viewed the vine at close range. She reached out a hand and touched a thorn, then drew her hand away and showed Sula the dot of blood on the pad of her forefinger.

"Greedy," she said.

Sula gave a shiver. "Nasty thing," she said. "We should clean up the blood."

Mazankosi licked her finger experimentally. "Hard to get rid of it all," she said.

There was a scrub brush in Sula's hand. She dropped to her knees on the green, spongy ground. The scent of blood seemed to clog the back of Sula's throat. With both hands she began scrubbing, bristles tearing at the mossy vegetation. The blood had soaked deep into the ground, and there was a lot of it. More vine tendrils snaked toward her.

"Poor Earthgirl," said a voice. Sula looked up sharply, and found Caro Sula standing by Mazankosi's side. Looking at Caro was like looking into a mirror: the same emerald eyes, the same porcelain complexion, the same silver-gilt hair.

"Earthgirl always gets the dirty jobs," Caro said. "Why is that?"

"Greedy," said Mazankosi. She licked her finger again.

Sula returned to her scrubbing. Her breath grated in her throat.

Blood dripped from the bristles of Sula's brush, welled up between her fingers. "Where's it all coming from?" she asked.

"Someone's heart, I suppose," said Mazankosi. Sula looked up and saw that Mazankosi's pale blue eyes were now a darker, more intense blue, like chips of sapphire. As blue as Lamey's eyes.

"Earthgirl's heart got broken," Caro said. "The blood might be hers."

"No," said Mazankosi. "It's her friend's."

"Which friend?"

"There are so many to choose from," said Mazankosi. "And they all ended up bleeding." She spoke with the voice of Gareth Martinez.

One of the vines wrapped around Sula's wrist. She could see the vine pulsing as it drew blood through the piercing thorns.

Sula could feel cold horror crawling up her spine, a scream rising in her throat . . .

"My lady! A message, Lady Fleetcom!"

Sula stared up into the face of Ricci, her signals lieutenant.

"Yes?" she said, and hoped she hadn't been screaming.

"You've been asleep," Ricci said. "Sen-thar has sent another message." His soothing baritone had never been more welcome.

The dream and its terrors withdrew slowly from Sula's mind, and she suspected that the dream's thorns were still firmly implanted in her psyche, and that she'd revisit the nightmare world ere long. She took a long, deliberate breath against the heavy gravity.

"Thank you," she said. "Let's see the message."

Sen-thar appeared on the display. Nictating membranes half-covered his golden eyes.

"Lady Sula," he said. "My staff has been analyzing your rather impressive armada, and we have come to realize that there *is* no First Battleship Squadron. The drive signatures are those of large transports. Other ships would seem to be smaller civilian ships, and a large percentage of your ships are decoys. We can confirm only two drive signatures as belonging to actual warships." The nictating membranes rolled off his eyes. "Perhaps *you* should surrender to *me*, Lady Sula. Or at least get out of my way. End message."

As the orange end-stamp filled the screen, silence reigned in the small beige room.

*Bluff called*, Sula thought. But there were more bluffs within the bluff.

She looked at the chronometer and saw that it would still be eleven hours before the two forces met at a hypothetical point in empty space. Of course, the encounter would be over before any such meeting took place.

Yet there was no time like the present to make her point.

"Message to all ships," she said. "Prepare for Ghost Tactics. Commence standard pattern centered on *Pride of Parkhurst* six minutes from now—*mark*." Then she felt the corners of her lips turn up in what she was confident was a self-satisfied, knowing smile. "*Splendid* and *Mentor*, prepare to release missiles."

The six minutes sped by on the chronometer, and then Sula felt a tug on her inner ear as *Splendid* shifted course and began to move in accordance with the unpredictable patterns of Ghost Tactics. She looked at her displays and saw the other ships begin to slot themselves into the pattern, and she knew that the weapons stations on *Splendid* and *Mentor* were busying themselves shifting the decoys into place. The pattern was centered on *Pride of Parkhurst* because *Parkhurst* was masquerading as the flagship, and the others would be doing their best to protect it.

And what would the enemy see? That the Ninth Division was neither offering to surrender nor get out of the way, but was prepared for combat.

Sula waited to see whether any of her command botched the shift into the Ghost Tactics pattern and saw they were performing well enough—it was necessary only to follow a formula, after all, and even a civilian pilot could do that.

"Message to *Splendid* and *Mentor*," she said. "Commence releasing missiles. Form the missiles into a defensive halo."

At which point missiles began appearing on the displays, hundreds of them—fired not from the warships' batteries, but apparently from *Parkhurst* and the other two giant transports that formed the purely notional Battleship Squadron One.

She could only imagine the horror that would flood Sen-thar's mind as he saw the long strings of missile flares racing from the ships he had just denounced as mere transports. In Sula's imagination, he recoiled from the display while shouting, like a villain in a melodrama, "*What witchery is this?*"

*My* witchery, Sula answered silently. And you have no idea how the magic was done.

The transports had not a single working missile tube. The missiles had been fired by *Splendid* and *Mentor* on the other side of the wormhole gate—they'd depleted their magazines by half—and then the missiles had been marshaled into small squadrons that rode alongside the big transports, like satellites orbiting their primaries. The missiles had duplicated the big ships' maneuvers, and Sula was reasonably confident their much smaller drive flares would have been invisible against the vast blaze of the transports' massive drives.

Sula closed her eyes and tried to relax into her acceleration couch. She felt a tug on her inner ear as *Splendid* performed a small shift in its trajectory, to make it harder for the enemy to score a hit with beam weapons. The apparent missile launches were her last bluff, and if Sen-thar didn't surrender, she would have to fight at a severe disadvantage.

She would, she thought, make use of the fact that Sen-thar's ships were shooting toward her and would overtake and pass Division Nine unless they did some very hard decelerations. She'd form all those missiles that now orbited Division Nine into several waves and send them ducking and dodging toward Sen-thar. The first wave of missiles would fall victim to antiproton beams and countermissiles, but their hot expanding fireballs would overlap and provide an opaque radio wall between Sen-thar's and Sula's ships until the fireballs expanded and cooled. Neither side would be able to see the other, but Sen-thar would be flying into the fireballs, and Sula would be flying away. Sen-thar wouldn't see the next set of missiles coming, and his defenses would have less and less time to acquire targets—and every time they destroyed an attacking missile, they would only add to the radio confusion that blinded them.

In the end, Sula thought, she'd need only three hits—and each hit would weaken the enemy's defenses and make the next hit more likely.

She thought she'd stand a fair chance of winning the fight, and if not, she'd have to be satisfied with the knowledge that she'd frightened the hell out of the enemy—though of course the satisfaction would hardly last, because she and her division would be wiped out.

*Everything dies*, she reminded herself. *Nothing matters.*

Time passed, and Sula drowsed, worked out battle plans, and drowsed again. She looked at the chronometer and decided it was about time to send the crews to general quarters.

"My lady," said Ricci. "Another message from Sen-thar."

Sula's heart gave a surge. The message would be surrender or defiance. It all came down to this moment.

"Let's see it," she said.

Sen-thar appeared. He'd changed from the fatigues jumpsuit into full dress, buttons and rank badges glittering. His expression was so fierce, golden eyes glaring, that Sula's spirits sank. *Battle after all.*

"Lady Sula," he said. "After a conference with my captains, we concluded that our only hope of avoiding unnecessary loss of life is to accept your offer of surrender. We trust that your offer of honorable treatment is genuine, and we now await your orders. End message."

The flag officer's station burst into cheers and laughter, which—as the message had been sent in the clear—was no doubt being echoed in every command and communications room in Division Nine.

*Conference with my captains*, Sula thought, and grinned. Committees almost inevitably chose the least bold course, and Sen-thar had been clever enough to make sure the responsibility for the decision to surrender was spread out among his fellow captains.

Which wouldn't prevent any of them from execution if the Zanshaa government got its hands on them.

After the celebration in the flag officer's station died away, Sula composed herself to reply.

"Captain Sen-thar," she said. "I hope this moment signals the beginning of a true partnership to rebuild the empire. Kindly fire your entire supply of missiles in a neutral direction and set them to explode at a safe distance. Be aware that we will be counting every single missile and every single explosion.

"Prepare also to receive shuttles that will transport new crews to your vessels, and which will take you to your new quarters. I shall look forward to making your acquaintance, and that of your officers. Message ends."

And now, Sula thought, she had to make all that happen.

While fountains of missiles raced from the Lai-own ships to blaze in the darkness like a vast array of fireworks, she arranged to send experienced crew to each of the enemy vessels, along with a much larger number of recruits. Two lieutenants from *Splendid*, and one from *Mentor*, would now be appointed acting captains.

She also sent armed members of the military constabulary, including a squad under the command of Macnamara, to make certain that order was maintained and that her commands were obeyed.

*Splendid* and *Mentor* would retrieve their own missiles only after the enemy ships were securely under Sula's control.

Officers, she decided, would be held in captivity on the *Pride of Parkhurst*, and the enlisted evenly split between the other two big transports. She arranged that in whatever quarters they were housed, there would be sufficient guards to keep them from mis-chief.

And then it occurred to Sula that she should probably tell her superiors what had happened. The crew of the wormhole station would have reported back through Zarafan on whatever they had seen, but they were observers, not participants, and it was time to make her triumph official.

She sent her report to Michi Chen, who would doubtless forward it to Wei Jian if Jian had managed to win the contest over who would command the forces of the Restoration. Sula sent it by way of the Fourth Fleet flagship and used the command cipher, which would allow Gareth Martinez to read the message as he forwarded it on, so that he could inform the Fourth Fleet of her victory.

"Lady Fleetcom," Sula said, "I am pleased to announce victory in the bloodless Second Battle of Colamote. Senior Captain Sen-thar surrendered his three heavy cruisers rather than face extinc-tion by Battleship Squadron One and its formidable escorts. We now have three more warships to add to the forces of the Resto-ration. I will send crews aboard immediately and begin training and integration."

She offered the camera a self-satisfied look. "The wormhole sta-tion to Antopone is still in enemy hands," she said, "so a report is undoubtedly now on its way to Zanshaa. We can hope that news of the loss will cause the enemy to overreact and do something fool-ish. End message."

The message was enciphered and shot away at the speed of light. "Message to all Division Nine," she said. "Reduce deceleration to point eight gravities. Maintain a high state of alert in Command and on weapons stations, but others may continue their normal du-ties and take their meals on schedule."

When the gravity eased, she tipped her cage forward and rose to her feet.

"Message from Fleetcom Martinez," Viswan said. "It uses the command cipher, so you'll have to decipher it yourself."

Sula returned to her couch and slotted her command key into the signals display. The brief message was deciphered in only a few seconds.

I'LL LOOK FORWARD TO YOUR REPORT, SO I'LL KNOW JUST HOW BADLY YOU THRASHED THEM.

She played the message twice, and at the sight of Martinez she felt a flush prickle across her skin.

At least, for once, he had expressed confidence in her judgment.

She climbed out of her acceleration cage and set out for her quarters. It was time to celebrate, she thought, and in her pantry there was an interesting-looking bottle of brandy to help her do it.

A WEIRD ELATION possessed Martinez as he trudged back to his quarters with his helmet under his arm. That morning's exercise split the Fourth Fleet into two forces that battled each other, and for the first time Sula's scheme to predict outcomes for ships using the Martinez Method had worked—for one side, though not the other.

Martinez had commanded the side that lost, but that didn't bother him as much as it might. His own ship had been destroyed by virtual missiles relatively early in the exercise, which meant he spent the rest of the time watching the battle unfold. The enemy missiles seemed to know just where his own ships were bound even when they were concealed by the exploding radio blooms, and even though most of the missiles were destroyed, *they just kept coming*, so accurate that it was impossible to swat them all.

Ranssu Kangas, who commanded the other side, had won his first virtual victory and proved it was possible, after all, to predict where the Method was going to take the other side's ships. The trick, of course, was to do it consistently, and so far the odds were not encouraging.

Yet Sula had pointed out that even wrong guesses produced data, and that the data could be employed in future exercises. And the fact that the predictions had worked once gave Martinez hope that they would work again.

At the thought of Sula, anxiety began to gnaw at his nerves with sharp little teeth. Whatever had happened in Colamote, he should be receiving word of it about now, if not from Sula, then from the wormhole station.

While he had been fighting his mock battle, she had been fighting a real one, and if it had gone against her, she would have been blasted into subatomic particles and scattered across the solar wind. He felt tension drawing a hard, fierce line across his shoulder blades.

Mpanza met Martinez in his quarters and helped him draw off the upper part of his vacuum suit. The lower part contained all the sanitary attachments, and Martinez removed those himself.

"I'm very sorry that we lost, my lord," Mpanza said.

"I'm not," Martinez said. "The way we lost was . . . illuminating."

"Was it?" Mpanza's eyebrows rose. "Well . . . that's good, my lord."

After wearing his vac suit, Martinez always washed away the scent of disinfectant and suit seals, so Mpanza helped Martinez into a dressing gown for his brief walk to the shower.

"What are our chances for the next round of the Fleet Quiz?" Martinez asked.

"Rigger Cusi is confident," Mpanza said, "but he wishes some-one on the team were more confident on history."

"Much of our history seems to be fiction, anyway," Martinez said. "Or covered up, like what happened to the Lorkin."

Martinez had been trying to provide diversion for his crews, to make the seemingly endless time on shipboard less dull and de-pressing. His first attempts were all competitions—he knew the crews were competitive anyway, and already competed in the fleet exercises. The Fleet Quiz had just started, with each ship fielding a team of six enlisted, answering questions on music, popular en-tertainment, history, science, sports, and stars and planets of the empire. The questions were submitted by officers, then distributed randomly among the various ships.

So far, the first round had eliminated half the teams, and there would be a new round every three days until a winner was declared.

Other contests were in the planning stages. There would be a gymkhana for pinnace pilots, each pilot trying to put her fast, nimble little vessel through a complex series of maneuvers in the smallest amount of time. There would be competitions in board games and video games. A talent contest had been announced, but the first event wouldn't take place for another five or six days, to give the talent a chance to rehearse.

There was talk of clearing away the tables and benches of the crews' messes to allow room for a dancing competition.

Other suggestions had been made and were under consider-ation, though Martinez had no difficulty saying no to numerous requests for drinking contests. Let the recruits puke themselves on their own time.

Martinez walked toward the shower, then looked at the Torm-inels on the walls and grimaced. In the more public areas of his quarters the Torminels were wrestling, but in his bedroom the murals were frank pornography.

And then he had a better idea.

"What do you think of an art competition?" he said.

Mpanza looked at him in surprise.

"The winner gets to redecorate my quarters," Martinez said.

Mpanza offered a thoughtful glance at the tangled Torminels on the walls. "Whoever wins could scarcely do worse," he said.

"Exactly my thought."

At that moment Martinez's sleeve display gave a chirp, and he felt his anxiety leap. His tunic was hanging on a wall hook, and Martinez took two quick steps to it, then picked up the sleeve and triggered the display.

"Yes?" he said.

Banerjee's grandmotherly face looked out at him. "Message from Lady Sula, my lord," she said. "In the command cipher."

"Send it to the display in my office."

The anxiety began to ebb at once. The very fact that Sula had sent him this message meant that she had survived whatever encounter had taken place.

He walked to his office and turned on the display. His commander's key, a viridian-green strip of plastic that concealed a small electronic ID feature, was worn around his wrist on an elastic band. He slipped the band off his wrist and inserted it into the slot on his desk.

*From the flagship of Battle Squadron One, I am pleased to announce victory in the bloodless Second Battle of Colamote.* Martinez's heart gave a leap.

The enemy had surrendered, and the Restoration now had three new warcraft without a single ship, or life, lost on either side. He appreciated the ironic reference to Battle Squadron One, which gave him a very good idea of how Sula had brought off her victory.

All his anxiety had been for nothing.

He decided to share the news at once. Realizing that the sight of him in his dressing gown was not appropriate to the occasion, he sent the message via audio only.

"To all ships," he said, "Lady Sula reports a complete triumph over the enemy at Colamote. Senior Captain Sen-thar surrendered his three heavy cruisers without resistance. The Restoration continues its unbroken tradition of victory, and I ask all personnel to celebrate with me today and raise a glass to Lady Sula and her command."

He sent the message, then leaned back in his chair and took a long breath. Something loomed over his right shoulder, and he gave a start.

"Shall I bring coffee, my lord?" Mpanza asked. "Or would you like wine or spirits to salute Lady Sula?"

"I can salute her with coffee," Martinez said. "And bring something to eat. Sandwiches or something simple."

"Yes, my lord."

He gave Mpanza a look. "You heard, I suppose?"

"Yes, my lord. You didn't close the door behind you, and I couldn't avoid hearing Lady Sula's dispatch."

Especially since he was hovering in the doorway, Martinez thought. "So what do you think?" he asked.

"Think?" Mpanza frowned in consideration. "I wondered why you sent her out with that ragbag collection of ships, but now I understand. You must have known the enemy was coming."

Martinez strove to look wise. "I'm afraid I can't say," he said.

"Of course not. I'll bring your coffee, my lord."

Mpanza made his way out and left Martinez alone with the thoughts that frothed through his mind like a spinning whirlpool.

# CHAPTER 5

The after-battle party was held aboard the immigration ship *Ideal*, which had kitchen and dining facilities large enough for every officer in Division Nine and a promenade big enough for dancing.

Sula required a couple glasses of wine before she was in a mood to do anything but catch up on her sleep, and even after she was in the shuttle she doubted she was in the mood for a large gathering. But when she stepped aboard *Ideal* and its captain escorted her to the promenade, hundreds of officers, cadets, and recruits turned to her and braced to attention, and a derivoo singer began to keen from speakers. Sula broke into laughter—apparently enough people had heard the music wail from her quarters every night to spread the information through the division. She gestured for everyone to stand at ease and walked into the great open room that now echoed with cheers and applause.

*They must have been frightened to death*, Sula thought. Most of those present had been stationed on civilian ships with no way of defending themselves—yet somehow, miraculously, the enemy had been talked and cajoled and bullied into surrender, and this had sent the crews into an explosion of mad joy.

Now over a hundred enlisted prisoners were berthed on *Ideal*, in third-class immigrant berths, and possibly in a position to hear the celebration going on a few decks away. By now they probably knew how their officers had been fooled.

Yet so far the captives had taken their situation well. A few of the officers had shot themselves rather than endure the disgrace of surrender, but the rest of the prisoners seemed resigned. Sula imagined they were pleased to be out of a war in which their own side hadn't won a single engagement.

The party was loud and raucous and skated now and again over the borders of propriety, even in the dining rooms reserved for officers. Lord Nishkad presided over a table of former Naxid officers, and Sula made a point of offering the Naxids a toast. She lost track of the toasts after that, and of how many times servants filled her wineglass. After the meal a live band struck up on the promenade and there was dancing. The first dance was reserved for the captain of the *Ideal*, and Sula rose from the table with her head spinning, but she managed to keep her feet and avoid disgracing herself. Afterward, Dr. Gunaydin asked her for a dance, and he proved expert at steering her around the promenade without colliding with the furniture or other dancers. His dancing was assured, his touch delicate, and she found herself revising her opinion of the doctor, deciding he might have hidden depths.

She wasn't sure she liked the shaved head, however. For a shaved head to be attractive, the skull had to be of a certain configuration, and she wasn't convinced that Gunaydin had the proper bone structure.

Other partners crowded around her, and she was obliged to dance with others less skilled than Gunaydin. She managed to avoid being trodden on, but only barely, after which a final round of toasts was called for, and Sula and *Splendid*'s officers were escorted back to their shuttle.

Next morning, Sula woke with a dry mouth, foul breath, and a head that felt as if it had been clubbed with a constable's truncheon. She drank a tall tumbler of water to counter dehydration, cleaned her teeth, then ordered tea and analgesics while she showered.

The timing could have been better, since she was to meet with engineers, weaponers, and the captains of the *Ideal*, *Parkhurst*, and *Lentrec* to make plans for converting their transports into warships. She barely felt able to manage pouring her tea, let alone leading a technical discussion. The analgesics were of limited help, and her stomach turned over at the thought of eating anything.

In the end she went to the liquor store. Macnamara had returned to his duties after escorting prisoners into captivity, and he radiated disapproval as she poured a slug of brandy into her tea and drank it off. A pleasing warmth began to spread through her body, and the headache faded. She found herself contemplating breakfast without revulsion and asked for a basket of sweet pastries.

By the time she left for the meeting aboard *Parkhurst*, she was feeling reasonably robust. The meeting went well, she thought, and she recommended that preliminary construction begin.

Division Nine was growing, both in size and in power.

SEVERIN CONTEMPLATED THE virtual battlespace projected onto his visual centers and thought a small adjustment was in order. "Division Two," he said. "Alter course to two-eight-three by zero-zero-one relative. Execution immediate."

Division Two had been Lord Jeremy Foote's command at Second Shulduc, where it had stood like a wall between the enemy and its escape route and had lost sixteen of its twenty-four ships. To provide replacements, two ships had been added from another division that had been broken up, but Foote's division was now no larger than a mere squadron. Division Two made the minor course change, and Severin felt a subtle shift in the flow of the exercise. He was gently inserting a wedge between two groups of the enemy.

"The enemy" at this moment was the other half of the Fourth Fleet, under the command of Gareth Martinez. Both sides had tried to predict where the Martinez Method would take the other side's ships, but both had failed, and now it was a case of two evenly matched forces employing the same tactics against each other.

Martinez launched a barrage that concealed an attempt by his vanguard to double Severin's lead ships, catching them between two fires, but Severin anticipated the maneuver and countered. In the meantime, Foote's command continued its subtle intrusion into Martinez's domain until it suddenly pounced, and Martinez's forces broke into three parts. This enabled Severin to overwhelm one of the three segments before the other two fought their way toward each other and reunited, though now they were outnumbered and at a disadvantage. Martinez tried his imaginative best, but in the end he was overwhelmed, and Severin grinned as he told his ships to secure from general quarters and reform while the casualties returned from the dead.

Martinez called him just after he had climbed out of his vac suit, and he put the video on his sleeve display. "Yes, Lord Fleetcom?"

"I'm not a fleetcom anymore," Martinez said. "And you're no longer a squadron commander, first grade."

"I'm not sure a Fleet officer has the authority to degrade me in rank," Severin said.

"But a Fleet officer promoted you in the first place."

"But that"—Severin smiled—"was something I chose to *consent* to. If I don't consent to a demotion, I don't know what Wei Jian can do about it."

"I'm sure she will tell you at length," said Martinez. "In any

case, I didn't call you to discuss promotions, I called to congratulate you on today's exercise. I'm not sure what happened—I'm
going to have to look at the recordings—but it was quite a surprise
when my command broke up."

"You recovered fast, though," Severin said. "I was hoping you'd
stay stunned for a few more minutes."

Martinez looked at him narrowly. "What happened was a surprise to *me*," he said. "But was it a surprise to *you*?"

"You mean, did I do it deliberately?" Severin grinned. "It was
all part of a plan. I hope to discuss it with you."

"Come to supper tonight," Martinez said.

"Certainly. Thank you."

"I'll invite Paivo, and you can break it down for us."

"Very good, Lord Captain." Severin hesitated. "That *is* what I'm
supposed to call you, yes?"

Martinez gave him a sardonic look. "According to some, yes."


MARTINEZ MET WITH his flag captain, Elissa Dalkeith, for an
analysis of the morning's exercise, then walked down the grand,
paneled stairway that spiraled around the officers' quarters, and
from there to his own suite. He opened the door to his dining
room, through which he could get to his sleeping cabin faster than
by going through his office, and then froze in surprise at the sight
of Agustin Mpanza in the embrace of a young woman. She was
seated on the dining table, her arms and legs wrapped around him,
and they were kissing with great enthusiasm. No clothing, Martinez judged, had yet been removed, but the removal of clothing was
definitely on the agenda.

*The moment awkward*, Martinez thought, and closed the door

with an authoritative thud that he hoped would sound through the pair's self-preoccupation.

He went to the door of his office, entered, sat at his desk, and waited. Mpanza entered after a few moments.

"My apologies, my lord," he said.

"I'm glad it didn't go any further," Martinez said. "If it had, I'd regret serving guests off that table."

"I'll give the table a good cleaning and polish."

Martinez was tempted to say that a good polishing of the table was something he hoped to avoid, but decided against it.

"Who was the young lady?" he asked. "I've seen her somewhere."

"Electrician Second Class Raju, my lord."

"Ah. I remember her now." He looked at Mpanza. "I'm all for spontaneity," he said, "but next time you should reserve a tube. They aren't as plush as a hotel, or even my dining room, but they're free . . . and not my dining room."

"Yes, my lord."

The so-called recreation tubes were intended for assignations among the crew and had been ordained, in a perfectly unsentimental way, by the Great Masters when they realized the variety, scope, and power of human sexuality and strove to direct it into a nondisruptive channel. Martinez had used the tubes himself at points in his career when he didn't have a private cabin and found they certainly helped to make a long voyage bearable.

"May I get you anything, my lord?" Mpanza asked. "Coffee, a drink, something else?"

"No, thank you," said Martinez. "You can get straight to polishing the table."

"Yes, my lord." Mpanza withdrew.

Martinez felt a stirring of jealousy as he recalled that he and Sula had never done anything as adventurous as polish the table—the bed had been too comfortable and inviting. Now the opportunity was lost forever.

He also reflected that the phrase *polishing the table* was on its way to becoming a euphemism that would stick in his mind forever, without his being able to banish it.

Martinez went to his sleeping cabin and viewed a video sent him by his son, Gareth the Younger, who in accordance with the time-honored rules of the Chen clan was known to the family as Chai-chai. The young genius spoke with rapid enthusiasm about his day, which involved praise from his art teacher and the triumph of his friends in some complex and ill-defined conspiracy against another set of children. It had all been Chai-chai's idea, apparently, though what had been done, and to whom, and for what reason was completely opaque to the elder Gareth. A file of Chai-chai's latest drawings was appended. Martinez printed one out and stuck it on the wall of his sleeping cabin, obscuring a grimacing, orgasmic Torminel.

Martinez checked that the table, freshly polished and set for him and two guests, was ready, then joined Paivo Kangas at the main airlock, where they waited for Nikki Severin's shuttle to dock. Martinez's attention drifted to the plaque inset in the vestibule, a memorial explaining that *Bombardment of Los Angeles* was named in commemoration of a heroic action taken by the Fleet during the Rectification of Terra—a euphemism for the conquest of Earth—where a large city was efficiently annihilated in under two minutes by bombardment from orbit, all to the everlasting glory of the Praxis.

Severin's shuttle docked and Martinez welcomed him to *Los Angeles*. Severin had straight black hair and narrow eyes above prominent cheekbones, and he and Martinez had known each other since the early stages of the Naxid War—when Severin, commanding a wormhole relay station, had physically shifted the wormhole out from under a Naxid squadron, sent them on a monthslong detour, and kept them out of the war for a crucial period. Since then, Martinez had tried to act as a kind of patron to Severin and had introduced him to several high-caste Peer ladies, who in turn introduced Severin, and his puppet shows, to the High City.

As they walked from the airlock, Martinez studied Severin for signs of grief over the loss of Lady Starkey, but Severin offered no clue. "Nikki," he said finally, "how are you?"

"I'm trying to stay focused," he said.

*So am I*, Martinez thought, though he found there were too many hours in the day to completely exclude his own sense of grief and loss, and he supposed that Severin was no different.

He walked with the others to his dining room and took his place at the head of the table. "Drinks?" he said.

"I'll have some of your Laredo whisky," Paivo said.

"I'd like wine, if I may," said Severin.

"What sort?'

"Whatever goes with dinner, I suppose."

Martinez didn't know what Mangahas planned to serve, and besides, he never understood why one sort of wine was supposed to go with a particular dish rather than some other kind of wine—unless the stuff was absolute rotgut he couldn't taste much of a difference. He summoned Mpanza, ordered whisky for himself and Paivo, and then told him to bring an appropriate wine for Severin.

Whisky and wine were poured and served, and then Mpanza brought out Mangahas's first course, a fish soup. The Fourth Fleet had left Zarafan weeks ago and the fresh food was almost gone, so Mangahas had to use frozen, canned, or dried ingredients.

The soup was sour, which was a surprise, but the comments of his guests told him that they thought the sour was a good thing. Martinez had no opinion concerning whether the sour was good or bad, but at least it was unusual.

He liked Marivic Mangahas as a chef, because her food didn't taste like the food of other cooks. Whether it was better or worse was a separate issue he felt unqualified to answer, but he was happy in its variety.

Severin sipped his wine. "I've been wondering, my lords," he said, "about the Peers, and since you both belong to that order, I thought I'd ask you my question."

Martinez and Paivo looked at each other. "Go ahead," Martinez said.

"What exactly," said Severin, "are you people *for*?"

The question caught Martinez by surprise, and he didn't have an answer ready. Severin spoke on.

"In primary school, they taught us that the Peers were a kind of intermediary between the Great Masters and the rest of us—interpreters, if you like. But now the Great Masters are all dead and don't need interpreters anymore. But somehow the former interpreters ended up in charge of everything, and where in the Praxis is that?"

"What choice is there?" asked Paivo. "You can't have the people choosing their own leaders—that's democracy, which is the same thing as mob rule, and it's absolutely forbidden by the Praxis."

"But the Peers don't seem to be doing very well," Severin said. "Two civil wars in ten years—the Peers aren't exactly covering themselves with glory, are they?" He hesitated for a moment, then added, "Present company always excepted."

Martinez stroked his chin as he formulated his answer. "Your question seems to assume that the Peers are uniform in some way.

In fact, we're as varied as any other group—we don't all think the same way, or make the same assumptions, or view one another with the same degrees of approval."

Severin looked thoughtful. "That's a little harder to see from my perspective," he said. "Until I got to know some of you, you looked like a very solid ceiling a very great distance above my head." He nodded. "And of course Peers compete with one another—if you didn't, we wouldn't be fighting a civil war, would we?"

"And naturally there are degrees of Peers," Paivo said. "Some come from prestigious clans and some don't, and though we're all supposed to be rich, some are very poor."

"Especially since the economy collapsed," Martinez said.

"I've noticed that you have a kind of informal stratigraphy," Severin said. "There's the absolute top rank, like Lady Terza and Lady Sula—the upper-upper-upper set of Peers. Whereas you two are upper-upper-middle, and the upper-upper-upper feel free to condescend to you." He turned to Martinez. "That's why you had to start your own yacht club, yes? Because you wouldn't have been allowed into the established clubs."

"I . . . won't disagree," Martinez said cautiously.

"And Chandra Prasad, I think, is middle-middle-middle, and Naaz Vijana is lower-middle-middle. Lord Gareth's aide Santana is, at best, lower-middle-lower." He raised his wineglass. "And I, of course, am a considerable distance below even the lower-lower-lower, because I'm not a Peer at all."

Paivo smiled as he swirled his drink in his hand. "You know," he said, "these categories are kind of fun."

Severin continued his dogged analysis. "But even though the peers no longer speak for the Great Masters, they still have a monopoly on certain institutions. Peers are two percent of the population, but have ninety percent of the money. The places at the Fleet academies are reserved for Peers, so even if I were the most talented applicant, I could never be an officer, unless I was promoted through the same kind of accident . . ." He hesitated, aware he was weakening his case. "The sort of accident that actually allowed my step to lieutenant."

"An upper-upper-upper gave you a field promotion," Martinez said. "Out of condescension, perhaps."

"I've always assumed you recommended me," Severin said.

"I recommended a reward," Martinez said. "It was Michi who decided you should be an officer."

"Really?" Severin thought that over, then waved a hand. "Well, I like you anyway."

Martinez smiled. "That felt just a little condescending."

"You're wrong about the academies," Paivo said. "There were commoners in my class. When I was a cadet on the *Standard*, there was a commoner in the wardroom."

"And how many commoners command warships, or any of the big dockyards?"

Martinez couldn't think of an answer.

"And there are no commoners in the Convocation, and the Convocation runs the empire," Severin said.

"Commoners have been co-opted into the Convocation," Martinez said, "but they generally get a peerage at the same time."

"At Harzapid," Paivo said, "Lady Sula was talking about awarding offices and promotions based on competitive examinations."

"Was she?" Martinez was surprised. She hadn't mentioned the idea to him. It seemed remarkably fair-minded of her—but then he remembered that she'd scored a First on her lieutenant's exams in her year and that if her ability to fly through exams became a qualification for office, she'd be running the empire in no time.

"There was some old empire on Terra that appointed officials based on exams," said Severin. "From my perspective, it seems an idea worth considering."

"The idea makes me wonder if we want everyone in charge of the empire to be so intelligent," Paivo said. "Those with, ah, lesser gifts can be depended on to provide a degree of stability, because they'll have enough imagination to do their jobs, but little else." He laughed. "But have you ever tried to get a group of very intelligent people to agree on anything? We might have a new civil war every week."

"So you're saying that the empire depends on the mediocrity of its officials," Martinez said.

Paivo blinked. "Apparently I am," he said.

"I'd like to point out that we," said Severin, "by which I mean the highly intelligent officers of the Fourth Fleet, seem to have collaborated very well with one another."

"We are under extraordinary pressure to work together," said Martinez. "To assure our own survival, for one thing. Once the fear of annihilation is over, rivalries and discord may well surface." He shrugged. "*May*? Let's face it, some will be at each other's throats."

"I for one would enjoy the sight of Michi Chen gnawing on Wei Jian's jugular," said Paivo.

Mpanza entered, and the conversation faded while he refilled everyone's glasses. Martinez applied himself to his sour soup.

It had never occurred to him, he realized, to ask himself what he was *for*, as a Peer or anything else. As a young man he'd had a choice, to remain with his family and develop into a less impressive version of his older brother Roland or to strike out on his own. As a Peer he'd had a free berth at the Nelson Academy, where upper-upper-middle Peers predominated, and so he opted for the Fleet. Which had turned out to be the right decision, because the Naxid War had shaken the empire just enough so that he had opportunities for advancement that wouldn't have otherwise been available. And of course the same wartime disruption had made it possible for a commoner like Severin to rise to the highest rank in the Exploration Service.

But what was he *for*?

He was for winning battles, he thought, fortunately for the right side. And he was for fathering genius children.

Anything else, he thought, could be left to specialists.

Once Mpanza withdrew, he addressed the matter. "It would be good if we found ways for people like Captain Severin to advance and exercise his gifts," he said, "and to do it without a war."

Severin's look was dark. "Indeed," he said. Martinez guessed he was thinking of Lady Starkey.

"One problem is that it's not up to us," Paivo said. "It's up to the politicians." He looked at Martinez. "Unless Lady Sula has her way and we establish a military dictatorship."

Martinez was aware of this element of Sula's program. "Remember when I said that conflicts and rivalries would surface after the victory?" he said. "Imagine how the knives would come out when everyone's competing to be sole ruler of the empire."

Paivo considered this. "I fancy Lady Sula could dispose of any rivals without much trouble."

Martinez felt a cold finger touch his spine, and he wondered how much Paivo knew, or guessed, about Sula's methods for dealing with those she found inconvenient.

Mpanza entered to collect their soup bowls, fortunately bringing an end to any more speculation on Sula or dictatorship. The next course was a kind of vegetable stew. This was followed by deep-fried pork, and lastly coconut and shellfish in a delicate fried wrapper. More coconut was present in the dessert, a kind of custard topped with fruit. Mpanza brought out coffee, its scent sharp in the air, and then Martinez called up the morning exercise into the displays and asked Severin to explain how he had won the morning's exercise.

The Fourth Fleet's last opponent, Lord Tork, had employed the Fleet's traditional playbook and strung out his squadrons in a long line. Martinez had been able to employ the third dimension to send his own formations north and south of Tork's line and achieve a local superiority that broke Tork's formation into pieces, each of which was then overwhelmed in turn.

There had been considerable discussion among the officers concerning how best to employ the third dimension in this new phase of the war—Martinez had initially favored stacking his ships into a formation resembling a flyswatter, and intended to be used in much the same way as a flyswatter, to bat enemy ships out of the way. His ideas had evolved as the fleet exercises had revealed more possibilities, and now he employed mobile reserves and detached squadrons flying in advance and in the rear, all to add flexibility.

That morning Severin's ships had been flying in a formation similar to that of Martinez, with detachments ready to reinforce the main body at any point, and every ship whirling in the unpredictable chaos of the Method.

"I call it a patchwork quilt," Severin said. "Each of the patches can be any size, and each can maneuver independently."

"Can you explain how that's different from what we've been doing till now?" Martinez said. "My subformations were also capable of independent movement."

"The difference isn't in their capabilities," Severin said. "But in my exploitation of transient movement."

Severin explained that he was always ordering minor shifts in his squadrons' headings, just to see how the opposition reacted.

Once the reactions became predictable, his own maneuvers could be used to shift the opposition out of position, after which he would pounce.

"Everything's a feint, until it isn't," he said, as he showed how Foote's Division Two had wedged apart Martinez's squadrons until he could dash in to disrupt Martinez's entire force.

Martinez took a sip of his strong coffee and hoped it would help him grasp Severin's tactics. "I'd like to think I would have noticed what you were doing," he said, "if I weren't so absorbed in trying to envelop your lead ships."

"If you'd countered Foote," Severin said, "I would have feinted somewhere else."

Paivo frowned. "It's a very subtle thing you're doing," he said. "All those micromaneuvers—how do you keep them all in your head?"

Severin spread his hands. "I just *do*," he said.

Paivo turned to Martinez. "I'm beginning to think that Squadcom Severin and I should change places," he said. "He might make a better tactical officer than me."

"That's a generous thought," Martinez said, "but it's premature. If what Nikki is doing forms any kind of system, we can learn that system. Just give us time." He turned to Severin. "Nikki, I'd like you to command the opposition again tomorrow, and we'll see if we can be ready for you."

Severin nodded. "As you like, my lord," he said. "I'll do my best to beat you again."

Martinez, as he took another sip of his coffee, resigned himself to once again being on the losing side.

But the next day Martinez surprised himself by winning. This time, Sula's scheme to predict where the Martinez Method would take the other side's ships had worked, and Martinez was able to target Severin's ships one by one until the computer proclaimed that Severin had been wiped out. The victory had been so swift and decisive that Severin hadn't an opportunity to develop his micro-maneuvers.

At present, the computers were predicting enemy actions about 30 percent of the time. If Sula was right, the computers would get better at it.

But if they didn't, Severin's system would be valuable indeed. At least assuming that anyone other than Severin could understand it.

"I HAVE VIEWED your report of the action at Colamote," said Wei Jian. From the video display her dark eyes bore on Sula like the barrels of a cannon. "I was shocked and disgusted to see you improperly dressed, insofar as you wore insignia belonging to a junior fleet commander, not a senior captain. If this appalling behavior continues, I shall be forced to take disciplinary action. End message."

*Well,* Sula thought. *Complaints about shoulder boards, and no congratulations for my bloodless victory. I guess we now know what's important to our new overlord.*

Thoughtfully, she reached for her toasted muffin and spread honey on it. The gentle fragrance of the honey failed to calm her.

She knew the answer she wanted to send: *Shut your mouth, you stupid fucking cow! You have no authority over me or over anyone else! You're a coward who spent months avoiding battle and skulking among the asteroids, and everybody knows it. You're lucky that you're allowed to breathe the same air as the rest of the Fleet! Any more lip from you, and I shall be forced to take disciplinary action, and I don't think you'll like that one fucking bit!*

By the time she'd finished her muffin, she'd decided that sending the message would not improve the situation. Documenting your mutiny on video was probably not the best prescription for continued health.

She decided not to reply to the message at all. What, after all, could be the point? She had an independent command, there was no way that Wei Jian could monitor her, and very shortly she would be out of communication, since between Colamote and Laredo most of the wormhole relays were occupied by the enemy.

Division Nine would be taking the route to Laredo instead of heading to Harzapid, since Sula wanted to stand between the six Laredo cruisers and any more enemy ships popping up from the direction of Antopone. So Division Nine would continue its acceleration out of the Colamote system and accelerate for ten or twelve days, after which they'd turn over and begin a deceleration, which eventually would bring their velocity to zero, followed by an acceleration in the direction of Colamote once more. The Laredo cruisers would catch them, the Fleet crews would be transferred aboard, and the civilian crews that had taken the cruisers from Laredo would get aboard Sula's excess civilian ships and head for home.

Staffing, however, was going to be a problem. Sula had brought sufficient trainees to crew six *Celestial*-class light cruisers, with several hundred extra volunteer crew that had to be evacuated from Zarafan anyway. But now she'd captured the three *Bombardment*-class heavy cruisers of Sen-thar's small squadron, each of which required a larger crew than any of the Laredo ships, and the result was that all her warships were going to be undercrewed, with an insufficient number of enlisted serving under newly promoted officers unused to, and possibly unqualified for, their jobs. The crews of the heavy cruisers had all trained on simulators of the light *Celestial* class, and now they were having to relearn everything.

Sen-thar's former ships were also undergoing refit. Furniture for Lai-own included an extra support for the Lai-owns' keel-shaped breastbone, and the chairs, over time, were excruciating for humans. Regular shuttles full of furniture, including acceleration couches, were moving back and forth between the immigration ships and the new prizes.

In addition, *Ideal, Lentrec,* and *Pride of Parkhurst* had begun their conversion into warships, a procedure that had so far gutted large sections of the ships' interiors with no increase in the ships' usefulness, at least so far. Heavy sheets of radiation shielding were being jigsawed into place, and the mechanism to feed missiles to the launchers were being fitted. Installing the launchers, which would involve cutting holes in the ships' hulls, would be saved for last.

Sula had called for one military exercise, *Mentor* and *Splendid* versus the new captures. As Sula suspected, the captures' new crews weren't yet up to actually maneuvering their ships in anything like combat; so the battle had been fought entirely in virtual, with the ships linked together by communications laser in a single computer-generated environment. Despite the heavy cruisers' advantages in numbers of missile tubes and maneuver elements, the result had been a complete rout, with the three heavy cruisers swiftly destroyed as they staggered through the simulation, unable to coordinate either maneuvers or missile fire.

Sula had assured the dejected officers of the losing ships that they would get better with practice, but privately she had her doubts. Division Nine was trying to do too much, and its resources were stretched too thin. Inexperienced crouchbacks crewed ships they hadn't trained for, major reconstruction was being carried out not in dock but on the fly, officers were either inexperienced demi-cadets or recycled retirees—and the nature of the squadron itself, with its heterogeneous collection of warships, transports, and the three giants, was all a great big radioactive formula for confusion and failure.

And what Sula's commander Wei Jian cared about was *insignia*. She didn't know whether to laugh or weep.

*Everything dies. Nothing matters.* Somehow that thought now seemed a comfort.

A door slid open, and Shawna Spence stepped in. "More tea, my lady?"

"I think I've had enough, thank you."

"More pastries, then?" Spence's eyes strayed to the image of Wei Jian frozen on the screen. "New orders, my lady?" she asked.

"None I plan to pay attention to," Sula said. "Why don't you get a cup from the kitchen and join me for tea?"

Spence fetched a cup and sat next to Sula at the wedge-shaped table. Sula looked at the battered beige walls. "I'm thinking of re-painting," she said.

"Good idea," Spence said. "Bright colors, so being on a ship again isn't so depressing."

Sula, who had been considering a dark viridian green, decided that perhaps Spence had a point.

"As long as it doesn't look like the set of a children's program," she said. "No red balloons, no cute animals, no wrapped presents with big bows."

"I *like* cute animals." Spence looked at her. "How about happy derivoo?"

"That would be too scary. I wouldn't sleep at all."

Sula saw Spence hesitate before answering, and she knew what thought was going through Spence's head: *Oh. No change then.*

"No derivoo," Spence said. "Check."

Sula looked at her teacup with its motif of tulips and pomegranates. "Maybe something like this," she said. "I can look up tra-ditional Anatolian designs."

"If they're all as colorful as that," Spence said, "we'll have the most cheerful flag officer's quarters in the Fleet."

Sula sipped her tea, felt the sweet liquid ease along her tongue, then returned the cup to its saucer.

"How is Macnamara faring?" she asked.

"Oh," Spence said. Her face adopted an ambiguous expression. "He's very much in love."

Sula had assumed as much. She had checked the logs of the ship's recreation tubes and found that since Macnamara had re-turned from escorting prisoners to their new accommodation, his name or Japutra Bliss's were found on reservations for the tubes.

"He knows Bliss is married, yes?" Sula said.

"Oh yes. *He* says that *she* says the marriage is over."

Sula gazed into her teacup. "We'll see if the husband agrees."

Spence was silent.

"Well," Sula said finally. "Whatever makes Macnamara happy."

Her own experience was that spouses turned up at the most inopportune moments, usually the happy ones.

"And yourself?" Sula asked. "Have you met anyone on this journey who might lighten your burdens?"

Spence shook her head. "No. But then I have to be careful."

Sula was surprised. "Careful? How?"

"There are ambitious people on this ship," Spence explained, "and I'm orderly to the commander of the division. Some might feign an interest in me in order to come to your attention, in hopes of getting a promotion or some other favored status."

Sula blinked. She hadn't considered this possibility. "Does that happen often?" she asked.

Spence shrugged. "Often enough."

"And this Bliss person?" she asked. "She's not ambitious in that way?"

Spence shrugged again. "She hasn't made any effort to cross your path, has she?"

"I don't think so. I'm not sure I've even been in the same room with her."

"So maybe her ambitions are confined to Gavin."

"Good for Macnamara, then."

Sula suddenly realized that this topic was making her weary. She had no advice about relationships to offer Macnamara, Spence, or anyone else.

All her lovers but one were dead, she thought. It's almost as if she had been careless.

WEI JIAN'S EXPRESSIONLESS face looked out of the video display on the wall of Martinez's office. Martinez gazed at her, the stranger on her way to take his job, with resentment.

"I reviewed your latest report," she said, "and I took note of the way you are dispersing missiles into ambush positions around the system. I see that all the missiles are in the same plane, hidden behind planets and amid asteroids and so forth, which—" Her lips gave a little twitch. "Which is adequate as far as it goes. Kindly send missiles north and south of the ecliptic plane, into empty space where the enemy is less likely to look for them. End message."

*Adequate as far as it goes.* Martinez clenched his teeth. His ambushes had worked well against Tork and had accounted for over a hundred enemy ships with no losses to the Restoration.

But Martinez had to admit that Jian was right. Do-faq's ships were much less likely to scan empty space for incoming threats, and there was a chance that missiles coming at unlikely angles could cause serious damage.

A scraping sound rasped against his nerves. The air had a fierce chemical tang. Martinez had held a competition to redecorate his quarters among those members of the Fourth Fleet who fancied themselves artists, and the winners were now at work in his dining room, stripping away the grappling Torminels before putting their own work on the walls.

Martinez tried to ignore the scraping while he busied himself with plotting missile launches, and then there was a chime on his video screen, and he saw the arrival of a message from Terza. He leaned back in his office chair, took a breath of the paint-stripper air, and triggered the video.

Wearing the brown tunic of the civil service, Terza sat behind a desk, dark wood with brass fittings. Martinez recognized on a corner of the desk a miniature of the allegorical statue *The Great Master Presenting Perfect Justice to the People*. Martinez detected an amused glint in Terza's eyes, as if she'd just brought perfect justice to someone who deserved it.

"I'm forwarding you a video of a message I sent to Wei Jian," she said. "I hope you find it diverting."

Martinez triggered the second video, and saw Terza sitting at the same desk. The camera focused on her more closely, and the allegorical statue had been moved closer into the frame. Her face, posture, and voice radiated serenity, one of those tricks of hers that had always made Martinez a little uneasy.

"Fleet Commander Jian," she said, "I have received your orders concerning the reorganization of the Harzapid government and the appointment of an official in Lady Governor Koridun's office to report to you on all decisions made or contemplated by that office."

She nodded gracefully. "Lady Wei," she said, "I find it my painful duty to tell you that *we do not work for you*. We—by which I mean the Select Committee for the Restoration—are the legitimate government of the empire until the war is won and a proper reorganization can be made on Zanshaa. As the Praxis clearly states that the military is subordinate to the civilian government, I'm afraid that *you work for us*, not the other way around—unless of course you do not recognize the Restoration as the legitimate government, in which case I wonder what you are doing here."

Again that graceful nod. "Naturally, we will do our best to comply with any requisitions sent to us, provided submissions are made using the proper form. End message."

Martinez grinned while his soul filled with admiration. Wei Jian had been out-Jian'd, and she who so enjoyed putting people in their place had been shown her own status, farther from the center of power than she would like.

*Select Committee for the Restoration.* The ad hoc committee that had been running things on Harzapid appeared to have gained a name, and perhaps new legitimacy.

The orange end-stamp faded from the display, and Terza reappeared, her face wreathed in a pleased smile. "We'll see if Jian answers by sending a flight of missiles my way," she said, "but short of that, I think we have ordered things rather well."

Martinez replied at once. "Congratulations!" he said. "Well handled!" He smiled. "Now, if the Select Committee is in charge, I wonder if the Select Committee could fire Wei Jian? Or perhaps recall her for consultation?" He smiled. "Just a little notion of mine. Well worth considering, I think."

He ciphered the message and sent it on, then decided to celebrate with a new pot of coffee. Mpanza arrived with coffee a few minutes later and poured Martinez a fresh cup.

"How are we doing?" he asked.

"On the whole we are pleased with events," Mpanza said. "We still worry about Wei Jian. What if she proves no better a commander than Lord Tork?"

*The question critical*, Martinez thought, but he preferred not to voice his own doubts to a servant.

"We're going to win no matter what," he said.

"We appreciate your confidence," Mpanza said.

"How is Electrician Second Class Raju?" Martinez asked.

Mpanza hesitated before answering. "She is uncertain whether to hold the wedding on Zanshaa, after the victory, or on Hy-Oso, so her family can attend."

Martinez was surprised. "You're engaged? Congratulations."

"I don't recall ever deciding on an engagement," Mpanza said. "Maybe I proposed while sleepwalking."

Martinez considered this. "Raju's jumped the gun where marriage is concerned?"

Mpanza's expression was tinged with melancholy. "My lord, she has already named several of our children. And what kind of name is Möxämmätcan anyway?"

Martinez lifted his coffee cup and inhaled the aromatic steam, a considerable improvement over the terpene scent of paint stripper floating in from the dining room.

"It's none of my business, of course," he said, "but perhaps you should try to alert Electrician Raju to her, ah, misapprehensions?"

"I've done my best," Mpanza said. "She seems impervious, but I'll keep trying."

"Best of luck with it," Martinez said. "And thanks for the coffee."

Mpanza withdrew, and Martinez gave orders for missiles to be fired and marshaled north and south of the ecliptic plane. Notice of another message appeared on his display, and he opened it to find it had been sent in text.

TO LORD COMMANDER MARTINEZ:
YOU ARE CORDIALLY INVITED TO DINE ABOARD THE AR-
GENTÉE AT A DAY AND HOUR CONVENIENT TO YOU.

And the message was signed, *Nikkul Shankaracharya.*
*The invitation cryptic,* Martinez thought.

Shankaracharya was married to Martinez's youngest sister, Sempronia. Sempronia had been engaged to PJ Ngeni, a minor member of the powerful Ngeni clan who had then served as patrons to the Martinez family, and when Sempronia and Nikkul had flown away together, the middle Martinez sister, Walpurga, felt it her duty to step into Sempronia's place and make a marriage with PJ, a marriage that Martinez devoutly hoped was a sham. Walpurga had fled Zanshaa just ahead of the Naxid advance, while a deeply humiliated PJ decided to stay behind. Both the Ngeni and Martinez clans had disowned Sempronia, and so far as Martinez could tell, Sempronia had disowned her own family in return.

Not that he was a party to anyone's decision. Yet Sempronia, who was Martinez's favorite sister, apparently blamed him for everything.

PJ died a hero when Sula stormed the High City with her army. As for Shankaracharya, he had been a junior officer in the Fleet when his patron had strong-armed Martinez into taking him aboard his frigate *Corona.* But Nikkul hadn't been ready, had frozen twice in combat, and Martinez had written a report that blew up Nikkul's career.

Nikkul, along with his bride, had returned to his family's electronics empire, headquartered at Harzapid, and there produced the superior sensor suites designed for the Exploration Service.

Nikkul and Sempronia had tried to contact Michi Chen about the sensors, but Michi had been sensitive to the prejudices of her in-laws and had refused to see them. They had approached Sula instead, and Sula had recognized the value of the new sensor suites and committed to installing them on every warship in the Fourth Fleet, where they would be an element in any victory.

And now Nikkul was inviting Martinez to dinner. Martinez wondered if he was being forgiven or if he would be offered as a target for his sister.

Martinez paged Aitor Santana. "Is a ship called *Argentée* near us? Can you tell me where?"

Santana came back a few minutes later. "*Argentée* is a private yacht licensed to the Shankaracharya Electronics Company (Harzapid). It was bound from Harzapid to Zarafan when we evacuated, and they flipped over and started a hard acceleration back to Harzapid. Currently they're ahead of us, and we're scheduled to overtake them in fifty-seven hours."

"Thank you." He mentally composed a message, and then said, "Message to *Argentée*, personal to Nikkul Shankaracharya. 'Would it suit to meet at 18:01 hours two days from now?' Signed, Martinez, etc."

Santana repeated the message back, then sent it. A reply came a few minutes later. "*Date and time suit very well.*"

Martinez viewed the text glowing in the display, and wondered if the flicker of optimism he felt would be justified or if it would fade like every other hopeful illusion.

"I WANT TO make it clear that this was all Nikkul's idea," Sempronia said, "and that I still hate you."

Martinez, who had just walked out of the airlock, felt his

tentative optimism flutter to the deck like a falling paper flower. "I don't know why I expected anything else," he said.

*Argentée* was a typical business yacht, with recessed lighting, silent, attentive crew in neat black uniforms, and paneling that smelled of lemon polish. Sempronia inhabited this environment well, in a leaf-green dress with a flounced hem and embroidered cherry blossoms. It was a dress that wouldn't suit her sisters at all, which might have been the point.

Martinez DNA favored certain traits: olive skin, dark hair and eyes, sturdy mesomorphic bodies, arms long in proportion to relatively short legs. Sempronia was the exception, with hazel eyes, light brown hair, and a slim silhouette.

"Nikkul's waiting for you," Sempronia said. "I'll be joining you for your meal, not because I want to be around you, but because I don't want Nikkul to do something stupid."

"I'm not interested in Nikkul's being stupid either," Martinez said.

"Too late," Sempronia said. "He invited *you*."

Sempronia showed Martinez to a small dining room with a table that could sit no more than six people. The chairs were plush with cream-colored aesa leather, and the walls were clad— *upholstered*, Martinez thought—in the same material. If *Argentée* was forced into high-gee maneuvers, the diners could carom off the leather-padded walls in something like safety.

Nikkul Shankaracharya had been working with a hand comm, but he dropped the device into a pocket when Martinez arrived and rose from his chair.

"Captain Martinez," he said. "Welcome to *Argentée*."

He was a slight man with cocoa skin and hair that tumbled in ringlets over the back of his collar. His eyes were liquid, brown, and attentive.

"It's good to see you thriving," said Martinez.

"Please take a seat," Nikkul said. "Would you like something to drink?"

"Whatever you're having," Martinez said.

A silent, black-clad attendant appeared with a bottle of silvery Cavado wine and poured. Nikkul raised his glass.

"To your very great success, Lord Captain," he said. Sempronia snorted and declined to raise her glass. Nikkul and Martinez sipped.

Martinez decided the wine tasted very much like wine.

"I've been testing your sensor arrays in fleet exercises," Martinez said. "They're excellent, and I anticipate they'll provide a crucial edge against the enemy."

Sempronia snorted again. "We couldn't sell them until we went to Lady Sula," she said. "Every door was closed."

"My door was open," Martinez said. "But nobody told me about your sensors."

"I knew better than to approach *you*," Sempronia said. "Even if you decided in our favor, Roland, Vipsania, and Michi would have overruled you."

Martinez considered this. "I wish I could disagree," he said, "but you're probably right." He turned to Nikkul. "You were bound for Zarafan when you had to turn back to Harzapid. What were you planning on doing there?"

"We have facilities on Zarafan," Nikkul said. "You acquired all the sensor suites they had in storage there—and I'd like to be paid for them, incidentally. But we were actually bound for Zanshaa, and would have stayed on Zarafan only if it wasn't safe to proceed directly for the capital."

"And in Zanshaa you would—what?—look after family assets?"

"That," said Nikkul, "and we hoped also to contribute to the cause of the Restoration."

"I'm sure any contribution would be welcome," said Martinez.

Nikkul looked thoughtful. "Possibly," he said. "But would Roland welcome any such contribution? Vipsania? Walpurga? Michi Chen? Lord Ngeni? Pierre Ngeni?"

Martinez felt his heart sink. "They're not about to forgive you," he said. He spread his hands. "I'll do what I can, but—"

"I told you this meeting was pointless," Sempronia said. "Gareth's useless, and the rest are bastards."

Nikkul frowned at his wine glass, then looked up at Martinez.

"But will they stand in my way?" he asked. "If the Restoration wins, your family is going to be in charge of—well, probably not *everything*, but you'll be dictating a lot of policy to the Convocation. You're going to need to rebuild the Fleet, and I have a lot to sell the Fleet besides the sensor suites. Improved electronics, missile guidance systems, advanced proximity fuses, point-defense weaponry. Will your family blacklist my products?"

"I don't think my family is going to be in charge of the Fleet," Martinez said. "I'm the only Fleet officer among them, and Terza serves the Fleet in the Ministry of Right and Dominion. All I can say is that I won't impede your progress in any way, but a great deal will remain up to selection committees and so on, and on who's going to serve on a reformed Fleet Control Board."

"My patron is Lord Pezzini," Nikkul said. "He *was* on the Fleet Control Board, but I imagine he's under house arrest now, unless he managed to get himself killed. Do you think he'll be back on the Control Board when and if he's released?"

"I don't know," Martinez said. He hoped not—Pezzini was an arrogant, argumentative man, a traditionalist who had stood against all the plans and reforms advocated by Martinez and his friends.

"That's not very helpful," Nikkul said.

"I didn't realize I am here to help you. If you haven't noticed, I've been concentrating on winning the war," Martinez said. "If there are plans for what happens after the victory, I'm not privy to them."

"You're *still* useless!" Sempronia said. She turned to her husband. "Look, we should just bribe our way to the contracts like we always do."

There was a moment of silence. Martinez looked at Nikkul with eyebrows raised. Nikkul sighed.

"I suppose it comes as no surprise that the selection process is largely corrupt," he said. "We must pay to play, and play we must." He rapped his knuckles on the table top. "We're doing well on provincial worlds," he said, "and we'd do better if not for the, ah, *flaws* in the selection process—but we haven't cracked Zanshaa. Traditional High City families and firms have locked up all the business there."

"If those families and firms are supporters of the current Zanshaa government," Martinez said, "at least some of that business will be unlocked following any victory."

"Again, though: Will your family stand in our way?" Nikkul asked.

"I imagine that they'll be too busy to examine every contract being awarded," Martinez said. "But Vipsania and Walpurga are dead set against you, and you should know that."

"I didn't tell Walpurga to marry that idiot," Sempronia said.

"*Nobody* was supposed to marry him," Martinez said. "The engagement was a sham, and if you'd played along for another year or two, we'd have worked out a way to make the engagement disappear. But once you ran away—" He waved a hand. "The Ngenis got very huffy about family honor, and that made Roland and the others get serious about *our* honor, and so . . ."

"Right," Sempronia said. "Blame me, then!"

Martinez looked at her. "I do," he said. "I absolutely do."

"For not following your stupid plan?" Sempronia demanded. "Of having to live a lie for *years*, when Nikkul and I were in love, and every minute was precious because it was war and we could have been killed at any time? Of all the hypocritical—"

"If you had been a little more hypocritical," Martinez said, "PJ Ngeni might still be alive, you'd still be married to Nikkul, and your family would be happy to welcome you to Zanshaa."

"I—"

"If you can't stand hypocrisy," Martinez continued, "maybe you should stop bribing selection committees and go home to Harzapid, because you are absolutely unsuited for life or politics in the High City."

Sempronia's face turned to stone. She turned to Nikkul. "Well," she said, "it seems we are dismissed to our sad little provincial home."

Martinez look at Nikkul. "You had questions for me. I answered them as honestly as I could. I hold you no ill will, and I wish you every possible success." He pushed back his chair and stood. "But I see no point in continuing this. If you don't like my answers, perhaps you need to find some new questions."

Sempronia just glared at him. Nikkul stood. "I'll walk with you to the airlock," he said.

They walked in silence for a few moments while anger and sadness chased each other through Martinez's brain.

Nikkul Shankaracharya had proved unsuited to combat, but otherwise he was a highly intelligent man, with an active, agile imagination and an abundance of technical knowledge and skills. He'd made a contribution to the Method, and Martinez had genuinely regretted shooting down his career.

"I'm sorry," Martinez said. "My family is broken, and I don't know how to fix it."

"I'm sorry too," said Nikkul. "The sad fact is that I genuinely believe in the Restoration and its cause, and I think I could contribute to the reforms the empire desperately needs. But now—" He waved a hand. "We'll have to see what we can do."

"Good luck," Martinez said.

Nikkul gazed at him with solemn brown eyes. "And to you. I think you'll need it more than I."

SULA BROUGHT A gift when she visited Lord Nishkad in his palatial quarters aboard *Pride of Parkhurst*. It was a statuette of Nishkad himself, each part created in an autolathe in *Splendid*'s workshop, then assembled and sprayed with a bronze microalloy plating. Nishkad stood nobly on his four feet in his old squadron commander's uniform, complete with decorations. A plaque on the base held an inscription:

To Lord Nishkad, in Gratitude for His Benevolent and Unflagging Support of the Restoration, from Caroline Lady Sula and the Officers and Crews of Division Nine.

Macnamara carried the heavy statuette from the shuttle and handed it to Sula at the door. A servant in livery met Sula there, took the statuette, and brought her to where Nishkad waited in his parlor. Naxids had only two speeds, *stop* and *very-very-fast*, and Sula smiled as the servant bolted ahead of her, shoes clattering on the tile, only to be forced to stop to allow her to catch up.

"I brought you something for your trophy shelf," she said as she entered the parlor.

The servant placed the sculpture on a gleaming, polished table, and Nishkad uncoiled from his sofa and approached the statuette, which he studied with his black-on-red eyes. The eyes turned to Sula.

"Thank you," he said. "This is most unexpected."

"I considered giving it to you in a public ceremony," Sula said, "and I still can, with your permission. But if the Zanshaa government wins the war, this award would be viewed as evidence of treason, and I thought perhaps you'd prefer to keep your contribution out of the public eye."

"If we win," Nishkad said, "my contribution will become known. It will also become known if we lose, and in that event—if my courage proves sufficient—I plan to cheat the executioners by taking my own life."

Sula approved of Nishkad's calm acceptance of his fate, whatever that would be. *Everything dies. Nothing matters.*

"Fortune attend you, my lord," she said. "And once I'm back in the Convocation, I will try to pass an act to award you a decoration. You and the other Naxids have provided our very best chance of success."

"Thank you, my lady," said Nishkad. He returned to his sofa and coiled his quadruped body on the plush cushions. "I have tea prepared, if you would like some."

"I would, thank you."

"Please sit."

Sula perched on an intelligent chair that adjusted itself to her human frame. Another liveried servant pushed in a tray with a setting for tea and with a selection of cakes and pastries.

"I remember that you like cane syrup," Nishkad said, "and I found some on Zarafan."

"That's very thoughtful of you, my lord."

For half an hour they sipped tea, ate lemon cake, and talked about progress made in training and in the reconstruction of the three great ships. The transformation that had begun in chaos was slowly beginning to take on a more concrete form, with crews that were learning their jobs and transports slowly turning into warships.

The Colamote system was well in their rear, and Division Nine had already turned and begun the deceleration that would allow it to rendezvous with the Laredo cruisers.

The three captured cruisers were still losing to *Mentor* and *Splendid* in any exercises, but their crews were growing more experienced and were making measurable progress.

"My problem is lack of trained crew," Sula said. "When the new crews board the cruisers from Laredo, they're going to find themselves in battle within months. That's hardly enough time for a shakedown, let alone for everyone to know their jobs. While Dofaq's ships and crews have served together for years."

"You must plan your tactics in accordance with the skills of your subordinates," Nishkad said. "Which I know is far easier said than done."

"I wonder," Sula said, "if we might use some of your veteran instructors as crew on our warships."

Nishkad looked at her in wary surprise. "That of course would be illegal," he said. "Would your superiors permit such a thing?"

"I don't plan to ask them," Sula said. "I didn't ask permission when I employed Naxids in construction, or when I called for

Naxid volunteer instructors—and as long as I produce results, no one will be in a position to complain."

"And if you fail," Nishkad said, "all evidence will be destroyed, along with the ships and the crews."

"It will hardly matter to either of us at that point."

Nishkad's expression turned inward. "I will call for volunteers," he said. "But I will resist any attempt at conscription."

"That is all I ask," Sula said. "If anyone prefers a free, safe ride to Laredo, they're welcome."

Inwardly she smiled. Nishkad certainly deserved the award she'd given him, and she was perfectly sincere when she told him she would try to get him a decoration, but her timing had been quite deliberate. She needed him to put his people at risk by agreeing to her latest scheme, and she knew that few people were immune to flattery.

Now if only the enemy delayed their attack long enough for her to train her crews.

THE FLAGSHIP *CRISIS* had any number of airlocks suitable for docking a shuttle, but only two that would support the dignity of a senior officer of the Fleet, so there was a queue, with shuttles hanging in formation near the cruiser until a new space opened up. Martinez courteously let others go first, not because he was feeling deferential, but because he hadn't wanted to experience the strained conversation between Jian's officers and his own, which he expected would be hesitant, dreary, and depressing.

Plus, he wanted to save his impressive entrance for last.

At the last minute, Martinez stepped aboard the *Crisis* to the flourishes of a military band playing "Sworn Ever to Serve the Praxis," its seven members crammed into a corner of the lobby and barely able to deploy their instruments. Martinez wore full dress, the tall collar scratching at the flesh under his chin, and he carried the Golden Orb in his right hand, the polychromatic liquid swirling in its transparent ball.

The welcoming party braced to attention when they saw the Orb, and he heard a hesitation on the part of the band, until with a gesture he told them to continue their playing. The others he let stand easy for a few seconds, then set them at ease. An elcap with the red triangles of a staff officer escorted him to the elevator, and then to Wei Jian's dining room.

The two largest elements of the Restoration fleet had finally united. Michi Chen, her new leg, and her nine freshly repaired cruisers had arrived ten days earlier, and Martinez and Michi had engaged in long discussions about how best to welcome Jian and her captains. Formally correct, they decided, and any informal dialogues, including the subversive ones, could happen behind the scenes.

Jian and her fifty-five warships had joined the Fourth Fleet only hours ago, and she had promptly called a meeting of the high-ranking officers of both commands. Martinez had the feeling that this wasn't going to be the usual service dinner, with the diners slogging through one course after another and the dreariness relieved only by wine, but something else—for one thing, it was being held in midafternoon and not at mealtime.

As Martinez stepped off the elevator, he saw two military constables braced at attention on either side of open double doors. Desultory conversation came fitfully through the doors The staff officer led him to the doors and stood aside, and he walked in.

Wei Jian sat at the head of the table, with Michi on her left, and a gray-haired squadron commander on her right. Jian's eyes lighted on Martinez as he stepped through the double doors, and without hesitation she leaped to her feet and braced to salute the Orb. The others followed, and soon Martinez gazed down the table at a double row of formally dressed officers standing frozen at attention, chins raised to bare their throats in a sign of submission.

"Be at ease," he said, and the others relaxed.

"Captain Martinez," said Jian, "a place is reserved for you here."

An orderly drew back Martinez's chair, and he walked to it and sat. "Coffee or tea, my lord?" the orderly said. "Or a soft drink?"

"Coffee will be fine." Silver jugs of coffee and tea stood ready on a nearby shelf. The orderly brought him a cup and saucer, then poured from one of the jugs. A sharp aroma rose from the cup—it seemed Jian preferred her coffee strong, and Martinez could only agree.

The room was very functional, the walls painted light green, with recessed lighting, video screens on the walls, and a floor tiled in a severe pattern in black and white. Wei Jian had lived in this suite for *years*, he knew, and Martinez found it strange that the room remained so impersonal after all that time.

He sipped his coffee, glanced over the assembled guests, and saw almost all the officers in the Fourth Fleet who had served as a squadron or division commander, including Severin of the Exploration Service, the Daimong Rivven with his immobile face frozen in a perpetual expression of indignation, and the Lai-own An-dar, Rivven's fellow defector. Amid the officers of the Fourth Fleet were their opposite numbers from Jian's force. All were seated in order of rank and seniority dating not after any promotions within the Fourth Fleet but from the first day of the rebellion.

Looking at the assembled officers, he saw at least three of Jian's officers who outranked him. Any of them could be placed over him at any time: Martinez might well find himself in command of a single ship—or perhaps not even that, because every ship already had its captain.

Chandra Prasad entered the room, her metallic red hair swinging, and then braced at attention. Jian directed her to a chair. Martinez suspected that Chandra had arrived late as an act of insolence, and he hoped that the insolence—or the perception of it—would not fatally poison the atmosphere of the meeting.

Jian rose to her feet. "Now that we are all present," she said, with a pointed look at Chandra, "I will present my plan for engaging the enemy." Video displays flashed on the walls, showing numbers and types of ships.

"The Fourth Fleet has ninety-four ships," Jian continued, "or at least it will once those under repair have joined us—and the last should join within the next few days. My own command stands at fifty-five. In addition, two light cruisers were constructed at the Harzapid dockyards, have taken on crews, and are now on their way to a rendezvous. Other ships have been built on Terra and other worlds, but will not arrive for some weeks.

"Lady Sula's command, when she joins us, will consist of eleven warships, most with crews new to their jobs, plus three, ah, *improvised* warships"—her lips gave a dismissive little twist—"which may be of some limited use."

Jian's eyes scanned the room, locking eyes, however briefly, with each of the officers in turn. Gazing back into that determined stare, Martinez felt a chill run up his back.

"That," Jian said, "gives us a total of over a hundred and sixty warships, and despite some of the crews' hasty training, we now have a fair chance of engaging Do-faq's hundred and sixty-six on something like equal terms."

Jian frowned at one of the displays. "But why did Do-faq give us a *chance* to engage on equal terms? After all, the enemy knew ages ago that the Fourth Fleet had only seventy-five ships at Zarafan, some of which were under repair, and if Do-faq had attacked then he could have outnumbered Captain Martinez more than two-to-one and destroyed him. So the question I must ask myself is, *Why did he hesitate?*"

"The politicians may have ordered him to stay and protect the capital," said Captain Conyngham. Conyngham was a dedicated officer who had stayed in the service despite the bad luck of being captured on the first day of the Naxid Rebellion, and at Second Shulduc had commanded *Perfection of the Praxis*, the Fourth Fleet's one and only battleship, protected by a squadron of cruisers. As intended, Lord Tork had assumed that *Perfection* was the flagship of the entire fleet and had personally led the attack with his own three battleships and their support, and in so doing fatally overstrained his own line. Conyngham had fought an extended defensive action and survived by the skin of his teeth, and it had been claimed afterward that the action had been so harrowing that his hair and goatee had turned white. Martinez happened to know that Conyngham's hair had been white before the start of the Accidental War, but he saw no reason to let trivial truth stand in the way of a good story.

Wei Jian, however, was not inclined to respect Conyngham's white hairs, and put him in the crosshairs of one of her cold stares.

"Kindly do not interrupt," she said. "When I wish to hear speculation, I shall ask for it."

Conyngham was taken aback. "Beg pardon, Lady Fleetcom," he murmured.

Jian ignored him and turned to the rest of the room.

"It may have been a political decision, yes," she said. "But I think the decision was a military one—a conservative decision, perhaps, but a decision that might have unwelcome consequences in the long run. I think that Do-faq had decided to await reinforcements."

She paused to let that calculation sink into the minds of the assembled officers.

"Recall that Tork had left nineteen ships to defend the capital," Jian said. "That raises Do-faq's total to a hundred eighty. And we may assume that the Zanshaa government has been building new warships, just as we have—casualties, after all, were foreseeable, and contracts for replacement ships would have been let out early in the war. The three cruisers that Lady Sula captured at Colamote were newly built at Antopone, and Antopone doesn't have a large, well-staffed Fleet dockyard. The enemy have more yards, personnel, and cash than we do, so if every Antopone-sized ring station was ramped up to produce three cruiser-equivalents, we may assume that at least twenty-one new ships may soon be reinforcing Do-faq at Zanshaa, if they haven't already."

There was a stir in the room as the assembled officers turned to look at one another. Calculations clicked over in Martinez's mind: ships, missiles, missile launchers. Jian's calculations were at least plausible.

"Furthermore," Jian said, "we can assume that the enemy co-opted ships of the Exploration Service, just as we did. A percentage of Service ships are on extended exploration missions, so probably no more than nine or ten will be both strong enough to stand in battle and available to join Do-faq."

Rivven had told Martinez that Tork, wanting the glory of victory to go entirely to the Fleet, had refused the offer of Exploration Service ships, but that meant there were now more available to Do-faq.

Jian leaned forward and rested her knuckles on the surface of the table. "Most important, however, are the forty warships formerly commanded by Nguyen at Felarus. The enemy boasts that these ships were captured, not destroyed, and that all Terran crew were killed without any damage taken by the enemy. While some of this may be an exaggeration, we should nevertheless assume that those forty ships would have been converted from Terran use to that of other species, and done as quickly as possible.

"Remember that Felarus is the headquarters of the Third Fleet, and in normal circumstances maintains and crews more than two hundred ships. If all available personnel were concentrated on converting and crewing those forty captured ships, the job could have been completed in very short order—anywhere from one to two months, and after the three-month voyage to Zanshaa all forty ships would be ready to join Do-faq. All these added together would make over two hundred fifty ships, which would leave us substantially outnumbered."

Martinez knew that if the captured Terran ships were assigned to Daimong or Torminel, a conversion was barely needed at all. Daimong and Torminel were roughly human-shaped, and at need could use furniture and acceleration couches designed for humans. Lai-own required fixtures designed for their own species, and any Terran ship given to Cree would also require every screen, console, and display altered to conform to the near-blind species' requirements. But if no ships were given to Cree, then Wei Jian's figures were more than plausible.

Jian straightened and looked out over the heads of her audience without even seeming to see them.

"Therefore we must prepare to fight an enemy that possesses a substantial advantage in numbers. I will accordingly make assignments based on successful investigations conducted by ships in transit, and by success in combat."

Martinez felt invisible fingers tug at his ears and draw his head upward at an inquiring angle. *Success in combat*. That seemed encouraging.

"But first," Jian said, "let me deal with a matter of designation. I have assumed command of all ships in the Restoration, whether they belong to the Fourth Fleet or not. I therefore propose to name this unified force the Combined Fleet of the Restoration. Please refer to this designation in all communications and reports henceforth."

Jian paused to pick up a glass of water and sipped. Martinez was relieved to see this sign that Jian was human—she had delivered her briefing thus far in a deliberate monotone, with every syllable distinctly articulated, like a primary-school teacher carefully instructing her charges.

Jian put down her glass and cleared her throat. "Experience has shown," she said, "that the greatest chance for success will be achieved by adaptation of the Foote Formula."

Martinez couldn't help but look at Lord Jeremy Foote, seated a little farther up the table. The Foote Formula was identical to the Martinez Method and Sula's Ghost Tactics, but Foote had very little to do with it—when Martinez and Sula, far apart on different ships, had created the system, Foote had been the censor on Sula's ship and had been able to read the correspondence. He'd subsequently promoted the system on his own, amid his higher-born friends—he'd claimed he was merely taking the Martinez and Sula names off a controversial proposal that would have got them in trouble, but Martinez felt free to assume a less noble motive.

Annoyed, Martinez saw a familiar invisible set of fingers pull on Foote's ears and draw his head nobly into prominence.

"The Fourth Fleet had different designations for different formations," Jian continued. "Squadrons, of course, and the new term *division* for formations made up of more than one squadron. I propose to leave these designations alone and create new Grand Divisions larger than any units heretofore."

*Heretofore*, Martinez thought. *Henceforth*. Wei Jian was certainly demonstrating her mastery of legalistic language. His son, Gareth the Younger, might well profit by her example.

"There will be four Grand Divisions in total," Jian continued, "designated van, main body, rear, and reserve. These Grand Divisions will not be uniform in size but will have the number of ships appropriate to their purpose." She cleared her throat again. "Also bear in mind that, in action, the ships' course may reverse so that the van may become the rear, and vice versa. Despite its altered role, the designation will not change."

Jian looked at Michi seated at her side. "The Grand Division of the Van will be commanded by Squadron Commander Chen," she said. She looked down the table at Martinez. "The rear by Captain Martinez."

Martinez felt the invisible fingers pluck again at his ears.

Jian looked at the squadron commander on her right. "Squadron Commander Farhang will command the main body." Again she looked up over the heads of her audience. "I will command the reserve in person." Her gaze dropped to the one figure at the table in the blue tunic of the Exploration Service.

"Captain Severin will command a division in the main body, where in action he will attempt what I believe he has called the Patchwork-Quilt maneuvers. He will also attempt to teach this method to other commanders, though I understand that so far he is the only person who has successfully deployed these tactics in fleet exercises."

Severin's narrow eyes widened. He looked stunned. In the last battle he had commanded a squadron, and now he would have more than one, and furthermore be expected to execute a difficult mission.

"In combat," Jian said, "the van and rear will accelerate or decelerate in order to attempt to draw the enemy van and rear out of formation. As the physique of Do-faq and the other Lai-own will not permit heavy accelerations, we may hope that an attenuated enemy force may be subject to swift and destructive attack. If the enemy fails to be drawn out of position, the van and rear will be in position to effectively surround the enemy and attack from multiple directions.

"All commanders," she added, "will also familiarize themselves with Lady Sula's system for predicting where the Foote Formula will maneuver enemy ships. You will employ this system in action at every opportunity."

Her eyes turned to Martinez, and alarm shot through Martinez's nerves. "Captain Martinez," Jian said, "I would like you to modify our own formula somewhat. It has occurred to me that the enemy may have been thinking along lines similar to ours and may have worked out a system similar to Lady Sula's for predicting the motions of our ships. If you can introduce another variable into our formula, it should prevent the enemy from any successful prediction."

A series of curses chased one another through Martinez's skull. He should have thought of that himself.

"Yes, Lady Fleetcom," he said.

Jian's attention shifted to the officers in general.

"You will all receive your units' specific orders later today. Please establish contact with your immediate superiors and subordinates and begin to work together. We will begin exercises based on these new formations in a few days."

She paused, then gave a brief nod, as if to herself. "My lords and ladies," she said, and gave a glance at Severin, "and *gentleman*," she added. "That is all. You are dismissed."

Jian turned abruptly and marched toward a door leading to her private quarters. There was a rustle and the sound of chairs being pushed back as the assembled officers jumped to attention. One of Jian's servants opened the door and the Commander of the Combined Fleet vanished from sight.

*Not the sort to call for questions, then*, Martinez thought.

The officers relaxed from their stiff braced posture and looked at one another. Severin still seemed stunned, Chandra's anger smoldered behind her long brown eyes, and Foote affected nonchalance, his hand brushing at the cowlick on the right side of his head. Ranssu Kangas fingered the pale patch of transplanted skin on his cheek. Jian's own officers seemed to take everything in stride: perhaps they'd had briefings like this before.

The visiting officers began to file out of the room and make their way to the airlocks. Martinez found himself walking alongside Severin.

"So what did you think of that?" Severin asked.

"I'd be far more annoyed if she wasn't adopting so many of my ideas," Martinez said.

He should, Martinez thought, be enjoying his triumph. He had set himself to create a system that would offer the best chance for a victory, a system backed by experience and data—a system that Wei Jian would be obliged to adopt whether she wished to or not. She had adopted the system wholesale, yet he felt no inclination to break out the champagne and celebrate.

Because he hadn't just created a system—he'd created an opportunity for Jian to adopt his ideas and then take credit for everything.

"I think Lady Wei is focused on the win," he said. "If it brings her a victory, she's willing to use people she doesn't know and possibly doesn't even like."

"She and I are complete strangers," Severin said. "And whether she likes me depends I suppose on how much she likes my puppetry. But suddenly I have a great deal of responsibility, and it's more than a little intimidating."

"You'll be fine," Martinez predicted. "Your crazy quilt is going to be brilliant."

Severin blew out a breath. "I hope so."

Martinez had developed an idea of Wei Jian from the communications she'd sent to him and to Michi Chen, but now he realized that his notions were simplistic. There was more to her than was apparent from her fussy insistence on rank and subordination—he had hoped that she would prove a blank surface on which he could impose his ideas, but now it was apparent that Jian had ideas of her own.

He didn't know whether he liked that or not.

# CHAPTER 6

Division Nine reappeared in the Colamote system as a much more impressive force than it had been during the last transit. The six Laredo ships were crewed and ready, as were the three captured cruisers and the three giant transports. *Splendid* and *Mentor* provided a cadre of veterans to support the newly crewed vessels.

The six smaller transports were on their way to Laredo, carrying the noncombatants, the prisoners, and armed crouchbacks to guard them—mostly crouchbacks too old for the high accelerations of combat, but still young enough to keep the prisoners in line.

One of the Laredo cruisers was now crewed exclusively by Naxid volunteers, and Naxids occupied key positions on another ship that was largely crewed by humans. If this produced resentment or friction, no report of it had so far reached Sula.

Lord Nishkad remained in the owner's suite on *Pride of Parkhurst*. Though he held no official position and was in no one's chain of command, he nevertheless had considerable moral authority over the Naxids, and Sula consulted him regularly. Nishkad could have gone safely to Laredo with the other noncombatants, but he claimed he was curious about how the war would turn out and wanted to see the end in person.

When Division Nine transited the Colamote system, no enemy force awaited them, and if any enemies were watching, they had no way to contact their government at Zanshaa. All the wormhole relay stations in the Colamote and Zarafan systems had now been occupied by Severin's Exploration Service techs, along with those on the far side of each wormhole. All the relays between Laredo and Zarafan had also been occupied, and there were now uninterrupted communications from Laredo to Harzapid via Colamote or Zarafan, and also to Division Nine and what Sula understood was now called the Combined Fleet.

The new relays allowed her to communicate with Ming Lin, the Restoration's economics adviser, and with Lady Koridun, the young Torminel who had been appointed governor of Harzapid. Through them she learned how the economy and the civilian government of the Restoration were progressing, which was better than anyone had a right to expect. Harzapid and other worlds in the Restoration were experiencing something very close to a boom economy.

She also received a brief text message from Lord Batur Khan-Niyaz, who commanded the dockyard on Terra. *Your instructions have been faithfully carried out.*

Sula hoped that the death of Lord Peltrot Convil would be just one killing lost amid the war's tens of thousands of deaths and would hardly be worthy of comment. Besides, the Restoration was under a form of martial law, and arbitrary actions were to be expected. No one was going to miss Peltrot Convil.

And if her arbitrary action came back to bite her, she felt she would be able to justify it. *Acted to prevent a violent criminal from causing further harm,* or some other rationalization.

*Everything dies. Nothing matters.* Not that this motto would constitute an appropriate legal defense . . .

She'd worry about it if she needed to. Such reckonings were a long way off.

Not so far off was her rendezvous with the rest of the Restoration fleet. In a little over a month, Division Nine would join Wei Jian's command, and Sula would find her division placed in one of the Grand Divisions. Commanders for the four Grand Divisions had already been appointed, and so Sula would find herself bossed not just by Wei Jian, but by a Grand Division chief.

Who, Sula hoped, would not be Martinez. That would put them in daily contact, the very thought of which was agony. Sula pictured the space between them littered with explosives mounting proximity fuses . . . There was no way they could avoid combustion, and the shrapnel would threaten to slice anyone nearby.

Martinez was now regularly invading her dreams. For the last three nights her sleep had been interrupted by nightmares, and though she couldn't remember all the details, she knew that each had ended with Martinez's big hands closed around her throat. The derivoo she played every night hadn't kept the nightmares away, and neither had alcohol, even when she drank to the point of passing out. Her suite's new paint scheme—cheerful yellow and bright green—had failed to brighten her mood.

Sula stared bleakly at the remains of her breakfast, then looked up as Gavin Macnamara entered. "More tea, my lady?" he asked.

"Thank you, no." Division Nine would soon take part in an exercise that would require Sula to spend several hours in her vac suit. She hated being confined to the suit, and having a full bladder would only make it worse.

"Shall I clear?" Macnamara asked.

"By all means." As he cleared her breakfast away, Sula heard him softly humming a tune she recognized as a ballad titled "The

Love That Never Dies." Sula gathered that his relationship with Rigger First Class Japutra Bliss continued along its rhapsodic track.

"The Love That Never Dies" was a saccharine, sappy ballad, one that had never failed to annoy Sula when she heard it, but now she found herself wishing that she might find herself humming such a love ballad in accompaniment to her own joy, surely preferable to waking with a shriek while derivoo wailed and sobbed in the air and a nightmare slowly faded from her perception.

But no. Her life was not a sappy ballad, it was a derivoo song, brittle, sharp, and dangerous.

So many around her had died that she couldn't believe that love wouldn't die too. In fact, she hoped that it would, and put her out of her misery.

MARTINEZ STRETCHED OUT on his bed, sighing as his bruised muscles sank into the soft mattress. The Combined Fleet had just concluded an exercise that involved firing real missiles and jinking through space at heavy accelerations, and after that a spell on a proper bed was the height of luxury.

His Grand Division of the Rear had done very well, better than the main body under Farhang. His command included Chandra Prasad's division and that of Ranssu Kangas and was made up of combat veterans who outperformed Wei Jian's crews, who— despite serving and training together for years—had never developed the confidence, dash, and elan that could be earned only by victory in combat.

Martinez rubbed a hand over the bristle on his chin and gazed at the newly painted walls and ceiling. The redecoration of his suite had concluded with the bedroom, in which the walls were spread with verdant and ruddy pigments meant to evoke the colors of Laredo. The chief ornaments of the room, however, were portraits of his family: his daughter, Yaling, known in the family as Mei-mei; Gareth the Younger; Terza; and his parents, Lord and Lady Martinez, seated with Mei-mei and her aunt Walpurga, who had been looking after her since the war had started.

Now that lines of communication with Laredo had been established, Martinez was receiving regular bulletins from Mei-mei and found himself perpetually astonished. They had been apart for close to a year and a half, and during that time Mei-mei had grown into a near-stranger. She was seven now and had developed from a potbellied near-infant into a genuine, curious person, with her own temperament and interests. She had developed a fascination with natural history and spent much of her time on the Martinez country estate of Rio Hondo, pursuing fauna and collecting plants. She showed him some of her cuttings, the leaves and berries and seed pods, and very seriously explained what the plants were called, and the sort of terrain they liked to live in, and what the parts of the plant were for.

Martinez watched his daughter in some amazement. She had developed this affinity for natural history on her own, had absorbed an astounding amount of information in a short time, and was able to relate it in a coherent way.

Gareth the Younger was not the only genius among the younger generation, he concluded.

When he was involved with Sula, he'd taken Terza's portrait down. Now it was back in its place, and Martinez had resolved that it would remain there.

Yet the thought of Sula, once she crept into his mind, refused to slip away. He experienced again that bewildering, horrific moment in the Celestial Court, the white flowers tumbling from his hand at the sight of Sula with Hector Braga dead at her feet. She hadn't offered an explanation, and Martinez hadn't asked for one.

Yet now he wondered why Braga was dead. There must have been a reason, even if Sula was too arrogant to disclose it.

He knew that Sula and Braga had known each other for a long time, having met on Spannan shortly after Sula's parents had been tortured to death for crimes against the Praxis. Spannan was famously an ill-managed world, with the Torminel Lady Distchin its patron. It had been generations since any head of the Distchin clan had visited Spannan, and they managed their interests through relations and lackeys tasked with squeezing as much money out of the place as possible, all to support the opulent lives of Lady Distchin and her immediate circle.

Everyone agreed that the situation with Spannan and the Distchins was a disgrace, but nothing had ever been done about it, nor about any of the other worlds being plundered by their patrons. Martinez had concluded that the High City Peers quietly agreed among themselves that while it was a shame about Spannan, a sufficiently high-ranking patron had the implicit right to ransack her own worlds if she wanted to.

The upper-upper-uppers, as Severin might call them, were a law unto themselves. At least right up to the point where they *weren't*, at which point the executioners started sharpening their skinning knives.

While Martinez knew that Braga and Sula had known each other on Spannan, he didn't know the nature of their relationship. Perhaps they had been lovers, perhaps something else. They were sufficiently intimate to refer to each other by nicknames, Lamey for Braga and Earthgirl for Sula.

Sula would have been quite young at the time—maybe seventeen in Shaa measure, or fifteen in the Earth years that Sula liked to employ. Martinez hoped that Sula's youth meant they hadn't been lovers, because if he actually thought Braga had taken advantage of a grieving, confused young girl, he might just decide that Braga deserved the two bullets that ended his life.

Martinez's eyes drifted to the portrait of Terza on the wall, then drifted away again.

He realized that he had been assuming that Braga's death had something to do with his past on Spannan, and he really knew nothing of the sort. Braga had shown up on Zanshaa as part of a delegation lobbying to get rid of the Distchins, and he had quickly attached himself to Roland Martinez as a kind of fixer and bag-man, someone who handled the unsavory errands that were beneath Roland's dignity as a member of the Convocation.

Martinez wondered exactly what Braga's employment had been back on Spannan. Certainly he had a gift for the underhanded side of politics, and possibly he had been some kind of criminal.

After the war had started, he had formed a planetary development company with Lord Mehrang, the patron of Esley, the home world of the Yormak species. Much of the planet had been reserved for the primitive Yormaks until they had rebelled, and now the few survivors of the rebellion were penned up on reserves and the rest of the planet had been opened to settlement.

Braga's company soon ran into trouble—the war certainly didn't help—and he fled to Zarafan ahead of a group of Lord Mehrang's less savory associates, who were bent on fetching him back to Harzapid to find out where Mehrang's investment had gone.

Sula, Martinez remembered, had been at home with gangsters and had allied with the Zanshaa cliquemen in the Naxid war. He wondered if Braga had been the first gangster to make Sula's acquaintance.

Braga's death surely couldn't have been a gangland execution, could it? That seemed too incredible.

Then again, walking into her apartment that night had been incredible too.

Martinez decided that he had too little information to reach any conclusions, and he could hardly make inquiries from his suite on *Los Angeles*. Spannan was in a part of the empire controlled by the Zanshaa government, and he could set nothing in motion there.

And as for Braga's present-day activities, he could simply ask his brother Roland—although Roland, in his turn, might wonder why he was asking.

Martinez then wondered why he was even *thinking* of trying to get to the bottom of Braga's death. Surely he couldn't think that if he managed to understand why Sula had killed Hector Braga, then everything would be all right between him and Sula.

No, he decided. He couldn't possibly be thinking that.

A knock on his door snapped him out of his musings. He rolled to one side and reached for a Fleet-issue jumpsuit that waited for him on a chair.

"Who is it?" he asked.

"This is Banerjee. I'm sorry to bother you, but—"

"Wait a moment, please." Martinez unfolded the viridian jumpsuit and aimed one of his feet at the opening of a jumpsuit leg. He couldn't help but think it bad form to be caught in his underwear by the grandmotherly Banerjee.

"It's important, my lord," said Banerjee through the door. "The relay station on the far side of Zarafan Wormhole One reports that Do-faq's fleet is coming."

Martinez froze with his foot halfway down the jumpsuit leg. "Did they say how many ships?"

"Over four hundred sixty, my lord." Many of which would be decoys, of course, but Martinez knew from the timing of the attack that Wei Jian had been right about Do-faq's waiting for reinforcements before moving, and that in any battle, the Restoration forces would be severely outnumbered.

"Thank you," Martinez said. "Put the original message in my queue—"

"Already done."

"And give me Lady Wei as soon as she calls."

The message would have been addressed to Wei Jian, as Combined Fleet commander, but as the former commander of the Fourth Fleet, Martinez had access to the command cipher and was able to read any message sent to Jian. Perhaps it had not occurred to Jian that her messages were not entirely private, or perhaps she was willing to share the dry, pedestrian reports that were sent to her every day. Either way, it was good for him to be prepared for when she did contact him.

Martinez rose from his bed and drew on his jumpsuit, and then he walked to his office as he drew on the arms. The merest whiff of fresh paint remained in the air, and Martinez paused for a moment to appreciate the absence of Torminel wrestlers on the walls. New murals showed aquatic scenes, all of them based on pictures of sea creatures drawn by Gareth the Younger and sent to his father. Gareth was nine and drew well for his age but was far from an accomplished artist, and so the winner of the Fourth Fleet's art contest had corrected and improved on young Gareth's work and provided convincing background and lighting effects, going to some effort to depict the shimmer of light on water. Martinez had sent his son photos of the murals as they were completed, and young Gareth had been delighted with the result.

Martinez turned from the mural to the video sent from the

wormhole station and saw another kind of light shimmer—a fire-fly swarm of antimatter drives, squadrons echeloned about their flagships, all surrounding two drive signatures much brighter than any around them, marking them as either battleships or very large transports.

It would probably be a month before the Combined Fleet and Do-faq's force came together, and during that time analysts would be very busy with these images. The longer a decoy was observed, the more it looked like nothing other than a decoy, so Martinez assumed that before very long they'd have a true estimate of the enemy strength, and know as well whether the two largest vessels were battleships or something else. Do-faq definitely had a battle-ship at Felarus at the start of the war, and there had been another battleship under construction at Zanshaa when the war broke out. Squadron Commander Kung, when he had defected from the Home Fleet to the Restoration, had comprehensively sabotaged that ship, but it could have been repaired in the months since.

Martinez was musing on the image of Do-faq's fleet shining against a background of stars when an image of Wei Jian appeared in the corner of his video display. He enlarged the image to full-screen, nodded, and said, "Lady Wei."

"Stand by," she said. A few moments passed in which Jian frowned into the camera, apparently making gestures that the camera didn't pick up, after which the screen split again to reveal three more people: Martinez himself, Michi Chen, and gray-haired Squadron Commander Farhang.

"I have included all the Grand Division commanders in this conference," Jian said, "so that we can coordinate our response to Do-faq's advance."

She was adopting the pedagogical tone she had used at that first meeting aboard the *Crisis*, and Martinez wondered if he and the others were intended not to participate in the meeting but instead to receive their orders and obey in silence.

"As expected, Do-faq is accelerating at a very deliberate one gravity," Jian said. "Fortunately, this makes his arrival predictable, so that we can coordinate our own movements so as to engage at Toley, Shulduc, or some other system this side of Harzapid."

Actually getting two large fleets into an engagement was a challenge and required a certain amount of cooperation from both commanders. If Do-faq came in too fast, he might overshoot the Combined Fleet, exchanging missiles as he raced past. He would then be able to take Harzapid, but only by enabling Wei Jian to strike unopposed at the capital of Zanshaa.

Since Wei Jian had joined, the Combined Fleet had moved toward Zarafan again, then decelerated, pulled hard gees as it swung around two gas giants and a sun, then accelerated toward Harzapid again, effectively patrolling back and forth across the same few systems.

"We have no way of knowing if Do-faq will continue to accelerate at the same rate all the way to Harzapid," Jian said, "but if so, we will have plenty of time to respond. Therefore, I propose that the Combined Fleet continue on its present course until Do-faq's intentions become more clear. I will also issue orders to Lady Sula to increase her acceleration in our direction, to make certain Division Nine can join us well before any engagement."

She nodded, presumably at Martinez's image on her screen. "Captain Martinez, as you have placed the missiles in ambush along Do-faq's presumed route, and since you have experience in this regard, I will put you in charge of harassing Do-faq's forces as they travel toward Toley."

"Yes, Lady Fleetcom," Martinez said, and then, before she

could move on to another topic, he added, "Lady Wei, I have some ideas for additional use of missiles. Shall I offer my suggestions now, or would you prefer to continue with your analysis?"

Wei Jian's eyes were focused a little off-center, as if she were still looking at Martinez's image on the video display and not at the camera.

"I have nothing to add until I get more information," she said. "Captain Martinez, you have the floor."

Martinez nodded. He realized that his mouth felt dry, and he wished he'd ordered coffee or a glass of water.

"My lords and ladies," he said, "it's occurred to me that Do-faq has to be experiencing a certain amount of anxiety over whether we're somehow going to get around him and strike at Zanshaa. For example, we could head from Toley to Colamote, and move on the capital from there while Do-faq is en route to Harzapid. Or we could retrace Lady Wei's route from Magaria, and again strike at the capital via Magaria—I believe a course of action that Lady Wei at one point contemplated."

"Indeed," Jian said, her gaze still focused off-center.

"We might prey on Do-faq's anxieties," Martinez said, "not by taking the route through Magaria to Zanshaa, but by making it *appear* that at least part of our force is attempting this. Lady Wei, I believe that you destroyed several of the wormhole relay stations near Magaria as you voyaged to Harzapid?"

"Correct," said Jian. Her responses, Martinez thought, were as curt as her speeches were prolix.

"We could blow up more relays," Martinez said. "Send missiles at relativistic speeds into the Magaria system, to destroy the relays connecting Magaria with Zanshaa. It will look as if we're covering an attack by Restoration ships."

Jian's gaze shifted to her camera, so that she now appeared to be gazing into Martinez's eyes. "To what end? We won't be making a real attack."

"It might encourage the Zanshaa government to order some of Do-faq's ships home to defend the capital," Martinez said. "In any case, it may make the enemy hesitate fatally."

"I will consider it," said Jian.

"Thank you, my lady," said Martinez. "My other idea was to have Lady Sula fire a barrage through Colamote to Zarafan, to strike Do-faq as he emerges into the system. But I decided against it, largely because Do-faq might be expecting it.

"Instead," he continued, "I'd suggest having Lady Sula fire a barrage, but to wait until after Do-faq has left the Zarafan system en route to Toley and Harzapid. The barrage would follow him through the wormhole—he might not be on guard against such an attack."

"We should launch the missiles from the Combined Fleet," said Jian. "The Fleet Train can replace our spent missiles much more easily than they can Lady Sula's."

Martinez felt a pang of chagrin as he realized that he should have thought of this himself. "Yes, my lady," he said, and then cleared his throat in an attempt to pump saliva into his dry mouth.

"We have such an abundant supply of missiles that we should use more of them," Wei Jian said. "Let our ambushes and strikes be reinforced."

"Yes, my lady."

Jian's gaze flickered away from the camera, as if she were looking at faces on her video screen. "Unless there are other comments," she said, "I will bring this conference to an end. Please refrain from informing your crews of today's developments until I send a general message to the Combined Fleet later today."

The faces vanished from Martinez's screen, and left him contemplating the mystery that was Wei Jian.

"I HOPE HER flagship takes a missile up the tailpipe," said Chandra Prasad. "I would be sorry to lose the ship, but if we are to lose ships, I'd prefer to lose certain ships over others."

"We can't spare any, unfortunately," said Martinez.

"It's up to the veterans to hold the Combined Fleet together," Chandra said, "and to keep Jian and her clique from making mistakes."

"She's made damned few," Martinez mused. "She started in a distant, barren system with fifty-five ships, and now she's the one in charge."

"Only because we didn't resist," said Chandra.

Martinez raised a warning hand. "One civil war at a time," he said.

He had been invited to dine with Chandra's captains aboard the flagship of Chandra's Division Three. Chandra's mutinous talk was alarming, particularly since she spoke in front of nearly a dozen witnesses, but then perhaps her captains were used to her blunt speech or were willing to forgive a tactless squadcom who had fought so well at Second Shulduc.

The conversation had been eased by the wines served with each of the five courses. Martinez felt too sated and drowsy for a vigorous discussion of Wei Jian and her faults and decided to steer the conversation away from the dangerous topic. He turned to Lieutenant-Captain Vonderheydte.

"How is the situation on the *Declaration*?" he asked. "Are the crew ready for the fight?"

"They resent having to refight a war they thought they'd already won," Vonderheydte said. "And they resent serving under Jian. But I think I can convince them to take their resentments out on the enemy."

"Remember that Do-faq killed Nguyen's forty crews at Felarus," Martinez said. "That's nearly ten thousand dead Terrans. Let's keep reminding our crews of that."

Chandra raised her glass. "Here's to the spirit of revenge," she said.

Martinez drank, the wine tingling across his palate. He looked at Vonderheydte and saw a degree of ease and contentment that was new in the younger officer.

Vonderheydte had been a cadet on the *Corona* during Martinez's escape from Magaria at the beginning of the Naxid War, and it was Martinez who had promoted him to lieutenant. Since then, Vonderheydte had served out the rest of the Naxid War, and after joining the Fourth Fleet had commanded his own ship, the frigate *Declaration*.

The blond Vonderheydte, with his delicate bones, had also proved popular with women. Martinez was a little vague about how many times he'd been married, but he knew the number of former wives stood at least at three, plus a number of engagements that had been abandoned before any marriage took place. At the beginning of the Accidental War, Vonderheydte had fled to Harzapid in the company of Marietta Li, the wife of a high-ranking Peer. Since taking command of *Declaration* and joining the Fourth Fleet, he had gotten involved with Chandra—or perhaps the volatile Chandra had chosen to get involved with *him*. Martinez was happy that Chandra had an outlet for her passions that did not involve either mutiny or Martinez himself, and if Vonderheydte was growing restless in Chandra's ferocious embrace, he wasn't showing it.

Martinez felt a moment of jealousy at the couple's happiness, and then he remembered that Chandra was involved and the jealousy vanished.

As the last of the dishes were carried away, Martinez asked for a cup of coffee and drank it, then made his excuses and went to his shuttle. Once aboard *Los Angeles*, he made his way to his suite, then paused as he heard angry voices echoing from behind his dining room door.

"You lied to me!" a woman shouted.

"Never once!" The voice belonged to Mpanza. "Never once!"

"We were going to be together forever!" the woman answered.

"When did I ever say that?" Mpanza demanded. "Never once did I say it!"

Martinez decided that it was time to end this second violation of his dining room and opened the door. Mpanza and a young woman stood by the kitchen door, Mpanza stiff with outrage, the woman blotchy and tear-stained. They both jumped as Martinez entered and turned to him with horrified expressions.

The woman's uniform told Martinez her place in the ship's hierarchy. "Electrician," he told her, "you have no business here. Go to your quarters."

He stood away from the door as she left in silence, then closed the door behind her. He turned to Mpanza.

"Consider my quarters off-limits to your girlfriends," he said.

"I beg your pardon, my lord," Mpanza said. "I felt our conversation required privacy, and—"

"Privacy is available elsewhere on this ship," Martinez said. "I do not run a hotel."

"I'm so very sorry, Lord Captain."

Martinez walked past Mpanza to the door of his sleeping cabin, then opened the door and stepped through it. Once alone in his room, he took a long breath, let it out hissing past his teeth, and thought, *Breakups are hard. But at least this time no one got killed.*

**DO-FAQ CONTINUED HIS** predictable one-gravity acceleration, which made it easy to coordinate a response. Sula's Division Nine increased its own acceleration to make certain it would reach Toley well before Do-faq.

Once analysts had deducted the decoys, they concluded that Do-faq had 261 warships, which was still more than expected. And the two large drive signatures were clearly those of *Praxis*-class battleships.

The wormhole relay stations along Do-faq's route had been abandoned, and their systems placed on automatic. Their crews had dispersed into the remote corners of star systems, where they could observe the enemy ships and pass the information through the wormholes to another shuttle carefully positioned to receive the signal. When possible, the shuttles were grappled to asteroids or moons, then powered down to avoid detection, leaving their crews shivering in the cold. Sending a transmission created heat, of course, and to avoid showing up on an infra-red scan they broadcast only at certain fixed hours.

Do-faq and his ships had barely passed through the wormhole leading from Zarafan toward Harzapid when five hundred missiles, accelerated to relativistic velocities, shot from Colamote into Zarafan, crossed the system in a little less than ten hours, and then flashed through the wormhole onto Do-faq's tail. Mere seconds before the scheduled impact, a distant Exploration Service shuttle painted the enemy fleet with its laser rangefinders, enabling the missiles to locate their targets and do final correction burns.

Do-faq, expecting this kind of ambush, had entered the system with radars and ranging lasers pulsing, but the attack from behind was discovered only at the last moment, because the missiles were traveling almost as fast as the return signal.

Automated point-defense systems blazed out and intercepted missiles exploded into a network of fireballs behind Do-faq's formation, a network that leaped closer to the warships by the second and finally engulfed the rear of the enemy formation. Nearly fifty strikes were observed, though Martinez assumed many of them would have been decoys.

Killing ships was ideal, but even the misses would have an effect. Martinez knew very well the sort of terror produced by this type of attack, the crew dashing for their stations while being hurled into walls and bulkheads by sudden, unpredictable accelerations, the officers staring in disbelief at their displays, captains shouting orders that were already too late.

*Welcome to the rest of your lives,* he thought.

The shuttle shut off its lidar, and Do-faq's fleet began to sort itself out. Decoys were launched and deployed rearward of the warships, and at the sight Martinez cursed.

Less than two minutes after the first attack, the laser range-finder flashed on again and nearly seven hundred missiles dashed into the system, their approach hidden behind the blazing radio wall of fireballs formed by the previous barrage. Again, the point-defense lasers and antiproton guns flashed in the void while the enemy ships jinked their terrified dance. Again, a torrent of fireballs blossomed behind Do-faq's armada. Again, strikes were observed among the enemy, but despite the larger number of missiles, Do-faq's defenses were better coordinated this time and hits were fewer and almost entirely on the just-launched decoys.

They enemy also found and destroyed the shuttle that had painted them with its lidar, an uncrewed craft controlled by a second shuttle hiding on the far side of an asteroid. Martinez had expected to lose the shuttle and had others in reserve.

By the time analysts reviewed the recordings of the fight, they decided that Do-faq had lost twenty-two ships, and that fourteen more were maneuvering badly and had probably been impaired in some way. Martinez was pleased with the result. He had many more missiles to spend.

Do-faq took eleven days to cross to the next wormhole, and Martinez launched more than one attack each day. Some involved small numbers of missiles that were all destroyed before they could do any damage, but these were aimed less at enemy warships than at enemy morale. Each attack, even if it offered little danger, still sent the ships into a high state of alert and triggered violent maneuvers, leaving the crews sore, exhausted, and increasingly on the edge of nervous collapse.

Do-faq and the other Lai-own crew, who could not endure high accelerations, would suffer more than other species. Each attack made them choose between broken bones and escape.

Clearly the enemy took the threat seriously. They proved far more adept than Tork had at finding the shuttles Martinez had hidden around the system, and then destroying them. Martinez could only imagine the horror of the shuttle crews as they watched, from half a system away, a missile as it streaked toward them, knowing they had no defense and there were only so many minutes left before the missiles turned them to blazing radioactive dust.

Eventually the shuttles' numbers were so reduced that Martinez decided, on the tenth day, to launch all remaining missiles while he still had some hope of coordinating them. The result was over a thousand missiles targeting Do-faq from all directions, all timed to arrive at the same moment, all dancing in frenzied zigzag patterns as they tried to avoid countermissiles and point-defense systems.

The enemy was able to see the missiles coming and launched countermissiles to intercept the attackers well away from their own ships, and so only a few of the Restoration's missiles whirled through the defenses to strike home on the enemy fleet.

Still, Martinez had every cause to feel satisfied with Do-faq's eleven-day transit. Analysts reported that forty-nine ships had been destroyed, and that two dozen or more had suffered damage.

In addition, the enemy had expended nearly two thousand missiles that could not be replaced, while the Fleet Train had already made up the Combined Fleet's missile losses.

Martinez planned a strike as Do-faq approached the wormhole into Roda, the next system—first a huge flight of missiles dashing through the wormhole as Do-faq came near, then another flight to meet Do-faq on the other side.

The entire effort fizzled. Do-faq anticipated something like Martinez's attack, and his ships began a surprise deceleration as they approached transition and also made an unexpected curve off the direct course to the wormhole. The result was that the missiles, traveling at relativistic speeds and with little time to find and track a target, completely missed the enemy ships. The follow-up strike was intended to meet the enemy in the Roda system, but Do-faq's deceleration meant they, too, raced through the wormhole without finding the enemy.

The missiles decelerated and turned to track Do-faq, but in slowing down and reversing course they made perfect targets for antimissile fire, and the attack proved a complete failure.

When Do-faq's ships curved back on track to the wormhole and made their transition into Roda, they did so unopposed.

Martinez shrugged. There were still plenty of missiles in his arsenal. He had hidden them behind planets, behind moons, behind Roda's sun. Some simply hung in space, waiting for the signal to launch themselves at the enemy.

And the enemy was here: Do-faq and the Combined Fleet were now in the same system. The Combined Fleet was halfway across the Roda system, decelerating and plainly offering battle, though Do-faq wouldn't catch the Combined Fleet until both forces were in the crossroads system of Toley.

Martinez looked at the plots anticipating the movement of the two fleets, then the intended meeting in Toley of the Combined Fleet and Sula's Division Nine. He frowned, then did some calculations of his own. He then messaged Captain Yoshida, Wei Jian's tactical officer.

Yoshida was a diminutive man with a shaven head and the smooth, gracious manner of the perfect courtier. His video image was seated at his desk in full-dress uniform, his face at polite attention, his glossy head framed with a perfect halo in the shape of a large round golden plaque or metal sculpture on the wall behind him.

"Lord Captain," Martinez said, "I wonder if you would look at this plot and give me your opinion."

"Yes? Of course, my lord." Yoshida looked down, toward the plot that had just appeared on his displays. "This is what it would look like if the enemy managed to get between us and Division Nine?"

"Not exactly," Martinez said. "This is what it would look like if Lady Sula slightly increased her deceleration, and appeared in Toley with her entire division in Do-faq's flank and rear."

Yoshida looked at the plot with increased interest. "Ah yes," he said. "I see what you mean. Very interesting, Lord Captain."

"If you think this idea worth considering," Martinez said, "you might present it to Fleetcom Jian at the next opportune moment."

"Ye-es," Yoshida said thoughtfully. "Ye-es, I believe I will." He looked up at the camera. "Thank you, my lord. It's a very interesting idea."

Later in the day, Martinez received a brief text message from Wei Jian, saying that she was ordering Sula to decrease her deceleration to Toley, and thanking him for the idea.

Martinez was taken aback. He had assumed Yoshida would have taken credit for the idea. More, he hadn't expected Wei Jian to thank him for anything, ever.

The woman never ceased to surprise.

Perhaps, he decided, she was in a benevolent mood, and this would be an ideal time to approach Jian on another matter. As this wasn't strictly speaking a tactical issue, he sent his next message directly to Jian instead of involving Yoshida.

"Lady Fleetcom," he said, "it occurs to me that we might take advantage of the fact that our two fleets are currently within sight of each other. During the campaign against Tork, he sent us a demand to surrender so that he could kill us, and in reply we sent messages to him in the clear, so that it could be received by any ship—actually it was Lady Sula who sent the message, and it consisted mostly of abuse, though it contained a good deal of matter for them to think about."

He smiled to himself as he remembered Sula's opening lines: "*How* dare *you invoke the Praxis, you senile, witless box of turd! How* dare *you make demands! You* started *this war, you imbecile, with your demented order to arrest every Terran crew in the Fleet, and your smug conviction that somehow we wouldn't find out about it! Your security was so perfect that we knew within* hours!"

And from there it only got better. And more vicious.

"We also sent some propaganda," Martinez said, "and some information, like a report concerning the eradication of the Lorkin by the Shaa. We knew we couldn't deter Tork in any way, but we hoped to shake his subordinates' resolve, and I think we did."

He nodded into the eye of his camera. "I know Do-faq personally, and I could try to speak with him if you don't want to do it yourself. Or if you would rather we entertain ourselves by telling them what idiots they are, we could again employ Lady Sula."

He rather thought that Wei Jian wouldn't approve of Sula's savage style of vituperation, even when used against an enemy.

He didn't receive an answer for another half hour, when one of Jian's signals officers asked for copies of the messages sent between Tork and Sula. Martinez complied, and pictured Jian's eyebrows crawling ever higher up her forehead as Sula's ferocity seared the air.

"Now you've arrived in person with thousands of crew who you're willing to sacrifice for your own vanity." She laughed. "I'm here to tell you that you still haven't realized who you're dealing with. We're going to cut up that fine fleet of yours, take it apart piece by piece, and we're going to do it on our time, not yours. You'll watch your fleet's life's blood drain away drop by drop, and there won't be a thing you can do about it. In the end, there will be just you, alone, in your flagship's magnificent ballroom wondering why no one else has come to the dance."

Martinez imagined that issuing from every speaker in every signals station in Tork's fleet, and could only speculate on the effect it had on the listeners.

Or, for that matter, on Wei Jian.

No answer came from Jian, so Martinez busied himself with planning the next attack, a pincer movement of missiles coming at Do-faq from north and south. It would be launched in two and a half hours' time, so he decided he might as well have his midday meal while waiting. Miraculously he hadn't been invited to attend a massive, hours-long dinner in the wardroom or on someone else's ship, so he called for a light collation, and asked Mpanza for coffee.

Wei Jian's answer, in text, came as he was finishing his second cup. *"Permission granted to contact Fleetcom Do-faq,"* Martinez read. *"Civility should be given high priority. Captain Severin's puppet videos may be valuable as propaganda, but no value can be derived from mentioning Lorkin."*

Martinez looked at the message and shrugged. While it was true that the news that a species called the Lorkin were wiped out by the Great Masters thousands of years ago was of dubious benefit to the Restoration, it at least might serve to shake up any pious certainties held by Do-faq's crews.

Nevertheless, Wei Jian had given him broad latitude in what he could say, so long as he retained civility. He would have to find a *polite* way to make the same points that Sula had made to Tork.

He decided to send the message after the next missile strike, when it might have greater impact on officers who had just survived alarms, terror, and tooth-rattling accelerations. It would also give him a chance to hone his text.

The advantage of both fleets being in sight of each other was that Martinez didn't have to sacrifice a shuttle to paint the enemy with lidar, because his whole fleet was doing it.

The attack, six hundred missiles in all, failed to account for any enemy ships, but it did succeed in its primary purpose of forcing Do-faq's command to jitter all over the sky as they tried to dance away from oncoming destruction. By the time the last missile had gone up in a scorching antimatter fireball, Martinez had changed from walking-out dress into full dress, the disk of the Golden Orb gleaming at his throat, and faced the camera with his message ready.

"This is Captain Lord Gareth Martinez," he said, "speaking on behalf of Fleet Commander Wei Jian and the government of the Restoration. I hope I am addressing Lord Pa Do-faq."

He paused for a moment, as if waiting for a response. "I trust you realize that these attacks can continue indefinitely. We are re-treating toward our base of supply, and at present the Restoration is producing more missiles than we can properly use. You, on the other hand, are using up weapons that you can't replace, and it's probably too late for you to turn around and go home."

Martinez offered the camera a solemn nod. "I fear, Lord Pa, that there is only one way that this can end. The Restoration has defeated Rukmin and her force, wiped out Force Orghoder—both without a loss—and the only elements of Lord Tork's great fleet to survive were those that joined our side. With all respect, I don't think your position is tenable."

Again, he performed his sage nod. "There are alternatives, how-ever. You might reconsider your position in regard to the Zanshaa government. Surely it has occurred to you that the government in Zanshaa is dominated by a corrupt clique of hacks and bankrupts who seized power from the legitimate Lord Senior, and that restor-ing the rightful government should be the first concern of any com-mander worthy of his commission.

"Rather than sacrifice your life and those of your crews to the thieves and fanatics in the Zanshaa government, I urge you to join the Restoration and work with us to bring about a peaceful reso-lution to a bloody civil war that shouldn't have begun in the first place."

He jabbed at his desktop with his finger. "The war can stop to-day, if you agree. *Today.*"

He realized that he had spoken with too much anger, and so Martinez composed himself and clasped his hands on his desk. "I look forward to your reply, and I hope we can engage in a construc-tive dialogue. In the meantime, I'm attaching some videos that might amuse you."

He appended Severin's satirical puppet programs and told Banerjee to send the message in the clear, so that every one of Do-faq's ships would receive it. Then he undid the top buttons of his uniform and sagged in his chair.

Being polite was *work*. Especially as he was being polite to someone who had opened this war by killing ten thousand Terrans.

It would take about twenty minutes for the message to reach Do-faq, and the same amount of time for any message to come back, and Martinez assumed that Do-faq would have to spend some time composing his reply, if he decided to reply at all.

Martinez had no idea whether Do-faq would view the puppet shows or not.

He decided to occupy himself with plotting ambushes.

He had a lot of time, because with the fleets in sight of each other, neither could practice realistic exercises, with the ships experiencing genuine accelerations and firing real missiles, because it would give away their tactics to the enemy.

Maybe he could spend the next several days making and sending chatty videos to the enemy.

Do-faq's reply came after three hours, sent in the clear. Like Martinez, he wore full-dress uniform, his medals glittering on his chest. When Martinez had served under him, Do-faq had been young for his post, but now the feathery hair on either side of his flat head had lost its youthful dark shade. Nictating membranes half-slitted his golden eyes.

"Captain Martinez," he said, "I reject your characterization of the legitimate government of the empire. Lady Gruum was chosen by a majority of the Convocation, and her ministers were appointed by the normal means. If there is blame to be laid for this war, it should be laid at the door of those who rebelled because they didn't approve of the new government."

He stiffened, his muzzle lifting into the air. "I am proud to be an obedient servant of the empire, and it is the empire that has tasked me with ending this treasonous rebellion, a task I have every intention of accomplishing successfully. If you wish to avoid loss of life, I suggest that you and your fellow criminals surrender your force immediately. End message."

Martinez glared into the camera. "Record, message follows," he said.

"Lord Pa, you seem to be rewriting history. The rebellion came about not because we objected to a new government, but because a doddering, senile, so-called 'Supreme' Commander decided to arrest every Terran in the Fleet, then torture them until they confessed to crimes against the empire—which they *did not* commit— and I'm sure that you received orders to do exactly that, so don't pretend you know nothing about it."

He had to restrain himself from waving a fist at the camera. "I had great respect for you, Lord Pa. You made all the right decisions in the last war, and you stood by them. But apparently Tork's diminished mental capacity was catching, and now you're determined to follow Tork's example even unto your own death."

He felt heat rise to his face. "We Terrans declined to be exterminated in the same obliging way the Yormaks died, and for that we're called criminals and traitors. By Lady Gruum, of all people, who lost her fortune due to her own incompetence, and who's now intent on getting her money back by killing Terrans and confiscating their property. Which I'm sure you also know about, by the way."

He raised his head and looked slightly to the side, as if he were addressing another person. "Since Lord Pa has demonstrated only mindless servility to the powers in Zanshaa, I would now like to address his officers and crew. I don't know why you're so intent on committing suicide—surely it can't be out of your great love and respect for the Zanshaa government—but I'd like to suggest an alternative. Should you join the Restoration, you will lose no rank or honor, and you will be welcome into the Combined Fleet.

"We are not a force for Terran domination. We do not plan for our species to hold absolute power in the way the Naxids intended—indeed, in the Combined Fleet there are Lai-own and Daimong squadrons, and Lady Koridun, a Torminel, is the Lady Governor of our temporary capital at Harzapid."

Martinez allowed himself a tight smile. "Consult with one another, pick your moment, and abandon your doomed fleet and your doomed commander. If you fly apart from the others and signal your surrender, you will not be molested, and after the conclusion of any fighting you'll be welcome in our ranks—or you are welcome to surrender and be interned, if you prefer."

His smile tightened. "And as for you, Lord Pa, up till now I felt great regret at the necessity of killing you. Now I confess I'm rather looking forward to it. End message."

Martinez realized only then he'd neglected to button up his uniform tunic, but then he decided it didn't matter. He was done with being polite. He had Mpanza bring him a shot of brandy and he downed it in one go, rejoicing in the fumes that filled his sinus and the fire that blazed through his veins.

A few minutes later Santana sent him a message. "Rivven's sending a message to the enemy, Lord Captain."

Martinez paused a moment in shock. "Put it on my screen," he said.

The Daimong was tall and imposing, and his gray face, as always, was frozen in an expression of hauteur. His vocal apparatus made his words sound like the magnificent, resonant conclusion of a symphony. "I wish to confirm what Captain Martinez has stated," he said. "The Restoration is not a movement aiming at Terran domination. When I joined the Restoration, for one example, I was promoted from the command of one squadron to the command of two. I have an honored and respected place in the Combined Fleet. We do not promote the domination of a single species, but the removal of the corrupt, useless government that provoked this war and that sent you here to die in order that they may hang on to the strings of power.

"*Join us!*" The words rang out like braying trumpets. "*Join us,* and together we will restore the righteous rule of the Praxis! No one need fear us unless they have committed crimes against the Peace of the Praxis, and together we can cleanse Zanshaa of the mad creatures who began this war!"

Martinez had barely begun to send his compliments to Rivven when Squadron Commander An-dar, the Lai-own commander who had defected along with Rivven, sent a message similar in content, but without the spectacular sonic effects.

Before long someone else transmitted a video of Lady Koridun, the young Torminel governor of Harzapid, delivering her inaugural address to the planet's legislative body.

"Some may say that I am too young to accept this appointment as Lady Governor of Harzapid." Koridun brandished an arm. "But I am not too young to fight for the Restoration!"

Her luminous blue eyes shone. "Some claim we are rebels!" the new governor said. "We *disdain and reject* the term!"

"Message from Lady Wei!" Santana called.

"Just as we were starting to have fun," Martinez said. "Well, put her on."

"I think we have given the enemy enough to think about," said Jian. "All ships to cease sending messages to the enemy for the present."

At least, Martinez thought, he wasn't reprimanded for failing to remain polite.

**ANOTHER MISSILE ATTACK** launched later that day, packs of missiles darting in from different corners of the system. All had accelerated while masked by planets, then went black just before they flew within sight of the enemy. Do-faq's rangefinders spotted most of them well out, but some came at the enemy unawares and were spotted only as they made final correction burns. Martinez rejoiced as he saw explosions among the enemy and was only slightly disappointed when the analysts told him that the kills had probably been decoys.

*At least they must be running low on decoys*, Martinez thought, and went on to plan his next attack.

This took place as Do-faq's fleet formed into single file to get a gravity assist from one of the system's gas giants. The gas giant in question had seven moons large enough to hide missiles behind, which leaped the short distance to the passing fleet to kill sixteen of them.

*Four more planets in the system*, Martinez exulted.

Then Martinez felt his exultation fade. After re-forming his forces, Do-faq ordered his ships to depart the system's ecliptic plane on a long curve to system south, which meant it would no longer trigger the ambushes Martinez had prearranged at each planet, but instead proceed in a long system-wide arc that would terminate at the wormhole gate to Toley. Martinez could still launch missile attacks, but the enemy would have a much greater chance of seeing them coming from far away and of intercepting them at a safe distance from their ships.

The next choke point, where missiles and enemy ships could

not avoid one another, would be at the wormhole between Roda and Toley.

Of course, Do-faq knew that. He'd evaded Martinez's ambush at the previous wormhole, and he would try to avoid getting hit on the way to Toley.

Martinez knew that there had to be a way to neutralize any possible action by Do-faq, and he set himself to work out what it was.

In the meantime, he continued to launch attacks with the missiles already in the system. None came close to damaging enemy ships, but each caused alarm and evasive action and served to keep the enemy bruised, exhausted, and paranoid.

The Combined Fleet transited the wormhole into the Toley system, which meant they no longer had Do-faq under direct observation, but rather depended on shuttles and remote sensors hidden in the system. Any information coming through the wormhole was delayed, and any attack was bound to suffer from a delay in targeting information.

What Martinez discovered, however, was that he could trigger evasive action on the part of Do-faq simply by lighting up enemy ships with lidar from a distant part of the system. Do-faq had no choice but to assume the threat was real, and his ships went through their mad evasive dance in order to escape purely imaginary missiles.

Martinez attacked with real missiles as well, just to keep Do-faq from growing complaisant.

Now that they were out of sight of the enemy, Wei Jian ordered the Combined Fleet to begin daily exercises in order to bring them into fighting trim.

The climax of the war, Jian had decided, would occur on schedule.

**A DERIVOO STOOD** onstage in her traditional flounced skirts, her whitened hands poised, her face marked by rouged spots high on her cheeks. Her dark hair was drawn severely off her forehead to form an elaborate chignon at her neck. Behind the singer, sequined curtains shimmered in the stage lights.

The derivoo would move, her lips would open to sing, and inevitable tragedy would soar out from the stage. That was understood. But for the moment, the performance was suspended, frozen, poised to begin.

The cocktail glass was cool against Sula's fingertips. She sat at her table, center front, the crisp white tablecloth bright under the lights.

Ice cubes clinked as Sula sipped. The cocktail had an astringent, herbal taste, and Sula wasn't sure whether or not she liked it.

The derivoo remained as motionless as a wax dummy. Sula searched her face for signs of life.

A wet plop sounded in the stillness. Sula glanced behind for the source of the sound. Tables with their white cloths rose in tiers into the darkness above, but no one sat there, and above was nothing but the glare of the stage lights.

Another plop sounded. Sula swiveled her head and saw only the derivoo poised on the stage above her.

A third plop echoed in the near-empty theater. Sula looked at the white tablecloth in front of her and saw a red stain at its center, a stain that expanded as another drop of red fell onto the tablecloth from above. The stain grew. Sula pulled her hands away from the table so she wouldn't get spattered. Anxiety began to creep like serpents along her nerves.

She looked up toward the remote, black ceiling, hoping to see where the red was falling from. She wondered if there was a corpse stuffed in the rafters somewhere.

The sound of spattering rose in the room. More corpses—if they *were* corpses—were now oozing. Table linens were speckled with red. A perfect red globule dropped into Sula's cocktail and hovered in the liquid like a fiery sunrise.

The reek of blood filled Sula's senses. She held her napkin over her head so it would shield her from the spatter.

Sula became aware that the derivoo had begun to move, but very slowly. Her whitened hands opened, then drew toward her, as if to invite the room into an embrace. Her head tilted, her eyes shone. Her painted lips parted in a malevolent smile.

Sula looked at the smile, and her blood froze at the realization that the derivoo was drawing breath, and that soon she would begin to sing. Somehow Sula knew that if the song was released, if the words were uttered, that would spell the end of everything, the whole world would drown in a rain of blood. She absolutely had to prevent the derivoo from singing.

But she could move no faster than the derivoo. She looked down at her hip and saw she had no sidearm. She threw her drink, but it only inched its way toward the stage, the ice and liquid floating out like a cloud, the red droplet still brilliant at its center.

Sula saw the muscles tauten in the derivoo's throat. The first words were about to come.

She could not stop them, so she had to drown them out. Her own mouth opened, and she screamed. And screamed. And screamed.

Sula came awake with derivoo pounding in her ears and her screams a searing in her throat. She fought her way free of the tangled bedsheets and sat up. Her pulse pounded in her throat, and the derivoo's feral smile floated like an afterimage in her mind.

She rose from the bergamot-scented sheets and put on her dressing gown. Her hair was damp at her nape, and when she turned on the lights the surfaces of her sleeping cabin had a hard-edged, brittle texture, the dream lingering in her perceptions. She opened the door to her dining room and the welcoming scent of hot tea.

Shawna Spence—straw-colored hair tousled, dressing gown belted loosely over sturdy hips—leaned over the table to take hold of the teapot.

"I expected you'd have a bad night," she said, "so I have the tea ready."

Sula searched for words. "How did you—?"

"You were about due."

"Ah. Hah. I suppose I was."

Tea poured. Cane sugar syrup oozed into the cup. Spence offered Sula a plate of pastries.

"Thank you," Sula said. The last vestiges of the nightmare shuddered through her nerves. The sweet and fragrant tea helped to settle her thoughts.

"You could see a doctor," Spence offered.

"That would have to be Gunaydin, since he's the only one in the division."

"See him about the nightmares. There must be . . . some medication that's appropriate."

Sula contemplated her teacup. "Military doctors aren't just doctors," she said. "They report up their hierarchy. They're as good as spies." She held the cup between her fingertips and inhaled the aroma. "Gunaydin could rule me unfit. He could denounce me to the authorities."

"Not a lot of authorities in this neighborhood," Spence said.

"There's Wei Jian," Sula said. "She might have some favored junior she'd like to promote into my place. And once we win the battle, she'd have no further use for me. She could use a report from Gunaydin to confine me to what they call a health ward."

"I don't like you having these screaming nightmares." Her eyes turned to Sula. "It can't be good for you."

"It'll taper off once the war is over," Sula said. "That's what happened last time."

Spence shivered. "I remember."

Sula sipped her tea. "Let's talk about something cheerful," she said. "Let's talk about Macnamara. He's always smiling and humming little tunes to himself."

"He's still in love," Spence said. "How long has it lasted?"

Sula tried to add up the days and hours of Macnamara's bliss, but the exact dates escaped her. "Months, anyway," she said.

"A long time."

What, Sula wondered, did Spence know about a long time? Sula had been obsessed by the same man for ten years, and the time she'd spent with him probably didn't even add up to a month.

"But, you know, clouds," Spence said. "Clouds. On the horizon."

"Hm?"

"The husband," said Spence. "His ship joined the Combined Fleet."

"Ah."

It might not matter, Sula thought. The husband might get killed, or Bliss might get killed, or Macnamara might get killed, or everyone in the Combined Fleet might get blown to pions, and the issue of who was happy or unhappy could become irrelevant.

Sula wondered if she'd much mind being killed.

She wondered if it was the drifting undercurrent of the dream that helped to propel these speculations.

At least death meant the dreams would end.

A FEW HOURS later Sula was at another breakfast, playing host to her senior officers. A dull ache had settled deep behind Sula's eyes, and a chance movement of her head, or a flash of bright light in her eyes, could bring on a savage, stabbing pain that could stop her in her tracks. She had countered with analgesics that had been worse than useless.

The officers stood around the wedge-shaped table, all but two in viridian green. One of the exceptions was Abasi of the *Ideal*, who had retained his grand civilian cream-colored uniform. The other was the Naxid commander of one of the new light cruisers, who was not legally an officer of the Fleet, because Naxids were not permitted in the Fleet. Technically she was a civilian who just happened to find herself in command of a warship.

On its journey to Toley, Division Nine had been divided into three squadrons: Heavy, Light, and—because Sula got to pick the name herself—the Very, Very Large. The Heavy Squadron consisted of *Splendid* and the three heavy cruisers captured at Colamote, and Sula commanded them in person. The Light Squadron were the frigate *Mentor* and the six light cruisers from Laredo, commanded by Lieutenant-Captain Lepp. The Very, Very Large were the three improvised battleships *Pride of Parkhurst*, *Lentrec*, and *Ideal*, so cumbersome that they couldn't maneuver with the other ships.

The best Sula could say for the Very, Very Large ships was that most of their missile launchers worked most of the time. None worked so badly that they jammed or exploded, and there were so many that even if a number failed, a truly impressive number of missiles could still be launched.

The VVLs would remain in the rear, with the other two squadrons protecting them from enemy fire—which, since the Very, Very Large ships were sitting ducks incapable of high-gee maneuvers, would be a challenging task.

"To the Restoration of the Praxis," Sula intoned, raising her glass, and her words were echoed by the captains. She tipped the glass toward her lips, and a blend of citrus and alcohol fizzed its way along her tongue.

"Be seated, please." The officers shuffled into their seats. She looked from one to the other and winced as a bolt of pain shattered her thoughts. She tried to reassemble them.

"This is our last chance to meet before entering the Toley system," she managed. "I would like to hear from each of you concerning the state of your command, and whether there are any concerns remaining." Her eyes rose to one of her officers. "Lieutenant Kavasia?"

Kavasia was a white-haired lieutenant brought out of retirement and placed in command of the three converted battleships. He was suitable for the task in part because he could not stand high accelerations, and neither could his ships.

"Thanks to the Fleet Train," he said, "we have full magazines. Our crews are new recruits buttressed by a disciplined core of civilian volunteers from the old crews." He flapped his hands. "Nothing works properly, but we've built workarounds where possible." He looked up and cleared his throat. "I think that's all."

Sula asked his captains—all civilians—if they had anything to add. They didn't.

Sula looked again at her officers. In previous commands her leadership style had been angry and derisive—she had heaped scorn on officers who were lazy, incompetent, or simply unlucky, and raged at foolish or inept decisions. She had openly questioned her subordinates' parentage and their right to lead and had predicted disaster for anyone unfortunate enough to follow them into battle.

That approach had been successful, but only because her subordinates had been overprivileged Peers who had never before been required to use their brains for anything more complicated than wagering on a football match. Never before had anyone called them vile names or questioned their right to expect absolute obedience from their social inferiors. Sula's scorching verbal assaults had shocked them out of their inbred complacency and compelled them to engage their underused brain cells.

She knew that this approach wouldn't work with Division Nine, not with her mixed crews of civilians, raw recruits, professionals, Naxids, and those brought in from retirement. She had been encouraging, helpful, and useful, and she had restrained the tongue-lashings that some of the imbeciles so thoroughly deserved. She knew that given time constraints the best she could hope for was a consistent mediocrity, and she flattered herself that this goal had been achieved.

Still, the fact that *no one* had anything to add set her teeth on edge.

Sula turned to Lepp. "Lord Elcap?"

Lepp favored her with one of his offhand smiles. "*Mentor*'s crew has trained together for years, and I daresay we're a very efficient ship. The Laredo cruisers are crewed mostly by new recruits, and in the last weeks they've become reasonably competent at their tasks, if not absolutely proficient. The fact that before going on their ships they spent the better part of two months training on simulators was a great help.

"That said, we're stretched for experienced officers and warrant and petty officers. *Mentor*'s sent three of its five lieutenants to other ships, and I've had to replace them with inexperienced cadets. On a ship like *Mentor*, with its well-trained crew, this matters less than it might elsewhere."

Which summed up the situation throughout Division Nine.

A lack of officers and senior NCOs meant not only that the ones she had were overworked but also that there were too few on hand to teach the recruits their jobs. All this meant that Sula was constantly bombarded with messages from officers asking her how to do their work, because their own seniors couldn't, or weren't available, to teach them.

The irony being that the two most efficient ships among the new Laredo cruisers were the two fully or partially crewed by Naxid veterans.

Sula hadn't appointed a tactical officer in part because all the officers in the division had more useful employment, and in part because of her considered opinion that she could do the job better than any of them.

Lepp raised a hand to his glossy waved hair, as if to make certain it was in perfect order. "Still," he added, "morale is good, and the crew are eager to avenge Squadron Commander Nguyen and the dead of Felarus."

"Thank you," Sula said. "Are there any other comments from the captains of the Light Squadron?"

The Naxid captain surprised everyone by speaking. "Only this, my lady," she said. Her black-on-red eyes glittered. "I wish to state that I am grateful to be given this opportunity to demonstrate my loyalty to the empire, and that I and my crew shall give their utmost in defense of the Praxis."

"Well spoken, my lady," said Sula, and then winced as pain lanced her skull. She paused and took a breath, then asked for comments from the captains of the Heavy Division. She could see from their expressions that they wished they'd been the first to make a noble little speech about giving their utmost in defense of the Praxis and were a little sorry that the Naxid had spoken first.

Last she turned to Dr. Gunaydin, who sat on her left. "A report from the medical department?" she said.

"Medical supplies are adequate," Gunaydin said, and touched a finger to a corner of his mustache. "We have qualified pharmacists aboard all ships," he said. "The pharmacists, and many of the damage control specialists, have taken basic and intermediate first aid courses. They can take care of routine medical emergencies."

He frowned.

"Unfortunately, I remain the only physician in the division, and if there are significant numbers of casualties, it is inevitable that I will be overwhelmed. I hope that in that event, the Combined Fleet will send us doctors to deal with the situation."

Gunaydin and Sula both knew that it was far more likely that entire ships' crews would be incinerated in a single blazing instant. Antimatter warheads didn't just knock people around like a conventional explosive, it flashed them into subatomic shrapnel.

Yet there had been cases of ships surviving, not a direct hit, but a hit on a nearby ship or a miss close enough to melt part of the hull. In that case there *would* be casualties, and a lot of them.

"The Combined Fleet has an adequate supply of doctors," she said. "I'll do my best to make sure they're available."

Gunaydin gave her a grave smile. His shaven head gleamed softly in the indirect light. "I would be grateful, Lady Sula."

Sula turned toward her other guests, and again winced as pain exploded in her head.

"I, ah—" she began, and then gathered her words. "If there are no more comments, then I think we can begin our breakfast."

As the servants came in with their plates, Sula looked at the chronometer on the wall.

In less than four hours, she saw, Division Nine would enter the

Toley system, appearing in Do-faq's flank and rear—presumably, she surmised, to the enemy's dismay.

**THE FLEET TRAIN** had supplied the Combined Fleet a perfectly absurd number of missiles, and there was no reason, Martinez thought, not to use them all.

When Do-faq came through the wormhole into Toley, he would find himself under assault from at least six directions, including from behind the wormhole itself. Since Do-faq was almost certain to order his ships into last-minute maneuvers that would make it difficult to predict the time of his transition into the Toley system, Martinez decided to send the missiles late instead of early—the enemy would have more warning, but they wouldn't have the chance to destroy missiles that arrived prematurely while they reacquired a target.

Do-faq's maneuvers brought him through the wormhole half a minute later than expected, which made Martinez glad he'd held back his attack. From the moment of transition, the enemy was completely lit by the Combined Fleet's sensors, making them ideal targets. Do-faq's own radars and laser rangefinders flogged space in search of something to shoot at, and found them in terrifying numbers just as the lead missiles were making final course adjustments prior to their run.

No sooner had the enemy fleet appeared than it was surrounded by a brilliant sphere of light as countermissiles and point-defense beams detonated incoming missiles. Radio hash formed an impenetrable wall between the combat and the sensors of the Combined Fleet, and so it was impossible to tell how Do-faq's fleet was faring, but the sheer number of detonations was impressive.

The fight went on for nearly six minutes as different flights of missiles arrowed in, and then the flashes died away, and after several minutes Do-faq's fleet appeared out of the expanding overlapping fireballs.

Martinez had watched the entire combat from his office while sipping a cup of coffee—he was such a distance from the fight, there was no reason to be in the flag officer's station—and he strained his eyes as he looked at the ships appearing on the displays. Their formations were ragged, and there were holes where ships—or decoys—had once been. At least one ship was tumbling slowly end over end. Do-faq had been hit hard.

When the analysts aboard Wei Jian's flagship reached a conclusion, they announced that Do-faq had lost 42 ships, leaving Do-faq with a total of 153, with a couple dozen of the survivors damaged.

The Restoration now possessed numerical superiority, at least once Sula's division was added to the Combined Fleet.

Martinez rubbed his long jaw while satisfaction warmed his bones. He had been invited to dine with the wardroom the next day, and now he and the lieutenants would have a great deal to cheer about.


"MY LADY? LADY Sula?"

Through her vac suit, Sula felt a soft touch on her arm. She opened her eyes and viewed her signals, lieutenant Viswan looking down at her through the faceplate of her helmet.

"Yes?" Sula said.

"I thought you should know. We've successfully transited to Toley."

"Ah. Hah."

Apparently she'd fallen asleep while awaiting the transition. Blinking gum from her eyes, Sula shifted her gaze to the displays locked down inside her acceleration cage. Division Nine shone in a corner of one display, the ships still sorting themselves out after the transition. The division now seemed much larger, for each of the warships had fired a pair of decoys just before diving through the wormhole. With luck, the enemy wouldn't have time to sort ship from decoy before the battle started and would waste missiles on the decoys that would better be aimed directly at Sula's vitals.

Across a distance of empty space was Do-faq's fleet, already arrayed for battle, the ships spiraling in the intricate knots of Ghost Tactics, with the Combined Fleet beyond. Toley was a largely barren system, with many asteroids and rocky planetoids, but no gas giants or places capable of supporting life. It was as empty a battlespace as anyone could desire, and it would be more than a day before the engagement would begin.

Sula felt weariness dragging at her eyelids. "I'm going back to sleep," she said. "Let me know if anything happens."

"Yes, my lady." Viswan withdrew as quietly as her boots permitted. *Splendid* gave a little graceful swoop as it maneuvered to avoid any enemy beam weapons, and to Sula it felt as if the ship were rocking her to sleep.

Sula supposed that her dropping into slumber during a crucial evolution might be a story that would soon escape the flag officer's station and become current in the Fleet. *Quite a cool head on that Lady Sula*, they might say, *going after the enemy while taking a nap*. Whereas the reality had nothing to do with sangfroid but instead involved her own exhaustion and the fact that she really had nothing important to do, and wouldn't for hours.

Sleep cast its net over her and drew her into a darkness untroubled by dreams.

# CHAPTER 7

From the displays in the wardroom, Martinez watched the appearance of Sula's division with more unease than he would have wished. When Sula had been far away, remote in a vast emptiness threaded together by a tenuous trail of wormholes, he had been able to keep his turbulent feelings in some kind of order. Now that her command was within sight, he felt a threat to his precarious emotional balance.

It would be worse, of course, after battle, when he would be obliged to see Sula socially. Perhaps he could see her in person without imagining a smoking pistol in her hand or without the cold, imperious glimmer in her emerald eyes.

Or perhaps not.

The lieutenants who were playing host in the wardroom burst into applause when Sula's ships shot through the wormhole to arrive on Do-faq's flank. Earlier in the day they'd seen the enemy fleet torn by antimatter bursts as it entered the system, and—between Do-faq's battering, Sula's arrival, abundant food, and even more abundant alcohol—they were inclined to be merry. That within two days they would all be facing death in the battlespace was not something they were inclined to contemplate.

The premiere lieutenant raised her glass. "To Lady Sula's timely arrival," she said.

Martinez raised his glass to his lips and drank without tasting the wine.

Sula was in his life again, whether he wanted it or not.

"LADY SULA," SAID Lord Nishkad. His rheumy black-on-red eyes gazed at Sula from one of her displays on her acceleration cage. "I hope this message hasn't added too much to the burdens of your busy day." He inhaled deliberately, his lungs fighting against nearly two gravities' deceleration as Sula's ships shed momentum so as not to engage prematurely.

"I wished only to express my confidence in your capabilities," he said, "and my belief that Division Nine will triumph in the coming battle. Your gifts are of a high order, my lady, and I hardly think the enemy can match you."

He raised a black-scaled hand. "Fortune attend you. End message."

A rising elation swept through Sula. She had been looking at the eighteen ships that had been sent to bar her path and trying to work out a way to bring her own forces into an engagement on anything like favorable terms. She was slowly coming around to the idea that she shouldn't engage at all—if she kept threatening the enemy rear without actually getting into a fight, she'd be keeping eighteen enemy ships out of battle, and her fourteen would suffer no losses.

Lord Nishkad's message had come at exactly the right moment to buoy her hopes. And he hadn't added to the burdens of her busy day, because her day was now almost leisurely. Everything and everyone was ready for combat, but the battle hadn't started. She couldn't order maneuvers or an exercise within full sight of the enemy, and all she needed to do was to catch up on her sleep, because when the battle started, she would be very busy indeed.

And for some reason she found it easy to sleep in the flag officer's station. The featureless gray walls, broken only by consoles and displays, were soothing. Her signals officers spoke only in hushed tones and padded quietly around her acceleration couch when they came and went.

And, more importantly, nightmares didn't come when she was drowsing on her acceleration couch. Maybe it was the presence of other people in the room that kept her from diving deep into the ocean of nightmare, or maybe it was the activity on the displays, or the miniwaves that pulsed through the couch that relaxed her taut muscles as well as prevented blood pooling under acceleration. Whatever it was, she was grateful.

Sula sent Nishkad thanks for his kind message, then closed her eyes and let herself fall into half-sleep, her breath regular, her awareness suppressed . . .

And then she thought, *Oh!*, and realized that she might have a way of dealing with those eighteen enemy ships.

FROM THE POINT of view of *Bombardment of Los Angeles*, the Combined Fleet was speeding toward Harzapid, their engines flaring in a continuous deceleration in order to let Do-faq overtake them and bring about a battle. The enemy followed, decelerating themselves, but at a slower rate.

Remote off the enemy's flank and rear, Sula's division sped toward an interception point. She was traveling fast in relation to the two fleets, as Sula needed to cover a greater distance to arrive at a rendezvous, and unless she did a hard, long deceleration burn, she would overrun Do-faq's fleet.

The start of any battle would depend heavily on timing. If Sula arrived prematurely, she would find herself facing the entire enemy force on her own, and if she arrived late, she could miss the entire fight. Orders went out from Wei Jian's flagship carefully regulating everyone's decelerations.

In the meantime, the Combined Fleet and Do-faq's force mirrored each other. Do-faq had duplicated Wei Jian's battle order of van, main body, rear, and reserves. The enemy's units had already adopted the shifting, stochastic-seeming dance of the Martinez Method, and Wei Jian had responded by ordering her formations to begin their own maneuvers.

Martinez thought it was like prizefighters dancing and ducking before closing the range and beginning the bout.

Except he could already start punching. Martinez launched one attack after another toward the enemy, accelerating missiles from remote corners of the system. None caused any damage, but each presumably sent alarms shrilling through the enemy ships and sometimes resulted in frantic jinking.

Do-faq made the first alteration in the order of battle, as he detached three squadrons, two from the reserve and one from the main body, and formed them into a wall between Sula and the rest of his fleet. The enemy squadrons were depleted but still amounted to eighteen ships against Sula's fourteen. The odds were more heavily against Sula than the numbers suggested, since three of Sula's ships were converted transports, and most of the rest had inexperienced crews. Martinez felt anxiety gnaw at his vitals with little rodent teeth. He had no way to help her.

The next alteration wasn't ordered by either commander. Martinez was sleeping when it happened and was awakened by a banging on the door and the voice of Lalita Banerjee telling him to look at the display *now*. His heart lurched wildly as he lunged from his bed, then shouted at the display to switch on.

"Banerjee!" he shouted. "Send me the feed!"

"It's already on Feed Seven!"

Martinez ordered Feed Seven onto the display and collapsed back onto his bed, expecting the video to show some catastrophe: missiles arrowing in from some unexpected direction, Rivven and An-dar defecting back to the enemy, Chandra Prasad engaging in ship-to-ship combat with Wei Jian . . .

What he saw was that one squadron of five ships had detached itself from Do-faq's main body and begun a high-gee acceleration in a direction orthogonal to the enemy's course, flying by itself into the emptiness of system north.

"Do we have any transmissions?" Martinez asked. There was no answer: Banerjee had returned to her place in the flag officer's station. He shrugged into his uniform tunic, triggered the sleeve display, and told it to contact Banerjee.

"Do we have transmissions from that enemy squadron?" he asked.

Banerjee gasped for breath, apparently having just run from Martinez's door to her station.

"Nothing yet, my lord," she wheezed.

"Are we overhearing anything?"

"All ciphered, my lord."

Martinez padded to his office, where numerous displays waited, and called up several views of the tactical situation.

Unless the squadron was engaged in some arcane tactical maneuver that Martinez had yet to comprehend, he had to assume that the five ships were in the act of deserting the enemy fleet. He hoped they would manage their escape, but he thought not. The rogue squadron was outnumbered thirty to one.

His heart sank as he realized that there was nothing he could do to assist. The Combined Fleet was too far away to engage the enemy, and the fleeing ships were entirely on their own.

For a moment, he thought about sending one of his distant packs of missiles racing for the enemy fleet, and at least distract them from what would soon turn into a very one-sided fight. Yet so far it *wasn't* a fight, and he didn't want to do anything that would send the enemy into a state of combat readiness if by some unlikely chance they hadn't yet noted the little squadron's escape.

Martinez remembered his own dash from the Second Fleet at the start of the Naxid War, in the stolen frigate *Corona*, and all the frantic methods he'd used for deceiving and delaying the enemy while he burned for the nearest wormhole. He imagined that happening in the fleeing squadron, the squadcom sending out a series of increasingly unconvincing messages explaining why his command was taking this unorthodox action.

An alert popped onto his screens, and he saw that one of the packs of missiles he had hidden in the system had received a command to burn for the enemy fleet at maximum acceleration. Wei Jian, who shared the codes that were able to activate the missiles, had undoubtedly sent them in the direction of the enemy.

*Well, here we go*, Martinez thought.

In the end the missiles made no difference. Do-faq's fleet began shooting at the breakaway squadron before Wei Jian's signal even reached the missiles, and suddenly both sides were launching missiles and countermissiles, and the ships were flinging themselves in all directions to avoid beam weapon attacks. Fireballs bloomed in the darkness between Do-faq's fleet and the escaping ships.

Banerjee's voice interrupted the silent action. "Message in the clear, my lord," she said, and put it over the video without waiting for Martinez's order.

"This is Squadron Commander Draymesh of Light Squadron Twenty-Two." Martinez could tell from the sonorous tones that Draymesh was a Daimong. "We have left the Unified Fleet in hopes of joining the Restoration, and now we are being fired upon. We request immediate aid from Wei Jian and others in service to the Restoration."

Martinez was relieved that he wasn't obliged to respond to that message. Draymesh had started his rebellion too early, and there was nothing Martinez or any else could do to help him.

It was possible, he thought, that Draymesh had no option. If he were engaged in a plot to defect, he might have had to move quickly before being denounced. It didn't change the fact that he was doomed.

Wei Jian chose not to respond to Draymesh's appeal. Perhaps she viewed the missile launch as the best signal she could send.

In any case, the missiles arrived too late. The rogue squadron twisted and darted and ultimately died in overlapping fireballs while anxiety gnawed at Martinez's entrails. The missiles sent by Wei Jian would have arrived ten minutes later, but counterfire blew them to bits long before they neared their targets.

Half an hour after the rogue ships had been turned into glittering dust, Wei Jian broadcast in the clear to Do-faq's Unified Fleet. Jian appeared on video as she always did: perfectly composed, expressionless, her eyes turned to the viewer as if estimating the range. The white stripes in her short hair were as perfectly ordered as the badges of rank on her uniform.

"I offer condolences to the friends of Squadron Commander Draymesh and his officers and crew," she said. "I would like to assure you that they will be amply avenged."

Something flickered behind her eyes, as if she were a machine calling up a new piece of code. "It is obvious that your so-called Unified Fleet is anything but unified," she said, "and that you are hardly in any state to fight a successful action. I would like to suggest to each captain again that you follow Captain Martinez's proposal and defect to the Restoration. I advise that you pick your time carefully, and choose a moment when the balance of the Unified Fleet is engaged and too busy to effectively respond. To preserve your own lives, it may be necessary to strike first, but in any case, I urge you to avoid the disaster that will soon engulf your entire fleet. End message."

*That wasn't so bad*, Martinez thought. Jian had certainly covered all the points he would have made himself, and he approved of how she had slipped in the suggestion that any defecting unit could best assure their escape through a surprise attack on nearby ships.

His respect for Wei Jian grew a little more.

Now he'd have to hope that Do-faq's commanders were listening.

SULA CLENCHED HER teeth against the heavy gees of Division Nine's deceleration. If she were going to engage a superior force, she had decided, there was no reason to hurry, and so she would be decelerating all the way.

The med patch she'd stuck to her neck chafed the sensitive skin on the underside of her jaw. The thought of shooting herself in the neck with an injector sent terror clawing at her nerves, so she used patches to deliver the drugs that would support her brain and circulatory system, keep her mind flexible and her blood vessels elastic, and help prevent the strokes and brain bleeds that could come with high accelerations.

She had donned the cap that contained her earphones and virtual reality projectors, but she'd left her helmet in the mesh bag attached to her acceleration couch. She hated the closed-in sensation of wearing the helmet and feared fastening the faceplate that locked her into a world of chemical smells, claustrophobia, and her own body stink.

She hissed as *Splendid*'s engines increased thrust, and her body sank deeper into her acceleration couch.

There would be some hours yet before the battle started, and Sula would be fighting gravity all the way.

*WELL*, MARTINEZ THOUGHT, *here I am again.*

He faced the camera in his office, the unwinking eye that seemed ready to indict him on any number of charges. He faced as well the possibility that he was about to send his last message to his family. The Battle of Toley would begin in a matter of hours, and if he was killed, this message would be the final memory his family would have of him.

He looked at the paintings of fish on the walls, Young Gareth's sketches enlarged and improved by an artist drawn from the Fourth Fleet. Scales, eyes, and teeth glittered in the spotlights, and Martinez felt a rising sense of well-being at the sight of his son's aquatic fantasies gleaming on his office walls. He turned to the camera and began recording.

"The fight against Do-faq's fleet will begin soon," he said. "I'm a little relieved that I'm not in command this time—my responsibility now is not to win a war, but simply to stay alive, and I think I can do that well enough."

He wondered if his false modesty sounded as false as he knew it to be. He *wanted* to be in charge. Every cell of his body was screaming at him to simply *take over*. He had built this fleet and won its two victories, he had developed every tactic that it would be using, and Wei Jian had supplanted him not by any virtue or ability, but by threatening to take her ships and go home if she wasn't put in command.

"Do-faq has been subjected to a series of ambushes that have gone on for weeks," he told the camera, "his crews are beaten down, and their morale has to be at rock-bottom. The Restoration will soon be able to announce another victory."

But it couldn't be *just* a victory, Martinez knew. The victory had to leave enough of a fleet available to the Restoration to advance on Zanshaa and anywhere else the enemy might be harboring ships. Even he had to admit his previous victories hadn't achieved that. He doubted that Wei Jian could manage it now.

But these doubts were hardly the sort of thing he should be sending his family right now.

Instead, he said, "I hope that soon we'll finally be able to see one another in person, in our own home in Zanshaa High City. Please send this video on to Mei-mei and my parents on Laredo. All my love, and you'll hear from me soon."

The unwinking eye dimmed, and Martinez viewed the video before he sent it. Watching himself perform always made him uneasy, and he rarely enjoyed the sight of himself on camera, but he decided the brief video was as good as it was going to get and forwarded it to be ciphered and sent on its way.

"MY LORD," SAID Aitor Santana. "We've broken the Method formula used by sixty-one percent of the enemy formations. When we engage, we'll know exactly where their ships will be even if our view is blocked by fireballs."

"It's too good to be true," Martinez said. "I'm sure Do-faq will order new patterns before any engagement."

"Still," Santana said. "It would be a relief if we simply got lucky for a change."

"I believe in luck," said Martinez. "But I don't believe in *that much* luck."

He and Santana were walking to the flag officer's station, both in vac suits and carrying their helmets. Wei Jian had decreed some preliminary maneuvering ahead of combat, in hopes of getting Do-faq to make a mistake—and though Martinez thought no mistake would be made, he reckoned that it was worth trying. He just had to hope he didn't make a mistake himself.

An alarm began to ring as Martinez was strapping himself into his acceleration couch. Elissa Dalkeith's lisping voice sounded through the ship. "General quarters. Now general quarters. This is not a drill."

Martinez locked down the displays in front of him and paused to assure himself that nothing unexpected had happened—which didn't take very long, as the situation hadn't changed except that the opposing fleets had crept closer to each other. He looked for a moment at Sula's Division Nine shedding speed as it approached the eighteen ships standing between it and the Combined Fleet, and wondered if Sula had any plan for dealing with the superior force.

Of *course* she did, he decided. Sula was the one person in the upcoming battle he didn't need to worry about. She'd already worked out a way to deploy her heterogeneous force in some unexpected and masterful way, because that was exactly the sort of thing Sula did. She'd blow apart the rear guard and come down like a giant hammer on Do-faq's flank and that would be the end of the battle.

Not that Wei Jian was likely to hand Sula any credit for her part in any victory.

Or to Martinez, for that matter.

*Stay alive, first. Claim the glory after.*

Martinez took the med injector from the mesh bag attached to his acceleration couch and pressed it to his neck. "Time to fire up," he said to the room in general.

There was a brief hiss, and Martinez experienced a slight coolness in his throat and a faint chemical taste on his tongue. Otherwise, he felt no difference, and he could only take it on trust that the drug was doing its job.

The others dutifully attended to their injectors. Martinez locked his helmet onto his vac suit and breathed in the scent of suit seals, disinfectant, and his own aftershave. He went virtual, the projectors in his cap sending an illusory battlespace into his optical centers. All Toley expanded to fill his skull. He studied the displays from this new perspective as he played different scenarios in his mind.

Wei Jian waited another ten minutes before issuing her first order. Martinez repeated the order to his own command, and then floated free in his straps as *Bombardment of Los Angeles* cut its engines. There was a shimmer in his inner ear as the ship rolled about its center of mass, and then a punch to his sternum as the engines fired. Gravities built quickly, and Martinez began deliberate breathing from deep in his abdomen, letting gravity drive the air out of him before he gulped it back in.

The Combined Fleet was now flying before the enemy in what looked like a disordered retreat. The tactic was intended to tempt the enemy into an overhasty pursuit, leaving behind any ships crewed by the hollow-boned Lai-own.

The tactic had worked at Second Shulduc, with Lord Tork ordering his entire command into a rash pursuit, the Lai-own squadrons lagging behind. Martinez thought this feigned flight was unlikely to work against a Lai-own commander, who would be reluctant to order his fleet into a pursuit that would leave him behind, but he thought it was worth trying.

Do-faq didn't take the bait, and after twenty minutes Wei Jian called off the retreat. Martinez sucked free, weightless air into his lungs while the ship rotated, and then the engines began their burn, taking the Combined Fleet toward the enemy. Two gees this time, a relief after the hard burn away from the enemy.

"Message from Lady Wei, my lord," said Aitor Santana. "Van and rear are free to extend the line."

"Acknowledge," Martinez said. He turned to Santana. "All ships in the Grand Division of the Rear to alter course to two-six-five by zero-zero-one relative, course change to commence in two minutes. Accelerate at two point eight gravities."

That would send his ships racing for the enemy's flank at the same time that Michi Chen's vanguard was dashing for the other wing. To Do-faq, it might look as if the Combined Fleet was intending to surround his command. Again, this was an attempt to get him to maneuver and try to match the velocities of the flanking forces and separate the Lai-own squadrons from the others. But, if he didn't, the Combined Fleet *would* be in a position to flank Do-faq.

The danger to the Combined Fleet was that its elements might separate to the point where the enemy could overwhelm a single isolated command before the others could intervene, so Martinez kept a close watch on the gap between his squadrons and the main body. He also had to keep from getting too close to the eighteen warships that had been detached to watch Sula, because if he wasn't careful he'd find them on his own flank.

He needn't have worried. The enemy rear tried to match his acceleration for several minutes, but in the end settled for adopting a defensive formation, its squadrons curving back and away to keep from being encircled.

Since the enemy wasn't to be drawn, Martinez canceled his own dash for the flank and arranged his squadrons in ways calculated to enrich his advantages. From a position hovering off the enemy flank, he could fire missiles at the enemy rear curving away from him, or he could fire straight into Do-faq's main body, with the missiles arriving from an unexpected direction. It wasn't a decisive advantage, because the enemy understood their situation as well as he did and would do their best to counter, but Martinez would happily employ whatever benefit the situation gave him.

His concentration on his own situation meant that he paid no attention to what was happening around Michi Chen's Grand Division of the Van, not until he heard Lalita Banerjee cry out. "Missiles fired! Missiles fired in the van!"

Martinez's heart leaped into his throat, and he frantically studied the displays. He let out a long breath when he saw that missiles had been fired within the *enemy* van, at one of their own squadrons. The targets had been in the United Fleet's lead squadron, and when the other units had abandoned the race and curved away from Michi into a defensive formation, the lead six ships had increased their acceleration and raced away from their own support. It had been several minutes before the enemy fully realized that the ships were defecting, and their missile launches had been ragged. The defectors managed to shoot down the first volley, and by the time the second was launched, Michi intervened with missiles and beam weapons of her own.

The six defectors got away, flying clear of both fleets.

"Now is the time," Martinez murmured. If there was ever a moment to take advantage of disarray and the collapse of morale among the enemy, it was now.

No sooner had Martinez spoken than orders came from Wei Jian. "Van, main body, and rear to engage. Fire a screening barrage, alter Method pattern, alter transponder codes as per instructions. Fire pinnaces and decoys."

This was followed by the boom of a massive orchestral chord, and from Martinez's headphones issued a massed Daimong chorus singing "The Praxis Is Our Only Goal." Martinez blinked in surprise.

Some commanders inspired their subordinates with speeches, some with the meticulous care and interest they showed in the welfare of their ships and crews. Some micromanaged subordinates to make them all a part of a single machine obeying a single will, and some gave their officers enough freedom to discover their own strengths and apply them.

Apparently Wei Jian relied on patriotic music.

Martinez wasn't sure whether he was supposed to obey orders immediately or wait till the song was over. He decided not to wait.

He ordered out a barrage, and when the enemy fleet vanished behind expanding spheres of blazing plasma, he ordered a change of course and for his units to alter their patterns. Decoys were fired, as well as pinnaces, yacht-sized vessels with a single crew originally intended to shepherd flocks of missiles but now used as observation platforms, intended to soar great distances away from the fight so they could see over the antimatter blasts and discover where in the battlespace the enemy might be lurking.

By the time the Daimong choir boomed out the triumphant

finale, "The Praxis is our only goooooooooal," the ships of the Grand Division of the Rear were beginning to enter the overlapping radio haze created by the missile explosions, and the Shankaracharya sensor suites were doing their best to find the enemy.

The Combined Fleet's tactic was based on another that had worked at Second Shulduc, to subject the enemy to a calculated psychological shock—when the fleet appeared out of the expanding plasma fog, the launching of decoys would make it look three times as large as it had been only moments before. The enemy would *know* that two-thirds were decoys, but what they would *see* was an overwhelming force bearing down on them, and that first impression would be a shock. In addition, they would have very little time to sort decoys from warships before the missiles started flying, and Martinez could hope that the enemy would waste a great many missiles blasting decoys to flaming pieces.

What Martinez saw as his ships passed through the radio haze was an overwhelming force driving straight at him. He stared for a moment in shock, and then he laughed.

Do-faq had unintentionally mirrored his enemies' tactics, taken advantage of the two fleets being hidden from each other to alter course and launch decoys, making his Unified Fleet seem much larger than it was. He had probably fired pinnaces and changed his Method patterns as well.

So far Do-faq had avoided panic, avoided plunging heedlessly into combat, and was reacting with tactical intelligence.

Damn. Martinez hated an enemy with brainpower.

**ON HER DISPLAYS,** Sula watched the Combined Fleet in its preliminary maneuvers—the feigned retreat, the attempt to extend the enemy flanks. She wasn't surprised that Do-faq made no fatal mistakes. The Battle of Toley was going to be a much more straight-forward fight than Wei Jian had hoped.

Sula's eyes sought out the nearest friendly force and found the Grand Division of the Rear on her display. Martinez commanded there, she knew, and she wondered if he was prowling through his ship like a caged animal. He was the most successful of the Restoration's commanders, had won the greatest victory in the empire's history, and now he had been superseded by a humorless, inexperienced senior officer obsessed with proper display of shoulder boards. If Sula had been in Martinez's position, she might well have reached for her pistol—whether to shoot Wei Jian or herself, she wasn't quite decided.

"Fucking hell," she muttered. She shouldn't be thinking about Martinez; he was a distraction that turned her insides to lead and half-paralyzed her brain. She needed to have her mind in the fight, not mooning over a lost lover.

Again, she scanned her display. Sula's plan to engage the enemy detachment had evolved since it had revealed itself to her, but enough time had passed so that she had begun to doubt the wisdom of engaging at all. She decided to pass the decision up the line of command.

"Message to Fleet Commander Jian," she sent. "Division Nine consists of fourteen ships, and the enemy has detached eighteen warships to face us. Even without engaging we have taken eighteen ships away from the enemy, and I question the wisdom of fighting at a disadvantage when we have already accomplished our objective of removing eighteen ships from the battle. I request permission to avoid a fight as long as the current conditions, ah, remain current. End message."

The med patch dug into her flesh again, and she pulled it off and reattached it.

"Message from Fleet Commander Jian." Ricci's soothing bari-tone. "Decrypting now."

Wei Jian appeared in Sula's display, her helmet's faceplate showing eyes leveled and unblinking, her face expressionless.

"Lady Sula," she said. "I note that you are improperly dressed. If your ship is at quarters, you should be wearing a helmet at all times. Also, patches are an inferior delivery system, and med injec-tors are preferred as more efficient."

Sula barked out a laugh. Wei Jian, she decided, simply couldn't help herself: everything in Jian's world had to be proper and pre-dictable, and even in the shadow of an apocalyptic battle she would go on assigning demerits to everything that didn't fit her notion of propriety.

Jian's proper milieu, Sula thought, was peacetime, when offi-cers were obliged to care about these exacting formalities because nothing else of any importance was happening in their sphere.

"As for your request," Jian continued, "I intend that every en-emy ship be engaged as soon as possible in order to win a victory as quickly as possible. When a general engagement begins, I trust that you will attack the enemy that is before you. End message."

Sula blinked, and when her eyelids opened Jian's image had vanished from her display.

"Acknowledge," she told Viswan.

She wondered if Jian would have reacted differently to her request if she'd gone to the trouble of donning a helmet before she sent it.

**"MESSAGE FROM LADY** Sula," said Banerjee. Martinez was startled—he hadn't received anything from Sula since her official report of the Second Battle of Colamote.

"It's addressed to the whole fleet," Banerjee added. "Deciphering now."

So Martinez wasn't getting a message for his eyes only. "Let's see it," Martinez said.

Sula appeared on the video, her near-translucent skin a pale backdrop to the burning green gems that were her eyes.

"Sula to Lady Wei and the Combined Fleet," she said. "A recording is attached of Do-faq's recent maneuvers. His ships weren't hidden from me, and if you analyze this quickly, you should be able to tell warship from decoy. End message."

*Brief and to the point,* Martinez thought.

"Make sure the attachment is forwarded it to weapons and tactical officers," he said.

He had even more cards to play. He spun his cage to face Paivo Kangas.

"Launch solar missiles," he said.

He had kept a flight of over four hundred missiles near Toley's sun, hidden within its glare. The two fleets were nowhere near Toley's sun, so the missiles would take about forty minutes to reach the battlespace, but Martinez hoped he could keep the missiles' drive plumes hidden in the glare of the sun until the very last seconds.

"Launch the other missiles as well," Martinez said. This was the decisive battle, and there was no point in hoarding weapons now. Besides, it was best to keep the enemies' heads swiveling and distracted by attacks coming from every direction.

The lightest touch of vertigo swam through Martinez's head as *Los Angeles* swooped to avoid enemy beam weapons.

"Squadrons have permission to engage," Martinez said. There must have been weapons officers hunched over their consoles with fingers poised above buttons, because missiles began leaping from warships almost instantly.

*Well*, Martinez thought. *It's real now.*

SULA PULLED A long, hard deceleration before engaging the enemy for the simple reason that she didn't want to fly haphazardly into a pack of hostile ships and bring about a melee that only the larger force would win. Just as she reduced her heavy burn to a mere one and a half gees Wei Jian's order to attack came, followed by the astonishing chorus of "The Praxis Is Our Only Goal."

Sula listened all the way to the final booming chords, in hopes that Wei Jian would appear at the finale and explain that it was joke.

Apparently, it wasn't. Or if it was, Jian wasn't letting on.

Sula drew lines on her displays with a finger and ordered her ships to launch a covering barrage into the indicated area. Missiles began hurling themselves toward the enemy, a spreading wave on a front both broad and deep.

"All ships cut engines," Sula said. "All ships rotate to new heading zero-three-zero by three-zero-zero relative. Light and Heavy squadrons accelerate at four gravities on my mark. Very, Very Large Squadron to accelerate as prudent."

And then she waited as the ship's engines cut and she floated in her harness as the ship rotated around her. She waited as the missiles began arrowing in on their targets, waited while countermissiles were fired by the enemy ships, waited until bright fireballs began to wink like gems across the darkness.

"Three, two, one, *mark*!" Her acceleration cage slammed to its dead point and gravity knocked the breath from her lungs. More fireballs splashed across the width and breadth of the enemy formation until the enemy was completely obscured.

She had deliberately rotated her ships when the enemy could see it, and lit off her antimatter torches before their view of Division Nine was completely obscured by the fireball screen. The enemy therefore knew her course and speed and would take countermeasures.

Sula took in a breath. "All ships cut engines," she said, and then gasped with relief as both she and the air she was breathing became weightless.

"Rotate all ships to a new heading at zero-three-zero by zero-seven-five relative. Lights and Heavies accelerate at three gravities on my mark, Very Large as prudent." She waited till all Division Nine had time to swing to their new course, then ordered the engines lit.

"Fire pinnaces," Sula added, as gravities piled weight onto her chest. "Squadron commanders shift Ghost Tactics pattern to one best suited to your mission. For the Heavy Squadron, that will be Revised Pattern Four."

Her inner ear felt a tremor run through *Splendid* as the cruiser shifted its pattern. Her hand, three times its normal weight, scribed a new pattern onto her display, and then she ordered the covering barrage to the new coordinates.

Sula had been inspired by the knowledge that many Fleet officers failed to fully comprehend how to employ the third dimension in maneuver—they tended to stay in the comfortable realm of two dimensions, and their maneuvers could be charted on a flat piece of paper.

Her first maneuver, then—the one she intended the enemy to see—would take Division Nine into the third dimension as it swooped in the direction of system south, as if it were planning on skipping over the enemy and racing for safety among the ships of the Combined Fleet.

The enemy, she assumed, would alter course to intercept, and so once her movements were masked, she altered course to send Division Nine north of the enemy, not south.

In the meantime, she kept hurling missiles, many taking a wide looping course around the enemy to attack them bow-on, all in hopes of convincing the enemy that she was in front of them.

She commanded an inferior number of ships with rookie crews, and her sole advantage lay in the sheer number of missiles she could fire. A battleship like Conyngham's *Perfection of the Praxis* had sixty missile launchers to the thirty of the *Obedience*-class heavy cruisers, and Sula's converted transports had been equipped with more than sixty, though with the proviso that not all of them functioned all the time. She was going to have to over-whelm the enemy with sheer firepower, and this would best be done if she didn't have to engage the entire enemy force at once. Martinez had won Second Shulduc by achieving local superiority over sections of the enemy's formation, and Sula hoped to do the same.

The enemy missiles that shot out of the fireball cloud con-firmed her guess—they were aimed at where Division Nine would have been if she hadn't made that last course change, which meant the enemy was looking for Sula in the wrong place.

And expecting fire from the wrong place too.

Suddenly Division Nine was in the clear, free of any radio clouds except those between Sula and her enemy. She could see Do-faq's main force strung out before a masking barrage, and be-yond that only hints of the Combined Fleet.

"I want sensors pointed at Do-faq's fleet," she said. "That's Jian's screen, but the enemy can use it too."

Division Nine was behind its enemies now, having launched itself into the third dimension, and was crossing their track. The enemy was invisible behind the fireball screen, but Sula had a very good idea where they were.

"Reduce acceleration to point five gees," she said. "Alter course to zero-three-zero by zero-zero-one relative."

Sula scribed lines on her display. "All ships fire into this area."

Her barrage began unfolding, some missiles boring directly for their targets, others looping to attack from unexpected angles. Sula worked for a moment to see that the Very, Very Large Squadron was covered by the defensive fire of the Heavies and the Lights. No one was shooting at them at the moment, but she knew that wouldn't last.

In the meantime, *Splendid*'s sensors were detecting missile flashes from out of the thick radio haze, as the barrage encountered countermissiles from the enemy. The fireballs were sweeping toward the enemy, and as Sula watched, two large explosions flashed out as the wave of missiles overran the enemy rear, marking ships going up along with their antimatter fuel.

"Just keep firing," she muttered. "And then fire some more."

MARTINEZ WATCHED IN something like awe as the enemy squadron evaporated in a blaze of overlapping missile strikes. One minute the enemy ships were coiling through the battlespace in the intricate motions of the Martinez Method, and then they were . . . nothing. Glowing dust on the solar wind.

It had been only minutes since Aitor Santana's voice echoed in his ears. "We've broken the pattern of one of their squadrons!" he called.

"All ships target that squadron," Martinez said. Missiles raced from their launchers, heading through the radio murk to a preprogrammed rendezvous, to a coordinate where the mathematics predicted the enemy would be found.

The target squadron was in the near-center of the enemy formation, and suddenly there was nothing there but a yawning gap. Martinez began giving orders to exploit this opportunity. Thanks to Sula's recording, the Restoration ships could ignore the enemy's decoys and concentrate entirely on their warships. Martinez could wedge their entire rear division apart, then crush the fragments piecemeal.

Elsewhere the fleets were engaged along the entire battlespace. Neither Do-faq nor Wei Jian had yet committed their reserves, but the main bodies and the van divisions were hurling matter-shattering warheads at one another with single-minded fury. In the very center, the fight between Conyngham's battleship *Perfection of the Praxis* and the enemy's two battleships was so intense with overlapping fire that it seemed as if a new star had blazed into existence in the middle of the warring fleets.

Some distance away on the flank, Sula's Division Nine was engaged with Do-faq's eighteen warships, with fireballs coming so rapidly that it was impossible to tell how either side fared.

Martinez checked his chronometer. The solar missiles were still twelve minutes out. But he had yet another surprise coming, and it would come at the enemy rear.

Days earlier, just after the Combined Fleet transitioned to the Toley system and could no longer be observed by the enemy, eight hundred missiles had been fired and directed at the wormhole leading to Colamote. The missiles accelerated to relativistic speeds, shot through the wormhole, raced past Sula's division as if it were standing still, then dashed through five star systems to Colamote, after which they passed into the Zarafan system, then through three more wormhole gates into Toley.

Because a large battle required a certain amount of cooperation from both commanders, it was possible to make certain that the Combined Fleet engaged Do-faq at a moment that would permit the eight hundred missiles to make maximum impact. Enemy sensors would be concentrated forward, on the Combined Fleet, rather than to their own rear. The radio haze of battle made detection even more difficult, and weapons officers, engaged in deadly combat with an enemy they could see before them, would be slow to react to a threat from an unanticipated direction.

And of course missiles coming at relativistic velocities would give only a few seconds' warning even to an alert target.

Martinez looked at the chronometer. *Less than two minutes.*

His mouth was dry, and he took a sip of water from his helmet dispenser. Digits flickered one by one on the chronometer. Missiles raced out from warships, were hit by counterfire, and erupted in a furious snarl of gamma rays, neutrons, and pions. Martinez was beginning to succeed in wedging the enemy rear squadrons apart. They were slow to react, possibly because they were so surprised by the sudden, sheer annihilation of one of their number.

Then the eight hundred relativistic missiles made their final correction burns and homed in on their targets.

A wall of fireballs blossomed behind Do-faq's fleet as his belated point-defense weapons fired. His reserves, still uncommitted, were the first target of the invading swarm, and Martinez saw ships blaze up in the night. Then the wall of fireballs advanced through the battlespace and began to consume the engaged ships.

The radiation counter leaped and leaped again as fireballs expanded throughout the enemy squadrons. Surviving ships scattered from the scene of destruction like wind-borne sparks blazing up from a bonfire.

Some of the missiles had been unable to acquire a target, and these raced through the Restoration ships without causing damage—the new transponder codes assured the Combined Fleet's safety. The missiles would turn around and make another pass at the enemy, but it required hours to take off all that velocity, and by that time the battle was going to be over. They had done their job, though.

Martinez looked at the squadrons opposing him and saw nothing but scattered ships flying in terror.

"Multiple messages of surrender, my lord," said Santana.

"Can you mark the surrendered ships on our displays?" Martinez said. "I don't want to waste ammunition on ships that aren't fighting us."

"I'll do it," said Paivo Kangas.

Green triangles began marking ships on Martinez's display, indicating those no longer a threat.

"Let me send this in the clear," Martinez said. "Message follows: 'This is Captain Lord Gareth Martinez. All ships wishing to surrender or to join the forces of the Restoration please clear the battle area. We'll sort you out later.' End message."

Within ten minutes he disposed of the enemy's rear division. Those still hostile were in flight. Martinez scanned the virtual battlespace in his head in search of his next target. The two fleets' main bodies still grappled with each other, ships buried in the haze of expanding fireballs.

He looked in the other direction and through the radio hash saw Sula's division still engaged with the enemy. It seemed a hard-fought action with no clear resolution in sight, and as he gazed, he saw one of Sula's giant converted transports turn into a miniature sun, and even at this distance the radiation counters maxed out. The transports were overlarge, awkward warships, but they mounted a colossal number of missile batteries, and Sula was going to miss all that firepower before the end.

He turned his attention back to the clash of the main bodies.

The enemy must have taken losses, but the battle-murk was so heavy that he couldn't judge how many had been hit. Calculations flooded his mind.

If he moved to help Sula, he would help win an action away from the main battlespace. But if he could crush Do-faq's main body, he would win the battle and the war.

And if he did attack the main body, he would have to do it quickly, before Do-faq's reserves could counter him.

He could help Sula or he could win the war. For a moment he was paralyzed, his mind whirring like a broken set of gears. Then he took a breath.

"All ships alter course to one-one-seven by zero-zero-one absolute," he said. "Increase acceleration to three gravities, on my mark."

His acceleration cage sang as it pivoted during *Los Angeles*'s course change. Red lines appeared across the virtual battle in Martinez's mind.

"Recommend course one-two-two by zero-zero-one absolute," said Paivo Kangas. "We'll strike the main body in center mass."

"Center mass is good," Martinez said. He issued the correction, and again the cage sang.

"All ships prepare for acceleration on my mark," he said. "Three, two, one, *mark.*"

Again, he felt the punch to his sternum, and the cage's song was cut off as it dropped to its dead point.

"All ships are free to engage," he said, his diaphragm and vocal cords taut against the increased gravity.

They would race behind the enemy main body, sandwiching it between themselves and the Combined Fleet, and they would be hurling missiles all along their path.

230  WALTER JON WILLIAMS

With luck, they'd avoid being trapped by the enemy reserve thundering down on them.


**RADIATION COUNTERS MAXED** as an enemy missile, dodging through defensive fire, found the converted immigration ship *Ideal*. The fireball was vast, the pulse of gamma rays and neutrons enormous. Sula's crossing the enemy's rear had destroyed four warships, but the enemy detachment had recovered from its surprise more swiftly than Sula would have liked, and now they were in pursuit of Division Nine. They were overtaking Sula as well, because the big converted transports weren't intended to accelerate at much more than a single gravity, though they could nearly double that figure at need.

It just took time. Too much time.

A vast radiation cloud hung in the space between the two forces, but at least the enemy was flying into the blinding cloud, and Sula was flying away from it.

Even with the loss of *Ideal*, Sula's ships had an advantage in numbers of missile launchers, and so she kept her ships firing, the missiles dodging and weaving to avoid counterfire. She was rewarded by an enemy ship blazing up, its fireball a cenotaph rising over the ionized remains of its crew.

Her elation was brief, because one of the light Laredo cruisers died in fire just a few moments later.

They couldn't go on exchanging ships like this, she thought. There would be nothing left.

But she couldn't think of anything to do but keep on slugging. Maneuver was impossible as long as the warships were obliged to screen the transports from the onrushing enemy. They were pinned in place.

*If we could read their Ghost Tactics patterns,* she thought, *then . . .*

But the computers told her that the probability of predicting the enemy's movements was still low.

"My lady," said Ricci, "Do-faq's rear division is coming apart."

Sula shifted her glance from one display to another that showed scans from the sensors she'd ordered trained on Do-faq's fleet, and she saw that Martinez had thoroughly shattered the enemy rear, and that the enemy's remaining ships were fleeing the battlespace as swiftly as their engines could drive them.

Relief flooded her. Martinez could come to her aid, if not with the whole Grand Division, then with a squadron or two. The survival of Division Nine would be assured and the enemy force destroyed, after which Sula and Martinez could turn and fall on the flank of the enemy main body.

But then the entire Grand Division of the Rear altered course, not toward Sula, but toward Do-faq's main body. Engine flares increased in brightness. Martinez was leaving Sula to her fate.

Outrage boiled up in her. "*That . . . arrogant . . . ballsack!*" she shouted, for once nearly at a loss for words. Ricci and Viswan turned to her in surprise.

Another enemy ship flared and died in the distant radio murk. A flight of enemy missiles came in from system south, and *Splendid* rolled to present more of its antiproton cannon. Beams sped through the darkness, and enemy missiles blew themselves to bits, the fireballs dancing closer and closer until they loomed over *Splendid* and its cohorts like a whole vast flaming world. Sula needed to buy more time for her defenses to find and target the incoming swarm.

"Heavy Squadron accelerate to eight gees for two minutes!" Sula called. "Execution immediate!"

Gravities dropped lead weights on Sula's chest. Her displays blurred before her eyes. She grunted as she fought for breath, as

*Splendid*'s old frame shivered to the sudden acceleration. Bleary brightness flashed on the displays, the missiles coming closer.

A loud, angry buzz sounded in her left ear, as if someone had switched on an electronic warning signal. Her hands hung in front of her, useless as those on a mannequin. The breath sighed out of her, and the sigh went on and on even though her lungs should have been empty by now. Blackness flooded her vision like a spreading stain. *Am I dying?* she wondered, and then her consciousness flickered, faded, and vanished like a snuffed candle flame . . .

MARTINEZ HAD FORGOTTEN about the missiles that had been hidden in the sun's glare. But now here they were, four hundred birds of prey tipped with blazing antimatter warheads, and another wall of fire was advancing through the enemy fleet.

The enemy had intercepted most of the swarm but not all, and now more ships blazed like supernovas in the firmament. The main body was hardest hit because, caught between Wei Jian's main body and Martinez's Grand Division racing across their rear, their defensive capabilities were already under severe stress.

"Squadron defecting," said Paivo Kangas. "North of the main body. Five ships."

Paivo marked the ships with green triangles as they made a mad dash for freedom. Their erstwhile comrades were so distracted that it seemed as if they'd make a clean escape, but whoever commanded the squadron had failed to consult his captains, and three ships fired upon the other two. Within seconds the squadron was obscured by overlapping fireballs. Martinez didn't know which of the ships to help or which to fire upon, so he watched the brief battle until the sole survivor spiraled out of the blaze and kept going, pulling hard gees all the way.

"Enemy reserves are coming up," Paivo said, and Martinez spun the virtual battlespace in his head, and saw the drive flares of Do-faq's reserves brighten as they accelerated toward him. Do-faq and the other Lai-own were restricted in how many gees they could suffer, but that wasn't the case with the hundreds of missiles that vaulted ahead of them.

"All ships," said Martinez, "alter course to one-four-zero by one-six-zero absolute, acceleration to commence in two minutes at 22:31:01. Accelerate at four gees on new heading."

He floated in his webbing as the engines cut and *Los Angeles* rotated onto its new course. Countermissiles began to lash out at the incoming barrage, along with antiproton beams and lasers. Bright detonations obscured the oncoming enemy ships.

Engines fired and Martinez's couch dropped to its new dead point. The new heading would take his command toward system south, out of the way of the oncoming enemy reserves, and capable of dropping on them from an unexpected direction if they maintained their present course.

It occurred to Martinez that Wei Jian, looking at the battle through the haze of expanding fireballs, might know none of this. He gasped in a breath of air. "Message to Fleet Commander Jian," he said. "Enemy reserves are now committing to reinforce their main body. I am shifting my command to system south in hopes of catching the enemy between two fires. End message."

He trusted the message, carried by powerful lasers, would be able to punch its way through the growing fireballs toward Jian. How she would respond was impossible to predict—maybe she'd send another patriotic tune.

Martinez turned his gaze from the oncoming reserves to the main body, just in time to see a part of the enemy formation come to pieces. Because he'd been subjected to it himself, he understood all too well the enemy's confused, belated, and altogether hopeless response, and he knew that Severin had employed his patchwork-quilt tactics and wrong-footed a whole division of the enemy.

He sent a message to Chandra Prasad. "Nikki's cracked open their main body. Help knock out his victims before they can get organized again."

Chandra didn't bother to formally reply, but her acknowledgment soon came in the form of a storm of missiles launched against the disorganized enemy. Martinez kept the rest of his Grand Division focused on defending against the barrage swooping in from the enemy reserves.

"As far as we can tell," Paivo said, "since Do-faq entered To-ley, we've whittled the enemy reserves down by nearly half." He sipped in air. "Some are decoys, so it's difficult to be certain, but it looks as if Do-faq's reserves have fewer than thirty warships remaining."

Fewer than thirty—Martinez could engage the enemy reserves on slightly better than equal terms.

"We'll have to keep whittling," Martinez said.

"Oh—and another seven ships from the main body are trying to surrender."

Martinez searched the confused battlescape and failed to find the seven ships. "Are they trying to run away, or—?"

"Six now," Paivo said. He gasped in air. "I think it was one of our missiles, not theirs. They're heading toward system north and trying to make their escape from the enemy reserves . . ." He gasped again. ". . . I don't think anyone's in a position to stop them."

The Grand Division of the Rear had driven far enough south to have escaped being trapped between the enemy reserves and what remained of their main body, and Martinez ordered his ships to turn around, with a deceleration of two gees, to keep too great a gap from developing between his own divisions and the Restoration's main body.

"Message from Fleet Commander Jian," said Santana. "Deciphering now."

Perfectly composed as always, her serene face revealed through the faceplate of her helmet, Wei Jian's image appeared in the virtual battlespace in Martinez's skull, appeared floating in a window above the battle, like a goddess contemplating creation.

"I am committing the Grand Division of the Reserve," she said. "Two squadrons will go to the aid of Lady Sula. The rest will reinforce the Grand Division of the Main Body by entering the battle to the north of that division. End message."

Messages of surrender were now coming from individual ships in the enemy main body. The rest were being annihilated.

With the enemy main body on the point of disintegration, there was little to stop the Restoration forces from creating a pocket in which to draw the enemy reserve force. Farhang's main body would hold the center, and Martinez and Jian, on the flanks, would be in a position to surround Do-faq. Do-faq's reserve, Martinez thought, wouldn't last long.

Only in the van, where Michi Chen and her opposite number confronted each other, raged a battle of near-equals.

Martinez watched as a furious line of fireballs came closer, moving with a speed both alarming and breathtaking. His heart lurched to an onslaught of adrenaline. Martinez could smell his own sour sweat inside his helmet.

Antimissile launches were continuous. The fireballs came closer, so close that Martinez winced with each explosion, and then the fireballs' momentum failed, exploding at a safe distance. The veteran weapons officers in Martinez's command had succeeded in fending off Do-faq's attack—the attack with the greatest chance of success, for the missiles had been launched in a great wave by officers who weren't distracted by enemy fire.

"All ships," Martinez said, "concentrate fire on enemy reserves."

Missiles raced away, burning into the murky no-man's-land between the rival fleets. A drumbeat of explosions throbbed in the radio haze, the wall of fire now advancing toward Do-faq. He had been caught between two fires, between the Grand Divisions of the Rear and the Main Body.

And soon a third fire entered, as Wei Jian's Grand Division of the Reserve appeared on the far side of the main body and launched a massive barrage from yet a third direction. A squadron of seven ships broke away from the enemy's reserves and began broadcasting a message of surrender. No missiles pursued.

"Message, my lord!" Banerjee's cry shimmered with delight. "Message from *Do-faq*!"

Do-faq materialized in Martinez's virtual battlespace, occupying the same window where Wei Jian had appeared. He wore a vac suit and helmet, with the faceplate up to reveal his muzzle, the lips peeled back to reveal peg teeth, and his golden eyes clouded by his nictating membranes. He looked half-dead, but when he spoke his voice was forceful.

"To Fleet Commander Jian and her crews," he said. "I wish to state that the battle has now reached a point where further combat will lead only to pointless loss of life without any chance of altering the outcome. I wish therefore to surrender the remains of the United Fleet. I hereby instruct my captains to fire only in self-defense, and to forego any offensive actions. I trust that Lady Wei Jian's offer of honorable and decent treatment is sincere, and I await her instructions. End message."

Whoops and cheers rang from the walls of the flag officer's station, but Martinez was busy sending his own message to his ships.

"All ships cease offensive fire, but defend yourself to the utmost. We're not quite at the end, so save the celebration until it's all over."

Then he lay back on his acceleration couch and tried to let the tension fade from his muscles. The war, he judged, was over.

SHE WOKE IN weightlessness. Viswan floated over her, holding her gloved hand, and Ricci was also there, one hand hanging onto Sula's acceleration cage, the other holding a hand comm from which he was reading. They swam in and out of focus.

Sula tried to speak, failed, then licked her lips and tried harder. "What . . . happened?" she managed.

"You were unconscious," Viswan said. Her large brown eyes gazed at Sula with concern. "Dr. Gunaydin and a stretcher party are on their way."

"Blood pressure's low, but within normal parameters." Ricci read from his hand comm, and Sula saw that it was cabled to the biomonitor on her suit. He turned to her. "You bounced back, my lady."

Sula slowly processed what had happened, and then she gave a start that sent her careening around within her webbing.

"We're not accelerating!" she said. "The engines have tripped!"

Viswan looked at her. Her voice was all concern. "We'll restart the engines once we get you to sick bay."

Crew suffering a stroke, cardiac arrest, or other life-threatening condition could trigger an engine shutdown. During combat the shutdown would be triggered only by a threat to senior officers, with ordinary crew left to live or die on their own.

"No!" Sula cried. "We're a sitting target now—we can't maneuver! Get back to your stations, and tell Gunaydin and the stretcher party to prepare for high gee!"

"My lady—" said Viswan.

"*Now!* I'm fine! Get moving! Missiles are on their way!"

"Those missiles were destroyed," Ricci said.

"*There are more missiles where those came from!* Get to your seats!"

Ricci looked at his hand comm again and gave Viswan a hopeless look. "Vital signs are nominal," he conceded.

Viswan sighed and pushed off for her acceleration cage. Ricci disconnected his hand comm from Sula's biomonitor, swung around Sula's acceleration cage, and pushed off toward his station.

Sula had already forgotten him and was absorbed in her displays. *Splendid* was currently drifting through a large, expanding, cooling bubble of radio noise, the remains of fireballs from destroyed incoming missiles. Sensors revealed the rest of Division Nine accelerating away, firing missiles that curled around *Splendid* before arrowing toward their targets.

*Splendid* was also firing, aiming into a patch of radio murk that was blazing hot, doubtless where the enemy force was lurking.

The door opened and Dr. Gunaydin floated in, saw Sula, then kicked out toward her. He caught her cage, and she and the cage swung as it absorbed his momentum.

"Doctor," Sula said. "Get to a couch. We're about to start acceleration again."

Gunaydin's face was stern. "My lady," he said. "That's impossible."

"It's very possible," Sula said. "I'm fine, and I need to get this ship out of danger."

"My lady," said Gunaydin. "*Your heart stopped.* Your blood pressure crashed, and you were unconscious for . . ."

"Twenty seconds to engine start," reported Ricci.

"I'm conscious now," Sula said, and pointed toward the acceleration couch where the tactical officer would normally sit. "If you don't want to be flattened like a pancake, you'd better take that chair. You can monitor me from there."

Gunaydin gave her another stern look, but Sula glared him into submission, and he threw himself nimbly toward the vacant couch, leaving Sula's cage tumbling behind him.

*A good dancer,* Sula remembered.

She had passed out in combat twice before, first as a pinnace pilot at the Battle of Magaria. Nothing had come of that episode, and no one else had ever found out about it. The second time she'd crashed was at the Battle of Naxas. Except that had been caused by high blood pressure, not low, and she awoke with a nosebleed pumping weightless scarlet drops into the room.

She felt an alteration in her perceptions. She was light-headed, and her vision was slightly distorted, as if viewed through a warped crystal. Her displays seemed to lean toward her, and they pulsed in an aggressive, menacing way.

The engines fired, and Captain Mazankosi built velocity slowly, slowly enough that Sula got impatient for the gees to start building. She ordered the rest of the Heavy Squadron to cut acceleration and wait for her. Enemy missiles dashed out of the radio cloud, then were tracked and destroyed—but, as she'd said herself, there were plenty of missiles where those came from.

No shame in calling for help, she decided.

"Message to Fleet Commander Jian," she said, and then remembered she wasn't wearing a helmet, and added, "Voice only, no video. Message begins: 'Lady Wei, Division Nine is closely engaged with the enemy as per your wishes. We caught them by surprise at first and destroyed four ships, but they've started their counterattack, and now we're trading kills back and forth. If you could send us a squadron I could guarantee victory here, after which I could take the rest of the enemy in flank. If you sent two squadrons I could do it all faster.' End message."

Sula was gasping for breath by the end of her report. Her distorted vision was making her inner ear swim. Gravities were building fast, and soon *Splendid* would be among the rest of the Heavy Squadron.

Her arrival wasn't as welcoming as she would have liked. A flight of missiles poured in from an unexpected direction, and the Heavy Division's antiproton beams lashed out at the dodging, corkscrewing targets. Antimissiles were launched, and antimatter erupted into bright new stars.

One enemy missile, jinking and whirling, penetrated the defensive screen, and one of the Heavy Squadron's cruisers flashed into angry, snarling, deadly light.

"Message from Fleet Commander Jian," Viswan said. "Message reads: 'Stand by.'"

*Stand by?* Sula thought. What the hell did *that* mean? Did it mean 'Fight it out yourself'? Or 'Help is on the way'? Or 'I'm thinking about important things, don't bother me'?

Still, it meant she couldn't depend on help arriving, so Sula looked at the displays and tried to rethink her position.

Missiles were still flying off the rails and diving into the murk, and presumably there were enemy ships somewhere in the radio clouds. Both sides were firing completely blind.

But that meant that Division Nine wasn't using one of its advantages, the Shankaracharya sensor suites. They should provide a superior view into the overlapping fireballs, but right now the radio fog was so thick that neither side could see through it.

"All ships," Sula ordered. "Cease all offensive action. Missiles are to be used only for countermissile fire. You may fire at enemy ships, but only if you *detect* them. Then shoot your barrage, and immediately fire a covering barrage so they won't see *you*."

Missile launches declined as captains and weapons officers worked out what all that meant in practice. Division Nine drew farther away from the overlapping haze of fireballs and developed a clearer view of the battlespace. Missiles continued to fly out of the cloud, but were destroyed by weapons officers undistracted by any attempt to hit the enemy.

The first view of enemy ships came not from any of the warships, but from a pinnace that had been fired far from the action. Its single cadet had been soaring weightless in a remote corner of the battlespace, her sensors trained on the enemy, she saw three drive signatures appear through the radio haze.

The pinnace pilot didn't even have the Shankaracharya sensors, Sula knew. She just happened to be in the right place at the right time.

Sula's eleven remaining warships fired over sixty missiles at the three targets, then spread more missiles out as a screen.

Before the screening missiles detonated, multiple Shankaracharya sensors detected four drive signatures emerging from the radio haze. Another sixty missiles were launched, and drove at the enemy through the fireball screen that had just splashed across the sensor battlespace.

Sula's first launch resulted in three hits, though—from the size of the secondary explosions—two hits were made on decoys, and only the third on a warship. The second wave, emerging from the wall of fire, made a single hit, the target's erupting fuel causing the radiation counters to tick over.

*This is better*, Sula thought. She scanned the displays for any more emerging enemies.

But then the big converted cargo ship *Lentrec* blew up, and Sula's heart gave a wild leap as she goggled at the displays in utter surprise. No enemy missile had been detected anywhere near the giant ship, and Sula wondered if the enemy had looped some missiles in from a completely unexpected direction, and if more of her ships were about to erupt in antimatter fire.

There were no more missile strikes. Sula considered the possibility that *Lentrec* had destroyed itself in some kind of monumental accident—with inexperienced crews and jury-rigged missile launchers, there was always that possibility.

However *Lentrec* had met its end, Division Nine had lost much of its firepower. Even so, Sula almost found herself hoping that *Pride of Parkhurst* would be next. Once free of the obligation to defend the converted transports, Sula could initiate a battle of maneuver that would give her a better chance of fighting the enemy.

"Message from Captain Hui of Light Squadron Four," Ricci said. "Deciphering now."

Within seconds Hui's face appeared on Sula's display. "Lady Sula," she said. "Light Squadrons Four and Seven have been detailed to your assistance. Please let us know how you wish us to proceed."

*About time.* Sula drew more lines on her displays, and split her reinforcements to take position on either end of the enemy formation, subjecting the enemy to envelopment.

What Sula needed now was to concentrate on staying alive until the reinforcements arrived. She told Division Nine that two squadrons were being sent to their assistance and to concentrate on defending themselves. "Take shots only when you have a good chance of hitting," she said. "Concentrate your offensive efforts at maintaining a screen."

Even with efforts concentrated almost entirely on defense, Division Nine succeeded in killing one more enemy warship before Hui and the reinforcements arrived. Hundreds of missiles began launching at the enemy from multiple directions, and as soon as they were under way Sula received word of Do-faq's surrender.

"Cease offensive action," Sula said. "Concentrate on defense until we can discover whether the enemy will obey Do-faq's instructions."

The missiles already launched scored hit after hit, and in the end only three enemy warships survived to surrender to Division Nine. Following Wei Jian's instructions, the surrendered warships unloaded their missile batteries in the direction of nothing at all, and as the missiles detonated in the far distance, they created a wall separating one part of nothing from another.

"Command and weapons systems should remain on heightened alert," Sula broadcast. "Other divisions may relax their alert status. Recall all pinnaces. Crews should be relieved in shifts in order to take meals and have some time to relax."

Having said this, she decided to follow her own advice. She unwebbed, unlocked the displays and pushed them out of her way, tilted her couch forward, and put her booted feet on the floor. She turned to Viswan and Ricci.

"I'll have some drinks and sandwiches sent up," she said. "If the message traffic isn't too heavy, you can stand down in shifts." She used the struts of the cage to help herself to her feet.

"Lady Sula," said Dr. Gunaydin. "I'll need you to go with me to sick bay. I must examine you."

"I'm going to take a shower first," Sula said. "And then I'll join you in sick bay."

"I think—"

"I think I need a shower, Doctor." Firmly. "I'll see you soon."

Sula retrieved her helmet from the net bag and marched to the door just as Captain Mazankosi announced the ship's relaxed alert status.

Securing from quarters meant the ship's elevators were unlocked, and so Sula didn't have to take the stairs to her suite. Her perceptions were still distorted, and the elevator walls leaned toward her in a vaguely menacing way. Once in her brightly painted suite she battled her way out of her vac suit, dumped it on the floor, and headed for the shower. The shower head loomed at her like a long-necked monster. She looked at something else and triggered the water.

When she had fallen into unconsciousness during the Battle of Naxas, she'd succeeded in covering it up simply by removing all mention from her ship's log, then adding a brief note that the engine trip had been caused by a power spike in a transformer overloaded by the radiation of a near miss.

Sula couldn't do that here, because Gunaydin was a witness. He wasn't a line officer and therefore wasn't in her chain of command—he reported to a separate authority. He had no reason to keep silent about Sula's collapse in the middle of a battle, and every reason to do his duty and report it.

She'd just have to pass any physical exam with the best score in history. Perhaps no one would pay any attention to Gunaydin's report. It would be buried in other reports from the battle, and by the time it cycled up his chain of command to his distant superior on Harzapid or even Zanshaa, her few seconds of unconsciousness might have dwindled into insignificance.

Sula rewarded herself with a long, thorough shower, pounding hot water breaking the tension in her muscles, and emerged from the shower cabinet wafting the aroma of vanilla-scented soap. She donned a fresh, clean Fleet-issue jumpsuit, checked the sleeve display for messages, and replied to those in need of an answer. She remembered to call the kitchens and have food sent to the flag officer's station.

Then she picked up the sweat-soaked clothing she'd worn in the battle and pushed it through the hatch intended for laundry, after which she retrieved her vac suit from the floor and hung it in its locker. Spence or Macnamara could swab it with disinfectant later.

She looked over her suite for something else to do, and then realized that the impulse to linger in her suite had to do with her indecision concerning whether or not to indulge in a recent habit.

She decided.

Sula went to the pantry, unlocked the liquor cabinet, and poured herself a shot of brandy. She drank it, then drank a second. And then, because she didn't want to go into a medical examination exhaling alcohol fumes, she drank a shot of mint-flavored liqueur, and hoped she could pass off the scent as mouthwash.

She finally reported to the sick bay, where a number of crew were being treated for bruises and sprains they'd received while in high gee. She was shown to the officers' section, then she waited amid the scent of disinfectant for Gunaydin to arrive. He had her lie on a bed that tracked most of her vital signs and deployed detectors to track the rest.

"Your brain is unimpaired, Lady Sula," he said. "No stroke, no hemorrhage. Your heart and respiration are nominal, and your nervous system is functioning normally. Your moment of incapacity has no obvious explanation—I would like to investigate further, but for now I will release you to duty."

"Thank you, Doctor," Sula said, and as she sat up she felt the brandy swirling in her head and took a breath. Gunaydin frowned and looked at her.

"Have you been drinking alcohol?" he asked.

"Celebration," she said. "Perhaps premature."

"That sort of celebration is best reserved for the time *following* a medical examination," he said. "The alcohol could have skewed any number of tests."

"Sorry," Sula said. "Shan't do it again."

He was about to say something, but she held her finger up, stalling him, when her sleeve display chirped at her, with a message from Wei Jian.

"From Toley," Jian said, "we will shape our course directly to Zanshaa. The Fleet Train will resupply us with missiles en route. Badly damaged ships will return to Harzapid for repairs. Ships able to repair without a dockyard will join us on our advance to the capital. If they are not too damaged, captured and defecting ships will be added to our numbers. I will give some hours for initial repairs to be completed, after which I will call for high-gravity accelerations to get us to Zanshaa as fast as possible. End message."

Another uninspiring recitation from Wei Jian, Sula thought. Not a word of praise or congratulations, no moment of reverence and sorrow for those friends who had been killed, only the next set of orders, delivered like the last in her precise schoolteacher's voice.

But, Sula thought, if Wei Jian wasn't going to offer praise or congratulations, that didn't mean that Sula couldn't. She'd praise Division Nine till the heavens rang, and include Captain Hui's two squadrons as well.

She'd send the message from her office, she thought. And on the way she made another stop at the liquor cabinet for a shot of brandy, and decided to bring the bottle along with her.

IT TOOK TIME for the battle to wind down. Missiles were already in flight, and these had to either be destroyed or called off before the opposing ships flew out of the zone of expanding and cooling fireballs and into clear space, where they could get a good look at one another. Wei Jian ordered all surrendered ships to fire their entire missile supply into empty space, instructed them to report their names, designations, captains, and status, and then told them to ready themselves to be boarded.

Shuttles were crewed. Boarding parties went out, composed mostly of weaponers and propulsion specialists, along with a few officers to make sure that Wei Jian's commands were followed. *Los Angeles* lost two lieutenants and sixteen crew to help captured ships.

Wei Jian sent a shuttle to bring Do-faq off his ship to her own flagship, the *Crisis*. There he would be treated as an honored guest, and gently debriefed, after which he would be transferred to a ship in the Fleet Train for the return journey to Harzapid.

Do-faq might be executed eventually, depending on how much the Restoration government wanted vengeance for Nguyen's ten thousand Terran dead. Martinez was still surprised that Do-faq had actually surrendered rather than going down, like his predecessors, in a blaze of antimatter fire. He would be adjudged a traitor by the government he'd sought to defend, and for their own part, the Restoration was unlikely to view him with anything like charity.

Martinez allowed a warm, quiet celebration to throb through his veins. He had done what he'd set out to do. With the Fourth Fleet he'd created a machine for winning battles and destroying the enemy, and when Wei Jian had taken command, she'd had the good sense to employ the machine as designed.

Figures were totted up. After enduring the relentless ambushes on the route from Zarafan, Do-faq had entered the Toley system with 195 ships, then immediately lost 42 to Martinez's massive missile strike. By the time Do-faq conceded the fight, he had only 63 ships left in his command, and half of those had already defected or surrendered. Nine were so badly damaged they had to be destroyed after what remained of the crew were taken off, and two dozen had suffered major damage.

Counting Division Nine, the Restoration had come into the fight with 163 warships. Fifty-four had been lost, the largest percentage of which belonged to Michi Chen's Grand Division of the Van, which had fought the enemy van on equal terms. Thirty-one Restoration ships had suffered damage, and of those eleven would need an extended stay in a shipyard.

High-ranking officers had paid the cost of victory with their lives. Farhang, the commander of the Grand Division of the Main Body, had died with his ship in the final moments of the fighting. Squadron Commander An-dar, the Lai-own who had defected with his whole command at Second Shulduc, had been blown to bits along with his flagship. And Conyngham, the white-haired captain of the battleship *Perfection of the Praxis*—he who had commanded a heroic defense at Second Shulduc and again at Toley—had died of a cerebral hemorrhage in the midst of combat.

His ship, however, had survived, while both Do-faq's battleships had been destroyed in the general massacre that had overtaken the enemy main body.

The Fleet of the Restoration had not only triumphed, but survived as a fighting force. Nothing would stop them now from advancing on Zanshaa.

**TWO DAYS AFTER** the battle, Sula received a message in text from Wei Jian.

*Lady Sula*, it said, *a report has reached me of your incapacity in the recent battle. Until the cause of your impairment can be determined and treated, I regretfully conclude that you are no longer fit to command a warship. You are hereby appointed captain of the Pride of Parkhurst, and will follow the Combined Fleet to Zanshaa, where you may receive medical treatment.*

Somehow she was not surprised.

# CHAPTER 8

Lord Pa Do-faq did not seem in the best of spirits. He slumped in the place of honor in Wei Jian's dining room, his tunic rumpled, his golden eyes half-shuttered by nictating membranes. Despite being presented with delicacies catering to the Lai-own palate he had little appetite, and he nibbled absently on intoxicating thu-thu pastilles without showing any signs of intoxication.

Perhaps, Martinez thought, he was regretting not having shot himself after surrendering, as had a number of his officers. Certainly he didn't have a lot to live for.

His doleful air contrasted with that of the officers of the Combined Fleet, who laughed, spoke loudly, made jokes, offered toasts to one another, and ignored their guest.

Martinez didn't speak to Do-faq. He had been placed too far down the table, and he didn't know what he'd say anyway. And Do-faq offered him no attention except when he had to, to stand in the presence of the Golden Orb when Martinez carried it into the room.

Martinez was happy when the dinner was over, and he could pick up his Orb and shuttle back to the *Los Angeles*. He was walking to the airlock when he heard heels rapping on the flooring, and he turned to see Chandra Prasad approaching.

"Gareth!" she said. "I've got some good news."

"More good news? Let's hear it."

She took his arm and steered him in the direction of the airlock. "Remember when we were retreating from Zarafan, and I had the idea of firing a couple hundred missiles at Do-faq's fleet when he was coming into the Zanshaa system? You told me to go ahead, but we never found out what happened?"

"Of course."

Chandra was practically skipping by Martinez's side. She held up a fist. "Twenty-eight ships destroyed! And eight damaged, with three having had to go into dock."

Martinez looked at her in surprise. "Congratulations!" he said. "How did you find out?"

"One of my lieutenants is now captain of a captured ship. He's been going through the records, trying to work out how many warships remain in the enemy fleet, and he found a report on what was reported as 'the treacherous rebel assault on the Third Fleet.'"

"Do-faq should have realized it was a preview of things to come."

"I'm glad he didn't," she grinned.

They approached the airlock's lobby and found it crowded with officers waiting for their shuttles. They halted, and Chandra's fingers dug into Martinez's biceps. "Think how more difficult it would have been to face twenty-eight more enemy ships in the battle."

Martinez frowned. "They replaced those losses, though. Where did the extra ships come from?"

"New ships built across the empire. Their shipbuilding capacity was larger than we thought."

"So how many ships can we expect to face at Zanshaa?"

"About forty. The officers will be experienced, but many of the enlisted will be new to the service."

"We'll have over a hundred. And we're all veterans now."

She gave Martinez a satisfied, catlike smile. "We are." Her smile disappeared, and her eyes widened. "I was so intent on congratulating myself I forgot about my other news. Have you heard about Lady Sula?"

The mention of Sula's name still had enough power to slam Martinez's heart against his ribs.

"Ah," he said. "I haven't heard anything."

"Jian's removed her from command of Division Nine. She's been reassigned to command the *Pride of Parkhurst*."

Outrage shot like plasma fire through Martinez's veins. "*What?*" he said. "For what possible—?"

"The rumor is that it's medical," Chandra said.

Concern tempered his outrage, along with annoyance at the way his emotions were tossing him around like a figure stuffed with straw.

"Was she injured in the battle?" he asked.

"*Splendid* wasn't hit," Chandra said. "But I suppose there could have been an accident."

"Or Jian wanted her out for some reason." He murmured the words, careful not to be overheard by one of Jian's clique.

"Could be."

*Pride of Parkhurst* belonged to his family, Martinez thought. He could shuttle there in order to conduct an inspection of his property, and make sure Sula was all right at the same time. And then the scheme came to a lurching halt.

What was he thinking? She might refuse to see him, and even though his impulse had been to rush to her side, he knew that it would be a very unwise thing to do.

He wanted answers first.

He saw that Chandra was observing him with care, concern

showing in her long dark eyes. Like the entire Fourth Fleet, she knew about his affair with Sula, and like the entire Fourth Fleet doubtless wondered what had caused their split. She had known him a long time and might make a shrewd guess as to his divided feelings. He spoke carefully.

"Nothing to be done, I suppose," he said. "But Jian's making a mistake, considering how effective a commander Sula has proven herself to be. And she's made a bigger mistake if she thinks that Lady Sula is going to forget this. She's a member of the Convocation, and she might be in a position to put a spike in Jian's projects."

"If she does, I'll be cheering from the sidelines," Chandra said.

*Me too*, he thought.

SULA GAVE A farewell address to Division Nine and told them how brave and brilliant they were, and how proud she was to have led them into battle. The words were conventional, but the feelings behind them perfectly genuine. In spite of the inexperience of so many of the crews, Division Nine had done well against veteran opposition, and they had earned Sula's admiration.

For the losses the division had suffered, Sula blamed Wei Jian for demanding an engagement, and Martinez for not sending aid, and instead going for glory and the credit for delivering the decisive stroke against the enemy.

*To hell with them both*, Sula thought.

Sula gave a farewell dinner to the surviving captains of Division Nine and was pleased that they were furious on her behalf. She had fought hard and won, and was now to be replaced by one of Wei Jian's staff officers who had never commanded anything larger than a frigate, and that in peacetime. The other captains found her supersession outrageous.

Captain Mazankosi offered to let Sula use her hunting lodge in the To-bai-to Highlands once she arrived on Zanshaa.

Sula thanked her, but rather thought she'd be doing her hunting elsewhere.

SULA VIEWED *PRIDE of Parkhurst* from over the rim of a cocktail glass. She had come aboard with Macnamara and Spence, her communications specialists Ricci and Viswan, her cook, and the engineer she'd brought aboard as one of the four orderlies she was allowed, but who she'd promptly loaned to *Splendid*'s engineering staff. Now the man toiled in *Parkhurst*'s engine bays.

The Combined Fleet began their heavy decelerations and outpaced *Pride of Parkhurst*, which was following at a prudent 1.2 gee, calculated not to overstress the vast ship's frame. Sula would arrive at Zanshaa weeks behind the warships.

Sula had very little to do, because *Parkhurst* already had a captain named Devindar Suri, who had commanded the ship on behalf of the Martinez family before being co-opted into the military. He seemed an intelligent and efficient officer and knew the ship much better than Sula did, so Sula adopted an attitude of noblesse oblige, and other than conducting a few inspections let Suri run things.

She did usurp his quarters, however, a luxurious suite intended for a rich passenger. Suri then took the first lieutenant's quarters, and the first lieutenant that of the second lieutenant, and so on down the line.

Dr. Gunaydin had also been ordered to shift to *Parkhurst*, which had surprised him and Sula both. The Combined Fleet had no shortage of doctors, and someone had decided that, since *Parkhurst* was being left behind, it should have a physician of its own, so Gunaydin shuttled to the big transport, and Sula's replacement brought his own physician with him.

Sula sat with Gunaydin on the promenade overlooking the ship's huge concourse. Below, she saw uniformed Fleet crew strolling or sitting in the concourse—many fewer than the disorderly mob that had thronged the deck when *Parkhurst* first set out, for most of that mob had been transferred to other ships. Those who remained had very little work now that the battle had been won, and so they spent their time in pleasant relaxation. Very much like Sula, in fact.

She sipped her cocktail—grain alcohol, citrus, and some indefinable herbal scent—and she looked at Gunaydin and wondered if he had been sent as a spy, with orders to keep her under observation and confine her to a health ward if possible.

She was inclined to think Wei Jian was too straightforward to come up with such a plot, but Jian had people on her staff, more devious perhaps, who might think it was in their own best interests to knock down Jian's rivals.

Gunaydin touched his mustache. "I've reviewed all the data concerning your episode, and I'm inclined to look more closely at the vagus nerve. The vagus affects the parasympathetic control of a goodly number of your organs—your heart, lungs, blood pressure, speech, stomach, degree of sweating, and even your transverse colon. It's been known to be responsible for vasovagal syncope— that's fainting due to a drop in cardiac output and blood pressure, and it's believed to be caused by emotional stress—and I doubt there's anything more stressful than combat."

*Combat stress plus every other damn emotion in the book*, Sula thought. "It's only happened the one time," she said. "What if it never happens again?"

"Then you're lucky."

"Can you certify me fit for combat?" Sula asked.

Gunaydin hesitated. "Not yet," he said. "Best to be cautious."

"Are there any more tests you can do?"

Since their transfer to *Parkhurst*, Sula had survived a whole battery of tests that had failed to detect anything wrong with her.

"Tests?" Gunaydin said. "There's nothing new I can do here, but I can refer you to a specialist once we return to Zanshaa."

Sula took another sip of her cocktail. "Nothing to do but enjoy ourselves, then."

Wei Jian had made herself invincible with her victory at Toley, even if all the planning and preparation had been done by others.

But invincible, Sula thought, only in the military sphere. Now that the battle had been won, other spheres might start to become important again.

*Maybe*, she thought, *I should change my uniform.*


**THE NEXT DAY** she changed into the wine-red jacket that marked her as a member of the Convocation, the empire's highest legislative body. She'd had the jacket cut like a military tunic, and wore her medals, shoulder boards, and the disk of the Golden Orb around her throat. From the communications center aboard *Parkhurst*, she sent a message in the clear to the entire Combined Fleet.

"I am Captain the Lady Sula. As a member of the Convocation, I wish to make myself available to anyone dealing with, or anticipating, civil or political issues. Anyone with problems, or ideas for solutions, should feel free to contact me."

*And now*, she thought, *for the caveat.*

"I should make it clear that if your issue concerns the military, solutions should be sought through proper military channels, and not through me. If your issue isn't to do with the military, I will look forward to any communication."

She had tried to make it clear that she wasn't challenging Wei Jian in her own sphere—though, in fact, that's exactly what she was doing, bypassing Jian's supreme position in the Fleet by shifting her ground to the political arena. Whatever Jian's merits, Sula thought, no one could claim she was a born politician.

Though Jian proved politician enough to recognize the threat. A response came within the hour, and Sula found herself staring into Wei Jian's emotionless face and unblinking gaze.

"Lady Sula," she said, "you have not asked or received permission to engage in political activity within the Combined Fleet—and indeed I forbid any such activity from this moment. You are aboard *Pride of Parkhurst* in order to recover your health, and for no other reason."

Sula saw that little familiar flicker behind Jian's eyes as she shifted from one topic to another. "I see that you are wearing the disk of the Golden Orb. As this decoration was not authorized by the appropriate authorities, I insist that you remove it. End message."

Sula smiled as the orange end-stamp filled the screen. Jian had responded exactly as she had hoped.

She sent for tea while contemplating her reply. *Parkhurst*'s communication center was enormous, built to provide service to the thousands of immigrants the ship carried to newly settled worlds, and there were several rows of matte-black consoles spotted with silent screens, with only a few of them occupied by Fleet signals techs. The comm center was lightly used even though *Parkhurst* had a large crew, as they were cut off from most of the empire and were unable to communicate with their friends and families—and of course any communications were subject to military censorship, which put a damper on things.

Sula was tempted to send her reply in the clear, but decided that would be too great a provocation and sent it instead using the command cipher, which meant it could be read only by Wei Jian, commanders of the four Grand Divisions, and their signals crews—and the signals techs, Sula knew, often collected interesting signals and shared them among their friends and one another. It was illegal, and the penalties were ferocious, particularly if the messages were classified as Highly Sequestered, but it was done anyway, and largely accepted.

Sula waited for her tea to arrive, then poured in a long stream of honey. She inhaled the sweet floral aroma, then sipped and felt a rising sense of well-being. When she recorded her message, she tried to match Jian in her unblinking gaze and expressionless face, though she knew she couldn't equal Jian's careful schoolteacher enunciation.

"Lady Wei," she said, "I am a member of the empire's supreme body, and so far as I know, I am the only convocate in the Combined Fleet. It is both my duty and my privilege to engage in political activity, and I will do so whenever I see fit. I have already stated that I will not intervene in military affairs, but will confine my activities to their proper sphere. When we arrive in Zanshaa, we will be facing many political challenges, and it is best to be prepared."

She allowed a touch of amusement to show at the corners of her mouth. "As for my Golden Orb," she said, "I'm sure you are aware that this award is granted not by the Fleet but by the civilian government. My Orb was awarded me by the government of the Restoration on Harzapid, and if I removed it, I would subject the Restoration to a grave insult.

"The Praxis states," she continued, "that we owe our firm and undivided allegiance to our civilian government. We of the Combined Fleet are obliged to consider the Restoration the legitimate government of the empire, and to follow their instructions insofar as they are consistent with the Praxis. If we disregard our government and the Praxis, we proclaim ourselves no better than pirates or bandits out only for our own benefit, and I reject that description utterly. End message."

After the message was sent, the signals techs in the room burst into applause. Sula grinned and waved her teacup in acknowledgment, then sipped while awaiting a reply. As no reply came, she rose from her chair and joined Lord Nishkad in the owner's suite, where he offered her a very fine dinner.

TERZA'S SERENE, LOVELY face was framed perfectly by the combination of a high-collared black velvet gown and the large chignon into which she'd pinned her long black hair. Gloves secured by silver buttons reached nearly to her elbows, and she wore a belt of silver links low on her hips. Martinez had to take a breath when he saw her, and a ghost of her vetiver perfume drifted through his senses.

"I'm dressed for tonight's victory ball," Terza said, "for which we may thank you more than anyone. I wish you could attend, but there will be more victory balls once we reach Zanshaa."

She stepped closer to the camera so that she could address him more directly. Her dark eyes gazed directly into his. "The Restoration government will be departing in a few days on the *Corona*," she said. "Since so much of the original crew has been dispersed into the Fleet, we'll be crewed by newly made Fleet officers and crew, and carrying out a hundred or so replacements fresh from the training schools. We'll be escorted by a new frigate built in the yards on Earth, so if the enemy tries again to sneak in some new-built ships from Antopone, we'll have some protection.

"At the same time, Walpurga, Girasole, and Mei-mei will be heading to Zanshaa on the *Ensenada,* so in three months or so our family will be reunited in our house in the High City."

She gave one of her poised, unruffled smiles. "I'll be looking forward," she said, "and I'll make sure to save you a dance at the ball. End message."

The orange end-stamp filled the screen, and Martinez leaned back in his office chair. With a wave of his hand, he turned off the display and stared at the sea creatures painted on his office walls. His bones ached for a reunion with his son and daughter, and now he would have to wait another three months.

At least, he thought, he'd made sure his family was out of danger. Even when his sole command consisted of the unarmed yacht carrier *Corona,* he'd managed to destroy an enemy cruiser in defense of his son. The Fourth Fleet and the Combined Fleet had stood like a wall between his family and the enemy, and in the end the wall had prevailed.

Now his task was to make sure Zanshaa was safe for his family by the time they arrived.

THANKS TO A combination of alcohol and derivoo, Sula's night had been free of nightmare, and now that she was awake and freshly showered, she felt only lightly impaired as Shawna Spence brought her pastry and fragrant tea.

"Get a cup and join me," Sula said.

Spence fetched a cup from the pantry, sat, and pushed her straw-colored hair out of her eyes.

"So you got downgraded by another superior," Spence said.

Sula laughed. "My next command will probably be a pinnace."

Spence poured tea. "You destroyed five warships with a pinnace once."

Sula was struck by Spence's bringing up that bit of her history, when she hadn't drawn the connection herself.

"Yes," she said. "I did. I hope Wei Jian remembers that before she thinks to downgrade me again."

"I heard you put her in her place."

Sula shrugged. "She won't stay there for long."

Spence held her teacup in both hands and brought it to her lips. She and Sula gazed at nothing for a while, and then Spence put her cup on the table with an emphatic gesture that suggested that her mind was made up.

"What is it?" Sula asked.

"Hm?" Spence seemed genuinely surprised. "I didn't say anything."

"You looked as if you'd made a decision."

"No. No decision at all."

Sula smiled. "We're in a low-pressure environment. No decisions necessary."

Spence looked at her. "You think the war is over?"

"The *fighting* is," Sula said, "unless a few ships try to hold out in some corner of the empire—and if that happens, we'll vaporize them." She looked down at her pastry. "But the *war*—the war will continue, just in a different form."

Spence's eyes narrowed. "That's why you've gotten so political all of a sudden."

"In part, yes. In part because I'm trying to amuse myself."

"I hope you're amused," Spence said, "because I'm just bewildered."

"So am I," Sula said. "But I'm trained not to show it."

Thoughts tracked slowly behind Spence's eyes. "So this war that we won't be fighting with the Fleet—who's going to be in it?"

"Let me think." Sula took a bite of her pastry, swallowed, then chased it with a sip of tea. "Three contenders at least," she said. "Those who want change for reasons that make sense to them, those who refuse to permit any change at all, and those who think change is inevitable whether it's wanted or not. And there will be divisions in each of these categories, all of whom will be contending with one another."

"Sounds like—" Spence began.

"Sounds like normal," Sula said. "But there will be new players on the scene—players who may have been around for a while, but who will have more power and prominence due to the Restoration's victory."

"The Martinez family, I suppose." Spence's voice was leaden.

"Oh yes," said Sula. "Along with their relatives, like the Yoshitoshis, the Ngenis, and the Chens. Our friend Lady Koridun is going to be pushed to the forefront, and so is Wei Jian."

"Hector Braga?" Spence asked.

A soft shock pulsed through Sula's system at the mention of Lamey's name.

"Very possibly," she said. "Though currently he seems to be missing."

"Is he a Martinez ally?" Spence asked. "Or one of yours?"

Sula contemplated her teacup. "Lamey's alliances are strictly temporary."

"Nikki?"

"I hope so. He knows how to fix things."

"I like his puppet shows."

"So do I." Sula frowned down at her teacup. "I'm only guessing about any of this, of course, and nothing's going to happen until we take the capital. We've got the entire journey to Zanshaa to work out who's going to be in charge of what."

"Are *you* going to be in charge of anything?"

Sula smiled as she raised her teacup to her lips. "I'm on the Court of Honor, remember," she said. "And the court decides who stays in the Convocation, and who gets kicked out."

"Ah."

"I may not be able to get my friends *into* the Convocation, but I can surely return my enemies to private life."

"They could install a revolving door," said Spence. "They put themselves in, and you bounce them out."

"It's an attractive picture," Sula said. She took a bite of her pastry and let the buttery sweetness melt on her tongue. She turned to Spence.

"How is Macnamara faring, now he's separated from his girl?"

"He's fretful," Spence said. "The distance from Japutra to her husband is a lot closer than it is to us on *Parkhurst*."

"Is the husband—Todd?—is he trying to arrange a meeting?"

"Of course. But he's on a ship that's suffered some damage, and the crew has to finish repairs before the captain will give anyone family leave."

"And Japutra will agree to see him?"

Spence rolled her eyes. "'To tell him the situation and say goodbye,' she says."

"She could do that by sending a message."

Spense nodded. "Yes, she could."

Sula leaned back and gave a sigh. "This situation is beginning to seem familiar," she said.

*Except this time there won't be any bodies*, she thought.

MARTINEZ, SLIGHTLY TIPSY after a supper with Captain Dalkeith and the officers of *Los Angeles*, hummed to himself as he walked along the dark-paneled corridors toward his suite. The corridor was circular, with doors leading to the quarters of most of the officers on the ship, along with storage rooms for the large amount of gear the officers were expected to carry with them from one posting to the next, and for the furniture, porcelain, and eating implements suitable for all the species of the empire.

As he walked, the curving corridor wall revealed a man and woman in a passionate embrace, the man pressing the woman against the dark wood panels. Martinez stopped his humming. He was not surprised to see that the man was Mpanza.

The two lovers were close to the door that led to his office, but not actually leaning against it. Martinez walked to the door, and he saw the woman open one eye, see his approach, and then frantically push Mpanza away so that she could brace to attention. Mpanza straightened his mustachio with a knuckle before bracing himself.

"You should get a tube," Martinez said.

"We have reserved one in four hours," Mpanza said. "It's hard to get a tube when you want one, since they're being overused right now. The crew is feeling . . . frisky."

"Ah." Martinez understood better than most—he and Sula had fallen into each other's arms mere hours after the victory at Second Shulduc.

Martinez turned to the woman. "May I know your frisky friend?"

"My lord," Mpanza said, "may I present Warrant Officer Second Class Filomena Juskiene."

"Lord Captain," said Juskiene.

Juskiene had shining black hair, now slightly disordered, and remarkable blue eyes. Martinez saw from her insignia that she was a specialist in maintenance for pinnaces, shuttles, and other small craft.

"Pleased to make your acquaintance," Martinez said. He turned to Mpanza. "I'll call when I need you," he said. And then, as he disappeared through the door, Martinez added, "Thanks for staying out of the dining room."

He closed the door, sat at his desk, and viewed his messages, which were routine except for a message from his brother, Roland. He deciphered the message himself—the family used a special cipher among themselves—and then brought his brother onto the display.

Martinez recognized the view behind Roland as the media center on *Corona*, the yacht carrier on which they had escaped from Zanshaa just ahead of the war.

"We've left Harzapid's ring," Roland said, "and hope to be in Zanshaa in three months. The ship is overrun, and recruits are stacked in bunk beds in the corridors—I'm afraid the Corona Club will have to spend a small fortune refurbishing the ship once we get to Zanshaa."

Martinez had thought he'd try to invoice the Fleet for the repairs, but the Corona Club was good for the money if that didn't work out. Certainly every other shipowner was going to be asking the government to cover their losses, and it was a show of financial power to *not* ask.

"We've received Fleet Commander Jian's official report of the battle, and you'll be pleased to know you are mentioned favorably."

Surprise warred with vanity in Martinez's soul. He had half-expected to be ignored.

"Michi was also mentioned, as was Farhang, and Yoshida, the tactical officer." Roland gave a significant nod. "Lady Sula was *not* mentioned, though I gather her division was present."

Martinez wondered why Wei Jian had taken against Sula, not only removing her from command but failing to mention her in the official report of the battle.

Roland adopted a puzzled expression. "Jian's report might be described as scanty. She praised your conduct, but didn't mention anything you did to earn her praise. She just reported the victory, mentioned you and Michi and a few others, and then went on to list casualties, captures, defectors, and so on. She finished by telling us she intends to proceed to Zanshaa, then ended with 'Long live the Praxis!'"

Roland shrugged. "If you could give us a few more details, we'd very much like to know what actually happened." He smiled. "Vipsania would like to proceed with her new documentary. We'll make sure to give her all the necessary access."

When Martinez's sister Vipsania had married the presumed heir to the Yoshitoshi family, she had taken control of Imperial Broadcasting, a Yoshitoshi possession. Among her other projects, she had created a meticulously crafted series on the Naxid War, which incidentally featured her brother as one of the war's heroes and made him a celebrity.

Martinez had no problem with being praised and celebrated once again, but wondered how he was going to get Vipsania the information she wanted. The easiest method would be to send her recordings of the battle, but the recordings were probably secret, and he didn't want to run afoul of the sequestration laws. He could of course write his own report, one more detailed than that of Wei Jian, but that wouldn't be the same as viewing the action from the point of view of a participant.

He told the camera to turn itself on.

"Vipsania's project would best be served through being privy to recordings of the battle," he said. "You can request that Wei Jian send them, and since you're the government, she'll most likely obey. So far as I can tell she didn't do anything in the battle that might embarrass her, so there's no reason for her to refuse. Oh—" He laughed. "Tell her you want to have the recordings so that her victory at Toley can be taught to cadets at the training schools. I think that would please her."

He ciphered the message and sent it on his way, then dealt with the rest of his correspondence. There was nothing quite so sleep-inducing as a heavy meal combined with routine messages, and once his eyelids started to droop, Martinez decided he might as well go to bed. He paged Mpanza.

"I'd like my cocoa now," he said, and he sent another message to Mangahas to tell her to get it ready.

Mpanza brought the cocoa a few minutes later. Mangahas had added spices, most of which were a mystery, though Martinez recognized red chile powder. Martinez let the liquid coat his tongue, then let the hot spicy liquid ease its welcome way down his throat. He looked at Mpanza.

"I hope Warrant Officer Juskiene remains frisky," he said.

"I hope so, too, Lord Divcom."

Divcom was presumably short for "division commander," which was not a rank recognized in the Fleet. Martinez raised an eyebrow. "Did you coin that word?"

"I did."

Martinez placed his cocoa cup on the surface of his desk. "I like it," he said.

"You fill the office, you might as well have the title."

Martinez took another sip of his cocoa, then made a grand gesture with one hand. "I dismiss you," he said, "to the arms of Miss Juskiene. I'll see you in the morning."

"Thank you, Lord Divcom."

"Enjoy your time in the tube."

Mpanza made a face. "We could get only half an hour," he said.

"We have a long journey ahead of us," Martinez said. "It's best not to reach complete satiation too early."

Mpanza considered this. "If you say so, my lord."

After Mpanza left, Martinez enjoyed his cocoa and was about to take his cup and saucer to the kitchen when he saw a new message appear on his screen, and his heart gave a lurch. The message was in the clear, he saw, and from Sula.

I AM CAPTAIN THE LADY SULA. AS A MEMBER OF THE CONVOCATION, I WISH TO MAKE MYSELF AVAILABLE TO ANYONE DEALING WITH, OR ANTICIPATING, CIVIL OR POLITICAL ISSUES. ANYONE WITH PROBLEMS, OR IDEAS FOR SOLUTIONS, SHOULD FEEL FREE TO CONTACT ME.

Well, Martinez thought. That would well and truly set Wei Jian's blood boiling.

And probably Roland's, too.

THE MESSAGES THAT Convocate Sula received after her appeal fell into several predictable categories. There were people who wanted help contacting their families in enemy space. There were those who wondered, now that the war was over, when they could expect to be discharged and take up their old lives. Some proclaimed the superiority of the Terran species and hoped other species would be plundered or reduced to servitude, and a subset of these voiced deep suspicions about Rivven and the others who had defected from the enemy fleet, and warned of some deep-laid treachery. Despite Sula's disclaimer that she would not deal with any problem belonging to the military, a large number of crouch-backs took the opportunity to denounce their superiors or complain of the way recruits were treated.

All these messages lent themselves to standard replies, and Sula assigned these replies to her communications staff.

Some asked questions about postwar arrangements: Were humans going to be in charge of everything? Would the government take the same form after the war? Would the Fleet be in charge? Could the sender get a job in the Ministry of Right and Dominion?

Sula sent replies echoing the Restoration's own public pronouncements: that the old government under Lord Saïd would be reestablished if possible, that those who were responsible for the war would be punished, and that it was hoped that the empire would return to normality as soon as events permitted. And everyone would have an equal chance as new jobs became available.

She felt free to doubt every one of those pronouncements, and she found that her ideas were echoed by another officer.

"The Restoration might have given itself the wrong name," he said. "I don't know if we will be able to restore anything at all. I think too much has changed."

Nikki Severin wore a rumpled blue jumpsuit and gazed from the display through his narrow eyes. He looked tired, pale, and stressed. Not only was he running the Exploration Service and the Restoration's entire communication network, he was still in mourning for Lady Starkey.

Severin had recorded the message in his office on his *Expedition*, with white walls marked by little splotches of color in the abstract Devis mode. The Devis mode really didn't seem Severin's style at all, but Sula knew he'd been promoted from the ranks and didn't have much money, and probably couldn't afford the expensive paneling and tiles installed by other captains. White paint with abstract daubs of color were far more economical, and she found herself respecting him for it.

"I've spoken to my own officers about what they expect the empire will look like after the war," he said, "and they think it will be much the same as it was before the war. I suspect they lack imagination on that score. I think the new order will be—*must* be—very different from the old.

"The advantage of the old order was stability," Severin continued. "Scarcely anything changed over the thousands of years the Shaa were in charge—and if anything changed, it changed slowly. In thousands of years, our society remained substantially the same, and our technology changed hardly at all.

"And then the Great Masters died, and the future became more uncertain. The Naxids launched their rebellion in hopes of replacing the Shaa with themselves—if they'd won, they might have had a chance at ensuring a stability equal to that of the Shaa. But they lost, and now change is bubbling up again. The war has forced an evolution in military technology. We're opening up new planets, with new opportunities for people willing to emigrate, and there's a new commercial class that developed after the Naxid War forced changes in the financial system."

Severin clasped his hands and leaned toward the camera. "This wealthy commercial class isn't part of the old social order, and they don't have any significant representation in the Convocation, but they have so much money it's hard to argue they don't have any power."

The Zanshaa government, Sula knew, had tried to turn the clock back by repealing the emergency financial measures enacted in the Naxid War and returning to the old method of directly taxing commerce instead of income. The result was that commerce came to a shivering halt, and Sula had to wonder how the Zanshaa government had raised the money it needed to fight the war.

"Since I saw the videos from Lorkin," Severin said, "I've wondered if the empire is somehow tilted toward the annihilation of entire species. How many times has a Lorkin happened?

"In the short years since the last Shaa died, we've as good as wiped out the Yormaks, and it could be that the Zanshaa government was aiming at getting rid of all Terrans." He shrugged and rolled his shoulders, as if he was cramped by his static position in front of the camera. "Is this a systemic problem? Is it built into the Praxis somehow? The Shaa presumably intended to be in charge forever, so they may not have viewed this as an issue—the loss of one species would be inconsequential to them. But the successor governments don't have the stability of the Shaa, and they may decide that every problem might be solved by xenocide."

He shook his head. "I'm probably sounding like I want the Shaa back, even though I don't. Yet I think a great many people crave the brutal certainties the Shaa brought—the certainty that evildoers would get what's coming to them, even if it's the population of an entire world, like Dandaphis."

Centuries ago, a group of Terran scientists on Dandaphis had tried to build a Shaa-killing plague, and the Shaa had bombarded the planet so thoroughly that it became uninhabitable for generations.

Sula knew that history, and she listened to Severin with some fascination, because so much of what he was saying paralleled her own thoughts. *Those who refuse to permit change at all* . . . Such people would justify Dandaphis, or vote to praise Lord Mehrang for his suppression of the Yormak rebellion, or justify Lord Tork's preemptive arrest of all Terran ship crews.

"The fact is that the empire has always used violence to solve its problems," Severin said. "Is it possible there's an alternative method? And can we discover it?"

Sula paused the recording in order to ponder this, freezing Severin's image in the midst of uttering a word.

The empire had been established by violence, Sula thought, and had always depended on violence to maintain its absolute authority. The Shaa had never lacked for subjects willing to inflict mayhem on other subjects, and some of those subjects got to be Peers.

When the only solutions you have are antimatter hammers, Sula thought, every problem looks like an antimatter nail.

When Sula was a girl, she had been fascinated by Earth history and the glittering parade of kings and princesses and exotic ways of living that seemed to offer an alternative to the dreary reality of her life in the Fabs. The passing of her girlhood, her time on Earth, and exposure to the people who ran the empire had brought a more realistic appraisal of Earth's history. It had to be admitted that all those shining kings and queens were despots, the nobility and the warrior classes trained killers, and the dreary parade of brutal dynasties only rarely relieved by a despot more enlightened than the others. Golden ages sometimes flowered in city-states, but the lessons of city-states could not be applied to something as large as the empire of the Shaa.

That left the oligarchic republics that had emerged in the centuries before the Shaa conquest, oligarchic republics that preferred to call themselves democracies. These rarely fought one another, but they did their best to conquer everyone else—allegedly to spread enlightenment and civilization, the same reasons the Shaa offered to justify their own conquests. Their empires fell apart after a few generations, but the oligarchs continued to provide peace and stability in their own homelands until the Shaa blew their world to bits.

The empire could never profit from the examples of these republics, for the Praxis absolutely forbade democracy, or anything like it. Power originated at the top and radiated downward, not the other way around.

Another problem, Sula thought, was that democracy was *stupid*.

One of the surprises of the time Sula had served on Earth was the subculture of Terrans who enjoyed reenacting Earth's history. They marched about in Roman armor or drove Qin Dynasty chariots over the plains or—in the case of Lady Camille Umri—restored the pyramids of Giza to their original splendor, cased in brilliant white limestone and tipped by capstones of shining electrum.

One group of re-creationists tried to enact democracy, with debates and votes conducted by specialists playing the roles of politicians. Sula had watched one of these events and been annihilated by boredom within minutes.

The problem with democracy, she decided, was that no one was really in charge of anything. The participants argued back and forth and voted on this and that, but no one actually seemed responsible for success or failure, because responsibility was spread out among so many people that it might as well not exist.

The only sensible way to deal with a problem, Sula thought, was to put someone in charge of that problem and give her the means to create a solution. That person could be rewarded or punished in accordance with her performance, and no debates or votes would be necessary.

A crucial problem with the empire as it now existed, Sula thought, was that if you came from a high-caste Peer family, there were no consequences for failure. If you failed, and your name was Foote, or Distchin, or Ngeni, Chen, Gruum, or Orghoder—or Sula—you might be transferred to another job, or actually promoted. It was only if your name was less illustrious that you could be sacked, or imprisoned, or executed.

*Well*, she thought, *there were going to be consequences* now.

She triggered the recording, and Severin's image resumed its soliloquy.

"I know you've argued for a permanent military dictatorship after the war. I don't know how much support you'll get for that idea, but I know we'll be running things for a while, at least until we can get a Convocation and a Lord Senior we can work with. So what I suggest is that if we want any kind of real change, it's got to happen in a period when no one will dare to oppose it. So we need to decide what that change is, and then make it happen as soon as possible.

"And I do mean *we*."

Severin gave a long sigh, then offered a weary smile. "How are you, by the way?" He laughed. "Maybe I should have opened with that. End message."

Sula pondered Severin's arguments as she stared at the orange end-stamp on the display, and then she waved a hand at the *record* button, and the camera eye winked on. She smiled.

"Hi, Nikki. I'm very well, thanks for asking," she said. "You look as if you could use a long vacation, but I know what it's like when your brain won't stop spinning its gears."

She took a breath. "I think that you're right that we need to move fast politically when we arrive at Zanshaa, and to that end we have to have our program ready before we arrive. Fortunately, we've got a couple months to get it in shape. I'll communicate my ideas to the political leadership on Harzapid, and you should do the same."

Sula nodded at the camera. "It occurs to me that our victory at Toley might be the first pebble falling in what could be a massive avalanche. We've argued that the government in Zanshaa is illegitimate, and that we're going to replace it with a government somehow more genuine, but the fact is that the Zanshaa government was chosen in the normal way, and our actual objection to Gruum and Tu-hon and the others is that they're stupid, greedy, overprivileged, and want to kill us. Do-faq might not have been wrong when he accused us of trying to overthrow a legitimate government by force." She grinned. "Not that I care about his accusations particularly."

She tapped her desktop with her fingers. "But say for the sake of argument that Do-faq was right. Once we're in charge, what's to stop others from doing what we've done, which is gather a fleet and make a dash for the capital?

"*We've proved it's possible.*" She shook her head. "That's another argument for us establishing a dictatorship," she said. "Put the power in the hands of the people who actually have the missiles, rather than a civilian government that depends on the missile-launching classes for their own safety."

She considered adding a digression on the transfer of power during the Roman Empire, but when she contemplated the lengthy list of emperors who were stabbed, strangled, committed suicide, died in battle, were killed by their bodyguards, or were drowned in their own bath, she began to doubt that these examples buttressed her case.

"We should continue these discussions with our friends in the Fleet and with our friends back on Harzapid," she said. "And I hear you: *we* should figure this out. I look forward to hearing from you. End message."

She loosened the collar of her fatigues jumpsuit and picked up her stylus while turning on her desk display. She called the kitchen and asked for tea, then made notes on her desktop till she had her arguments in order. Macnamara delivered her tea in silence, then withdrew. Ignored, it silently perfumed the air. Sula instead stayed focused, writing an outline for what she planned to say, then faced the camera and readied herself to say it.

It was then that she considered who would be viewing her message. The most energetic members of the Restoration's council were Roland Martinez, Vipsania Yoshitoshi, and Terza Chen—in other words, Gareth Martinez's brother, sister, and wife. She supposed they might listen to her message, but she doubted they would take it very seriously. They had plenty of ideas of their own.

She needed to give them a reason to treat her ideas with respect. She revisited her message, made a few more notes, then waved the camera on.

"This is Caroline, Lady Sula, with a report to the Restoration council. Greetings."

She waved a hand to indicate her convocate's jacket. "You will notice that I appear in the raiment of a member of the Convocation. I am the only convocate in the Combined Fleet, and I am already consulting with members of the Fleet to gather their ideas about the future of the empire."

That *should get their attention*, she thought. There was nothing like the news that a potential rival was harvesting clients from among the missile-launching classes.

"I presume that our intentions include reforming the Convocation as well as promoting a new Lord Senior in line with our ideas. I should like to point out that I serve on the Court of Honor, which rules on whether or not a given member is suitable to remain a convocate. If I were to chair that committee instead of Lady Tu-hon—who I presume we're going to shoot in the head once we find her—I can find reasons to ease any number of people out of the Convocation without any fuss and without any executions."

She smiled. "I also have some ideas for how the empire might be ordered after the end of the war."

*Now*, she thought, she might be listened to.


MARTINEZ WATCHED SULA'S video, then considered sending her his ideas about the future of the empire, but in the end decided against it. He preferred to avoid giving Sula a chance to exercise her talent at savage mockery, and besides, Roland was in charge of the political side.

When he thought about it, he really didn't have a political program, just a set of personal goals. He wanted his promotion to fleet commander back, he wanted to be co-opted into the Convocation, and he wanted a seat on the Fleet Control Board, preferably at its head.

All reasonable and warranted, he thought.

Once this war was over, there was no point in having a large field command, because the Fleet would be in a rebuilding phase, replacing the hundreds of ships lost in the war. The Fleet Control Board would manage that rebuilding, as well as supervise the training of new recruits to crew the ships. Martinez wanted to be in charge of all that, because though he had no firm ideas of where to take the empire, he knew where he wanted to take the Fleet.

He'd leave the political dimensions to Roland, Terza, Vipsania, and Walpurga.

And Sula, apparently.


SULA CONSIDERED WEI Jian handing out prizes for the Combined Fleet trivia contest and smiled. She couldn't imagine a scenario in which Jian would be more uncomfortable.

Yet that scenario would soon present itself. The Combined Fleet would be engaged in a lengthy series of intership competitions—quizzes; concerts; and contests in making art, music, short videos. There would be competitions in board and video games and gymkhanas for pinnace pilots. It was all a way of keeping the crews from being too idle, and of keeping their competitive spirit high. Apparently the Fourth Fleet had done much the same thing on its route to Toley.

And Wei Jian would hand out the prizes. Delightful.

Sula strolled along the mezzanine overlooking *Parkhurst*'s gleaming concourse. Bright banners hung from the mezzanine rail and the walls of the restaurant and bar. The sound of the ship's orchestra tuning came up like scattered birdsong from the bandstand below. *Pride of Parkhurst* was about to enjoy its victory ball.

*Parkhurst* was in a much better condition to host a ball than the Combined Fleet's warships. For one thing, the ship normally carried an orchestra, and enough of the musicians had volunteered for the Restoration Fleet to form the core of a new ensemble that included brand-new recruits who just happened to be musicians. Too, the concourse was large enough to make a dance floor, whereas in warships any dance would have to be held in the crew's dining area, with the chairs and tables removed.

Sula saw Dr. Gunaydin ahead, leaning on the mezzanine rail and looking at the growing crowd below. He wore civilian dress, more practical for dancing than formal military wear, and his head had been freshly shaved.

"Doctor," she said. "I hope to see you dancing tonight."

He turned and nodded. "I hope you'll reserve a dance for me." She couldn't help but notice that he'd failed to salute.

"Of course," she said.

He looked at her wine-red tunic. "You seem to have become a convocate again."

She spread her hands. "I do what I can."

"This might explain the queries I'm getting from the fleet commander's staff. They are very eager to discover the state of your health."

"Have you been ordered yet to confine me to a health ward?"

He seemed amused. "There is no health ward on the ship, though I suppose I could improvise one. But in any case, I am not in the fleet commander's chain of command and she—or her staff—have no business giving me any such order. I could appeal to my own superiors on Harzapid." He laughed. "But, the truth is, anyone who gives me such an order might qualify for a health ward herself."

She laughed with him. "I applaud your resolution, Doctor," she said, "though I think few people would resist such an order."

Gunaydin shrugged. "What could they do to me? Nothing."

Sula thought that Gunaydin was lacking in certain kinds of imagination.

"Let's hope so," she said. "I'll see you on the dance floor."

She went to the bar and ordered a couple of cocktails to get herself in the mood for dancing. She was finishing the last of these when she was approached by Devindar Suri, *Parkhurst*'s original captain. He was a tall, rugged-seeming man going gray at the temples and exuded a strange mixture of confidence and bonhomie, intended perhaps to be reassuring to wealthy paying passengers.

"Lady Sula," he said. "A pleasure to see you here."

"Please join me."

"Thank you." He eased himself into his seat. "I think the music is about to begin," he said. "Will you be giving an address to the crew beforehand?"

"No," Sula said. "I've already praised them in a formal address, so now they can lose themselves in celebration. *I* certainly intend to."

And then, because Suri seemed surprised, she added, "If you wish to speak, by all means do so."

He shook his head. "I haven't prepared anything. I assumed you would open the celebrations."

Sula considered the matter, then drained the last of her cocktail. "Why don't we open the event with the first dance? That should get everything started."

"I'd love to."

The two of them went out onto the concourse, stepped onto the dance floor, and Sula signaled the orchestra to begin. The opening chords of Mortak's "Lush" rolled out onto the concourse, and Sula and Captain Suri began to dance. For the first few minutes they had the dance floor to themselves, and then others began to join them.

Suri was a relaxed and expert dancer, which Sula thought might be almost a requirement for the captain of a large passenger ship. He bowed to her as "Lush" faded away, then turned to applaud the orchestra.

Sula danced with all the ship's officers in turn and managed to avoid being trampled by the clumsier of the cadets. The orchestra was in fine form. A succession of cocktails sent a warm wave of relaxation through Sula, and the easing of the tension she'd felt for so many months set her soaring onto the dance floor.

Eventually she found herself dancing with Gunaydin, and he steered her expertly around the other dancers. Colored spotlights reflected in his eyes and haloed his shaven head.

"How's my vagus today?" she asked.

He laughed. "Vagus function nominal," he said.

"That's what I thought."

Her sleeve display lit, and she saw that she'd just received a message from Roland Martinez. Roland's image floated through Sula's mind, so like his brother Gareth's. She scowled at the display.

"Bad news?" Gunaydin asked.

"Annoying news," Sula said. "It can wait till tomorrow."

Now Gareth Martinez had lodged in her head, and she couldn't get rid of him. The orchestra played a series of triumphant chords and the song came to an end. Sula applauded, then took Gunaydin's sleeve and led him off the dance floor.

"Come with me," she said. "I have an idea."

She led Gunaydin to the living area of her suite, closed the door, put her arms around his neck, and kissed him hard. It took him a few seconds to respond—he wasn't surprised, she thought, but he had to work out how best to respond.

The kiss went on for a while. Gunaydin's lips tasted of salt, and his mustache bristled against her upper lip. His arms wrapped around her.

The kiss came to a satisfying end, and they regarded each other from the distance of a handsbreath. His expression seemed quizzical.

"Are you sure about this?" he asked.

"I can't tell you to do anything," Sula said. "As you keep pointing out, you're not a line officer and not in my chain of command. So I suppose I'm just calling for a volunteer."

"What do I do?" Gunaydin asked. "Take a step forward?"

She grinned and pressed her hips into him. "You could try."

The second kiss was an improvement on the first. When it ended, she drew him toward her sleeping cabin and her bergamot-scented sheets.

"I'm going to take a shower," she said. "Make yourself comfortable. There's a selection of drinks in the cabinet."

He looked at her. "We could bathe together. A suite like this, I imagine there's room in the shower stall."

Sula considered this. There *was* room, though a part of her wanted the indulgence of a shower to be hers alone. But still, she had to admit that the thought of a shared bath was alive with possibility.

"I'll want the water really hot," she said.

"I'll manage."

"Give me a few minutes, and I'll call you."

She pinned her hair atop her head, used mouthwash, hung her clothes with care on the pegs provided, and put on a wine-red bathrobe that matched her convocate's tunic. She started a hot shower, then opened the bathroom door and summoned Gunaydin.

They kissed for a pleasant interval, collaborated in removing Gunaydin's clothes, and then she stepped out of her robe and into the shower, drawing him after. The gods of the Fleet had banished cake soap from its ships—hapless recruits could slip on them, fall during heavy accelerations, and break bones—but the liquid soap produced abundant lather and had a pleasing herbal scent.

The shower was a preview of things to come. Gunaydin demonstrated that he knew his way around a woman's anatomy, which was only to be hoped for in a physician. Sula found it amusing that while his head was shaved, his chest was thickly thatched, and soon heavily soaped. They rubbed against each other, skin sliding freely against soapy skin. Steam rose in the small cabinet.

When Gunaydin's arousal became impossible to ignore, Sula showered all the soap away and led him to her bed. They lay atop the scented sheets and kissed. Gunaydin's skin was cool and fresh after his shower.

"Maybe I'll achieve vasovagal syncope," she said. "It sounds like fun."

"I'll do my best to make you swoon," he said. "But no promises. It's *your* vagus nerve that has to cooperate."

Sula's vagus nerve offered neither encouragement nor trouble. The results were otherwise satisfactory: Gunaydin knew how to please a woman, and Sula knew how to please herself. He wasn't Martinez—there was no mutual extravagance of need and desire and pleasure, no rapture that stopped just short of anguish—but then that was probably the point.

She didn't think there would be nightmares tonight.

There was another agile embrace before sleep stole upon them, and again upon wakening. After which Sula showered, put on her robe, and called for breakfast.

Macnamara was startled to find Gunaydin sitting with Sula, his tunic partly unbuttoned, her feet resting casually in his lap. Sula could see calculation speeding through his head as he placed the basket of pastries and the teapot on the table, along with Sula's bottle of cane-sugar syrup.

"Is tea all right?" Sula asked Gunaydin. "Would you rather have coffee?"

"Tea is fine," Gunaydin said.

"I'll bring you a cup, Doctor," Macnamara said, and vanished into the pantry.

Sula knew that Macnamara was suffering from the absence of Japutra Bliss and hoped that the picture of satiation that she and Gunaydin presented wouldn't increase Macnamara's loneliness and misery. *Be happy for me*, she commanded mentally.

Macnamara returned with cups, plates, silverware, and napkins for two. The floral scent of the tea rose as he poured for them both. If he was suffering, he concealed it well.

"Thank you," Sula said, and Macnamara returned to the pan-

try. She turned to Gunaydin. "Would you rather have a more substantial breakfast?"

Gunaydin helped himself to a pastry. "This is more luxury than
I'm used to," he said. "Normally by this time of day I have an energy drink and go to the gym."

"We're not on a warship now," she said. "We won't be engaging
in high-gee burns or dangerous maneuvers. You don't have to be
in the gym every day, and you can award yourself a treat now and
again."

He looked at her. "I already have," he said.

After breakfast she took him to the door and kissed his buttery-
tasting lips.

"Do we get to do this again?" he asked.

"I hope so."

He smiled. "Me too."

She showed him out, returned to her sleeping cabin to put on
clothes, then went to her office. Roland Martinez's message still
waited in her queue. She contemplated the message, then decided
she needed more fortification before facing it and ordered more
tea. She dealt with routine correspondence until Macnamara arrived with the teapot.

"How are you this morning?" Sula asked as he poured the fragrant tea.

"Very well, my lady. Thank you for asking."

She stirred a long golden ribbon of cane syrup into her cup.
"How is Miss Bliss?" she asked.

"She reports herself well," he said carefully.

"And is she?"

Macnamara blinked. "I can't tell. I don't think she's happy,
but—" He looked down at her. "Do you mind my talking like this?"

"No, not at all." Which wasn't exactly true—it wasn't that she didn't want to help Macnamara, it was that she knew she wasn't very good at these sorts of conversations. *Human warmth not my specialty*, she thought.

"Say what you want to say," Sula said.

Macnamara hesitated, then spoke. "I know she's seen her husband. But she hasn't told him that she wants to divorce, and I'm sure she hasn't told him about me."

Sula slowly stirred her tea. "Has she said why?"

"Just that it's very hard."

"I'm sure it must be," Sula said. She sipped the tea. Welcome sweetness flooded her tongue.

"You have more experience with adultery than I do," Macnamara said. "I thought you might have some advice."

His words caught her by surprise. *Experience with adultery.*

*Well*, she thought, *true enough.*

"I turned out not to be very good at adultery," Sula said. "But I'll offer the advice I can." She sipped her tea again, then spoke.

"If you love her," she said, "prepare to forgive her, and always be honest."

It was advice she wished she'd given herself months ago. Macnamara considered it. "That's . . . sort of a challenge."

"Which? The forgiveness or the honesty?"

"Both," Macnamara said. "I'm a lot more angry than forgiving right now, and if I'm honest about how I feel, I could hurt her."

"Tell her what you need to tell her," Sula said. "If she doesn't know how you feel, she can't take your feelings into account."

"I suppose that make sense," Macnamara said. "Thank you, my lady."

Sula waved a hand. "Nonii."

After Macnamara left, Sula sat in the silence for a moment

and contemplated the shimmering reflections in her teacup. She supposed her advice had been sound enough, but she suspected it wouldn't make any difference. Good advice never did. The affair would take its course, and the finale would either be happy or not, and it wouldn't matter what the people involved thought or intended.

Roland's name blinked on her display again. She sighed. Time to see what the Martinez Machiavelli wanted.

"Lady Sula," Roland said, "we've been considering your message, and we'd like some ideas of how best to implement your ideas. We would also appreciate your notions concerning the reorganization of the Convocation, and suggestions for who should be co-opted and who should be eased out. We also wonder how you envision your future in the Convocation and the Fleet."

Sula paused the recording and laughed.

It seemed as if the Restoration council had decided to take her seriously.

# CHAPTER 9

The finale of the Combined Fleet trivia contest was held aboard *Perfection of the Praxis*. The vast empty space that was the battleship's unfinished ballroom was large enough for the contestants, judges, and all the audience who cared to watch. Since the Grand Division of the Rear had two ships providing teams for the finals, Martinez considered it an agreeable duty to attend.

*Perfection*'s ballroom was intended to have polished panel walls, a floor laid with custom tiles, graceful light fixtures, and a bandstand set up before a backdrop of inset scalloped shells. Instead, the flooring was cheap plastic panels, the walls were bare, and wires hung from the distant ceiling, each marked with a dangling tag. The lighting was improvised, and Martinez was surprised that it hadn't all come crashing down during the ship's radical accelerations and maneuvers.

The four final teams sat on a raised platform at one end of the room, with the three judges in the middle. Wei Jian presided from a separate platform at stage left, where she sat with a number of her officers and friends. Including, Martinez noticed, Jeremy Foote, who sat on Jian's right side and who offered her what seemed to be a series of amusing asides.

Foote was angling for a promotion, Martinez thought, and Fleetcom Jian was the only dispenser of promotions available.

Though Foote certainly had his work cut out for him. So far as Martinez could see, Wei Jian had never been amused by anyone, ever.

Foote might find this his hardest campaign.

Fleetcom Jian opened the contest with an introduction that managed to be both brief and awkward, and the contest began. The audience, composed of crew from the battleship as well as personnel shuttled from other ships, were loud in their appreciation, applauding and cheering their favorites. A few had to be cautioned after shouting out the answers.

One of the Rear's ships scored enough points to remain in the running for first place, against the Division Nine cruiser *Splendid*. Captain Mazankosi, whose bright yellow hair stood out like a shining beacon from the front row of the spectators, led the cheering for her team.

In the end, it came down to a single tie-breaking question: "Who won the Vandrith Challenge Race in the Year of the Praxis 12,476?"

Both teams knew the answer, but the Rear's sports expert beat his rival to the buzzer.

"Ehrler Blitsharts," he said. "And of course his dog Orange."

Blitzharts had been one of the great yacht captains of the age, always racing with his dog companion in the cockpit. He had died of asphyxiation in a subsequent Vandrith race, an occasion that had resulted in the first meeting of Martinez and Sula, who respectively coordinated and executed the failed rescue.

At the team's victory, Martinez stood and cheered, and leaned toward Chandra Prasad, who stood next to him.

"Join me for a drink after? I can shuttle you home afterward."

"Nonii," Chandra said.

The cheers and applause died away, and Wei Jian stepped forward to present the trophy, again with a brief, awkward speech. She really wasn't very good at being spontaneous.

Chandra sent her crew home on their shuttle and joined Martinez for the flight to *Los Angeles*.

Martinez informed the cruiser's watch officer that he didn't require the formal welcoming party to which he was normally entitled, and so he and Chandra walked from the airlock to be greeted by silence. They took the stairway to the officers' decks, stepped into the corridor, and immediately encountered a sobbing woman who dashed past them and eventually disappeared around the circular corridor.

Chandra watched her go, then turned to Martinez. "Is this the normal amount of drama for your ship?"

"I'm beginning to think it is." Martinez thought he had recognized Electrician Second Class Raju, who he had once discovered in Mpanza's embrace on his dining table.

"I thought *my* emotional life was complex," Chandra said.

Martinez went into his dining cabin and summoned Mpanza.

"Why is there a weeping woman running along the corridor?" he asked.

"That was Electrician Raju, Lord Divcom," said Mpanza. "She wanted me to take her back."

"Do all your romances have to play out in my quarters?"

"Not in your quarters, Lord Divcom. Our conversation was held out in the corridor."

Martinez sighed. "Choose more stable women in the future, Mpanza."

"I already have, Lord Divcom. I apologize for any interruption."

"Right," Martinez said. "We'd like drinks. I'll have Laredo whisky."

"Kyowan and Spacey," said Chandra.

"Right away, my lord. My lady."

Chandra and Martinez sat at the broad end of the keystone-shaped table. She looked at him and raised her brows.

"'Lord Divcom?'"

"Mpanza enjoys inventing new posts for me."

"Has he got to 'Lord Omnipotent' yet?"

"Well," Martinez judged, "I *am* fairly omnipotent." He waved a hand. "Are you hungry, by the way?"

"If you were omnipotent, you'd know I could do with a snack."

"Mangahas usually has some kind of fruit custard ready in the refrigerator. I'll send for some." Martinez contacted Mpanza and told him to bring the dessert along with their drinks.

Mpanza arrived a short while later, bringing the items on a tray. The custards were huge, served in large cut-glass goblets, decorated with candies and dried fruit that had been plumped with rum. Martinez decided that his whisky and the custard would provide too violent a contrast, so he decided to eat his dessert first. He took a spoonful and enjoyed the crunch of the candy between his teeth followed by the explosion of a rum-soaked cherry. He swallowed and turned to Chandra.

"I'm assuming you didn't just ask me here for sweets."

"I've heard from the Restoration council," he said. "And I've been asked to quietly sound out various officers concerning what awards they'd accept at the end of the campaign."

Chandra's eyes widened. "You mean I get to pick?"

"We wouldn't want to give you a political job if you don't want one, or an administrative role if you'd like another field command. Or maybe you'd like a city named after you, or a mountain range."

Chandra sipped her cocktail and gave him her sidelong smile. "I'll take promotion, a fistful of medals, a field command, and Vonderheydte as my personal and adoring slave."

"I thought you already had that."

"Well, yes." She waved a hand. "But it should be made official."

Martinez picked up another spoonful of custard. "I'll convey your wishes to those on high."

"Who is it that's on high, exactly? Your brother, your sister, and your wife?"

Martinez had to swallow his custard before he could answer. "There's also Ming Lin, Lady Koridun, Lord Mehrang, and a few others."

Chandra took a bit of custard, then gave him a thoughtful look. "So what rewards can *you* expect?"

"Assuming agreement from those I noted, membership in the Convocation and a seat on the Fleet Control Board. Plus"—he nodded—"promotion and a fistful of medals."

"How are you going to get all that past Wei Jian?"

Martinez spread his hands. "Some of those items aren't within her purview. As for the rest? I've no idea."

"I'd suggest finding out what she wants and making it a part of the package."

Martinez considered this. "I'm going to assume that promotion and a fistful of medals will be involved."

"Good guess, but I think she'll want more."

Martinez decided he'd didn't need any more dessert, and pushed the goblet away. He reached for his whisky.

"What else would she want?"

"Maybe she'll want to be Lady Senior of the Convocation."

Martinez frowned. "That would be a mistake. She's not a politician. She's comfortable only when she can give orders that can't be questioned."

"Maybe she thinks that's what a Lady Senior does."

Martinez sipped his whisky. The phenolic compounds in the drink promptly attacked whatever sweet dessert components remained on his tongue, and for a moment there was blazing warfare in his palate. He coughed, then cleared his throat.

"Lady Senior Jian would be a disaster, but that might be a good thing." He grinned at her. "The Convocation could then vote in someone else, and Jian could be put out to pasture."

"Unless she decides to bombard Zanshaa from space."

"Well." Martinez shrugged. "There's always that possibility."

THE COMBINED FLEET traveled with enough momentum that they passed into the next system, Sennola, while still undergoing deceleration. There, the warships were met by the cargo carriers of the Fleet Train, which filled the ships' magazines with brand-new missiles, distributed food and entertainment, sent in drafts of new recruits to bring ships up to strength, and took off the injured and the prisoners, including the unfortunate Lord Pa Do-faq. Captured enemy ships were given skeleton Terran crews to take the ships to Harzapid for refit, while defector ships were resupplied with everything but missiles. They would travel to Zanshaa with the Terran ships, but Wei Jian wasn't willing to trust them with full magazines . . . though to any observer from outside the Combined Fleet, they'd look as formidable as any other ship.

After a week in Sennola, the Combined Fleet finally shed enough momentum so that they could at last start their accelerations toward Zanshaa. Heavy gravities were laid on to get the warships up to speed as soon as possible, and crews spent most of their days in their couches, doing their best to breathe against the extra weight that sat like crouching monsters on their ribs.

*Pride of Parkhurst*, unable to inflict heavy gravities on itself, followed the Combined Fleet like a faithful dog panting after a speeding automobile. It was unable to finish its deceleration in the Sennola system and passed into Shulduc, where Martinez and Sula had annihilated Lord Tork's fleet in the largest battle in imperial history.

It was in the aftermath of that battle that Sula had drawn Martinez into bed and begun the months of happiness and hope that led to her current misery, anger, and exile. Being back in Shulduc did nothing to improve her heartache.

Sula's prescription for her wretchedness and self-loathing involved alcohol, sleep, exercise, and Serdar Gunaydin. He was candid, amusing, and unconventional enough to be interesting—he wasn't a career Fleet physician, he was a civilian who had volunteered for the Restoration, and in his brief time in the service he hadn't adjusted to life in the military. He still thought like a civilian and directly pursued answers to his problems without consulting the thousands of years of Fleet precedent that would have told him what the proper answer was, whether it was correct or relevant or not.

Her nightmares faded when she was with him, and even when she wasn't. No doubt her staff appreciated their nights uninterrupted by screams.

Sula didn't love Gunaydin, but maybe that, too, was the point. Certainly she had a brighter future with a man she didn't love than with the man she did.

She considered her other current relationship with a man she didn't love: Sula remained in contact with Roland Martinez, who had realized that she would be the first member of the Restoration Convocation to arrive on Zanshaa, and so the first member to represent the new political order. She would have to initiate the transition on her own for several weeks, balancing Wei Jian, the distant Restoration government, politicians like Lord Chen and Lord Saïd, who had spent the war under arrest, and whatever loyalists remained of the Gruum/Tu-hon clique. After which *Corona* and its cargo of politicians would arrive, possibly to undo all her work.

Roland had ambitious plans for the future of the empire, including replacing many of the Convocation with new faces, often drawn from the provinces, who could be counted on to form a loyal party around the Martinez clan. He also intended to establish local industry-based councils throughout the empire to balance entrenched interests and to serve as a check on traditional sources of power. Sula had jokingly called these "workers' soviets," and she didn't think she was far wrong. Roland's plans would stand or fall with these organizations, and with his ability to control them once he'd established them.

She didn't know where she stood on Roland's plans—she was still convinced that it was far better that she arrive with a pistol on her hip and Wei Jian's planet-shattering fleet overhead and simply tell everyone what to do.

And perhaps she would do exactly that. Her dictatorship might be brief, but she would make the most of it while it lasted.

SEVERIN WAS GLAD that the Torminel wrestlers were gone from the walls of Martinez's office, and though the incandescent fish that replaced them seemed just as strange, they were easier to live with.

He took a sip of Laredo whisky and listened as Martinez asked him what he might want after the war. The question didn't surprise him, since it was known that Martinez had been polling the Fourth Fleet's senior commanders, and he'd had time to think about his answers.

Severin sent another fiery taste of whisky down his palate.

"I'd like the Convocation," he said, and he saw Martinez's surprise at the answer. "I'd like a promotion within the Exploration Service," he continued, "but since I'm already at the highest rank, I'm not sure how that can happen—would it require an act of the Convocation, do you think? And I'd like Lorkin—or Garden, or whatever it's going to be called."

Martinez looked at him, his heavy brows contracted. "If you're already a Squadron Commander, First Grade, why do you want a promotion?"

"Because of seniority. There are other First Grades out there, they're senior to me, and I don't trust any of them."

Martinez nodded. "And Lorkin? Do you want to be governor, or patron, or—?"

"Being a governor would require my being absent from the Convocation. Being a patron is more flexible, I think. Though what I really want is to be in charge of the archaeology."

Martinez spoke slowly, as if he were working his way through the idea. "Digging through the ruins of the civilization that the Great Masters destroyed."

"And controlling how and when any discoveries are revealed."

Martinez nodded. "And you want this . . . why?"

"I think it's important."

"Whatever happened there is long past. Thousands of years ago. You might not find anything at all."

This was a reaction Severin had encountered before. "The

founders of our civilization destroyed an entire intelligent species," he said. "What does that say about them? About the empire we inherited? We've already as good as wiped out the Yormaks, and the Zanshaa government did their best to wipe out *us*. What if it's the Praxis that's at fault?"

"Do you think you'll find that out?" Then Martinez shrugged and waved a hand. "Nonii. I'm sure you can have Lorkin, if that's what you want. No one else is going to jump at it."

"Thank you." Severin raised his glass.

"I'm surprised you want the Convocation," Martinez said, "but I'm sure you can have it if you don't mind the rest of your life being politics." He shrugged. "You might be bored, but at least you'll be a Peer."

"I'm never bored," Severin said. "And I'm not sure I want to be a Peer."

Again, Martinez was surprised. "Well," he said on reflection, "that's your first political decision, isn't it?"

"Being the only commoner in the Convocation might give me a higher profile. Below the lower-lower-lower."

"I expect it will." Martinez nodded. "It might also make you a high-profile target."

"Of who? The old High City families?"

"They might view you as a jumped-up entertainer."

Severin laughed. "They'd do that whether I was a Peer or not."

"True." Martinez nodded. "It seems you've thought this through."

"I've given it some consideration, yes."

"I'll relay your wishes on to those on high. I'm sure you'll get what you want."

This was only the beginning of what Severin wanted, he thought, but he was willing to take it one step at a time.

There was a warning tone from one of the office monitors as a high-priority message came in. Martinez glanced at the monitor, then put the text message on the screen. "Reply to Captain Dalkeith," he said. "'Keep me informed.' Message ends."

"Something urgent?" Severin asked.

"One of *Los Angeles*'s crew got killed," Martinez said. "Murdered by her husband. Dalkeith's the captain, so it's her business, not mine, but she let me know because the husband might direct an appeal to me."

"It's clear he did it?"

"He admits it. He says he loved her."

"Of *course* he does," Severin said. "Because that justifies everything." A pang of misery rose in him, an endless longing and horrid emptiness where Lady Starkey had once been. He had lost his lover to an enemy missile, and that was terrible enough, but to lose a lover to brute, personal human violence was incomprehensibly harrowing. The very thought left him ill.

"People have been on these ships far too long," he said. "Stuck in a can with all the wrong thoughts chasing through their heads on an endless loop."

"I know what you mean," Martinez said, "but it's not just on shipboard. That's why you'll be useful in the Convocation. They've been on an endless loop for centuries."

"I KEEP THINKING it's my fault," Macnamara said. Tears trembled in his eyes. He turned to Sula. "I did what you said. I told Japutra what I felt. She said that she'd tell her husband the next time they met. And now . . ." The tears overfilled his eyes and spilled down his cheeks.

"It's not your fault," Sula said. "It's the fault of the husband, Todd Bliss."

"And he's going to get what he deserves," said Spence.

Which would either be poison or a shot to the back of the head. Normally it was the captain's choice, but sometimes it was left to the prisoner.

"But if I hadn't told her," Macnamara said, "she wouldn't have told Bliss about me, and she might still be alive."

"You don't know that," Sula pointed out. "You don't know if she even mentioned you, or if she asked for a divorce, or what other thing might have triggered it."

Spence and Sula were huddled beside Macnamara at the dining table in Sula's suite. News of Japutra's death had come from one of *Los Angeles*'s officers, who was informing anyone with whom Japutra had been in contact.

*Except this time there won't be any bodies*, Sula had thought, when she'd been told of Macnamara's situation with Japutra. It was unsettling to realize how wrong she'd been—that even at her most optimistic, she was wrong.

Bliss had started with his fists, and then grabbed her head and smashed it into a bulkhead, cracking the skull like an egg.

Sula put her hand on Macnamara's arm. "You are absolutely not to blame," she said.

She was doing her best against her own sense that her words were meaningless. The story of Japutra Bliss would have ended this way no matter what she or Macnamara said or did. Lamey had dropped dead on Sula's apartment floor in spite of anyone's intentions. Martinez hadn't intended to walk out of her life, and she hadn't wanted him to, but he walked out anyway. People were thrown together and apart and into extinction by some unknowable random process, and nothing so random could ever be meaningful.

The only true answer to life was that of the derivoo, to broadcast your defiance right to the instant of death.


**MARTINEZ DENIED THE** appeal of Todd Bliss, and so did Wei Jian. *Los Angeles*'s physician, a young woman barely out of medical school, prepared the fatal dose and fired it into Bliss's neck with a med injector. Then Bliss was stuffed into a Fleet-issue body bag and stuck in a freezer, where he would remain until the cruiser docked at some Fleet facility and he could be offloaded.

Martinez wished he could just eject Bliss from an airlock and let him be burned to atoms by *Los Angeles*'s blazing antimatter tail, but that was a punishment reserved for treason.

Bliss had died insisting that he loved his wife—she just needed correction, to cure her of her erring ways. Martinez pondered the crimes that lurked beneath the cloak of love, the murders and atrocities and betrayals. Out of love and horror he had helped Sula to conceal her murder of Hector Braga, and he wondered if Braga died because he had loved Sula, or Sula him, and that love had turned into something terrible.

He would try to find out, Martinez decided. He knew nothing about Braga, and apparently he knew nothing about Sula, either. As soon as the Restoration landed on Zanshaa and he had some control over the apparatus of government, he'd be able to use government resources to find some answers. The answers might already exist, in some government file that no one had viewed in years.

There was a polite knock on his office door. "My lord?"

The voice was muffled and Martinez didn't recognize it. "Come in," he called.

The man who entered was tall, dark-skinned, and wore the red armband and belt of a constable. He carried a large pouch of dark fabric in one hand. He braced.

"Constable First Class Hadad, my lord," he said. "I beg pardon for the interruption."

"Is there a problem, Constable?"

Hadad approached Martinez's desk, then reached into his pouch and produced a large round plate, which he placed on Martinez's desktop.

"Does this belong to you, my lord?" he asked.

Martinez recognized the plate easily enough: it was one of a set of silver chargers engraved with images of *Corona* and *Illustrious*, the two warships he had commanded in the Naxid War.

"Yes," he said. "This is mine."

Hadad picked up the charger and dropped it back in the pouch. "I'm afraid it's now evidence, my lord," he said. "It will be returned after the trial."

Martinez looked at Hadad in surprise. "Evidence of what?" he asked. "And whose trial?"

"This plate was stolen from your pantry, my lord," Hadad said. "It was found in the possession of one of the crew."

Martinez was surprised. He couldn't imagine who would do such a thing. "Who had it?" he asked.

"Warrant Officer Juskiene, my lord."

The name sounded familiar, but Martinez couldn't place it. Were he captain of *Los Angeles*, he would have done his best to know all crew by name, but the cruiser was captained by Elissa Dalkeith, who dealt with the crew on a daily basis. Martinez commanded the entire division, had little to do with the ordinary crew, and knew only a few of them.

"And Juskiene had the plate in her possession?" Somehow he knew that Juskiene was a *her*.

"She wasn't carrying it around, of course," Hadad said. "It was hidden in her rack, under the mattress."

"Did she say why she took it?" Martinez couldn't understand why anyone would have stolen such an identifiable piece, let alone a single charger out of a set of ten.

"She denies taking it at all, my lord," said Hadad. "But there's no doubt that—"

"Were her fingerprints on the charger?"

Hadad seemed startled. "The what?"

"The charger. That kind of plate is called a charger. Were Juskiene's fingerprints on it?"

"We don't do those sorts of technical investigations, my lord. I wouldn't know how to—"

Martinez knew perfectly well that shipboard constabulary were trained in breaking up fights, dragging crouchbacks out of bars, guarding access, and apprehending crew engaged in illegal drinking or gambling. They hardly ever saw a case more complicated than that, and their resources in such cases were extremely limited.

"You can make fingerprint powder out of graphite or aluminum powder," Martinez said. "Though possibly, the way you've been handling it, most of the prints on the plate will be yours."

Hadad gave an uncomfortable look at the charger within its pouch.

"Yes, my lord."

Martinez frowned as he considered the situation. "How did she get it out of my pantry?" Martinez said. "Only a few people have access, and Juskiene isn't one of them. And once you've stolen it, you can hardly walk around with a large heavy plate under your arm."

And then he recalled where he had encountered Filomena Juskiene before and remembered the startled blue eyes looking at him over Mpanza's shoulder.

"Oh," he said.


"SO YOU SAY that Filomena Juskiene was never in my quarters?" Martinez said.

"No, my lord," said Mpanza.

"Not like the other one? Raju, was it?"

Mpanza straightened and assumed a dignified air. "My lord, I learned my lesson on that one occasion."

Martinez narrowed his eyes. "I hope so."

A warning tone warbled along the corridors. The Combined Fleet was due to increase acceleration to two and a half gravities in just a few minutes.

"Better strap in," Martinez said, and pushed his chair back.

He went to his sleeping cabin, made sure his bladder was empty, then took off his tunic and shoes and strapped himself into his bed. He reached for his injector and fired the prep shot into his neck. A sharp chemical taste touched his tongue.

The high-gee warning clattered again, and then came the sensation of lead weights dropping, one by one, onto his chest. A video screen sat above his head so that he could work under acceleration, but there was little he had to do other than acknowledge reports submitted by his captains. He had entertainment options as well, and so he called up a video of Spate in the comedy *Good People with Bad Ideas*, which features his hilarious Cotillion routine, in which roughly sixteen setups inserted earlier in the production

302 WALTER JON WILLIAMS

paid off in the space of about four minutes. Martinez laughed until his ribs ached. It was the first time he had laughed unrestrainedly in months, he thought, and it had to be at a time when heavy gees made laughter painful.

He told the audio system to play music, closed his eyes, and tried to sleep. Under heavy acceleration boredom was sometimes worse than the heavy gravities.

HE MUST HAVE slept, because he had to brush crusty sleep from his eyelids when he woke. He looked at the chronometer and saw that *Los Angeles* would be under high acceleration for another forty minutes before an hour's break for supper.

Martinez saw he had a few messages, and he could tell from their subject line that they were routine except for a message from Roland. He then had to decide whether he really wanted to view a message from his brother. Roland had taken to sending him long messages consisting largely of things he wanted Martinez to do, mainly after he reached Zanshaa. Martinez was willing to do his best, but it was entirely up to Wei Jian whether he would be allowed to do anything at all. If Jian ordered him to take his division on to Magaria and secure the headquarters of the Second Fleet, he would have no choice but to obey, and then Roland would have to find someone else to run his errands.

He shifted inside his webbing to relieve a cramp, then decided the metaphor of having to be tied down in order to hear Roland was an appropriate one. He triggered the message.

The new dispatch was similar in content to the others, but Roland mentioned Hector Braga and asked Martinez to do another search for him.

It was a perfect certainty that Roland knew more about Braga than Martinez did.

Martinez replied to the message, discussed Roland's latest list with as much enthusiasm as he could manage, and then brought up the matter of Hector Braga.

"So far as anyone knows he's completely vanished," he said. "He's certainly not in my command. Lady Sula reports that he's not with Division Nine. The ships carrying civilians from Zarafan to Laredo don't report anyone of his description. So far as I can tell, he never left Zarafan at all, and though it's possible he joined the Fleet under a false name, that really doesn't seem in character for him."

His head swam with the effort of speaking for so long, and he took several breaths before continuing. "I realize I know next to nothing about Braga. We know he was from Spannan, and that he met Lady Sula there, but I don't know what he did there"—he gasped again for breath—"except for a strong suspicion that it was illegal. Does he have any old friends or contacts? Might someone from his past have caught up with him on Zarafan? I know Lord Mehrang blamed him for losing money in his planetary development scheme." He gasped again. "What other schemes was Braga involved with? Do you know?"

*And were any of them yours?* he added mentally, but knew better than to speak the words aloud, not when his message would be going through relays where it might be intercepted.

He ended his response, coded it with his family cipher, and sent it on its journey from star to star.

MACNAMARA WAS A wreck, but he insisted on carrying out his duties.

Sula understood his decision perfectly well—maintaining his routine meant he didn't have to be alone with himself, or with his grief. After Division Nine's departure from Zarafan, Sula had driven herself without mercy in hopes it would help her forget Martinez—which in fact it did, sometimes for whole minutes at a time.

She could drive herself as long as she had a division to command, but since she'd been aboard *Pride of Parkhurst* Sula had little to do but sink far down into her own misery, at least until Dr. Gunaydin came into view.

Gunaydin had become the most stable element of her life. They regularly supped together, they attended dances together, they slept together, they worked out together in the gym. Somehow it was all very easy, and Sula had a terrible suspicion that it was easy because she didn't care that much.

Yet she seemed to be content, or at least as content as it was possible for her to be. Sula was managing to keep the misery at bay, though she was aware that this took a certain amount of mental effort that was wearing over time.

She hoped Macnamara didn't resent this appearance of happiness, and she made a point of trying to connect with him at least once each day, to get some idea of the state of his mind and to try to drag him out of whatever anguished mental space he currently lived in.

Sula was also aware that she wasn't very good at this. She depended on Spence for information and hoped that between the two of them they could guide Macnamara out of the abyss.

And at some point, she knew, she'd have to drag herself out as well.

CONSTABLE HADAD REPORTED to Martinez during break-fast. The Combined Fleet got two hours of normal gravity for breakfast, and besides the meal, the time was also intended to be used for bathing, visits to the toilet, and—for the lucky—a visit to the recreation chambers.

The other meal breaks were shorter.

Most meals during heavy accelerations were stews or casse-roles, because they could be put in the oven for the length of the acceleration, then broken out for a brief meal. The two-hour span for breakfast gave Mangahas a chance to cook something to order, and she produced a fluffy omelet, spicy sausages, garlic rice, and an assortment of pickled vegetables. Martinez, who liked protein with his breakfast, approved.

Hadad arrived just as Martinez was finishing and Mpanza was clearing away the plates, leaving Martinez with his cup and flask of coffee.

"I found instructions for fingerprint powder in the constabu-lary's database, my lord, along with instructions for its use," he said. "I made some powder and dusted the charger, but—" He seemed embarrassed. "You were right, my lord. My own prints were the only ones I found."

Martinez considered this. "That means the charger was wiped before you found it," he said. "So why would the thief wipe her prints, then store it in her own bed?"

Hadad frowned for a moment. "My lord, are you suggesting that the thief hid the charger in Juskiene's bed, intending to remove it later?"

"I don't know enough to suggest anything," Martinez said. "What is Juskiene's sleeping compartment like?"

"She shares the compartment with another warrant officer. It's a small cabin with two desks, a bunk bed, a fold-down table, a pair of closets, and not much else."

Martinez remembered living in similar quarters when he was a cadet. There were few places to hide anything as large as the silver charger, and under the mattress was probably as good as any.

"Do they normally lock their door?" Martinez asked.

Hadad seemed resigned to being obliged to conduct further investigation. "I have not inquired, my lord."

Mpanza had been hovering in the room, unable to drag himself away, listening and standing with the breakfast plate, sitting on its silver charger, still in his hands.

"I never took Filomena into Captain Martinez's suite," he said. "And the pantry is always locked."

Hadad turned to Martinez. "Are the doors to the corridor kept locked?" he asked.

"My office door is often open when I'm working in the office," Martinez said, "but no burglar is likely to get by me when I'm at my desk. The door through the dining room is used mainly by the staff." He turned to Mpanza. "Do you normally lock that door?"

"When we're at quarters," Mpanza said, "and during sleep periods. The rest of the time . . ." He made an equivocal gesture with his free hand. "I don't think we have a set policy. When we're not in our racks under acceleration, Marivic and I spend most of our time in the kitchen or the pantry, and there's not a lot of point in locking ourselves in. Banerjee and Santana are often in the captain's office, and sometimes they stop by for one of Marivic's snacks and to say hello."

Martinez was not surprised that Mangahas's snacks were very popular among his staff. He turned to Hadad. "I don't see how anyone could get in," he said. "Even if one of the doors to the corridor was open, the pantry would always be locked."

"Unless I was moving plates and cups in and out," Mpanza said. "And if that were the case, I'd be in the room myself."

Martinez pondered the impossibilities of the theft, and then an idea flashed through his mind, lighting every brain cell like a strobe.

"Mpanza," he said, "you said yesterday that you'd learned your lesson about taking your lady friends through my suite."

Mpanza seemed uneasy. "Yes, my lord."

"'*On that one occasion,*' you said. The occasion when I found you and Raju together."

"Yes, my lord."

Martinez looked at him closely. "Are you sure there was just the *one* occasion?"

Mpanza's eyes turned uneasily toward a corner of the office. "Well, my lord . . . ," he began.

"You brought her here more than once?"

Mpanza made a visible effort to maintain his dignity. "Yes, my lord. I showed her around—she was interested because she'd never seen a ranking officer's suite. And we used my sleeping cabin now and again."

"Better than the dining table."

"Over time, certainly."

Hadad seemed intrigued by mention of the dining table. Martinez rubbed his chin. "Did you show her the pantry?"

"Well, yes. I wanted to show her all the specialized plates and glassware and so on. That big silver boat used for chilling wine, with all those allegorical figures—you have to admit that's impressive, my lord."

Martinez frowned for a moment into the middle distance, then gave Mpanza a searching look. "Do you think," he said, "that Raju might have stolen the silver charger in order to get Juskiene arrested and somehow win you back?"

Hadad was bewildered—he hadn't heard about Raju till now,

and Martinez could see a hundred questions building up behind his eyes. Mpanza's answer was immediate.

"I think she's crazy enough, my lord," he said. "But I don't see how she could have done it. She doesn't have access to your suite, or the pantry."

Martinez turned back to Hadad. "How did you know to search Juskiene's quarters?" he asked.

"Anonymous denunciation, my lord," Hadad said.

"How often do you *get* anonymous denunciations on *Los Angeles*?"

Hadad hesitated. "It's a happy ship, my lord. Now, I mean. There were a lot of denunciations at the very start, when people didn't know their jobs and had complaints about their officers or their fellow recruits, and they seemed to expect the constabulary to solve their problems. But that all died away when they finally realized they were complaining to the wrong people."

"How many anonymous accusations of criminal activity?" Martinez said.

Hadad frowned. "Just the one, my lord."

"Well then," Martinez said. "I think we should give serious consideration to the notion that Filomena Juskiene was framed."

Hadad let out a long sigh and seemed to diminish, as if he'd lost some of his mass. Martinez turned to Mpanza.

"Put the plates back in the kitchen, then bring Constable Hadad whatever he wants to drink." He turned to Hadad. "Have a seat, Constable. This may take a while."


"COULD RAJU—OR ANYONE—have watched you unlock the doors with a code?"

Mpanza shook his head. "I use a thumbprint, never the keypad."

Cabin door locks on *Los Angeles* were standardized, a fingerprint reader next to a standard eleven-key numerical keypad. Those authorized to pass the doors, like Mpanza and Martinez himself, would have their thumbprint in the system, and would be able to use their print to gain access. Others not normally authorized to be in the area would be able to get a code from an officer and would punch the code into the keypad to open the door.

The lock to the pantry was a different model, with the keypad and no thumbprint reader.

Mpanza and Hadad sat with Martinez at the breakfast table, Hadad with his Citrine Fling and Martinez with his third cup of coffee.

"Constable," Martinez said, "can you look into the records and see if Raju—or anyone else—might have thumbprint access authorized for my suite."

"I never gave her access, my lord!" Mpanza was indignant. "In fact, I couldn't! I'm not authorized!"

"I never said you did," said Martinez. "But Raju could have wrangled it from someone else."

Hadad made a note to himself on his sleeve display. "I'll look into it, my lord."

"And while you're looking, see if anyone was authorized a keypad entry who wasn't supposed to be here."

It might be too early to focus entirely on Raju, Martinez thought. There might be instead an unknown actor—though, he thought, it would have to be an actor with a grudge against Juskiene, and how many could there be?

A warning tone sounded through the ship. "Ten minutes to

high acceleration," Martinez said. He rose from his chair. "Constable, I'll talk to you during the next meal break. In the meantime, we'd better get to our couches."

Martinez returned to his sleeping cabin, took off his shoes and tunic, and then made sure his bladder was empty. During his conversation with Mpanza and Hadad he'd had too much coffee, and he had the feeling that sometime in the next few hours he'd be dragging himself out of bed under two and a half gravities, then creeping to the toilet. It was perfectly possible to walk under 2.5 gee—it was like carrying an overweight person on your back—but he had to take care not to injure himself.

He lay on his bed and strapped himself in, stared at the ceiling, and then felt a sudden, desperate longing to be off this ship and standing on some green world—Zanshaa, Laredo, Harzapid, it didn't matter—to feel the touch of wind on his cheek, to smell vegetation and freshly turned soil and the scent of rain, to be able to walk free beneath a sky of blue or viridian green or star-spangled night, breathing air that had not been filtered and processed.

He wanted to hear the laughter of children. To stand on a shoreline and watch the waves roll in from the far horizon. To see a plant that grew from the ground and not a pot. To kick off his shoes and feel grass beneath his bare feet.

Martinez had spent over two years in artificial environments, ships or ring stations, and the dreadful monotony of living in a habitat so resolutely *fabricated* was dragging him down as assuredly as a 2.5 gee acceleration.

Another warning sounded, and as the engines ramped up he felt the surge, and then the smothering weight.

With every second of acceleration, he was getting closer to Zanshaa.

Once he got down to the surface of the planet, it would take another war to drag him off it.


SULA WOKE WITH a gasp and a sudden spasm. Derivoo blasted from wall speakers. Pain blazed behind her eyeballs, and her mouth tasted foul. She blinked gummy eyes and saw that she was lying atop her bed in her jumpsuit, with the bedroom lights still shining.

She gave a groan and rolled onto her side, and only then realized she had rolled into a pool of vomit. She jerked away, but not before the smell of the vomit hit her, and for a moment it was all she could do to avoid throwing up all over again.

With exaggerated care Sula rose to hands and knees and climbed off the bed. One foot kicked a bottle, which then knocked into another bottle with a clank. She peered down at the floor and saw the two empty gin bottles lying next to a glass fogged with dregs and fingerprints.

*A slight miscalculation*, she thought.

She looked up at the wall chronometer and saw that her breakfast would be brought into the dining room in fifteen minutes or so, and thought she'd better clean up before that happened.

Another rocket of pain exploded in her head as she tried to walk to the bathroom, and she stumbled and grabbed the door frame with one hand to keep from falling. There was a trail of vomit, she saw, between the bathroom and her bed. At least she hadn't stepped in it.

Sula tried to remember the previous evening, but it eluded her. She'd spent the evening by herself, she remembered, and she was thankful that Gunaydin wasn't in the picture.

Though if Gunaydin had been there, she thought, she probably wouldn't be in this situation now.

She stepped into the bathroom and stripped off her jumpsuit and underwear. As she raised a hand to trigger the shower she got a whiff of body odor, sour sweat touched with the juniper scent of gin.

*I smell like Caro Sula,* she thought, and then her gorge rose, and she lunged for the toilet and threw up again.


"LORD SQUADCOM," SAID Martinez, "I've been asked by the Restoration government to find out what rewards you might accept for your service during the conflict."

Senior Squadron Commander Rivven was a Daimong who had defected with his entire command at the Second Battle of Shulduc, then fought with the Combined Fleet at Toley. Rivven was shorter than Martinez, which was unusual for a Daimong, and his gray immobile face was frozen in an expression of hauteur. Occasionally a whiff of his ever-dying flesh came to Martinez's nostrils.

"I should like to be promoted, of course," Rivven said in his beautifully modulated Daimong voice. "But more than anything else, I should like a place in the Convocation and a seat on the Fleet Control Board."

"Everyone I've spoken to wants to be on the Fleet Control Board," Martinez said, "and some are bound to be disappointed. I think your other requests are more than reasonable, though I hope you understand that I'm not the one making the decisions."

"I understand, Lord Captain." Rivven's round black-on-black eyes stared at Martinez with relentless intensity. "Though I think it would be awkward for the government if rewards went only to Terrans."

"I agree, Lord Squadcom," said Martinez.

Martinez understood that the way to please Rivven was to agree with him on all points, and it helped that he *did* agree that Terrans shouldn't hog all the rewards. He also knew that he wouldn't enjoy sharing the Control Board with the prickly Rivven, but supposed that the cause of interspecies solidarity would exact a price.

"This stuff is rubbish, isn't it?" Rivven said. There was a hint of a snarl in his voice.

"Some of it eludes me," Martinez said.

They were at another prize-giving aboard the battleship *Perfection of the Praxis*, this for the Combined Fleet Festival of Visual Arts. Paintings, photographs, and sculptures were on display in the cavernous ballroom, the room smelled of paint and polish, and Wei Jian and other judges wandered from one to the next, taking notes. Martinez noted that Jeremy Foote hovered purposefully at Jian's elbow.

"What is *this* thing supposed to be?" Rivven asked. "It looks like junk taken from the recycler."

The object in question was a bell-shaped structure, tall as Martinez, that had either been corroded in some way or treated so as to seem corroded. Video screens were visible through rents in the sculpture's surface, on which warship crew were seen capering, dancing, or making faces at the camera. The object was plastered with photographs, mostly of politicians or senior Fleet officers, all defaced with the same stuff that had corroded the main structure. Martinez was relieved not to find himself there. Also pasted onto the exterior were labels from products available on the ship, snack foods, drinks, and staples like flour, dried noodles, and canned vegetables.

"Perhaps it's supposed to be satire," Martinez offered.

"Satire is inevitably the product of a rebellious and disordered mind," Rivven said. "Such minds should be suppressed, not encouraged."

Martinez shrugged. "Whatever it is, I think it's fun."

Rivven gave him a long black-eyed stare, and Martinez received the distinct impression that Rivven viewed fun as the inevitable product of a disordered mind.

"If you'll excuse me, Lord Squadcom," Martinez said. "I see another officer I need to speak to."

"Of course, Lord Captain."

The other officer was Chandra Prasad, who was walking with Vonderheydte between two rows of pictures. Both carried cocktails and seemed as interested in each other as in the art on display. Chandra smiled at Martinez's arrival.

"Lo," she said, "the glorious steersman approaches."

Martinez was puzzled, but answered as seemed appropriate. "I'm pleased my achievements have been recognized."

"And *immortalized*," Chandra said. "Have you seen your statue?"

"*My* statue?"

"Come," she said with some glee. "I'll show you." She led Martinez through the rows of art until Martinez came face-to-face with himself.

He was caught in motion, right leg advanced, a stern expression on his face. One hand held the Golden Orb, the other a hand comm. He was in full dress, with the double row of silver tunic buttons and his medals on his chest. The statue was painted in brighter-than-lifelike colors, and next to the more subdued works in the vicinity seemed practically incandescent.

Martinez was unable to find words.

"It's called *The Glorious Steersman*," Vonderheydte said.

"It's a little startling," Martinez said. He searched the statue for any hint of irony, for the sense that he was being *mocked*, but so far as he could tell the work seemed a straightforward piece of homage.

Not that he was any kind of expert, of course.

Maybe he could *buy* it, he thought. Not to keep—it was too garish for anyplace he actually lived—but to donate to somewhere or other. To the city of Garethport on Chee, perhaps, the town his father had named after him. It could sit in the lobby of the city hall, shining in all its fluorescent glory.

"It must be wonderful to be so adored," said Chandra.

"Adoration is something we glorious steersmen must learn to live with." Martinez raised an eyebrow. "Did Wei Jian get a statue?"

"Not that we've found," said Vonderheydte.

"Of course," said Chandra, "if there *were* a statue of her, she'd have to recuse herself as a judge."

"She'd just appoint a flunky to vote for her," Martinez said. "And where did you get those cocktails?"

Chandra pointed toward a corner of the vast room.

"Thank you," Martinez said. "If you see any more adoring impressions of me, let me know."

"I'll be sure to do that," Chandra said.

The drinks, Martinez discovered, were not complimentary and did not include Laredo whisky. With his thumbprint, Martinez paid for a Kyowan and Spacey, and carried the drink into the exhibition, where he found another officer he needed to speak to.

Lord Naaz Vijana had a pointed face, caramel skin, and a pencil-thin mustache that outlined his upper lip. His black eyes darted from one object to another, restless as a sparrow. He had won the thanks of the Convocation for his annihilation of the rebel Yormaks on Esley, a job made easier by employing automatic weapons and fuel-air bombs against a species whose most advanced weapon was a stone-tipped spear. He had fought well in the current war, and had become spokesman for a faction that openly argued for Terrans becoming the dominant species in the empire, replacing the Great Masters.

Martinez didn't like him—his monomaniacal obsession with Terrans ruling the empire had grown tedious—but he also knew that Vijana was a gambler fond of high play and had already lost the money and mortgaged the property the grateful government of Esley had awarded him. He would be wanting more cash to lose at the gambling tables, and Roland Martinez would be willing to provide it if Vijana fell in with Roland's schemes.

So Martinez approached Vijana to ask what rewards he might accept from the Restoration government, and was told Vijana would take a seat in the Convocation, membership on the Fleet Control Board, and a promotion.

"*Everyone* wants the Control Board," Martinez said, "but the rest is perfectly possible."

Vijana was prompt in his response. "In that case," he said, "a seat on the Promotions Subcommittee." Which would give him a say in every promotion in the Fleet, an ideal base for building patronage.

"I'll pass it on," Martinez said. He wasn't sure he wanted Vijana building patronage—he much preferred a malleable bankrupt to the leader of a faction.

Though another consideration was that Vijana's patronage wouldn't go very far if he had no money to support his clients. But then, if he was a member of the Convocation, plenty of people would be offering him money and other sweeteners.

Martinez spent another hour at the exhibition, drifting past the exhibits while meeting and chatting with his fellow officers. He left before he had to listen to Wei Jian's awkward speeches congratulating the prize winners.

Once in the shuttle back to *Los Angeles*, he checked his messages and found an audio report from Constable Hadad. It had been two days since the breakfast meeting with Hadad and Mpanza, and very little had been discovered in the time since, only that the warrant officer who shared a cabin with Juskiene reported that Juskiene was always leaving the door unlocked, and that she'd complained to Juskiene about it.

"I'm unlikely to discover anything new, my lord," Hadad said. "I'd like to suggest I pick up Raju with a couple constables and subject her to an interrogation. It's possible she'd crack and confess."

Martinez considered this, then sent a return message. "Let's meet tomorrow for breakfast and talk about it."

After returning to *Los Angeles*, he gave a supper for Captain Dalkeith and her officers, and afterward he read reports and answered correspondence until it was time for Mpanza to bring in his cocoa. Mpanza arrived, but he didn't bring the cocoa, instead rushing into the study with an expression of fierce joy on his face.

"I just remembered something!" he said. "A few months ago, the fingerprint reader on the dining room door malfunctioned, and I had to use the keypad to manually input the code."

Martinez looked at him as the revelation cascaded through his head, toppling one assumption after another.

"Was Raju with you at the time?" he asked.

"I'm sure of it, my lord. She could have looked over my shoulder."

And then a revelation detonated in Martinez's head with the force of an antimatter collision.

"Do you know what we've been forgetting?" he said. "Raju is an *electrician*."

# CHAPTER 10

Martinez was able to use his command key to get into the records of the electricians' department, and he discovered that the repair on the dining room door had been signed by Master Electrician Park, who headed the electronics division. But then he noticed that Park had signed off on every single repair conducted by his department, leaving the impression that he spent all his time dashing about the ship repairing switches, faulty fixtures, and malfunctioning control panels while his staff played dice games in their office.

Hadad and Mpanza wathced as Martinez called Park. He knew on sight of the man's white hair and waxed mustachio that he was a retiree who had gone back into service when the war began. He also knew this because Park seemed completely unimpressed by his division commander suddenly appearing on his sleeve display.

"Yes, my lord?" he asked.

"Electrician Park, may I ask if you are alone?"

"I'm in my sleeping cabin. My watch just ended."

"Very good." Martinez considered his words. "Electrician Park," he said, "I notice that you sign off on all the work done by your department. Presumably you don't carry out all that work personally."

"I perform tests remotely when one of my staff reports a job done," Park said. "When the test is successful, I sign off on it my-self."

"I'm glad you're keeping on top of things," Martinez said. "I wonder—do you remember who happened to perform the repair on the lock on my dining room door?"

Park suddenly seemed hyperalert, as if he were aware that one of his juniors might be challenged. "Has the lock malfunctioned again, my lord?"

"No, the lock works well," Martinez said. "But I wonder if you remember who was assigned to carry out the repair?"

"That would be Electrician/Second Raju," said Park.

Martinez saw the triumphant smiles on the faces of Mpanza and Hadad. "Thank you, Electrician Park," he said. "I would appreciate your not mentioning this conversation to anyone."

Park seemed concerned. "Is Raju in trouble, my lord?"

"I don't know," Martinez lied, "but there's no sense in worrying her, so please don't bother her about it."

He assumed that Raju had looked over Mpanza's shoulder to learn the combination when he had opened the dining room lock. It was possible she'd done the same for the pantry lock, though he also thought she might have planted a small camera.

When the conversation ended, Hadad was all for arresting Raju immediately, but Martinez wanted conclusive evidence, so he had Hadad bring up his homemade fingerprint kit to find whose prints were on the dining room and pantry locks.

Any fingerprints on the dining room lock had been polished away, but one of Raju's was found on the pantry lock—not on the keypad, but just above it—right as the alarm sounded for high gravities.

"Strap yourself into your couch for now, Hadad," Martinez said. "Then arrest Raju on your dinner break."

"My lord?" Mpanza ventured. "Might he also release Juskiene?"

"He may," said Martinez.

Raju was arrested just as Martinez was sitting down to the casserole that had been simmering in the oven during the hours of high acceleration. Raju didn't bother to deny the accusation and seemed to think that any reasonable person—this would include Constable Hadad—would agree with the necessity of framing Juskiene so that Mpanza would fly back to Raju's arms. She seemed to think that now she had explained her grand design, Hadad would keep Juskiene in lockup and help convince Mpanza that an early marriage to Raju was in his best interests, and she was outraged that Hadad wouldn't fall in with her plan.

"She's still protesting, my lord," Hadad said. "The noise is going to make the constables' station a very unpleasant place if she keeps this up."

Martinez could hear the protests loud in the background. "Fight fire with fire," he advised. "Blast her cell with loud music."

"That won't make my station any more pleasant, my lord."

"But at least you'll have the satisfaction of taking action," Martinez said. "Good luck with it."

He returned to his casserole—ground Hone-bar phoenix, tube noodles, vegetables, and trek-tubers all wafting an undercurrent of allspice.

As casseroles went, it seemed better than most. He called Mpanza.

"You can have the rest of the lunch break for your reunion with Juskiene. I'll ask Mangahas to clear the dishes."

Mpanza brightened. "*Thank* you, Lord Divcom!"

Mpanza hastened away. Martinez's sleeve display gave a chime, and he saw that Roland had sent him a message.

"Of course I have a dossier on Hector Braga," he said. "I

wouldn't be in business with him if I didn't know what there is to know about him. I've attached it to this message. It's very prosaic, and I doubt you'll find it useful."

Roland gave him a searching look, as if he could read Martinez's face across all the distance that separated them.

"If you're engaging in detective work," he said, "I'm going to assume you don't have much to do. Perhaps you should satisfy your detective longings by watching the *Doctor An-ku Mysteries*, then ready yourself for your business on Zanshaa once you arrive."

Your *business*, Martinez thought, *and I seem to be doing all right in satisfying my detective longings—in fact, I just solved a knotty mystery and freed an innocent woman.*

Which he would tell Roland when next he had the opportunity.

The Hector Braga dossier would make suitable reading for the next period of high acceleration.

**SULA LOOKED AT** Dr. Gunaydin over the rim of her lowball glass.

"By the way," he said, "I've certified you as fit for duty."

She looked around the mezzanine with its bar, polished floor, and tented ceiling. "What duty?" she asked. "Even if I'm fit, I'm not assigned to anything but this single ship, and Suri runs it better than I could. I'm not about to get my division back."

Gunaydin raised his drink to his lips. His shaven head gleamed in the spotlights. "Sorry this took so long, but I had to wait for the Combined Fleet to get far enough ahead of us so that Wei Jian couldn't easily send someone here to replace me and certify you into a hospital." He gave a thoughtful nod. "Assuming, of course, that she'd want to do that."

"That was a not uncunning thing to do." Sula narrowed her eyes as she gazed at him. "What do you look like with hair?" she asked.

He laughed. "I'll send you a picture if you like. I shaved my head when I joined the military. I thought it might make life simpler."

They had met for drinks on the mezzanine before another victory dance. *Parkhurst*'s band had been relieved of most of their military duties and reverted to their original civilian function of entertainment, and now there were dances every two or three days.

"Shaving your head makes life simpler?" Sula said. "Maybe I should cut off my hair as well."

Gunaydin's expression showed dismay. "I hope you don't. Besides, you thrive on complexity."

Sula frowned into her drink. "I'm not sure I'd use the word *thrive*."

"I don't know how anyone thrives in the military," said Gunaydin. "But then I'm not best suited for it." He leaned closer, a smile touching his lips. "I don't know if you've noticed, but I'm not a very militant person."

She almost broke into laughter. "Really?"

"I'm still not used to it. When I meet with a patient I want to get to the source of his problem, not have to spend time working out who salutes who."

"But you hardly salute anyone ever, so I don't see why that's a problem for you."

Gunaydin's brows drew together in thought. "I don't salute?" He made a vague gesture. "Sometimes I forget, I suppose."

Sula drank the last of her Bitter Heart, then signaled the waitron for another.

"How is your Macnamara faring?" Gunaydin asked.

Sula shook her head. "It's hard for him. I don't think he's suicidal, so that's something to the good."

"You could send him to me. I could offer something to elevate his mood."

"I've broached the subject," Sula said, "but he's not interested having his mood chemically altered."

"He's determined to suffer, then." Gunaydin seemed resigned. "This sort of thing happens all the time. I don't understand it. We know everything about how the brain works except why people want to live in misery."

A Bitter Heart appeared at Sula's elbow, the color of blood bright with oxygen. She picked it up and sipped, a warming mixture of spirits and sweet wine with a touch of some bitter herb. The spirits were töldo, not gin. She couldn't drink gin, not since she'd whiffed Caro Sula's juniper scent drifting out of her pores.

Gunaydin watched with his mild brown eyes.

"Speaking of mood alteration," he said, "do you normally drink so much?"

She had been drinking less since she'd awakened in a bed spattered with her own vomit. She put that down to an unfortunate experiment, one she had no intention of repeating.

Still, it seemed that even though she was drinking less, she wasn't drinking so much less that Gunaydin had noticed.

"I normally don't drink at all," she said, and then wondered if that was even remotely true. A new normal may have taken hold in the last months.

"But now I seem to be on an enforced vacation, so—" She shrugged. "I drink. I dance. I consider my options."

"You do politics."

Sula shrugged. "It passes the time, and it annoys Wei Jian. Two things to be said for it." She considered her words, then sighed. "When I was in the Convocation before the war, I was frustrated that nothing ever seemed to happen, nothing ever seemed to change. Those six hundred–odd convocates had a *colossal* amount of inertia, and you couldn't shift them. But now meaningful action through the Convocation might be possible, and if it has to be enforced by the Fleet's monopoly on antimatter weapons, well . . ." She shrugged again.

The sound of musical instruments tuning echoed up from the concourse. Gunaydin interlaced the fingers of his hands. "I've heard some of your program. I can't help but think it will be difficult to carry out."

"That's why I want to be dictator. The problem is that too many people have to agree that I should run things."

He laughed, then waved a hand. "Who could blame them? You'll leave them with nothing to do."

Sula took a hearty swig of her Bitter Heart. "Let me finish this," she said. "We'll dance for a while, and then I'll give *you* something to do."

Gunaydin tilted his head and smiled. "I'll look forward to that something," he said, "whatever it may be."

TWO AND A half gravities pressing on his chest, Martinez reviewed Hector Braga's file as it glowed on the video screen above his head. Compiled by a retired detective on Spannan, the report was notable more for what was left out than for what was in it. Braga was from a place called the Fabs, a district of Maranic Town on Spannan. Spannan was a famously ill-run world whose patrons—the Distchin clan—hadn't visited the place in generations, and who used the planet's resources to support their extravagant High City lifestyle.

The Fabs, named after the prefabricated housing into which its residents had been crammed, was the sort of place that bred criminals, and Braga—or Lamey, as his friends called him—had been a mid-level executive in what were called linkboys, because they were part of an illicit chain that connected the lowest elements of society with the highest. His gang of hijackers, extortionists, loan sharks, and con artists had a few good years before one of their bosses was arrested, and Lamey's organization went into hiding before their higher-up informed on them.

When they reemerged, it was with a new protector, a fixer who called himself Lord Gurov—apparently Gurov actually *was* a low-rent Peer, though he was the younger brother of the *real* Lord Gurov. Lamey modeled himself on Gurov, who was paid mainly for settling disputes among linkboys, his job being to stop the linkboys from preying on one another, and instead unite in preying on everyone else. Apparently whatever Gurov did, it wasn't considered a serious enough crime for the authorities to concern themselves with.

In remarkably few years, Lamey exceeded his mentor and became associated with a group of local figures who wanted to get rid of the Distchins and find the planet a less larcenous patron. A large slush fund was raised and a delegation was sent to Zanshaa, and soon Hector Braga became a fixture in the back rooms of the Convocation. Among other things, he'd recruited Roland and several other Peers to co-opt Lady Sula into the Convocation.

The compiler of the dossier had dutifully recorded all Lamey's known associates, the vast majority of whom were part of his crew and had died young. But among those listed were "Lady Sula and her sister, Lady Margaux Sula."

*Margaux Sula?* Martinez stared at the screen while messengers on motorbikes raced up and down his nerves, their dispatch bags all empty.

The association between the Sula sisters and Lamey, the report said, "ended when Braga went into hiding and Lady Sula left for the Cheng Ho Academy."

After he recovered from his shock, Martinez checked the ship's files for a register of the Peerage and found it. Peers were very particular about guarding their genealogies and fussy about what sorts of respect and high regard they were entitled to, and the register was found in the data storage of every ship in the Fleet because no officer wanted to make the mistake of treating a lower-upper-upper as a mere upper-upper-middle.

The record insisted that Caroline Sula was an only child. Martinez cross-referenced the register with every other record he could find, and none mentioned a Margaux. The only relation who appeared in the record was a cousin named Ermina who had been murdered on Terra when Sula had been stationed there. The killer had shot the wrong cousin in a case of mistaken identity, though why he had shot anyone at all remained obscure.

Yet Sula had a cousin who looked enough like her to fool a killer, and this set Martinez to musing on the subject of identity. How many Sulas were there? And who was this Margaux? He wondered if Margaux could have been Ermina using another identity.

Further investigation showed that Ermina—whose surname had been changed to Viswani when the Sula clan fell into disgrace—was in school on Zanshaa when Lady Sula was associating with Hector Braga on Spannan. Assuming of course that this was the real Ermina.

He decided he was growing far too paranoid. Martinez resolved to start from the beginning.

How old had Sula been when she knew Hector Braga? A brief calculation told him that she'd been seventeen years imperial, and—because he couldn't get Sula's conversion algorithm out of his head—fifteen in Terran years.

At which point a solid hatred and contempt of Hector Braga burned like a brand into Martinez's soul. Braga had taken advantage of a girl barely older than a child, and furthermore a girl who was in mourning following the very public execution of both her parents. That she had been involved with a gangster at all showed how confused and vulnerable she had become.

And that swine Lamey had insinuated himself right into Sula's life, probably with the intention of taking possession both of her money and her body.

Martinez paused to indulge in a moment of purest hatred.

The mystery of Margaux remained. Margaux had disappeared at the same time that Sula went to the Cheng Ho academy and seemed never to have reappeared.

Martinez decided to trace the members of Lamey's circle in hopes of eventually interviewing them, but that proved futile. Nearly all mentioned in the dossier were dead, either murdered or executed. The rest were missing, including a girl identified only as Gredel, insignificant save that her disappearance had occurred at approximately the same time as that of Margaux.

She and Margaux might well have been murdered, Martinez thought, and the bodies never found.

The dossier included photographs, but none of either Margaux or Gredel.

Notions of identity continued to circle in Martinez's head, but there was no more information available, because though Fleet vessels had every reason to keep track of Peers' genealogies, none bothered to track schoolgirls on distant planets.

Further inquiries would have to wait till the authority of the Restoration reached Spannan, and then Martinez could commandeer the archives.

MPANZA DEFTLY PLACED Martinez's pickled mayfish before him, set a small bowl of congee decorated with pickled vegetables next to it, refilled Martinez's cup of coffee, then brandished a napkin, which he floated into Martinez's lap. Martinez looked up at him.

"You seem jaunty this morning," he said.

"I have some time off today with Juskiene," Mpanza said, "while you're a guest at Lady Chandra's supper."

"Have a lovely time," Martinez said. "And stay off my dinner table."

Mpanza seemed offended. "My lord," he said, "it was only the once."

"Only the once," said Martinez, "but she was a madwoman."

He would be glad once they got Raju off the ship. She continued to harangue the constabulary from her cell, and the sooner she was transferred to a Fleet-owned labor camp on a fifteen-year sentence, the better.

"Are you going to miss Juskiene when we go to the capital?" Martinez asked. *Los Angeles* was half a day from entering the Zanshaa system.

"I'll miss her a lot, my lord."

Martinez sipped his coffee. "I might be able to get her transferred to Zanshaa, if you'd like that."

Mpanza's eyes brightened. "In your household, my lord? Another orderly?"

"No," Martinez said, "but she's a specialist in maintenance and repair of small vessels, and we'll be coming in and out of Zanshaa City on shuttles. We're going to need ground crew, and Juskiene is suited for the work."

"I'd be ecstatic," Mpanza said.

Martinez picked up his fork. "I'll see what I can do," he said.

"Thank you, my lord!"

Mpanza practically bounded from the room in his happiness.

Martinez stared at the starscape on the wall as the mayfish oozed over his palate. *At least* someone, he thought, *might get a happy ending.*

# CHAPTER 11

"Senior Squadron Commander Tantu has recognized the authority of the Restoration, and offers us the new ships building at Felarus." Banerjee looked up at him from her console, and Martinez could see the joy and relief in her eyes.

"Relay the news to Fleet Commander Jian," Martinez said, "just in case she hasn't seen it."

Felarus was the last major Fleet base that hadn't recognized the Restoration, and Tantu's submission had for all intents and purposes ended the war. A few warships on detached duty, or traveling from one base to another, were still unaccounted for, but they were scarcely a threat to the Combined Fleet or its plans.

Martinez took a brief circuit around his new office in the Commandery, then paused before its broad window to enjoy the view of Zanshaa High City. He could see aides and cadets bustling about their affairs, birds flitting from tree to tree, clouds drifting through Zanshaa's viridian sky. Pure delight tingled through him. He could scarcely believe that, after all those months aboard a ship, he had finally set foot on a planet and was breathing air that hadn't been stored in a bottle.

The Combined Fleet had passed through the Zarafan system in silence and sent no ships to occupy the ring station. From that point the Combined Fleet was under observation by the enemy, and theoretically in communication with Zanshaa, but Wei Jian had sent no demands, and offered no opportunities for dialogue, but instead let the Gruum government observe the torches of over a hundred warships aimed straight at them. The ships were on high alert, ready to fend off any ambushes such as those Martinez had prepared for Do-faq, but no ambushes materialized.

When Jian finally entered the Zanshaa system, she sent to the capital the video of Do-faq surrendering his fleet—then waited developments, which came rapidly. The thirty-eight enemy warships detailed to guard Zanshaa, which had with a degree of cunning placed themselves on the far side of the system from the Combined Fleet and were in no position either to engage or defend the capital, surrendered within hours. Lady Gruum's government lasted only half a day before being voted out of existence by a Convocation more interested in survival than in retaining solidarity with the greedy hacks they'd supported for two years.

The Terran Lord Saïd, who had led the fight against the Naxids and headed the government until overthrown by the Gruum faction, was released from house arrest and appointed Lord Senior. Lord Chen, Terza's father, was then appointed Minister of Right and Dominion, head of the civilian agency that supported the Fleet. Lord Ngeni, the Martinez family's long-time patron, was put in charge of security and the police at the Ministry of Right-Mindedness. One of Wei Jian's relatives, a judge, was made Minister for the Defense of the Praxis, which put him in charge of the black-clad fanatics of the Legion of Diligence.

Saïd sent Lord Chen and a squad of police straight to the Commandery to relieve the officers on duty, to cut off computer access for all personnel, and to make certain that no data was destroyed. Lord Ngeni was sent to the Ministry of Right-Mindedness on a similar errand, and the headquarters of the Legion was likewise secured.

Days before any element of the Combined Fleet docked at Zanshaa's ring, Lord Chen had sent Wei Jian complete information on those forces still pledged to the Gruum government, all warships with their officers, crew, and armaments, and every ship building at every yard scattered through the empire. Demands for the submission of these elements were transmitted.

While most of the Combined Fleet was deployed in the system to defend the capital against counterattack, nineteen ships docked with the ring after eleven days of deceleration. The ships included *Los Angeles*, Michi Chen's flagship *Judge Kasapa*, and Wei Jian's *Crisis*. Military constables debarked to secure the dockyard ahead of the ranking officers, and met there with hundreds of Terran constables shipped up from the planet or released from detention on the ring.

Having taken the ring, the next step had been to secure Zanshaa City. The elevators that connected Zanshaa's ring with the planet dropped on or near the planet's equator, and from the elevator terminal to Zanshaa was a long and vulnerable ride even on a supersonic train.

Accordingly, it was determined to send the first wave by shuttle down to Wi-hun airfield outside Zanshaa. This was where the Naxids had landed their occupying forces in the last war, and Martinez regretted the necessity, because the sonic booms rattling windows in the city wouldn't be heard as the trumpet-blast of liberation, but a reminder of a miserable, murderous, and oppressive occupation.

Martinez came down first, with his suite, and was met by a company of the constabulary—all Terran—and another Terran company of the Motor Patrol. The easiest route from Wi-hun into

Zanshaa would be the Axtattle Parkway, but Naxids had been ambushed there in the last war, and a Daimong named Fer Tuga had made a great reputation for himself as "the Axtattle sniper" for the casualties he'd inflicted on enemy convoys. For all Martinez knew, Fer Tuga was back in business, on the other team, and crouched in his sniper's nest waiting.

Martinez chose a less efficient but far more discreet route into the city, and was driven without incident through the Lower Town to the switchback road that climbed to the High City through the Gates of the Exalted, and from there to the Commandery. The city seemed shabby and depressed, and there were a great many listless people on the streets. Apparently, the economic crisis that had helped to trigger the war was still ongoing.

The atmosphere at the Commandery was disturbingly normal: people—not all Terran—going quietly about their business, doing the jobs that kept the Fleet in being, and the ships in touch with one another and their commanders. But there were armed Terran constables patrolling the big building, and an unnatural quiet pervading the halls, the dining rooms, and the communications center. Many of the staff, perhaps, expected to be arrested at any moment.

Martinez met his father-in-law at the latter's office in the Commandery. Maurice, Lord Chen, had gained weight during his period of house arrest and suffered from a slight tremor in his hands, perhaps not unconnected to the brandy fumes he trailed behind him. The office, with its lemon-yellow walls and pictures of long-dead Fleet heroes, seemed not to have been altered since his predecessor, Lady Tu-hon, had inhabited it. There was even a portrait of one of Tu-hon's ancestors, though it had been taken from the wall and partly hidden behind a credenza.

Lord Chen dropped heavily into his office chair and invited Martinez to take another seat.

"By the all, it's been hard," Chen said. "Everything's changed. I've been viewing the orders issued from the Commandery—issued by people I'd thought were friends of mine—and I've discovered what bloodthirsty little horrors they all were. Now, of course, these same people are all in orbit around me, telling me how great I am, how they were always on the side of the Restoration, and offering the names of former colleagues who should be arrested and interrogated."

"That sounds like business as usual," Martinez said. "I thought you said everything has changed."

Lord Chen snarled. "I'd suggest killing them all, except that it would be too reminiscent of their own tactics. Instead, we should deprive them of rank and honor, and send them out to labor farms to harvest soybeans for the next fifty years."

Martinez had to admit that Chen painted a pleasing picture. "None of that is up to me," he said. "But you should send the files to Wei Jian and to Terza, if you haven't already."

Chen seemed not to have heard, but instead turned away and looked at an ornamental sculpture attached to the wall. It was made of dark wood and featured peaks and troughs similar to the waves of an ocean—or, Martinez thought, like a three-dimensional representation of spacetime.

Hypnotizing, in its way. Certainly, Lord Chen seemed hypnotized. When he spoke, his words seemed to rise from the black depths of a singularity.

"It's all slipped away from me, somehow," he said. He waved a trembling hand. "I may resign soon—not just the office, but the title. Terza will make a fine Lady Chen." He turned to Martinez and raised one eyebrow. "You could be Lord Chen, if you want it."

"You're the only Lord Chen we need right now," Martinez said.

Chen offered a melancholy smile. "That's very kind of you, Gareth." He turned to face Martinez. "I haven't been a good host, I suppose. Would you join me in some brandy?"

Martinez rose from his chair. "I would, but I have to pay my respects to the Lord Senior."

"Of course," said Lord Chen. "And please convey my own best wishes."

"I'll send you videos of Chai-chai and Mei-mei," Martinez said. "You can catch up with your grandchildren."

Chen brightened. "That would be lovely," he said.

Martinez headed for the Commandery's exit. His guards, armed military constabulary in their red belts and armbands, followed behind, not bothering at all to be discreet.

He mused on his relationship with Lord Chen, which had always been uneasy. At the beginning of the Naxid War, Roland had put Chen under a considerable financial obligation, and then demanded Terza for his brother as part of the payment. Martinez knew that Chen resented his daughter's being married to a man he considered a hayseed from a distant, unimportant world, and he absolutely hated the idea of one of that hayseed's children being in line to become Lord or Lady Chen, spoiling centuries of the scrupulous managing of bloodlines with other High City families.

When he'd learned that he would be expected to marry Terza, Martinez's relationship with Sula had just blown apart, and he had gone through with the marriage in a state of stunned hopelessness. But he'd realized that Terza was the real victim of this arrangement, and he'd sworn to treat her fairly and to be a good husband to her.

Except, of course, now he wasn't.

After two years of war and house arrest, perhaps Lord Chen had reconsidered his position, or at any rate reordered his priorities.

Perhaps, in the face of a long, bloody, and destructive civil war, a pure bloodline was no longer the most important thing in the world.

Or perhaps Lord Chen was simply a mellow drunk. Time would tell.

Martinez walked from the Commandery to the Convocation along the Boulevard of the Praxis, and his heart soared at the sight of the flowers planted in their rows, the impressive façades of the government buildings, the warmth of the sun on his face, the smells of earth and living things. He even delighted in the statues of *The Great Master Delivering the Praxis to Other Peoples*, an allegorical piece he normally viewed as a heavy-handed atrocity.

Thanks to his victories at yachting and his prominent role in the documentary series about the Naxid War, he was very recognizable, especially as he was wearing full dress with the golden disk of the Orb at his throat. People on the boulevard for the most part regarded him with caution, and some stepped aside for him as if they were afraid they'd be shouldered off the walk. A few humans cheered and applauded. He gave them a nod and a wave.

When he passed into the foyer through the iconic bronze doors of the Convocation, with the famous relief *The Many Species of the Empire Being Uplifted by the Praxis*, he was met by aides who escorted him past multiple layers of security to the office of the Lord Senior. Unlike Lord Chen's office, hardly changed from its occupation under Lady Tu-hon, Lord Saïd now firmly inhabited his quarters. The dark-paneled walls held portraits of ancestors and former occupants of the office. Lord Saïd's rayed badge hung in a place of honor, and his desk was covered with carvings of fruit and grain, symbols of abundance. The floor was deep with bright, handwoven carpets. Saïd's red ceremonial cloak hung on a special stand, adja-

cent to another stand that held the ornate copper wand with which
he controlled debate in the Convocation. The room held a slight
musky smell, something like sandalwood.

The Lord Senior himself was an ancient, wizened figure, his
oversized beak of a nose dominating a shrunken, wrinkled face.

"I bring good news, Lord Senior," Martinez said. "Tantu's surrendered the ships at Felarus. I think that means the fighting's at
an end."

Saïd's eyes glowed--- in contrast to his frail appearance, Saïd's
eyes seemed to gleam with youth and intelligence.

"I shall celebrate with tea and lemon cake," he said. "Perhaps
you will join me? If you would prefer something other than tea, I
would be happy to provide it."

"Tea would be very welcome. And the lemon cake also."

Martinez sat in a chair that quietly adjusted itself to his physique as he and Saïd exchanged pleasantries. The tea came in on
a trolley, pushed by a Cree servant nearly as old as Saïd himself.
The Cree poured from a distinctive eight-sided cobalt-blue teapot,
and a smoky scent rose in the room. Sula, Martinez thought, would
know who had made that teapot, and how many centuries old it
was, and what kind of tea was being served.

For himself, he knew the teapot was a teapot, and that it had
tea in it, but he also knew the sort of reception that was expected,
so he took the cup, inhaled its aroma, and took a taste.

It tasted very much like tea. "Exquisite," he pronounced. "I
don't believe I've tasted anything quite like it."

"It's a first cutting from my estates in the Lossing Highlands,"
Saïd said. "I'm so pleased you like it."

The lemon cake tasted like lemon cake, but then Martinez
liked lemon cake and had no objections.

After tea, Martinez circled back to the business at hand. "How can the Fleet help you, Lord Senior?" he asked.

"You can send more recruits down to the planet's surface," said Saïd. "We're outnumbered here. I've disbanded Tu-hon's militia, the Steadfast League, and they're supposed to turn in their weapons, but they might decide to turn them on us instead, storm the High City just as Lady Sula once did."

"What about Tu-hon herself?"

"She and Gruum and the other chieftains of their clique are under arrest," Saïd said. "The best thing would be to get them on a shuttle and up to the ring station as soon as possible, to prevent any possibility of rescue."

"We could simply shoot them," Martinez said.

"Oh, they will certainly be executed," Saïd said. "But I want them humiliated and disgraced first."

"I can't say I disagree."

Saïd's eyes turned solemn. "We are surrounded by felons and thieves," he said. "So many people were denounced as being in league with the Terran criminals . . ." His eyes flickered. "In league with *you*, and with your family."

Martinez felt a flush warm his skin. "I'm sorry that my family was used as an excuse for . . ."

Saïd waved a hand. "That doesn't matter. They would have found an excuse no matter what your family did." He leaned forward. His head suddenly seemed very heavy, and it sank down deep into his thin shoulders. "Many of those denounced lost their lives," he said, "and the rest lost money and property. Gruum's clique didn't victimize the highest ranks of Terran Peers—*I* was safe, and Lord Chen, and the Yoshitoshis and Ngenis and so on—but they felt free to prey upon those who were less prominent, and whose disappearance wouldn't create a big fuss."

"Lost money and property can be returned," Martinez said. "I presume there are records of all these dealings, and I imagine the executions were broadcast on the Punishment Channel."

"Yes, yes." Again, Saïd waved a hand. "But it will be an enormous undertaking to straighten all this out, and the crimes took place from one end of the empire to the other. The only way to counter the round of denunciations will be to call for a new round of denunciations, this time of the Tu-hon clique. It won't be pretty, and it will go on for some time."

"It will be a very large task," Martinez said. "I would offer the Fleet's assistance, but I'm not sure how the Fleet can help."

"As I said, send down more constabulary," Saïd repeated. "The government must be made safe, and those who prosecute our enemies must be safe as well."

"I'll transmit the request to Fleetcom Jian," said Martinez. "We'll soon have no lack of personnel. We can bring retired crew back to the service, and train new volunteers." He shook his head. "We're going to have to train a lot of new recruits in any case, to crew the ships we build to replace losses."

"I imagine Fleetcom Jian would approve of any projects that would increase the number of ships and personnel under her command."

"I can't think otherwise." Martinez turned to the door as the ancient Cree entered and offered to refill their teacups. Martinez held out his teacup wordlessly, and as the Daimong poured, he turned back to Saïd.

"Is there any other way I can help you, Lord Saïd?"

Saïd frowned. "Your brother's messages have been urging me to consider the economic policies of someone named Ming Lin. Yet Miss Lin's program is opposed to everything my advisors and the Imperial Bank are telling me."

"The economy of Harzapid is booming," Martinez said, "along with the economies of all the planets in the Restoration's sphere. You still seem to be in an economic depression here, which would cause me to question the policies of all your banks and advisers."

Saïd considered this. "There is something in what you say."

"Michi Chen knows more about this than I do. She was part of the committee that implemented Lin's policies, so you might contact her."

Martinez sipped his tea. It still tasted like tea.

"Perhaps. Most importantly," Saïd said, "we have to get rid of Tu-hon's tax laws. She repealed the tax on income she so hated, and replaced it with the old tax on shipping. As a result, shipping came to a stop, and even in the High City there are shortages of imported items. We need to get the economy flowing again, and we need to bring in income to the government."

It was the Convocation that could change the law, Martinez knew, and Saïd was the Lord Senior of the Convocation. He didn't need Martinez or the Fleet to do it, and Martinez wondered why Saïd was raising the issue.

"The Convocation can change the law," Saïd continued, "but the Convocation needs to be *safe*."

Martinez understood—three times were more than enough to drive the point home. "I will tell Wei Jian to make the constabulary her priority."

"Thank you, Lord Fleetcom." Saïd's benign brown eyes gazed at Martinez. "But for now, would you like more cake?"

LORD SAÏD'S REQUEST for more constabulary was relayed to Wei Jian, and the next wave of shuttles was packed with constables as well as Michi Chen and her suite. When the shuttles rocketed from Wi-hun and returned to the ring station, they carried Lady Gruum, Lady Tu-hon, and others of their clique to confinement on the ring. Martinez made a point of being present, so that he could see the leaders of the former government shuffling to the shuttle in fetters.

Seeing the captives, he felt pleased and righteous at the same time.

Michi was installed in the Commandery, which left Martinez with enough free time to consider his own situation in the High City. Lord Saïd had mentioned money and property being confiscated, and he decided it was high time he viewed his house. After all, his family was coming and would need a place to live.

His palace was modest in size for the High City, with only twelve rooms, but it was perched on the northern edge of the acropolis, with a glorious view of the Lower Town below. The thought that the Tu-hon clique might have confiscated it and then sold it to one of their lackeys made Martinez grind his teeth.

He called for three Hunhao sedans, packed them with constabulary, and set out for his home. To his relief, the house seemed unchanged, with its pale gold marble exterior and the contrasting green malachite pillars, but when he approached the front door he noticed some vases in the windows that weren't his. The door wouldn't open to his thumbprint, so he knocked. A Lai-own female in livery answered.

Martinez pushed past her into the foyer. "I need to speak to the master or mistress of the house," he said.

"I will see if his lordship is available."

Martinez didn't wait in the foyer, but followed the servant through the front rooms and into what had formerly been his office. Along the way he viewed the home and furniture with a critical eye. The pale marble was untouched, as were the carnelian pillars veined with red, but everything else had been changed, and for the worse. He and Terza had bought a building half-wrecked in the storming of the High City, and she had conserved and decorated the palace with superlative taste.

Terza's carefully chosen Devis mode furniture was gone, replaced with elaborately carved, vulgar pieces that seemed guaranteed to grow shabbier and sadder with each passing year. Valuable artwork had been replaced with commonplace paintings and the usual undistinguished portraits of ancestors. The palace's most unusual feature, the brass star-shaped plugs that had been used to seal up the bullet scars from the High City battle, had been removed, and the scarred marble subject to dubious repairs or hidden behind paintings or tapestries.

*And people think* I'm *a parvenu,* Martinez thought. *I've got nothing on this fellow.*

Martinez hadn't ever thought of himself as a snob, but apparently he was, at least where his own decor was concerned.

The master of the house was a plump Lai-own who was found bent over his desk, inhaling a dy-chi intoxicant. He looked up in surprise as his servant entered.

"Lord Dop," said the servant in haste, "this gentleman has—"

"This gentleman," said Martinez, "is Lord Gareth Martinez, commander of the Grand Division of the Rear in the Combined Fleet." He gave Lord Dop a glare. "You are in my house. Kindly remove yourself, your family, and your trash from my home."

Lord Dop rose from his chair, his inhaler still in his hand. "I am Lord Dop Kas-la," he said, "and I purchased this house legally—"

"From someone who had no right to the title," Martinez said. "I suggest you ask for your money back."

"I purchased it from the *government*," Lord Dop said. "At auction, for sixty-three thousand zeniths."

"You were robbed," Martinez said. "As was I. Do you know what happened to my furniture?"

Lord Dop stared with his golden eyes. "The house was empty when I bought it," he said. "All except for some rubbishy old painting of a Fleet officer. I kept the frame and threw the rest out."

The painting, Martinez knew, was of himself, the young victorious captain of *Illustrious*. He stiffened with rage.

"I'll find out what became of my possessions. In the meantime—" He waved a hand. "Push along, will you? I've got a building to get ready for my family."

Lord Dop stared for a few moments, then sat down in his chair with an emphatic gesture. His nictating membranes slid closed over his eyes. "I refuse to leave," he said. "This is my palace. The title belongs to me—" He gave Martinez a triumphant look. "From the *government*." As if that settled things.

Martinez laughed. "You might consider whether you can buy a legitimate title from an illegitimate government."

"Leave at once," said Lord Dop. "Or I'll summon the police."

"Oh," Martinez said. "The police? Allow me." He called for a pair of military constables and pointed to Lord Dop's chair. "Take this chair," he said, "and throw it into the street. If Lord Dop remains in the chair, throw him into the street along with it."

The constables swung Lord Dop into the air and began to carry him toward the door. Dop's inhaler clattered to the floor as he clutched at the arms of his chair.

Lord Dop didn't actually make it as far as the front door, because at that point his wife appeared, uttered a series of shrieks, and hurled herself at one of the constables. Servants and children clustered about, gobbling. A loud, chaotic scene followed that could end only one way, given that one party had guns and stun batons and the other didn't. Lord Dop, his family, and his household ended up outside on the sidewalk, watching while military police carried all their belongs out into the street. Lord Dop eventually conceded and hired some vehicles to take his stuff away.

In the meantime, Martinez called Aitor Santana and asked him to find out what had happened to his furniture. "It must be on record somewhere," he said.

It was. The furniture had been consigned to a warehouse in the Lower Town belonging to a company called Stellar Properties. Martinez put guards on the door of his palace to keep Lord Dop from creeping back in, put the rest of the constables back into the Hunhao sedans, and sped to the Lower Town.

The warehouse had its own guards who faded away as soon as they realized who had just appeared on their doorstep. When Martinez entered the building, he stopped in his tracks and gazed in wonder at the cornucopia stretching out before him. The place was full of furniture, paintings, sculptures, carpets, and ornamental bits of architecture—cornices, caryatids, capitals, medallions, grotesque faces, roundels, carved flowers and ferns—possibly rescued from demolished buildings but perhaps just ripped from façades.

Light flashed from dozens of grand mirrors. A procession of chandeliers hung from the metal roof beams. Sideboards, buffets, and cabinets were stuffed with porcelain, gold and silver plate, glassware, and cutlery.

There were several large safes lined up in one part of the warehouse, and Martinez had no way of knowing what they contained. Jewels, he thought. Possibly bonds or some other form of tradable asset. It wouldn't be gold or silver because the gold and silver were lying in plain sight.

Martinez hadn't been in the warehouse long before he realized that he wasn't viewing items stowed away by their owners, but a vast pile of someone's loot. Someone had used the government to confiscate wealth and transfer it to Stellar Properties.

He called Santana and told him to find out who owned Stellar Properties. In the meantime, he went to the warehouse office and told the manager to locate all his property. The manager, a powerfully built Daimong who smelled liked a ten-day-old corpse and looked as if he might have stolen some of the items himself, viewed the constabulary with their sidearms and batons and complied with great speed and efficiency.

Sula had argued for a military dictatorship, and Martinez was beginning to see her point. It made for efficiency in getting things done.

Martinez set the warehouse workers to carrying his belongings to the heavy trucks parked in the warehouse lot. Several of the firm's drivers were present, and Martinez had the manager summon more. While this went on, Martinez called the Ministry of Right-Mindedness, spoke to Lord Ngeni, and reported the warehouse and its contents.

"I imagine this will be the first warehouse of many," Ngeni said. Martinez could imagine the scowl on Ngeni's round cannonball head.

"They left a fairly easy trail for us," Martinez said. "If you follow the bureaucratic trail of where confiscated material goods were sent, I imagine you'll find any number of these places."

Ngeni gave a sigh. "I'm not sure I have the personnel for any of this. Personnel I can *trust*, I mean."

"I understand." It was the Ministry of Right-Mindedness that had confiscated the goods in the first place, and perhaps some of the police had profited from their actions.

"The Fleet might be able to help," Martinez said. "Let me give it some thought."

He left guards in the warehouse when he led the convoy of trucks and Hunhao sedans back to his house. En route he received a message from Aitor Santana concerning the ownership of Stellar Properties.

"The principal shareholder is someone named Simone Beckwith," he said.

"Wait," said Martinez. "She's a *Terran*?"

"Indeed. And interestingly enough, a minority shareholder is Lord Troom Lamong."

The Torminel name triggered a faint sense of recognition. "Lamong? How do I know that name?"

"He is the former minister of right-mindedness."

Martinez almost laughed aloud. "Do we know where he is?" he asked.

"I checked. He's under house arrest, my lord."

"Well," said Martinez. "We'd better haul him to jail, then."

# CHAPTER 12

"I've received information from the Naxids in the Combined Fleet," said Lord Nishkad. "They are ordered off their ships and are being sent back to Harzapid or Zarafan, wherever it is they came from."

Sula wasn't surprised. "I'm very sorry to hear it," she said. "They helped to achieve victory, and their contribution should be acknowledged."

Nishkad had invited her for a meeting in his suite aboard *Parkhurst*. The walls were pale green and gold, with landscape paintings in elaborate frames. Nishkad was coiled on a small settee designed for his centauroid species, and Sula sat in a comfortable armchair breathing in the flower scent of the tea that Nishkad had served her. An oblong table with a mosaic top sat between them, and tension simmered in the air.

"Is this the gratitude we can expect from the new government?" Nishkad asked. "Will nothing change?" Suppressed anger tautened his voice.

Sula sipped her tea as she calculated an answer. "I think the government is removing a possible source of contention," she said. "It would be difficult for them to flatly deny the Naxid contribution to the Restoration, and so they strive to limit the opportunities for the contribution to be discovered."

"I and my people are a 'source of contention,' then?" Nishkad said.

"A *possible* source," Sula reminded him. "When we try to reform the Convocation and the organs of government, it's best to concentrate on one job at a time. We must get the Convocation we need, and then more things are possible." She put down her cup, leaned toward Nishkad, and looked into the black-on-red eyes.

"I *have* given you a promise that I will do my best to ease restrictions on Naxids," she said. "And I further promise to give those who worked for the Restoration credit for their accomplishments." She touched herself on the chest. "*I* put Naxids on warships," she said. "I did it on my own authority. I knew it would be controversial, but I knew it was necessary for the success of the Restoration—and you know it as well." She nodded. "One day everyone will know it. This I promise you."

Her arms and legs tingled with the elation of her argument. She knew she was radiating sincerity, and that meant she probably *was* sincere.

Nishkad seemed unimpressed by her sincerity.

"I will submit to this humiliation," he said, "but only because I must. Yet it is a sad day when our new government cannot even acknowledge our contribution with a mere thank-you."

She knew that feeling all too well. And planned to remedy it for both of them.

THE DISCOVERY OF the warehouse with its booty was widely broadcast on Zanshaa, and video of the spoils and the arrest of Simone Beckwith and former minister Lamong were sent throughout the empire. An investigation of Stellar Properties found two more warehouses filled with plunder, and the money trail showed that Lamong had received nearly 40 percent of the cash from sales of the spoils, a figure that far exceeded his stake in the company.

The willingness of the Terran chairman of Stellar Properties to plunder her own species became a ten-minute sensation.

Martinez was surprised that the owners of Stellar Properties hadn't really bothered to hide their actions. They'd assumed they would be immune to all consequences, they'd assumed they had rights to the plunder, and they'd assumed they'd ride to riches on the backs of the dispossessed. Martinez was happy to disappoint them.

It was soon discovered that Stellar Properties, as befit its name, owned real property in addition to warehouses stuffed with loot. Confiscated homes had also shuffled to the custody of Beckwith, Lamong, & Co.

The scandalous revelations were reported daily in all media and served to blacken the Gruum administration's image. Other revelations weren't long in coming. Lady Tu-hon was found to have taken kickbacks on contracts to supply and support the Fleet. Lord Minno, the former minister of finance, was found to have used government money to finance his own private speculations and was discovered to have taken bribes to order the government to buy dubious securities. Gruum, the Lady Senior, had charged people who wanted to meet her for the purpose of obtaining contracts or other government business. She was far too proud and imperious to handle the money herself—for that she had minions, who got 10 percent of whatever they could collect.

She also had bought a number of confiscated Zanshaa City properties for a fraction of what they were worth.

None of this was exactly surprising—trading favors and the

offering of sweeteners to those with the power to give out government contracts was common enough. What was surprising was the
*scale*, the fact that they were *all* in on it, and that they didn't even
bother to hide the transactions.

Arrogance and stupidity on a galactic scale—literally.

The Fleet was able to aid the investigations, mainly by reviewing and processing data. Now that the war was over, the Combined
Fleet had a great many communications techs and analysts with
very little to do, and they were happy to dig through government
files for information that would blight the lives of those who had
supported war and the persecution of their species.

Wei Jian had been equally happy to loan her crews for this duty,
in exchange for receiving credit for any revelations. Martinez, used
to other people usurping his ideas, didn't even bother to be surprised.

With Lord Chen and his sister Michi running the Commandery, Martinez now had a great deal more time to devote to his new
hobby of fighting corruption. He led raids in person, usually trailed
by cameras from his sister's Imperial Broadcasting, and was seen
frog-marching guilty parties into custody. Such people as he encountered seemed to think well of this. *We might be holding you hostage with our many missiles*, he thought, *but at least we're arresting
bad people and returning stolen property. Which is more than the other
side did.*

Mpanza helped put Martinez's palace in order. Mangahas was
installed in the kitchen. Hirelings carried furniture and decorative objects from room to room. Martinez was pleased to rehire
Doshtra, the Daimong butler he'd left behind when he fled to Harzapid.

He had retrieved most of his possessions. A few objects had
perhaps been stolen by police, or by employees of Stellar Proper-

ties, but nothing of great value was missing. The object he most greatly missed was his portrait by Montemar Jukes.

In any case, it was perhaps time to have another portrait painted, one alluding to his victory at Second Shulduc. And a second portrait, of a family group, with Terza and his two children.

In addition to taking back his own home, Martinez also reclaimed the Martinez Palace, the residence of his brother, Roland. The great pink limestone house overshadowed the Street of Righteous Peace in the High City, and it had been confiscated and sold early in the war. The building's new master had moved to the country after the Combined Fleet appeared in the system, and only a few servants were in residence, which made it easy for the building to be repossessed. Much of the contents had been sold in a series of auctions, and Martinez recovered what he could from yet another stash house. If Roland wanted to track down the rest, Martinez would leave it to him.

He paid a call on his sister Vipsania's husband, Lord Oda Yoshitoshi, who had spent the war under house arrest, but who had otherwise suffered no losses. As Lord Saïd had said, the Yoshitoshis were too highly placed to plunder openly.

Martinez returned from this visit to his palace to find a young Daimong officer waiting for him in the parlor. The stranger wore red staff tabs on his collar, and the insignia of a lieutenant-captain. His gray-skinned face was frozen in an expression of surprise. Martinez did wonder if he was here on a mission of assassination, but he knew the guards outside would have searched him thoroughly. Just in case, he stood a good four paces away.

"I'm very sorry to bother you at home, my lord," said the stranger in his melodious Daimong voice. "But you seem not to spend a lot of time in the Commandery, and I thought it best that I introduce myself. I am Lord Ethgro Tribe."

"Lord Ethgro," Martinez said. "What can I do for you?"

"I hope we can keep our conversation in confidence, at least for the present. I may be in some danger if my information is prematurely revealed."

"Unless your information has some urgency," Martinez said, "I'll certainly keep it quiet."

"It's no longer urgent," said Lord Ethgro. "It deals with events that took place almost two years ago." He paused for a moment, and a hint of determination entered his words. "I wished to reveal to you that I served on the Fleet Planning Staff under Lord Tork and was privy to his plan of seizing all Terran ships in the Fleet."

Martinez felt his curiosity rise. "Continue, Lord Ethgro," he said.

"It was I who revealed Tork's plan to the Inspector General of the Fleet, Lord Ivan Snow. It was he, I believe, who alerted you and other officers of Tork's scheme and enabled your escape to Harzapid."

Martinez considered this. "Snow informed my father-in-law, who informed me. But it seems I owe you a great many thanks."

"Tork's plan was mad," said Ethgro, "and that the government chose to back him was even madder." His vocal apparatus made a buzzing noise of disgust. "We are well rid of them," he said. "The great shame is that so many brave and dedicated officers and recruits had to die before Tork's insane ideas were suppressed."

"You're fortunate that you escaped," Martinez said.

"Most officers wanted to fight, as a road to promotion," said Ethgro. "I didn't, and so had no difficulty staying in desk jobs until the end of the war."

"Where are you situated now?"

"I've been furloughed. Before that, I was part of a unit trying to estimate the resources available to the Restoration." He made the buzzing noise again. "We were useless. The leadership told us what conclusions they wished us to draw, and we obeyed." Light glittered in his motionless black eyes. "Even so, my personal analysis, which was suppressed, said you couldn't hold out. I failed to account for the Restoration's economic rebound."

"You were right about the important thing," Martinez said. "Are you looking for employment? And if so, where?"

Ethgro's voice was as melodious as birdsong. "For now, a return to intelligence work. I think I was good at it. Eventually, when the Fleet builds up its numbers again, I would hope for command of a ship."

If his story checked out, Martinez thought, that was exactly what Ethgro would get.

"I will do my best to get you back into the Investigative Service," Martinez said. "My personal recommendation can get you that far. But for the rest, I would have to tell your story to my superiors."

"Let us take it one step at a time," said Ethgro. "At this point I prefer discretion." He gracefully inclined his hairless gray head. "You have won the war in space, but have uncertain control of this world outside of Zanshaa City. You may be able to protect yourselves, but allies such as myself will be more vulnerable."

The beautiful voice was at odds with the chill analysis delivered from the gray expressionless face. Martinez found himself resisting Ethgro's conclusions. *Surely*, he thought, *we are loved. We have brought freedom, economic opportunity, and the blessings of peace.*

But yet.

"As you wish, my lord," Martinez said.

"SO IS IT time to have one of those conversations?" asked Dr. Gunaydin.

Sula had known that such a conversation was inevitable. *Pride of Parkhurst* had finally entered the Zanshaa system and would dock with the ring after ten days of deceleration.

"I suppose we ought," she said. She kicked off her shoes and put one of her feet in Gunaydin's lap. He seemed a little surprised, but then he smiled and dropped a hand to stroke her instep.

One of the great advantages of being on a ship like *Parkhurst* was that Sula's suite was much larger and grander than quarters on a warship. She and Gunaydin were in her lounge, a symphony in shades of white and beige, and relaxing on plush beige chairs. They had been enjoying drinks and snacks—*snacks* because Sula had been stuffed with food at far too many banquets and formal dinners, and a few nibbles artfully arranged on small plates were a welcome sight.

"Well," Sula said. "What do you want? Or hope?"

Gunaydin's tone was carefully neutral. "I hope to be separated from the Fleet as soon as possible," he began.

Sula nodded. "I can probably arrange that."

"And then I could return to Harzapid, perhaps to start a practice. Or I could stay on Zanshaa to try to find work here." His brows lifted. "What do you advise?"

Sula took a sip of her silver Cavado wine, the taste light and airy on her palate. "I would be pleased if you'd stay," she said.

"But stay as what?" Gunaydin said. "I don't quite understand my status. Am I the rebound man, the wartime man, or something else?"

The question caught Sula by surprise. "Your categories are just a little reductive," she decided.

"Possibly." Gunaydin sipped his wine. "But it's a question that's been on my mind for a while."

"Well," Sula said, "you can't be the wartime man if I invite you to stay on Zanshaa after the war is over."

"You haven't actually invited me," said Gunaydin.

"My mistake." Sula made a graceful gesture with her wineglass. "Consider yourself invited."

"Thank you." Gunaydin stroked Sula's shin and ankle. "But I'm going to have to remain reductive for a moment. I'm happy to be invited, but as what?"

"As whatever suits you. I can help you find your footing. I'm wealthy, if not as rich as the High City families. I can get you an apartment. I can set up your practice."

Now it was Gunaydin's turn to be surprised. He held up a hand. "Let me stop you before you promise to buy me many pretty things. My ambitions never extended to being someone's fancy man."

Sula grinned. "There you go with your reductive categories again."

"But still—"

"I *did* say 'whatever suits you. If being a fancy man doesn't suit, I won't turn you into one." She gave him a critical look. "You're insufficiently decorative anyway."

Gunaydin began to massage Sula's foot. She sighed and shrugged herself deeper into her plush chair. "I'm offering to make your arrival on Zanshaa easier, that's all. If you'd rather do it all yourself, I'll stand back and applaud."

He frowned down at his hands and dug strong fingers into the pad of her foot. "Say I establish myself on Zanshaa, however I do it," he said. "What happens then?"

"Too many variables," Sula said.

"I realize," he said, with a kind of plodding insistence, "that I would make an unsuitable spouse. I'm a commoner, I have only a modest amount of money, and I have no military or political power that could help you in your career. Whereas you are from a family of the highest rank and your career stands at a high point. You would want a husband who could help you rise."

"I don't want a husband at all," Sula said. "Honestly, it's the furthest thing from my mind." She put her other foot in Gunaydin's lap. "Do the other one, would you?"

He shifted to the other foot. "So there's no one to chide you about an unsuitable relationship?"

"*Chide?*" This time she laughed out loud. "If you only knew about relationships in the High City! There's no chiding, believe me."

"Well then," said Gunaydin. "I'm pleased to volunteer for an unsuitable relationship."

Sula made a throaty sound of ecstasy as his fingers dug into her foot. "Honestly," she said. "You are the most *reasonable* man I've ever met."

"Am I?" He looked at her in surprise. "I suppose that's a good thing."

"Trust me, it is."

She could keep on with Gunaydin for as long as she cared to, Sula thought. She liked him, she got on with him, he made no insane demands on her. He was confident but lacked arrogance. He didn't try to manipulate her, and she had no reason to manipulate him.

She didn't love him, she felt no great passion, but that made it easier. No one would ever write a derivoo song about them. They were *reasonable* together.

When she and Martinez next met, she thought, she'd need all the *reasonableness* that Gunaydin could give her.

FROM *PARKHURST*'S COMMAND center, Sula watched Zanshaa crawl across the video displays. She was nearly weightless and strapped in her couch, a mere observer. Devindar Suri bossed the approach, aided by a staff experienced in wrangling the big ship into dock.

Zanshaa, the war's ultimate prize, shone in the darkness like an iridescent opal, dark greens and blues contrasting with the brilliant white of clouds and the polar caps. The antimatter-generation ring drew a black line along the equator, and the ring's shadow could be seen on clouds below.

Gradually the ring grew nearer and larger, and soon eclipsed most of the planet. From close range the ring seemed a perfectly flat highway stretching to infinity in either direction.

The actual mooring was so smooth that there was no tug, no vibration, just gravity returning as the ship absorbed the momentum of the ring. Sula unwebbed herself from her couch and waited while Suri and the engineering staff went through the checklist that shut down *Parkhurst*'s massive engines.

The operation complete, Sula said goodbye to Captain Suri, thanked him for his hospitality, and formally transferred command of the ship to him. Once the ship's massive armament had been transferred to Fleet armories, he would resume his civilian identity and *Parkhurst* would be returned to the Martinez family and once again carry thousands of immigrants to newly opened worlds.

Sula returned to her suite, where Macnamara and Spence waited with her packed belongings. The nonessential gear would be taken by Spence down the elevator, then shipped to Zanshaa City by supersonic train. Sula and Macnamara would take a shuttle to Wi-hun so that she could get to the Convocation more quickly.

"Transport's on the way," Spence said.

Lord Saïd had already appointed her to chair the Court of Honor, the committee possessing the power to expel a member from the Convocation, and Roland Martinez had already sent her a lengthy list of convocates that he felt needed to be booted from the empire's highest legislative body. She had her work cut out for her.

Despite her resentment at Roland's treating her like a lackey, Sula was inclined to agree that most of these people needed to go. Either they had fallen in line behind the Tu-hon clique or they were bankrupt, addicted, useless, stupid, or all of the above.

Sula would consider it a personal pleasure to eject Lady Distchin, the absentee patron of her home world of Spannan, but it occurred to her that booting her out of the Convocation wouldn't be nearly enough.

"I'm happy to kick Distchin out of the Convocation," she sent to Roland. "But how about a bill that puts an end to her patronage of Spannan? Along with some of the other infamous absentees? We could appoint our own allies in their place, and we'd become very popular on those exploited worlds."

Roland sent his approval of the idea, but said that the Convocation would have to be purged first, to make certain that the Distchins and the others couldn't recruit enough allies to block the bill's passage.

That was all right with Sula. She'd waited years for her revenge on the Distchins, a revenge she'd long believed was impossible, and now that it was likely she could wait a little longer.

Sula turned toward the door as Dr. Gunaydin entered. He did not salute.

Gunaydin would not be going down to Zanshaa for some time yet, as he was still an officer in the Fleet, and still the doctor of *Pride of Parkhurst*. Sula was trying to hasten his separation from the Fleet, but returning volunteers to civilian life was turning out to be a difficult task. There were plenty of doctors assigned to the Fleet dockyards, but they were overwhelmed by the crews of the Combined Fleet and the Fleet Train, who had been nursing their injuries aboard ship for months, often without proper medical care. The older crew, the retirees who had rejoined, were particularly prone to injury and other issues. Gunaydin's demobilization depended on the Combined Fleet returning to prime health.

"I envy you the planet," Gunaydin said. "I can see it so very close, but I can't go there."

"You'll join me soon enough," Sula said.

"I hope so." He took her in his arms. Macnamara and Spence turned away to give them a little privacy.

"Once you get down to Zanshaa," Sula said, "you'll find out just how busy and how boring the life of a politician can be."

"I can't imagine you ever being boring." He kissed her. The kiss lasted a while—a *reasonable* length of time, Sula thought.

"I must be going," she said.

"I'll see you soon, I hope."

She offered her lips for a brief kiss. She turned to Spence and Macnamara. "Do you have my sidearm?" she asked.

Spence produced the pistol on its belt, and Sula remembered the familiar weight, the way she'd cleared the pistol from its holster, pressed it to Lamey's chest, and fired it twice.

It was a good pistol, and it had done its job. Sula was less than good, and had paid with her happiness for the work her pistol had done.

Was that justice? she wondered. Was *anything* justice?

"The Mark One?" she asked, meaning her machine pistol.

"Packed," said Macnamara.

"Let's hope we don't need it, then."

Spence looked at her sleeve display. "Transport is at the airlock."

Bags and trunks were moved through the airlock and into a six-wheeled Fleet van. She and Macnamara took their places in a Hunhao limousine and pulled away. The van went straight to the elevator terminal with Spence and Sula's chef, while the Hunhao went to the Fleet Records Office, where Sula deposited the data foil that contained *Parkhurst*'s log, and then to the shuttle hangar.

The shuttle ride was noisy and exhilarating, the vehicle banging and shuddering as it crashed through Zanshaa's atmosphere while storms of blazing ions flashed like heat lightning in the view ports. The violence ended when a series of S-turns slowed the vehicle and the wings deployed, but the shuttle was still traveling with such speed that Wi-hun's runways appeared below the shuttle before Sula saw the spaceport on the horizon.

She'd been in touch with the Department of Property Transfer to find out who actually owned her property now, and discovered that nearly all of it had been confiscated by the state, but hadn't yet been sold. Because she had escaped to Harzapid in disguise, with government-issued ID in a fictional person's name, the Gruum government hadn't known Sula had joined the Restoration until she'd captured the enemy squadron at Colamote, and her transmissions to Captain Sen-thar had been forwarded to Zanshaa. All her property was then taken, but the years-old financial crisis meant that the property market had been depressed, and only a few properties—an apartment building in the Lower Town, a winery in the southern hemisphere—had found buyers.

Well, it was all hers again, or soon would be.

Fleet vehicles met Sula at Wi-hun and transported her to her own front door in the Petty Mount, the modest hill that leaned against the High City's granite escarpment. She stepped out of the car and looked up at her apartment building, and breathed in the scents of the Petty Mount: meats grilling on skewers, flowers in window boxes, tobacco and hashish drifting from the smoking den across the street, the odor of glue and wood shavings from the nearby shop where antiques were restored.

A pair of Terran guards were deployed at the door. The doorman, a Lai-own in a uniform more grand than any in the Fleet, swung the door open and bowed.

"Welcome, my lady," he said.

"I'm delighted to see you, Let-kwai," Sula said, and found she *was* delighted to see the familiar face with its halo of feathery hair.

Let-kwai helped Macnamara wrestle the luggage through the Devajjo-styled lobby into the elevator, and then Sula was lifted in silence to her apartment on the top floor.

She walked through the door, turned on the lights, and her heart lifted. The room was unchanged. Light glowed on the parquet floor, and off the glazed ancient porcelain set in niches. The celadon vases were empty, but that would change.

Sula told the drapes to open, and Shaamah's light streamed in through the curved window that wrapped around a corner of the building and provided a view of the Lower Town. She stepped into the room and lifted a hand to touch a hard-paste Qing Dynasty bowl with a design of brilliant red hydrangeas. Its cool glossy surface caressed her fingertips. She let out a slow breath. She had missed this.

The building's management knew she was coming, and the apartment had been polished and dusted. Her clothes had never left the closet; her shoes gleamed on their racks.

For years she had hidden herself away in these rooms, doing her mathematical puzzles and being obsessed with the perfection of her porcelain, until Lamey had arrived with his plan to get her co-opted into the Convocation, and her whole existence had changed. Now the temptation to hide away again was palpable, but was also impossible: she would have to be in the Convocation tomorrow, working through the list of convocates she would either dismiss or convince to resign.

It would, she suspected, be a thankless task, and it would be a relief to be able to retreat to her refuge in the Petty Mount when her life grew too burdensome.

Macnamara arrived in her bedroom to unpack her trunk. "I'll do that," she told him. "Why don't you go out and get us something to eat?"

Macnamara turned his melancholy face to hers. His mourning for Japutra Bliss still gnawed at his spirit.

"What would you like, my lady?" he asked.

"The grilled proteins smelled good," she said. "Maybe some olives, some salad, some cheese."

"Very good, my lady."

Macnamara made his way out, leaving Sula alone in her apartment. She wanted to skip and dance through every room, but instead she went to the pantry where, before she'd let alcohol into her life, she kept wine for her dinner guests.

Sula found a bottle and opened it, then got a glass and sat in the main room, drinking as she watched the sun set over the Lower Town.

# CHAPTER 13

"Lady Convocate, I see that you are an investor in the firm of Do-jin & Company, and also, with Lord Minno, in the Precious Jewel Auction House."

"Yes, Lady Sula. Though I was unaware of the connection to Lord Minno."

The Torminel sitting across from Sula's desk had fur of alternating cream and chestnut. Her large night-adapted eyes were protected from glare by bubble-like dark spectacles.

"The problem, Lady Tongin," said Sula, "is that Do-jin was the receiver of goods plundered by the previous administration, which were then auctioned off by Precious Jewel. You might be accused of profiting off the confiscations."

"I had no idea that those things were happening," said Lady Tongin.

Possibly she didn't, Sula thought, though it seemed unlikely. The confiscations weren't kept secret—the Gruum administration trumpeted them as justice against the wicked Terran criminals. And even if Lady Tongin had never connected the dots between the confiscations and the auction house, she'd never seemed to wonder why her profits went up.

But as profiteers went, Lady Tongin was minor, and as a politician she was negligible. When Saïd was Lord Senior, she had voted with the government on those days when she bothered to come to the Convocation and register an opinion. She had voted with the majority to depose Saïd and elevate Lady Gruum, and then voted with the new administration. When the Combined Fleet entered the system, she voted to depose Gruum and return Saïd to office.

She was lazy and stupid, and the Convocation would do well without her. Better that she would be replaced by someone more dynamic, and with convictions less likely to change with the shifting wind.

"Unfortunately," said Sula, "I won't be able to prevent these revelations from reaching the public. I'm not in charge of the investigation. Once the investigation is completed, I will chair the Court of Honor and conduct a public hearing, and if you're found guilty of profiteering, you will be removed from the Convocation."

"Lady Sula!" Tongin was so shocked that her precise diction failed, and she began to lisp around her fangs. "My clan has been in the Convocation for sixteen generations!"

"So has mine," Sula said. Absently she rubbed the pad of scar tissue on her right thumb.

"In that case," Tongin said, "surely a person of your illustrious heritage would understand that—"

"I may chair the court," Sula said, "but I'm only one vote. Others will serve on the court with me, and not all have been appointed. Some, I suspect, will be drawn from those convocates that suffered from confiscations and arrests." She offered her most soothing manner.

"You can oppose the proceedings, of course," Sula said. "And I wouldn't blame you if you did. But you *did* profit from the confiscations, and that is going to count against you. Perhaps the best alternative would be for you to resign your seat in the Convocation before the hearings ever begin." She put on a helpful tone. "That will also make the authorities less likely to prosecute you for profiteering—they're pursuing high-profile cases, and if your profile is suitably lowered . . ." She made an equivocal gesture with one hand.

Lady Tongin looked at her in bleak silence for a moment, then spoke. "You won't help?" she asked.

"I may not be able to," Sula said. "If I'm outvoted, there's nothing I can do. Plus, I can't control a police investigation." She tapped her fingers together and feigned having an idea. "You know, my lady," she said, "that there are any number of funds being set up to relieve dispossessed Terrans and to help them recover their property. A large donation to any such organization might serve to ease any feelings against you." She nodded. "Still, any decision is entirely up to you. Any resignation should be transmitted to the Lord Senior. Thank you for stopping by, and I wish you the best of luck."

Sula stood and guided Lady Tongin to the door, then returned to her desk, sat in her chair, and spun idly in circles. Her last office in the Convocation complex, before her escape to Harzapid, had consisted of two cramped rooms wedged into the rear of the building. Now she occupied a much larger office that had once belonged to Lord Troom Lamong, who now resided in a single cell at the Blue Hatches Prison. Sula had soft carpets, a broad and impressive desk, and a view of the Boulevard of the Praxis. The valuable porcelain she'd kept in her old office had been taken in one of the confiscations, and she'd already demanded its return, but in the meantime, she'd bought a group of celadon vases, placed them about the room, and filled them with flowers. Their scent rested lightly on the air.

She'd also tried to reassemble the staff she'd had before the war.

The law professor Ashok Suresh had returned as her legal adviser, and for the moment she was using Spence, Ricci, and Viswan in the front office to wrangle communications and appointments. And, of course, Macmanara commanded her bodyguard, a group of Terrans who followed her through the day with a silent efficiency that was just robotic enough to be annoying.

Her hand comm buzzed, and she answered to find Spence looking at her out of the screen.

"Lord Hottash is in the waiting room, my lady," she said.

"Send him in, by all means."

Hottash was another useless convocate, a Torminel, degenerate gambler, brawler, and drunk who daily consumed enough methanol to blind or kill fifty humans. He rarely attended the Convocation, and when he did, he was usually too soused to make any sense in a debate or to register a vote.

The only thing to be said in his favor was that he seemed not to have actually done anything criminal, and he hadn't profited by the war in any way.

Those characteristics that rendered him obnoxious—the drunkenness, the bellicose behavior—were not against the law, or even that uncommon among convocates, and it would be hard to find a pretext for ejecting him from the Convocation. Sula would suggest that he quietly resign and continue enjoying his debased life without the necessity of attending boring debates and committee meetings, but she had the feeling that Hottash was belligerent enough to insist on a full hearing before the Court of Honor.

Which Sula would provide—she would sandwich him in between some genuine criminals to make him look even less savory—and in the end she would remove Hottash from the chamber on the grounds of conduct unbecoming a convocate. It annoyed her that the sham trial would be a waste of time, but then, most of her days in the Convocation had been a waste of time, so she was reconciled to it.

Hottash came lumbering into the room, a vast ponderous furry profligate with his large eyes turned toward Sula in anger. Apparently word had got around about what she was up to.

It occurred to Sula that at some point in the interview he might come lunging over her desk with fangs bared. In which case, she decided, she'd bash him over the head with the Golden Orb she kept on a stand on a shelf behind her chair. Searching for an alternative, she reached behind her for a methanol-based liqueur.

"Lord Hottash," she said. "Please sit down. May I offer you a drink?"

SULA AWOKE SCREAMING from a nightmare of bulkheads breaking, air shrieking out into space, blood spattering the displays, and the voice of Gareth Martinez in her headphones proclaiming that the catastrophe was all her fault.

Knowing that she would not fall asleep anytime soon, she wrapped herself in a dressing gown and walked to the kitchen to make herself some tea, and found Shawna Spence already filling the kettle.

"I'm sorry if I woke you," Sula said.

Spence hitched the belt of her robe above her sturdy hips. "I'm used to it," she said. "Maybe you should see a doctor."

"I *am* seeing a doctor," Sula said.

"Well," said Spence, "what does he say?"

"Nothing," said Sula. "I don't have nightmares when he's with me."

Spence looked at Sula over her shoulder. "So all it takes to stop the nightmares is to have someone in the bed with you?"

Sula shrugged. "Apparently."

"Maybe you should get a dog."

Sula surprised Spence by considering the suggestion. "Do I like dogs?" she asked herself aloud. Possibly she did. She didn't *dislike* them, but then, she'd never owned one. She looked at Spence.

"What kind of dog should I get?"

"A large one, I suppose. I don't see you as the owner of a toy pup."

Sula considered the idea. "The little ones yap, don't they?"

Spence filled the teapot with hot water, rolled the liquid around to warm the pot, then poured it out. "The little ones yap," she said, "the big ones bay. It's a matter of preference."

"Maybe I should get a shepherd of some sort. Herding dogs are smart, aren't they?"

"Ask Macnamara. He was a shepherd himself once."

Macnamara had been born in a particularly idyllic part of Kupa, and had indeed spent his summers minding sheep in the highlands.

"I'll ask him," Sula said.

Macnamara's advice, when it came after the break of dawn, was unexpected. "Shepherds are smart," he said, "and often as not that means trouble. They'll get round you if they can. I like dogs that are stupid, but good-natured."

"Certainly something to consider," Sula said. "But right now I've got to go to the Convocation to convince a drug addict, two minor profiteers, and a creepy stalker to resign."

"Why not just shoot them?" Macnamara asked.

"Too reminiscent of what the other side was doing," Sula said. "Plus, no one's appointed me dictator yet."

**THE PROFITEERS WERE** happy to protect their loot by resigning; the drug addict arrived out of his mind, shed fur on Sula's desk, and signed a resignation without realizing what the document contained; and the creepy stalker—and Sula didn't know that a Cree *could* be creepy, but this one definitely was—remained defiant until Sula called up the photographic evidence.

"Resigning from the Convocation will allow you to concentrate on your criminal defense," Sula said, and he signed.

Sula's efficiency resulted in an afternoon with nothing to do, so she went to the Convocation's restaurant, sat at the bar, and ordered a piece of cake along with a Hairy Roger, a cocktail she hadn't yet tried. As the alcohol spread its warm tendrils through her body, she wondered how long she'd be stuck in her splendid, flower-decked office intimidating her fellow convocates—weeks and months, perhaps. Roland had come up with a list of more than two hundred that needed to be squeezed out of their seats before he'd be able to steamroller the Convocation with his new legislation, and she seemed to have been appointed head squeezer.

"Lady Sula." Sula turned to see Lord Chen standing behind her. Since she'd last seen him, he'd added a couple chins and a great deal to his waistline. Chen offered an amiable bow and a sweep of his hand. "Would you join me at my table?"

"With pleasure," Sula said. Apparently, Chen hadn't heard any rumors about her affair with his son-in-law—of if he had, he approved, probably in hopes of getting Terza back in play and marrying her to someone more suitable.

Like *that* was going to happen. Terza would cling to Martinez like a limpet until they were both nothing but a tangle of bones in their tomb.

After they were seated in the leather-padded booth, Chen

looked at the cocktail in Sula's hand and raised his eyebrows. "A Hairy Roger?" he said. "I thought you didn't drink."

Sula sipped her cocktail, a hot beverage loaded with warm sharp flavors. She felt as if her tongue were growing fur.

"I've found it's the only way to deal with Wei Jian," she said.

Chen nodded sympathetically. "Gareth's told me about his troubles with her. And I can hardly forgive her for usurping Michi's command."

"Or refusing to recognize my promotion," Sula said.

"Or Gareth's." Chen signaled the waitron, who brought a small glass filled with mig brandy. "Though Gareth seems to have consoled himself by turning into some kind of freshly minted crime buster."

Sula grinned. "It's not hard to find criminals when they keep such good records. So far as I can see, they never hid *anything*."

And it kept Martinez in the news. With his division command on hold, and his career as a convocate not yet begun, he could manage his own story in the media and present himself as a hero bent on recovering stolen property from the war's victims.

A very good pose it was, too. Sula was probably doing more good tossing deadwood out of the Convocation, but Martinez was getting his handsome face out before the public, and by the time he took his seat he might be the most popular convocate in the empire.

Not that it would make him popular among his fellow convocates. Half the convocates probably had something to hide, criminal or not, and they wouldn't appreciate a self-appointed investigator poking into the lives of members of their class. The old, traditional Convocation wouldn't put up with some provincial newcomer telling them what to do.

Which was why Sula had been told to shove as many of them overboard as she could.

**SULA HAD ARRIVED** in Zanshaa's system, drifted in *Parkhurst* to the Fleet dockyard like a floating thistledown, then boomed through the atmosphere on a shuttle, rattling windows to announce her arrival. Now she was reshuffling the Convocation like a pack of cards.

Martinez hadn't seen her, but that just left her a niggling irritant in the back of his mind, as much an obsession as ever.

Now that communications had been opened with Spannan, Martinez sent a request from the Commandery to the same inquiry agents that Roland had used for his file on Hector Braga. He asked for all information related to the girl Gredel, and Lady Sula's supposed sister Margaux. He particularly asked for photos or video.

Having sent the request, he realized that there was a good deal of research he could do without leaving his office in the Commandery. So he sent Mpanza out for coffee and some sandwiches, and he dove into public records. As a big shot in the Restoration, he had an override that would let him get into sequestered files, but he couldn't think why anyone would sequester the information he was looking for.

He knew that Braga came from a place called the Fabs in Maranic Town on Spannan, and he likewise knew that Gredel, at least, should have been in school in that district. So he called up the school records. No one named Margaux had attended that school, but someone named Gredel had attended elementary and secondary school in the Fabs. Detailed records required a higher priority to view, so Martinez employed his override and found Gredel's complete school record.

She was about the right age to be Caroline Sula's contemporary. She came from a broken home—father a criminal on the run, mother in a labor camp—but Gredel had done well in school anyway, with near-perfect grades until she reached adolescence, when her grades and attendance fell off rapidly. She never graduated and disappeared from the record about the time that Hector Braga went on the run and Lady Sula went to the Cheng Ho Academy.

Martinez became aware of the odor of coffee floating in his office, and realized it had been placed at his elbow along with a pair of fish fillet sandwiches. He picked up a sandwich, bit into it, and chewed with satisfaction as he looked over Gredel's records.

He wondered then if he really ought to be viewing these records. He had no official reason for looking into the files of a long-lost schoolgirl from a distant world, and he felt an uneasy suspicion that if he pursued this course of action, he might find answers he wouldn't like.

*The hell with it*, he decided. *The world owes me a few answers.*

He finished his sandwich and turned to another section of the record, the official class and individual photographs, and there he found Gredel looking back at him.

More than Gredel, really. Because even though the girl in the photo had been born on a distant world, and Martinez had never officially met her, he recognized at once the pale, near-translucent skin, the emerald eyes, and the pale golden hair.

*Well*, he thought. *So here you are.*

**LORD SAÏD'S OFFICE** spoke of long tradition and continuity. Sula remembered the musky smell, the polished dark wood, and the ancient Cree servant pushing the tea trolley. The smoky tea was familiar, too, poured from the cobalt blue Guraware teapot with its creamy tin oxide glaze.

Saïd remained familiar as well, his skin a web of fine lines, his alert brown eyes bright on either side of his beak of a nose.

The only obvious difference was that Sula remembered lemon cakes, and today's pastry had chuchu-berry filling.

Saïd took a bite of his pastry and smiled. "I think that half my diet consists of sweets," he said. "At my age, I feel that I've earned them."

Sula raised her teacup, as a salute. "You certainly have, Lord Senior," she said.

Saïd had another bite of pastry and then put his fork down and gave Sula a speculative look.

"I wish to congratulate you on your successes with the Court of Honor," he said. "Some of the resignations, I confess, surprised me. I'd supposed they would put up more resistance."

"The more resignations I procure," Sula said, "the more formidable my reputation becomes. I hope that soon convocates might resign the second I look at them."

"But Lord Hottash? You must have done more than just look at him."

"I got him stinking drunk, then told him the Convocation was about to become a serious, earnest body intent on spoiling everyone's fun, and that he wouldn't enjoy it. I made it seem like a colossal joke. He signed with a high heart, and staggered out."

She didn't mention that she'd slammed down a lot of töldo in the process of getting herself and Hottash on the same wavelength, and that she'd spent the next hours nearly paralyzed, unable to get out of her chair without toppling back into it. Eventually she'd crawled to a settee, curled up, and waited for the agony to end.

At least she was getting better at drinking. She'd managed to avoid vomiting on herself.

Saïd pursed his lips. "Lord Roland," he said, "has urged me to fully empanel the Court of Honor so that hearings proper could begin. He gave me three names—all convocates who were denounced under the last administration and who were being held in jail awaiting trial when Gruum's administration fell."

"That should get the job done," Sula said.

"I fear that the specter of vindictiveness might hover over the proceedings," Saïd said.

Sula hoped that it would, but knew better than to say so. "I don't know them," she said, "but I am the chair, and I'll keep them in order if I have to."

Saïd tilted his head. "Perhaps," he said, "all three will not be necessary."

"Your lordship knows better than I." They were Roland's choices, after all.

Sula lifted her cup to her lips, inhaled the smoky aroma of the tea, then took a sip. Saïd continued to regard her with assessing, contemplative eyes.

"You will be playing a much more prominent role in the Convocation than previously," he said.

Sula laughed. "More prominent than being accused of blowing up the economy?"

Saïd's eyes twinkled. "Events have served to acquit you," he said. "No—I think I'm not wrong in saying that you wish an independent role in the Convocation, leader of your own faction, rather than being a supporter of some other leader."

*By which he means Roland*, Sula thought.

"I prefer not to be ordered about," Sula said. "I've had enough of that in the Fleet."

"I wish you every success," said Saïd. "But I fear you do not have sufficient resources. I believe you are quite well-off, but building a faction costs money, and you don't have nearly enough."

Sula rubbed the pad of scar tissue on her right thumb. "I have a very old name," she said.

"That name will open many doors," said Saïd, "and you will be able to join a great many exclusive clubs, but that alone won't convince many to follow you."

Sula sipped her tea again. She thought she knew where this was going, but decided that Lord Saïd should be the one to raise the issue.

Saïd gave a little smile, perhaps appreciating Sula's choice of silence.

"Before the war," he said, "I believe I mentioned to you my grandnephew Eveleth. He is an accomplished young man, a sportsman, and already bears a great name. He is very wealthy—wealthy enough to support a faction in the Convocation."

"He is also in want of a wife," Sula finished.

"That is truly the case," said Saïd. "For the most part he's an exemplary fellow, but there are certain realms in which he lacks maturity, and marriage would serve to season him in important ways."

Sula was not about to become the designated seasoner for some rich, overprivileged, overbred ninny.

"It is very kind of you to consider me," Sula said, "but as I told you before, I'm not interested in marriage at this time."

Dr. Gunaydin had finally achieved his separation from the Fleet and would soon arrive in Zanshaa City, and marriage was the very last thing Sula had in mind.

"If your ladyship is certain . . . ?" Saïd asked.

"I'm afraid so."

"Well then," Saïd said. "I'm a little sorry for the both of you, as I think you'd be well matched."

Sula bade farewell to Saïd and left his chambers. In the soft-carpeted corridor she met Captain Naaz Vijana, the victor of the Yormak Rebellion and the tireless advocate of Terran supremacy. His pointed face brightened as she approached.

"Lady Sula!" he said. "I wanted to congratulate you on your purge of the Convocation."

"Thank you," Sula said. "But there's a long way to go."

He fell into step beside her. "There certainly is," he said. "How many more before we achieve a Terran majority?"

"There won't be a Terran majority," Sula said. And at Vijana's scowl, she said, "We've calculated that we can dominate the Convocation with a forty percent minority, and it won't be so obvious that we're in charge."

She and Roland Martinez had arrived at that figure after a certain amount of discussion.

A confiding smile broke across Vijana's face. "Oh, excellent!" he said. "I understand. Sneak up on the animals before you conk them on the head and toss them in cages."

He made it sound like one of Captain Mazankosi's animal hunts. "Plenty in cages right now," Sula said.

Vijana rubbed his hands. "More to come!" he said cheerfully.

She couldn't get away fast enough.


"MY LADY," SAID Viswan, "we have a call from a Mr. Naveen Patel. Do you know the gentleman?"

"I'll take the call in my office." Sula closed the door behind her before taking the call on her desk comms.

"Hello, princess," Patel said with a white smile. "We seem both to have survived."

"And thrived, I hope," Sula said.

Patel's dark eyes gleamed. "Thrived more than not," he said.

Patel was a glossy, stylish man with gleaming black hair that tumbled in curls to his collar. He was also a leader of the cliquemen, a member of the commission that ruled Zanshaa City's gangsters. Sula had been allied with the commission in the Naxid War, and they had provided a hard, violent core to her Secret Army.

When Sula ran for Harzapid, she'd left the cliquemen—the Terran ones, least—at war with Lady Tu-hon's Steadfast League, originally an organization of those unemployed and impoverished by the economic collapse, but which had evolved into Tu-hon's very own not-so-secret army.

"How is Julien?" Sula asked.

"Julien's fine," Patel said. "He's doing a bit of recuperating in the country."

"Recuperating?"

"Caught a bit of shrapnel," Patel said, then shrugged. "He was in fine spirits last I heard. But he's deliberately made it hard for anyone to find him, so we'll just have to wait for him to surface."

Julien Bakshi was another member of the commission. Julien and Sula had been close allies over the years, particularly when a crisis occurred and the military governor of Zanshaa needed to be assassinated, or when Lady Koridun's older brother needed to meet an accident along with numerous other members of her family.

"The reason I called, then, princess," Patel said, "is that over the last two years we've acquired a lot of good intelligence on the Steadfast League. In the beginning they were a bunch of losers and pushovers who made a lot of noise but who ran away when things got tough. But Tu-hon moved a lot of hard cases into Zanshaa, and lately it's become something of a fair fight—*too* fair, if you ask me."

"The fighting isn't still going on, is it?"

"No, the league's officially disbanded. But we figure some of them are biding their time, just like your Action Groups did in the last war, and we have a pretty good idea who they are and where they're based."

Sula considered this. "How do you know this?"

Patel gave a laughing grin. "Because we infiltrated them, of course!" He saw the question in her eyes and laughed again. "No, we didn't slip any Terrans into their ranks. But not all cliquemen are Terrans."

"Ah. Hah." Sula nodded. "So you talked Sagas and the others into helping you?"

"They protected their turf but otherwise didn't fight," Patel said. "But they gathered intelligence and provided logistical support. We were able to hide arms and our bomb factories on their turf, where the league and the Urban Patrol wouldn't look for them."

Sula gave the matter some thought. "Send me the information you have," she said. "I'm not in a position to act on any of it directly, but I'll try to send it to where it'll do the most good."

Patel grinned. "You could send it to that Martinez geezer," he said. "He's been arresting Tu-hon's friends left and right."

Sula winced. She had no intention of providing more opportunities for Martinez to glorify himself.

"I think I can do better than that," she said.

"SECURITY REPORTS THAT there is a Lieutenant Lady Benedicta Kelly at the door, my lord," said Doshtra.

Martinez sprang to his feet. "Pass her!" he said.

He followed the Daimong butler to the door and watched him admit Kelly, who walked carefully into the house with the aid of a pair of canes. Her color was good. Her smile, which Martinez remembered as being a white shining blaze, was subdued and a little shy. Her black eyes were bright, and her fair, short hair was brushy on top and short in the back and on the sides. Martinez found himself looking for scars beneath the cropped hair.

He approached her with arms outstretched, and then hesitated. She was dangerously thin, and he didn't want to crush her.

Her smile broadened. "Let's take the hug as read," she said.

"Let's call it *postponed*," Martinez said. "Come to the parlor and we'll talk."

Kelly adjusted her canes, aimed herself at the parlor door, and began to walk. Martinez hovered alongside, uncertain whether to offer her an arm.

"I can walk perfectly well," Kelly assured him. "My legs are strong. I don't need the canes to walk, but they help with balance."

"I was afraid you'd never wake up," Martinez said.

Kelly found a Devis mode chair and swung herself into it with a practiced, agile movement. "The coma lasted five months," she said. "Then I woke, and I was in a hospital in the country, and they told me you'd sent me there and paid the fees."

"I didn't want you in the city," Martinez said. "Not with a war brewing in the streets."

"I don't remember the riot at all," said Kelly. "But they said you saved my life."

"I carried you to safety," Martinez said. "But a *lot* of people saved your life. Particularly Kosch Altasz, who was killed."

Lady Kosch, Kelly, and Martinez had been involved in the hermetic world of yacht racing, as members of the successful Corona

Club team. Kelly was emerging as the team's best pilot when she'd been struck down, as rioters from the Steadfast League tried to storm the Corona Club building.

"I know about poor Kosch," Kelly said. "When I was finally able to use a hand comm, I called up all the original news reports about the riot. The articles said the club burned down and was a total loss."

"It was insured," Martinez said. "We were going to rebuild it, but instead we all decided to have this big war."

"Can you tell me about my friends?" Kelly said. "I'd like to know if they're all right."

"I'll do my best," Martinez said. "But may I offer you something to drink? To eat?"

"A Citrine Fling?"

Martinez called Doshtra and asked for Citrine Fling and a pot of coffee. The butler bowed and withdrew.

Kelly and Martinez had served together only briefly, on the *Corona*—and in fact had been lovers for at least forty-five minutes during the frigate's perilous escape from Magaria. Martinez didn't know all Kelly's friends, but he was able to tell her that Vonderheydte, another *Corona* veteran, was captain of his own ship and was now en route to Magaria, part of a division under Chandra Prasad that, with two others divisions under one of Wei Jian's officers, would take command of the Fleet dockyard and, ultimately, the planet below it. Another division was on its way to Felarus, and small groups of two or three ships would occupy the smaller Fleet dockyards.

That division featured a newly promoted Squadron Commander Jeremy Foote, whose assiduous courtship of Wei Jian seemed to have borne fruit.

In the meantime, Wei Jian would remain at Zanshaa with most of the Combined Fleet, which in time would become the core of a new Home Fleet.

"Vonderheydte and Chandra Prasad are now a couple," Martinez added. "Though I don't know if you know her."

"Only by reputation," Kelly said. "Isn't she a kind of carnivore?"

"She has sharp teeth, that's certain."

Kelly looked dubious. "Well, I hope Von survives."

"And do you remember Garcia?" Martinez asked. "She got a command, but was killed at Second Shulduc."

Sadness crossed Kelly's face. "She had no luck at all," she said.

"No."

Doshtra brought drinks, and the scent of coffee drifted into the room. Martinez was able to tell Kelly about some more of her friends, and for others he used his command privileges to access the Commandery's database. Many had been interned for the length of the war, and of those who escaped to fight with the Restoration, at least half had been killed.

"Maybe I'm lucky," Kelly said finally. "I spent the war being looked after in a hospital. The government never bothered me because I was disabled and unimportant."

Kelly was a lower-lower-middle, Martinez knew. She had been talented enough to get into the Nelson Academy, but she lacked the family or service connections to advance in rank, and had been a lieutenant for the last ten years. Fighting with the Restoration would have given her a chance for promotion, and about an even chance of being killed.

"Are you fit for desk duty?" Martinez asked. "I could offer you a job."

"Doing what?"

"Communications. I always need more signalers, and Banerjee—she's my best—will be returning to civilian life as soon as the Fleet lets her go."

Kelly seemed pleased. "I'd be very happy to do it," she said.

"It won't interfere with your . . . your recovery?"

"I do most of my therapy at home, so my schedule is flexible."

Martinez raised his coffee cup. "Welcome back to the Fleet, Kelly."

Her broad brilliant smile blazed out, the same smile he remembered from long ago.

"WELL," SULA SAID. "If it isn't my fancy man."

Gunaydin walked through the barred platform gate at the Zanshaa terminal, looked for her, and smiled as he found her in the crowd. He looked just a little strange in civilian dress. She stepped to him, embraced him, and ran a hand over his no-longer-shaven scalp.

"You're starting to grow out your winter coat, I see," she said.

"You asked me what I looked like with hair," he said. "Now you know."

She looked at him critically. "You don't have enough hair yet for me to judge."

He raised a hand and touched his short brown bristle. "It will grow," he said.

Gunaydin shifted his luggage to a robot bag carrier that followed him to Sula's car. He took in the two Hunhaos, one ahead and one behind, both packed with bodyguards.

"You're in danger?" he asked.

"I don't know," Sula said. "No sign so far. But it's better to be prepared than not, and heavily armed police may act as a deterrent."

"You're carrying a sidearm."

"I'm being careful." She looked at him. "You want me to be careful, yes?"

He considered this. "I suppose I do. Though a careful Caroline is someone new to me."

Macnamara drove Sula to her building and parked in s reserved for Sula and her security detail. Let-kwai swept open the door and allowed the party to enter. Gunaydin followed Sula into the elevator, then to the apartment with its faint scent of lemon polish. When he came into the main room, he walked to the curved corner window and gazed out at Zanshaa Lower Town, with the Apszipar Tower standing tall on the far horizon.

"My reflexes are all wrong for this," he said. "I still can't believe I'm on the surface of a planet. I keep looking for walls and bulkheads, and I can't see them."

Sula stepped behind Gunaydin and put her arms around him, resting her chin on his shoulder. "Oh, the walls are there," she said. "Most of them are invisible."

He turned to her and put his arms around her waist. "Are you free this afternoon?" he asked.

She sighed. "No. I've got meetings with four senile or otherwise demented convocates in hopes of convincing them to resign. The problem being that dementia in a convocate has always been perfectly acceptable."

Gunaydin was surprised. "You find the most interesting employment," he said finally.

Sula shook her head. "It's not interesting at all, it's sad and pathetic. And dull, like everything else that happens in convocation." She slid out of their embrace and drew her hand comm out of her convocate's jacket. She tapped it awake, then sent Gunaydin a message.

"I've done some research," she said, "and I've found a number of apartments that might suit you. I've sent you a list. I don't exactly know what you can afford, so I found places across a wide price range. If you're not too tired, you can view some this afternoon."

"Ah," Gunaydin said.

She looked up and him and grinned. "Of course, if you really *are* my fancy man, take whichever apartment you want and don't worry about the cost."

Gunaydin seemed puzzled. "Need I move into a new apartment right away, or am I staying here tonight, or . . . ?"

"You'd *better* stay here tonight," Sula said. She turned to leave, and then halted. "I'm sorry to be so abrupt," she said. "You got to know me when I was on the *Parkhurst*, on what amounted to a vacation. But now the vacation is over, my life is busy, and I'll look forward to relaxing with you as soon as I can. Tonight, I hope."

Tonight might be the last chance to relax for some time, because she knew that tomorrow everything was going to change. *Corona* would berth on the ring and disembark Roland, Terza, Ming Lin, Lady Koridun, and the others who made up the guiding committee of the Restoration. There would be a formal arrival and ceremony at the Wi-hun airport, where the government of the Restoration would formally resign their posts to Lord Saïd, and hand over the Restoration archives.

Not that any of this would stop Roland from telling Sula what to do, of course.


**MARTINEZ WOKE WITH** a start. His senses were drenched with Sula's scent, her Sandama Twilight perfume. For a moment he stared wildly into the darkness, heart racing, his mind struggling to anchor itself in time. Was he with Sula? Aboard a ship perhaps?

Terza placed a cool hand on his shoulder. "Gareth? Are you all right?"

Sandama Twilight began to fade from his senses. "Yes," he said. "I had a—a falling dream."

*Falling head over heels*, he thought. True enough.

"Landed right on my face," Martinez said. Which was also true.

"You're all right now?" Terza asked.

"Nonii. Sorry I woke you."

Terza turned on her side, her hand still brushing his shoulder. Her breathing deepened, and Martinez presumed she was asleep.

His own sleep was more elusive. His day had been full, and the next day would be busy.

Clouds had darkened the ceremony at Wi-hun and scattered showers pelted the participants. Martinez had worn a uniform cap and overcoat and felt superior to those who hadn't. Lord Saïd, wearing the scarlet brocade cloak of the Lord Senior, accepted the resignation of the leaders of the Restoration, and he and Roland and a great many others felt the necessity of marking the occasion with boring speeches. Martinez, watching while rain spattered the brim of his cap, could picture Sula viewing the ceremony on video and laughing herself sick.

After the ceremony Martinez was reunited with his family. His heart swelled to bursting as he saw Gareth the Younger running through the puddles to embrace him, and he picked up his son and held him close.

"Salutations, Progenitor," Chai-chai said.

"Salutations," Martinez responded, and buried his face in his son's dark hair.

Through strands of hair, he watched Terza approach, walking slowly and with her usual unearthly tranquility. She was wrapped in a rain-spangled belted coat, carried an umbrella, and looked absolutely superb.

Who brings an umbrella on an orbital shuttle? he wondered. Only Terza. Because she checked the weather, to make sure Chai-chai was dressed appropriately, and no one else bothered.

Martinez threw out an arm to gather Terza into the family embrace. She kissed his cheek, and he inhaled the vetiver scent of her perfume. "Let's go home," he said.

When they arrived, Gareth the Younger dashed through the house, taking stock. He delighted in the familiar furniture and fixtures, but was taken aback by how few of his own possessions remained. His clothing, his toys, and his stack of drawings were all missing.

"You'll have to go shopping," Martinez said. He turned to Terza. "And you, too, I imagine."

"I'm so heavily scheduled I don't know when I'll have time," Terza said. "Fortunately, our baggage is coming down the elevator and will be arriving in two days. We brought enough with us to last until then." She walked through the parlor, noting the devastation that had been wrought on her interior design by Lord Dop. "It's all reparable," she said. "Though I wish I had time."

"Hire someone," Martinez said. "Then if it goes wrong, you'll have someone to blame."

Mpanza served supper to the three of them that night. Martinez watched with interest as Terza and young Gareth tasted Mangahas's cooking for the first time, a stew of vegetables, pork, fish, and shellfish served over rice in a sour sauce flavored with fruit. Chai-chai was enthusiastic, but Terza's response was more measured.

"That's a new taste, isn't it?" she said. "Very complex. I wonder what sort of wine goes with it."

"Let's open a few bottles and find out," Martinez said.

They opened only a single bottle and Terza seemed to think it complimented the stew very well. To Martinez it tasted like wine.

After young Gareth was sent to bed, Terza and Martinez returned to the parlor and sat on a sofa. He put his arm around her, and she rested her cheek on his shoulder.

He felt as awkward as he had when they were first engaged, hustled by Roland into marriage when Terza was still mourning a fiancé killed in battle, and he was in shreds from his breakup with Sula.

Not that he wasn't in shreds now, of course.

"It's been over a year and a half, hasn't it?" Terza said. "Since we've seen each other in person?"

"Yes," Martinez said. "But at least we could send video messages to each other. Not like the last war, when we were out of touch for so long."

Terza held a wineglass in her hand, with the last of the ruby-red wine gleaming in its crystal embrace. She swirled the wine, brought it to her lips, and drank it off. She put the glass on a side table, then leaned toward Martinez and kissed his cheek. He turned to her and tasted the wine on her lips.

"You aren't tired?" he asked.

"Some things are worth staying awake for," she said.

He took his beautiful wife to bed. The awkwardness he felt did not entirely disappear, in part because he couldn't quite imagine what he wanted—but since he didn't know what might please him, he set himself to pleasing Terza, and eventually her fire kindled his, and his unease faded beneath a torrent of purest carnality. Afterward, he and Terza fell asleep in each other's arms.

Until Sula's perfume crept into his senses and blasted his sleep to bits.

# CHAPTER 14

Severin sat in the small visitor's gallery and looked down into the Convocation, a covered amphitheater with rows of rising, concentric desks, all focused at the dais from which the Lord Senior conducted the business of the assembly. Severin could see Roland Martinez and Lady Sula below, in their wine-red convocates' jackets, waiting for the session to begin.

A surprising number of the desks were empty. Sula had been doing an excellent job of driving out selected convocates, particularly after the first few sessions of the Court of Honor. Lord Saïd had packed the court with convocates who had suffered under the Gruum administration, and these had led the assault against the accused while Sula confined herself to the role of moderator. In the end, the accused suffered public humiliation and lost their seats anyway. Some left the chamber only to be arrested by police waiting outside the doors.

After this, there were a lot of resignations and no more hearings. Some convocates resigned before they were even interviewed, and those interviewed submitted their resignations meekly.

Which meant that there were now plenty of seats to be filled by newcomers like Severin. He looked left and right in the small gallery and saw Gareth Martinez and Naaz Vijana, each wearing full dress, waiting for their nomination by the Lord Senior. Most of the new appointees were Terran, though not all: the Torminel Lady Koridun and the Daimong officer Rivven were among them. Koridun, at twenty-five, would be the youngest member of the Convocation.

The selection of convocates was not by the choice of those they would govern, because such an election might produce an incorrect result. Only the Convocation could decide who was worthy to be a convocate, and the selection was made by co-option, with the full Convocation assembled for the purpose of approving its new members.

Usually this was done one appointee at a time, but Lord Saïd was bringing all thirty-odd candidates to a vote all at the same moment. He had also filled his government with provisional appointments that the Convocation were expected to approve. Gareth Martinez and Squadron Commander Rivven were appointed to the Fleet Control Board, and were working on a plan to bring the Fleet back to full strength. Sula, in addition to chairing the Court of Honor, had been appointed to the Promotions Subcommittee, where she would approve—or not—the advancement of every officer in the Fleet.

Terza Chen now headed the Ministry of Right and Dominion, the civilian ministry that supported the Fleet; and Roland Martinez was in charge of the Ministry of Finance, and of the recovery following the economic catastrophe of the last few years.

Their appointments would be approved by the full Convocation in time, but in the meantime they were already busy with their departments.

Severin was surprised that Wei Jian wasn't going to become a convocate. It was probably a good decision—Jian would never make a politician—but it meant that she was now able to devote herself full-time to interfering in the Fleet and raising the blood pressure of juniors like Sula and Martinez.

Severin himself had been appointed acting head of the Exploration Service and was facing decisions about how to recover from the losses of war. Fortunately, the Service had lost a much smaller percentage of its vessels than the Fleet, partly because many of the ships had been on missions of exploration, and partly because Tork had wanted to achieve victory with the Fleet alone.

Severin gazed past the Lord Senior's dais to the tall glass windows that looked out onto the terrace and, beyond the low stone wall that marked the edge of the High City escarpment, the Lower Town that extended all the way to the horizon. Dark gray clouds swirled overhead, and the first snowflakes of winter were drifting to land on the terrace. Guards—military constables—patrolled the outside, rifle barrels directed at the ground until such time as saboteurs or criminals turned up. The constables were Terran, and Severin wondered what members of other species saw as they watched the guards pacing up and down—was it an armed threat? The advanced guard of a newly dominant species? Did they think the guns would be pointed at a threat outside, or aimed at them?

Severin viewed the great amphitheater again and pictured it in ruins, the hangings afire, the windows shattered, the desks collapsed under rubble. He found the image pleasing.

It was like his patchwork-quilt tactics. Probe here, probe there, eventually you will find the other side's keystone. Remove that, and their defense would go to pieces.

Everything was a feint until it wasn't. And by then it would be too late.

The windows dimmed, and spotlights lit the Lord Senior's dais. The sergeant-at-arms entered in his elaborate uniform, rang a handbell, and called for order. "All hear the Lord Senior!" he called.

Lord Saïd entered, his frail form shrouded in the heavy cloak of scarlet brocade. He walked to stand behind his desk and raised the long copper wand he used to control the assembly.

"I am honored to bring this assembly into session," he said.

There followed an automated roll call, assuring that a quorum was present, and then the sergeant-at-arms again rang his bell.

"Attend the Lord Senior!" he called.

"I hope the distinguished convocates will forgive me," Saïd said, "but I am postponing the other business of this assembly in order to introduce a recommendation from the Credentials Committee concerning the co-option of new members. The distinguished convocates will find the Credentials Committee report on their screens. Is there any discussion of the matter?"

There was not. Anyone who misliked the clutch of nobodies and climbers nominated for co-option was either staying away or keeping silent. There had been many opportunities for convocates to practice cowardice in the Gruum administration, and apparently the habit would continue.

Once the committee's recommendations had actually been accepted, however, the assembly's tongues were loosened. One convocate after another rose to congratulate the newcomers on their appointments and to express confidence that their wisdom and sagacity would lead the empire into a new era of peace and prosperity.

*Wisdom?* Severin thought. *Well, at least I'm wiser than most of* them.

Afterward there was a reception for the new arrivals. The new-minted convocates mixed with a few hundred of their seniors in a plush meeting room with red velvet hangings and brass fixtures. Bottles glittered under spotlights behind the bar. Severin found himself a pale silver wine from Cavado and drifted through the room until he was approached by a Lai-own named Par-kai, who said she was chairman of the Protocol Committee.

"Now that you've been co-opted," she said, "we'll have to make certain that you're raised to the Order of Peers as soon as possible."

"No, but thank you," Severin said. "I plan to remain a commoner."

Par-kai blinked her large golden eyes. "Are you certain? You would be the only commoner in the assembly. Some people might consider your position insupportable."

"I'm sure I'll be fine," Severin said.

"If you'd allow me to suggest . . ."

"Thank you," Severin said, "but if you'll excuse me, I have urgent business with Lord Roland."

Roland had just entered with his brother-in-law and fellow convocate Lord Oda Yoshitoshi. Severin approached and offered greetings.

"Congratulations, Squadron Commander," said Lord Oda. He was a distinguished older man with a shock of black hair going white at the temples, and his manner mingled assurance with nonchalance, a combination made easier by the centuries of breeding that had produced him.

"Thank you, Lord Oda," Severin said.

"Do you have your committee assignments yet?" Oda asked.

Severin smiled. "Yes, I do. I'll be chairing the Committee for Exploration and Planetary Settlement, and also the Committee for Ancient Monuments."

Roland was amused. "That should help you move forward with your various projects," he said. "Though I'm not sure if the entire world of Lorkin can be considered an ancient monument."

"It's clearly a monument to *something*," Severin said, "but to what? That's the question."

Oda nodded thoughtfully. "The Lord Senior must trust you a great deal to offer you two committee chairs."

"They fall within my specializations," Severin said. "My knowledge is narrow but extremely deep."

Oda was amused by this self-assessment. "I'm glad the assignments suit," he said. "They so often don't—for years I was stuck on the Meteorology Committee, and I had nothing to do with weather on this or any other world, and nothing to contribute."

"I suppose your current assignments are more to your taste?"

"Oh yes. I'm on Transportation, and also Broadcasting, Media, and Censorship." The latter of which would enable him to help his wife, Vipsania, Roland's oldest sister, who headed his family's possession Imperial Broadcasting.

"But I'll soon be promoted," Oda said. "I'll be leaving the Transportation Committee to become minister for Transportation."

"Congratulations, my lord," Severin said. Oda would be in charge of rebuilding the transportation networks severed by the war and would be in a position to award contracts, make appointments, and keep a good deal of commerce under his thumb.

Oda smiled. "My young nieces and nephews won't forgive me if I don't ask when we might expect another puppet serial," he said.

Severin laughed. "If Ancient Monuments can spare me the time," he said.

"Of course," Oda said.

"If you'll forgive me, my lord," Severin said. "I'd like to talk to Lord Roland for a brief time, if I may."

"Of course. Congratulations again, Lord Squadcom." Oda bowed and withdrew.

Roland turned to Severin. "Can I help you with something?" he asked.

"The more I have looked into being a convocate," Severin said, "the more I realize how much money I'll be needing."

Roland waved a hand. "You saved Chee from destruction," he said. "You only need ask."

"You've been generous enough," Severin said. After Severin had managed to turn off the pulsar and save the world that the Martinez family had only begun to settle, he had been rewarded with cash and valuable grants of land, enough to assure that he'd be well off for the rest of his life. But that was not nearly enough for a career as an independent convocate, let alone as Lorkin's patron.

And he very much wanted to be Lorkin's patron. Lorkin was Lady Starkey's discovery, and he wished to turn the world into a monument to her.

True, Roland was offering financial support, but he suspected that the support would come with obligations he might not care for.

"The two traditional ways to acquire money are to inherit it," Severin said, "or marry it. I seem not to have won the inheritance lottery, but I wonder if you might know a suitable bride."

Roland was surprised, but Severin saw calculation glinting behind his eyes. "What do you need besides pots of money?" Roland asked.

"I've been a convocate for less than two hours," Severin said. "You should tell me."

Roland mused aloud. "An ambitious family who will want to benefit from a convocate in-law, but not so large and ambitious that you'll be captured by their ambitions. A family sufficiently far down the hierarchy that they've been unable to produce a convocate of their own or to marry into the established High City families."

"Lower-middle-middle," Severin said helpfully.

Roland understood Severin's meaning, and smiled. "Amusing," he said, "and apt."

Gareth Martinez walked up, drink in hand, and greeted Severin. "Who's lower-middle-middle?" he asked.

"Nikki's bride," Roland said.

Martinez was surprised. "Who's the lucky lady?" he said.

"We don't know yet," said Roland.

"Ah." Martinez took a sip of his Laredo whisky, then turned to Severin. "What do you think of a young widow?"

"I've known a number of widows," Severin decided, "and had nothing against any of them."

He was something of a young widower himself, Severin thought. It was a thing they might have in common.

"Ismir Falana was one of my signals officers in the last war," Martinez said. "The Restoration promoted him to command of the *Courage* and he and his ship died at Second Shulduc. He was married for less than three years, I think, and now Alaya's en route to Zanshaa to settle the estate. She's a Bellanti from Devajjo."

"Ah," said Roland. "Transportation, electronics, infrastructure. If you want a town built on a new world, you'd give the Bellantis a call—" He smiled. "After you called *us*, of course, at the Chee Company."

"They compete with you in outfitting new worlds?" Severin wasn't certain he wanted to become an out-and-out rival of the Martinez clan.

Roland shrugged. "Plenty of new real estate to go around," he said. "More to the point, the Bellantis are very rich, but their operations are confined to the Hone Reach. They haven't got the muscle to win the big contracts handed out at Zanshaa." He looked at Severin and raised his glass in salute. "But if they are connected by marriage with a convocate who happens to be the patron of a world like Lorkin, I'd think it would be a cause for celebration all around."

Severin looked at Martinez. "And the lady?" he asked.

Martinez gave him an equivocal look. "I barely know her," he said, "but she seemed a pleasant person." He gave the business a moment's thought. "Now that I'm a convocate I'll be forever attending receptions and parties, or giving them. I can invite Alaya and introduce you."

Severin gave Martinez a look. "Do you know if she's even looking for a new husband?"

"No idea. I can ask her, I suppose, in a theoretical sort of way, without mentioning you." He gave an insinuating little smile. "Unless you *want* to be mentioned."

Severin was surprised and a little intimidated by the efficient and enthusiastic manner in which the Martinez brothers had jumped into the matter of his matrimony. He hadn't been entirely serious when he'd asked if Roland knew a suitable bride, but apparently Roland had taken the question at face value.

Though that was, he imagined, how the upper-upper-whatevers viewed matrimony. He supposed that Gareth Martinez had hardly hesitated when given the opportunity to marry Terza Chen, whose family connections could guarantee him promotion, employment, a rise in status, and a wider scope to exercise his talents.

Love was not an issue that arose in these sorts of discussions, but Severin supposed he was all right with that. He had bade farewell to love when Lady Starkey died, and now his life was a series of problems to be resolved rather than an exhilarating series of experiences to be lived.

Existence, without the addition of Lady Starkey, was drained of color.

"Well," he said. "I'll see her."

"Good. That's settled, then." Martinez turned to Roland. "Do you know," he said, "I'd like to be a fleet commander again."

Roland gave him a narrow glance. "Becoming a convocate isn't enough for one day?" he asked.

"What we need is legislation," Martinez said, "making all promotions within the Restoration permanent with seniority from date of promotion."

"That will make you senior to all Wei Jian's top officers," Roland said. "She'd never approve."

"Last I heard, the Convocation was senior to Wei Jian," Martinez said. "Her approval isn't necessary. But to avoid her objections, at the same time we can offer Wei Jian something she'd jump at."

Roland gave his brother a suspicious look. "Yes?"

"We can appoint her Supreme Commander."

Roland's suspicion deepened. "You've always said the office of Supreme Commander was useless and ridiculous," he said.

"I have, and frequently," Martinez said. "If Wei Jian accepts, it won't change a thing—she's already the most senior active officer in the Fleet, so all she'll get is the title. So if she chooses to accept the office, it will change nothing, and gratify nothing but her vanity—and she'll be seen to abandon her own officers who will see the Fourth Fleet commanders raised over their heads."

"How badly do you want to split the Fleet?" Roland asked.

"Wei Jian split the Fleet when she insisted on taking command of a victorious force that didn't belong to her," Martinez said. "The split was plastered over for the duration of the war, but those of us who fought while Jian was hiding at Tai-ma would very much like recognition of our efforts, thank you."

"Let me think about it," Roland said.

"You could also give her a parade or something. I bet she'd like a parade."

Roland gave him a pointed look. "I'm sure *you* wouldn't turn one down."

Martinez grinned. "Who would?" he asked.


"**CONGRATULATIONS, MY LADY,**" said Lord Saïd. "You are the youngest convocate in centuries. I'm sure your career will be both long sand brilliant."

"Thank you, Lord Senior," said Lady Koridun. She wore a Chesko gown shining with blued metal mirrors that reflected a shimmering world blue-shifted to a higher frequency. Her eyes shone a different shade of blue, and her gray-and-cream fur had been brushed to a high gloss.

Putting Koridun in the wine-red jacket of a convocate, Sula thought, would serve only to diminish her glamour.

Saïd's dark, discerning eyes turned to Sula. "Lady Sula," he said. "I hope the expanded Convocation is to your liking."

"It is, mostly," Sula said. She felt a prickling in her nerves at the knowledge that Martinez was in the room, barely visible near the gleaming podium near the top of the chamber.

Saïd nodded. "I have led the empire now through two wars," he said, "and I recognize the need for change. Such changes must come now, if they are ever to come at all." He gave a glance in the direction of the Martinez brothers. "The old cannot stand, yet the new is fraught with danger. Too radical a change might be as dangerous as no change at all."

"In my opinion," said Sula, "radical change is necessary, though perhaps not the radical change others are planning."

Saïd's eyebrows lifted. "Yes?"

"I think it's foolish to put all governance into the hands of two percent of the population," Sula said. "The talents of the remainder are wasted. I would open government office to all qualified candidates regardless of their origin."

"And qualifications are determined how?"

"Competitive examination."

Saïd considered this with a frown. "That *is* radical," he said. "Not to say revolutionary. You might have another war on your hands. Peers take pride knowing that certain positions belong to them by right."

Sula dismissed the privileges of the Peers with a shrug. "We can start slowly, with lesser offices. Once the lower offices are filled with talented personnel, there will be pressure from below to enlarge the pool of candidates, as well as—let's hope—pressure from above."

Lady Koridun's large night-adapted blue eyes gazed unblinking at Sula. "You aim to make the Peers obsolete," she said.

Sula could have wished that Koridun hadn't said this right in front of Saïd. As someone from the absolute top rank of Peers, he might not appreciate being turned out to pasture by an upstart officer.

"Not at all," Sula answered. "I think the Peers, as always, should lead the empire to a glorious and prosperous future."

Cynicism touched Saïd's smile. "It is a future I will not see," he said. "It is time to admit that age will soon bring an end to my service to the empire."

Sula felt a slow shock move through her nerves, not so much at the knowledge that Saïd would soon retire, but at the fact that he was willing to discuss it with two very junior convocates. *Has he told everyone?* she asked herself. Because once it was known that he would soon retire, people would no longer fear his displeasure, and he would lose a degree of his authority.

"I will remain in my present position," he said, "long enough to assure that suitable reforms are passed and that they are made as permanent as possible, but I will retire as soon as that is accomplished. You should give some thought to my successor."

A sardonic thought rose in Sula's mind. "I'm sure Roland Martinez would be happy to succeed you," she said.

"He is very able," Saïd said. "But too young, and too junior. The next candidate should be more seasoned, and preferably from one of the old High City families."

Possible candidates flashed through Sula's mind. Most of them, she thought, were too conservative, or too unimaginative, to make a suitable leader in a time of transformation.

"I hope your lordship's tenure may continue," Sula said.

"Ah, Lady Sula, you would condemn me to eternal misery," said Saïd. There was sorrow in his brown eyes. "To command the state, particularly in these times, is to steer a battered barque through an endless storm, only to find a safe harbor ever receding on the horizon."

"That is why I don't want to change captains," Sula said. "You have the authority to stand by a decision and enforce it."

"As I said, I will remain at the helm for a while longer. But mortality claims even the most skilled of captains." Saïd smiled. "It is best to plan for a successor now, rather than surrender the choice to fate." He offered a brief laugh. "Having survived the hazards of this last war, I desire nothing so much as to retire to the country and enjoy my vineyards and the shade of my orange groves."

Sula hoped those orange trees wouldn't burn in a new war.

"You've earned your retirement," Sula said. She glanced again at the Martinez brothers across the room, involved in an intent discussion with Nikki Severin. "I wish you a long and peaceful retreat."

She wondered how many others would so willingly give up the kind of power that Lord Saïd possessed, and whether it was even wise to do so. He could so easily become the target of a successor, who would blame Saïd for any unforeseeable, challenging problems that arose.

"And now," Saïd said. An expression of mischief crossed his face. "If you'll forgive me for raising the matter, I wonder if you have given any further thought to my grandnephew Eveleth."

Sula burst into laughter. "I haven't had the time, Lord Senior," she said.

"An exemplary young man, as I believe I have stated."

"I have no doubt," Sula said. "But I also have no time."

LATER, AS SULA and Lady Koridun left the hall through its doors inlaid with arculé wood, Koridun turned to Sula and asked, "Is this a typical day in the Convocation?"

"Not at all," Sula said. "And I wonder if Lord Saïd is announcing his upcoming retirement to everyone, or just to us."

Koridun blinked her luminous blue eyes. "Why would he tell just us?"

"That's just what I'm wondering." She frowned as she considered. "He wants us to do something, maybe. But what?"

She considered his words again, and something clicked for her.

*Find your own candidate,* she thought, *and match him against whoever the Martinez family puts forward.*

Interesting.

# CHAPTER 15

"My lady," said Sula, "Distchin mismanagement of Spannan is so well known that it's almost proverbial. How do you imagine this idea became so widespread?"

Lady Distchin—elderly, with large dark bubbles protecting her night-adapted eyes, brown and white fur combed beautifully to cover the bald patches brought by age—had not taken Sula's hint to resign her seat in Convocation, and instead had insisted on a full hearing before the Court of Honor.

Sula was delighted at the opportunity. Crucial years of her childhood and adolescence had been spent on Spannan, probably the most mismanaged planet in the empire, and she had wanted for years to tell the head of Clan Distchin exactly what she thought of her.

Glittering in the spotlights, Lady Distchin sat alone before her panel of judges. Jewels and biliments were braided into her fur, and an aigrette with a spray of gems was fixed in her cap. The scent that drifted from her was musk and spice. The chair in which she had settled was plain, possibly the least ornamented chair in which she had ever planted her plush bottom.

At the question, Lady Distchin wrinkled her nose as if in response to a bad smell. "Others are jealous of us!" she said. She

spoke with the languid High City drawl that was guaranteed to ir-
ritate Sula. "We are one of the oldest and most respected families
among the Peers. We have been patrons of Spannan for dozens of
generations and have raised what was once an unpopulated world
to a productive planet that is the envy of the empire."

"I've never heard of anyone envying Spannan," Sula said, "and
when I lived there myself, it's safe to say that no one envied *me*. It
was clear to me even as young girl that the place was a stew of corruption, incompetence, and crime." She waved a hand. "Everyone
complained about how every time anyone wanted to start a business or produce a new product, some agent of the Distchin family
was there to collect a fee or a tax or a bribe. Everyone there *hates*
you and your family." She offered a brief laugh. "Though of course
you wouldn't know that. You've never been on Spannan. Neither
was the previous Lord Distchin. Neither was *his* predecessor."

"Jealousy!" sniffed Lady Distchin. "We are one of the grandest
families in the empire! The opinions of anonymous, carping members of the lower orders are of no consideration!"

"Do you call me a member of a lower order than yourself?" Sula
asked.

Distchin's snarl revealed one pendant fang. "Out of courtesy to
a member of this august body I shall not respond to the question."

"You deny allegations that your family profits from extortion?"
More fangs flashed. "Of course!"

"Let's look at your finances, then," Sula said. "I've sent the Treasury a warrant for your financials, and the staff has been sorting
through the public record as well."

Imperial citizens had paid a 1 percent tax on their income for
only ten years or so, as a response to the need for paying for the
Naxid War, but the ten years' information revealed much. Sula reported the sums flowing into Distchin's accounts and compared

404 WALTER JON WILLIAMS

it with the amount spent on Spannan itself—on improvements, maintenance, and salaries.

The amount coming out of Spannan was colossal. The amount going in was a very small percentage of the returns.

The only thing that frustrated Sula was that she couldn't tie Distchin to the extortionate activities of the Tu-hon clique. Apparently, Lady Distchin was far too grand to ally herself with a seedy group of politicians, however grasping.

Sula reported the final figures with a flourish, then glanced up at Lady Distchin.

"The thing I find most astonishing about these figures," she said, "is that year after year, you somehow manage to spend it all."

Distchin made a gesture of contempt. "This morbid emphasis on my finances is in the worst of taste," she said. "I am proud to say that I have no knowledge whatever of my financial affairs."

"The money arrives, and you spend it. Does that sum up your attitude?"

Lady Distchin waved a hand. "I have no 'attitude,' as you put it. That would be vulgar."

"The inhabitants of Spannan have the lowest per capita income of any settled planet in the empire. Do you in any way hold yourself responsible for that?"

Distchin sniffed. "I can only imagine that the people of Spannan lack ambition."

Sula grinned. "As opposed to being systematically robbed by a family of grasping, gluttonous racketeers and their money-grubbing sycophants?"

Distchin tottered to her feet. "I have no intention of being insulted any further!"

Sula laughed. "I have not *begun* to insult you, Lady Distchin!" she said. "I remind you that you *requested* this hearing." Triumph fizzed in her blood like sparkling wine. "Now I suggest," she said, "that you sit your fat ass back on that chair before I have the sergeant-at-arms return you by force."

The fur on Distchin's head and body stood on end, making her resemble one of the plush Torminel dolls so popular with Terran children. But she smoothed her hair with an act of will and returned to her seat. Sula looked at her and smiled.

"Are you aware, Lady Distchin, that criminals on Spannan are known as linkboys?"

Distchin sniffed again. "I have no acquaintance with criminals."

"Are you not acquainted with your own family, then?"

As there was no response, not even a sniff, Sula continued. "Can you guess why these criminals are called linkboys, my lady?"

"I can't imagine."

"Because they are all linked to a network that runs from the criminal underworld to the highest echelons of society—and to *you*, Lady Distchin."

Distchin's lips twisted. "I can only repeat that I know no criminals."

"At this point I would like to call as a witness a native of Spannan, Mr. Am-tra."

When Lamey had arrived on Zanshaa he was a member of a delegation hoping to end Distchin patronage of their world, and though Lamey was quietly rotting in an abandoned refrigerator on Zarafan's ring, his delegation was still present, and still eager to tell their story. Am-tra, a former police official, stepped in to testify to the numerous links between criminals and members of the Distchin clan, and with a series of graphics showed how the money moved from account to account, with each handler taking a piece of the profits.

Another member of the delegation testified to numerous accidental deaths due to failure to maintain Spannan's infrastructure, while another delivered statistics on the spread of poverty and the large number of emigrants leaving Spannan in hopes of a better life.

Lady Distchin was offered a chance to respond and promptly claimed that the witnesses were insurrectionists who were a menace to society.

"I am before you as a Peer of the highest order," Distchin said. "The accomplishments of my family ring down the ages, unmatched by any other Peer household." She brandished a furry fist. "These ill-judged efforts to slander our achievements are impertinent and mendacious, and I am mortified that a Peer of the highest rank such as yourself should demean herself by participating in this charade! I suggest this hearing be ended before you embarrass yourself further!"

Sula found this performance hilarious, and managed to avoid laughter only by an extreme act of will.

"I think you may be mistaken concerning who finds themselves embarrassed by this hearing," she responded. "You've been shown at this hearing to be a thief, a liar, and a complete disgrace to the Convocation and the Order of Peers. The Convocation offered your family the great honor of becoming patron to a whole world, but you have abused your privileges and dragged your honor in the dust. No matter the outcome of the vote today, you will leave this room an infamous figure, and a subject worthy of contempt."

The night-adapted eyes glared at Sula. "You are impertinent. You have shown yourself worthy of the example of your parents, who died in disgrace on the scaffold."

Sula laughed. "I find it curious that you've not been on the scaffold yourself!"

Distchin's lip curled, revealing a single fang. "No one would *dare*," she said.

"Stand by," Sula said. "Events may surprise you."

Sula then let the other four members of the committee offer comments. All were from families that had suffered under the previous government, and all were very angry at the Convocates who had permitted the robberies and murders to go on.

If Distchin thought that Sula had been brutal, she soon discovered that Sula was nothing in comparison with her colleagues, who denounced the Distchin family in terms usually reserved for vermin. As they ranted on, Lady Distchin's fur kept leaping erect, but she managed to smooth it down.

Finally, Sula called for a vote. With a score of five to zero, Lady Distchin was removed from the Convocation. Sula called for the sergeant-at-arms.

"Throw this bitch out of the Convocation," she instructed. "And if she tries to come back in, shoot her."

She watched with great pleasure as Distchin was hauled out of her chair and marched from the room. Sula thanked her colleagues and brought the hearing to an end, then left to walked to her chambers. She entered her flower-scented office and found Roland Martinez waiting for her. He spun toward her in his chair.

"Well done," he said. "I'm surprised Lady Distchin's fur wasn't scorched."

Sula put her hands in her trouser pockets and strolled to her desk.

"Humiliation now, flaming fur later. Do you want tea?"

"No, I just came by to express my delight at your performance. I hope it will inspire others to resign ahead of their hearing."

"I trust it will." She looked out the window at the Boulevard of the Praxis, where a freezing cloudburst was driving people into shelter. She looked at Roland. "It's all very well to get Distchin out of the Convocation," she said. "But she's *still* patron to Spannan, and she and the Orghoders and the other great absentees will remain in control of their various ill-gotten empires until the Convocation votes to remove them."

"Which it will," Roland said. "And by the way, would you like to become Spannan's new patron?"

Sula laughed. "I hardly think so! Besides, I'm not rich enough."

Roland shrugged. "Don't say I never offered." He shrugged himself deeper into his chair. "I've been counting votes," he said. "With you taking out the dead wood, and with the Convocation co-opting more of our friends, I think I'm very close to introducing the industry council plan."

Which would allow participants in certain segments of the economy—agriculture, transportation, industry—to self-organize into units independent of the formal hierarchy dictated by Zanshaa. These would hold no formal power—that would be against the Praxis—but they would have the right to appeal directly to Zanshaa if they thought they were unjustly suffering at the hands of local authority.

Sula thought this would create massive chaos and uncertainty, but then, she wasn't altogether certain that Roland hadn't intended chaos all along.

"Congratulations," Sula said. "I'll vote for it, I imagine."

Roland gave her a thin smile. "We thank you," he said.

Sula viewed him. "I wonder if you'll support my notion of competitive examinations for members of the civil service."

"I will," said Roland. "But not this session. We have a lot to do in a short amount of time, and I think we can only tackle one major reform per year." He nodded at her. "Next year we'll put it on the calendar."

"It seems to me that we're doing a *great* many major reforms all at once," Sula said. "But if you can give me a firm promise to take up the civil service proposal next session, then I think we're in agreement."

Sula called up the next session's business onto her screen. Roland was planning to introduce a resolution co-opting more names into the Convocation, which made Sula frown.

"I see you're planning on putting Lord Mehrang in the Convocation," she said.

"Yes." Roland made an equivocal gesture with one hand. "I know he's not the most personable candidate, but he's been a supporter of the Restoration since the very beginning."

"He's also killed millions of Yormaks."

Roland looked at her blankly. "They rebelled."

"The Yormaks were framed," Sula said. "Mehrang wanted to get them off his world so that he could confiscate their land and develop it. He arranged for some Yormaks to be caught on video while angry and for certain civilians to die, all of them members of the Yormak Bureau who were supposed to look after the Yormaks. That gave him an excuse to round up the rest of the bureau 'for their own protection.' Then the slaughter began."

Roland considered this. "You have proof?"

"I have a witness," Sula said. "Though proof wouldn't be hard to find—any investigation wouldn't have far to look." She waved a hand. "And if any of this comes out once Mehrang's in the Convocation? It wouldn't look good for one of the stalwarts of the Restoration to be revealed a mass murderer."

Roland frowned. "If this gets out, we'll be very, very shocked at the allegations, and advise Mehrang to resign from the Convocation."

"And the mass murder? Do the Yormaks deserve justice?"

"Justice won't bring them back."

Sula looked at him. "You want Mehrang because he's broke."

Which meant that Roland could offer Mehrang a subsidy in exchange for votes. Roland was acquiring an expanding circle of impecunious convocates who depended on him for support. It was a traditional way of building a faction, but Sula resented it, in part because she couldn't afford to create a faction that way. Instead, she'd have to talk people into agreeing with her, and that was a lot of work.

Much better, she told herself, to be a dictator.

Roland showed irritation. "He's not broke. Hector Braga took a lot of his money, true, but Mehrang's still patron to an entire planet."

"A planet that will need massive investment before it can really start to pay large dividends. How long will it take to melt all those glaciers? And in the meantime, Mehrang will have to somehow support a High City lifestyle."

"Mehrang's a capable individual, I imagine he'll survive some-how."

"He killed Hector Braga, you know."

Roland affected surprise. "You have evidence?"

"No. But isn't it obvious?"

Roland shook his head. "Braga took too many chances." He made a gesture of finality and rose from his chair. "Thanks for the offer of tea," he said. "And once again, congratulations on driving Distchin out of the Convocation." He gave her a half-salute. "And many more," he added.

He left, and Sula frowned as she looked at the door he closed in his wake. She didn't like the idea of Mehrang sitting fat and greedy in the Convocation, profiting from his slaughter of Yormaks in the exact way that members of the Gruum government had intended to profit from the massacre of humans.

She couldn't go to any of the news channels with the story, because they were all censored and her message wouldn't reach the public. She couldn't complain in the Convocation because she had no evidence.

But she also couldn't do nothing.

She would have to think hard about how to approach this . . . and when.

THE FLEET CONTROL Board met in a large, shadowy room, and sat around a black-topped table. Martine thought it could do with a bit of sunshine, and wondered if the light level had been set ages ago by a nocturnal Torminel.

Wei Jian gazed down at the room from a video screen. "I am sending a plan for rebuilding the Fleet," she said. "The Control Board should begin implementation immediately, and any necessary enabling legislation should be introduced in the Convocation. Message ends."

The Fleet Control Board was understaffed and overchallenged. Traditionally the board consisted of three civilian politicians and three Fleet officers, with a chair drawn from the Convocation or the Fleet, depending on the preferences of the Lord Senior.

At the moment, the Fleet Control Board consisted of two politicians: Lord Chen, who was already distracted by his being in charge of the Commandery, and his daughter Terza Chen, who was Minister of Right and Dominion and busy with running a large civilian agency that had until recently been as divided as the Fleet.

The Fleet was fully represented, by Martinez, the Daimong

defector Rivven, and Wei Jian. Jian still commanded the Home Fleet from her flagship *Crisis* and had never attended a meeting in person. Usually she was present on a hookup from the ring, sometimes she sent only an agenda she expected to be followed, and today she'd sent a massive document that she assumed the Control Board would implement without question.

The Control Board had no appointed chair, but Wei Jian had assumed the role more or less as she had assumed command of the Combined Fleet: without being asked, and without tolerating dissent.

Now the board, which had been struggling to round up enough data on financials and building capacity to put together a plan for the enlargement of the Fleet, would be asked to approve an enormous plan to which they hadn't contributed.

Lord Chen looked as if he'd just bitten into a rotten apple. "Well," he said, "I suppose we should look at it."

"Who wants hardcopy?" Martinez asked. They all did.

The scent of ink wafted into the room as an aide brought in stacks of freshly printed paper. Martinez spread the plan before him and began to read.

The plan was comprehensive and enabled the Fleet to reach a goal of eight hundred warships within six years, growing building capacity so that each year would launch more ships than the last. Training schools were to be expanded to help make up the shortage of trained recruits and NCOs, while the venerable academies that produced new officers would also be ramped up, with new instructors drawn from among Fleet veterans.

No giant battleships, with ballrooms and steam baths, were contemplated. Wei Jian was vain, but her brand of vanity didn't extend to lodging in a floating palace.

Procedures were described whereby non-Terran officers and

crews could be evaluated, and those deemed reliable would be put in positions of responsibility. New non-Terran graduates of the academies would be employed in the Fleet without prejudice. As a result, the upper ranks of the Fleet would be dominated by Terrans for a generation, with non-Terran junior officers gradually working their way up the ladder of promotion until their numbers grew to prewar levels.

The plan even included what to do with excess production capacity once the eight-hundred-ship Fleet had been realized.

The plan was everything Martinez had been striving for in his own inchoate plans, and employed all the information that he lacked.

*Damn*, he thought. *I wish I had Jian's staff.*

He had the sinking feeling that this was going to be a preview of the next decades of his life—sitting at a table implementing Wei Jian's plans for the Fleet, with no chance to make his own mark. Resigned, he looked up at the others, and indicated the plan with a wave of his hand.

"If we study this very carefully," he said, "we might find a mistake. Let's do our very best."

THE LAST NOTE of the derivoo hung suspended in the air. As it faded it was replaced by a long, profound silence, and then the small theater filled with applause. The derivoo offered her audience a dignified bow, then withdrew along with her musicians.

Captain Alana Haz let out a long breath. "Lady Sula," she said. "I had no *idea*. I've never seen derivoo in live performance before."

"Did you like it?"

"I don't know that it's something to *like*," said Haz. "It's more like something to *experience*."

"True," Sula said.

Haz looked at Dr. Gunaydin. "Did you enjoy it, Doctor?"

Gunaydin gave a private smile. "I listen to derivoo all the time." Unspoken was the detail that he listened to derivoo at Sula's apartment, where he could scarcely avoid it.

The Rose and Dagger Club was on the north side of the High City, overlooking the park in the Lower Town below. Sula had decided on an evening with friends, with no one in uniform, and as discreet a security presence as possible.

Captain Mazankosi had been visiting friends in the High City on her way to her hunting lodge in the To-bai-to Highlands, and so was invited. Sula had asked Lady Koridun, but Koridun was committed to yet another reception for new convocates and couldn't attend.

Sula also asked Ming Lin, who had been her economics adviser before the war, when Sula had served on the Committee for Banking and Exchange. Lin's policies had created a booming economy in the worlds of the Restoration while the rest of the empire was still mired in the worst recession in recent history, and now she sat on committees that advised Lord Saïd and the Imperial Bank.

Alana Haz was a different case. War had caught her halfway out of the chrysalis, shifting from one identity to another, from Alan to Alana. Now she was on Zanshaa to resume that process, which required some fairly specialized medical treatment.

Haz and Mazankosi should get to know each other, Sula thought. Each had been Sula's flag captain at different stages of the war, and they could compare notes about how impossible she was.

Sula had seen that Mazankosi had been restless during the derivoo performance, and she thought that Mazankosi would probably rather face a charging penthrad in the jungle than sit through another set.

Too bad. Sula was the host, and she was paying.

She signaled the waitron for another Kyowan and Spacey. Cool fire blazed its way down her throat. "Would anyone like another drink?" she asked.

Drinks were ordered. Mazankosi turned to Gunaydin.

"Have you settled in Zanshaa, Doctor?" she said.

"I've got an apartment," he said. "I've decided it's unrealistic to start a practice on my own here, where I know so few people, so I'm looking to join an established practice or to get on staff at a hospital. I've had some promising interviews, but so far no job offers."

"What's your specialty?" asked Haz.

Gunaydin sipped his cocktail. "Internal medicine," he said. "When I was in the Fleet, I also did trauma care and general surgery, but that's because there weren't enough surgeons."

"Serdar also worked on Naxids," Sula said.

Gunaydin smiled. "Sprains and broken bones," he said. "Nothing serious."

Growing out his dark hair had actually made him look younger, and Sula thought it made his head more shapely. Sula was glad he had an apartment, because if he'd stayed in her place, with her working so many hours at the Convocation, he would have had nothing to do most of the day. She didn't want someone kicking around waiting for her to return, counting the minutes until she arrived too exhausted to pay attention to him.

Now their time together was relatively rare, and thus valued. Sula felt comfortable with Gunaydin. She was still pleased not to be in love, because love was obsession and frenzy and madness, and she never wanted that in her life ever again.

She turned to Ming Lin. "My investments seem to be climbing," she said. "You're probably responsible, so I thank you."

"The optimism in the markets has little to do with the current situation," Lin said. "It's barely changed, though at least we're low-ering interest rates. But investors are anticipating gains once new policies take hold. And if you could get the new tax law passed, we'd all be obliged, I'm sure."

During the Naxid War, Ming Lin had been a teenage member of Sula's Secret Army who specialized in tossing bombs into rooms full of Naxids. She was a graduate student in economics when Sula had hired her as her adviser, and then Lin saw the financial crisis coming and predicted its sad trajectory until the moment to leave Zanshaa or be killed arrived

Since the start of the war, she had with a degree of reluctance abandoned her black drill student gown and her pink updo to re-fashion herself as a glossy adviser to the rich and powerful, but she'd retained the broken nose she'd suffered in the fight to cap-ture the *Striver* from a company of Legion fanatics. The crooked nose gave her a piratical appearance and enhanced her image as someone not to be challenged. How many economists had ever thrown bombs or shot down the empire's formidable political po-lice?

"The new book?" Sula asked.

"No time to work on it. And I don't like writing about myself anyway." Lin's publisher had offered a substantial advance for a his-tory of Lin's adventures in the war, from the storming of the *Striver* to her revival of the Restoration's economy.

"Ghost writers are common on autobiographies, I believe." Sula knew this because she'd been receiving offers from publishers to relieve her of the task of doing her own writing, which she had no intention of doing anyway. She always refused them—there was too much of her past she didn't want to revisit—or want any-one else to know.

"The real problem is lack of time," Lin said. "I had more time when I was writing my thesis—in retrospect, it's amazing how much free time I had when I was a student."

Sula laughed. "And now you have credentials that entitle you to work yourself to death."

"Oh," Lin said. She shook her head. "No credentials at all. I never got my degree—I had to flee before I could defend my thesis, remember."

Sula stared at Ming Lin in surprise. "And they haven't given you your degree?"

"Well," Lin said, "I didn't show up for the defense, so . . ."

"And they can't reschedule?"

"My adviser's moved on. I've been told it's too late."

*Too late for* them, *maybe*, Sula thought.

"Tell me who to call," Sula said, "and I'll see what I can do."

The Rose and Dagger's manager, a small man with slick, glossy hair, arrived at their table to ask if the service was satisfactory, and he received a favorable answer.

"Lady Sula," he said, "I know that you're an aficionado."

"If I'm not," Sula said, "I'm wasting a lot of money in here."

The manager offered a brief laugh. "I wonder if you would consent to do us a favor."

Sula nodded. "If I can."

"In six days' time we'll host a competition from among the derivoo academies on Zanshaa. Would it be possible for you to join us as a judge?"

Sula blinked. "I'd be happy to."

"Delighted, Lady Sula! We'll so look forward to your participation."

"Gracious," said Mazankosi after the manager left. Her eerie blue eyes seemed glazed. "So many hours of such . . . extraordinary music."

"Yes," Sula said happily. "So many!"


**MARTINEZ LOOKED DOWN** at his daughter lying asleep, and love and tenderness rose in him with such sudden ferocity that it nearly stopped his breath. He reached out and took Terza's hand.

Yaling, his Mei-mei, had arrived that morning in the company of Roland's daughter, Girasole, and their aunt Walpurga, who had looked after them in their Laredo exile. Yaling had arrived with a trunkful of souvenirs in the form of leaves, twigs, pressed flowers, and dead insects, all the keepsakes she'd acquired in her investigations of Laredo's natural history.

Martinez had spent the day watching as his daughter had run madly over their palace, reassuring herself that the building still existed, that her bedroom was as she left it, that the small elevator with its brass accents was still in its shaft, that her favorite objects were still in place. All her toys were gone save for those she'd taken with her, and some of her best-loved art was gone from the walls, including her father's portrait. When she asked where her favorite things were, Martinez answered simply, "The enemy took them."

"Did you blow up the enemy, then?" Yaling asked.

"A lot of them, yes."

"And did you get my things back?"

"Some of them," Martinez said. "But I'm sure the rest of your things are making other little girls happy, and we should be pleased for them."

With that Yaling was reasonably satisfied.

Now, exhausted, Yaling lay asleep in her own bed. Martinez reached out a hand to brush a strand of dark hair from her face, and he felt her warm breath on his palm.

"I missed her so much," he said. He looked at Terza. "I missed you all."

"We're so busy," Terza said. "I keep thinking we deserve a vacation, just the family."

"We'll have one," Martinez said. "Soon, I hope."

Terza drew him out of Yaling's bedroom, and he closed the door behind him as he left. Terza's vetiver scent floated in the air, and her unhurried walk down the staircase displayed to his vision her slightly unearthly quality of calm and grace.

She led him to the lounge on the ground floor. "Drink?" she asked.

"Sure."

"Brandy sunflower?"

"Why not?"

She drew a chilled pitcher from the freezer and moved with her usual economy and elegance as she mixed the drinks. Accustomed to spending her days in the brown uniform of the civil service, she had changed to domestic wear, a pale poplin shirt over a pleated skirt that draped her hips and legs with casual ease. Martinez watched her with interest, as her manner seemed to confide that something of significance was about to happen, or at any rate be discussed.

Terza poured, then put the pitcher and crystal tumblers on a tray and placed it on the low table by the sofa. Martinez took his place on the sofa, and Terza smoothed her skirt as she settled next to him. Martinez took the drinks, handed one to Terza, and raised his glass.

"To family," he said. They touched glasses.

Terza tilted her head. "It was family I wanted to talk about," she said.

"Go ahead."

She sipped her drink. "When I was on Harzapid you suggested that we have another child," she said.

Martinez nodded as a warm glow kindled behind his breastbone. "You said you were not averse."

She gave him an appraising look. "Were you just feeling lonely and sentimental when you made the suggestion?" she asked. "Or do you still want another baby?"

The glow brightened. Martinez had suggested a child as part of a plan to help Terza disregard anything she might have heard about Sula, and to let her know that he was committing to their marriage. But though the idea originated as a strategy, the thought of another child had taken hold, and now he wanted a baby not as an element on a game board laid out between himself and Terza, but as a precious and irreplaceable object in itself.

"I would very much like another child," he said. "But not if you think the timing is wrong. It's you who has to carry the baby, after all."

Terza gave a little sigh. "My father tells me he's going to retire soon and leave me the title. That means I'll have to deal with all his clients and a very complicated business empire. And if I'm Lady Chen, I'll be in the Convocation, and that will take up even more time."

"Maybe we should have a baby as soon as possible," Martinez said, "before you get too busy even to think about it."

Amusement touched her lips. "There's something to be said for that idea," she said.

"It's a pity your family demands natural childbirth instead of using an artificial womb," Martinez said. "Or do they still?"

Terza sighed. "Of course they do."

"It's an upper-upper-upper thing, I understand," Martinez said. "But once you're Lady Chen, aren't you in charge? Can't you change the rules?"

She shook her head. "I'm afraid not. Or rather, I *could*, but it's not worth the trouble." She waved a hand as if chasing insects away. "All the *cousins . . .* ," she muttered.

He put down his drink and took her hand. "I'm sorry it'll be so much trouble," he said. "But shall we venture into parenthood once more?"

She bent her head, her long black hair shrouding her face, and then she raised it in a gentle gesture of acquiescence. "I'll see my doctor and get my implant removed," she said. "And then we'll let nature take its course."

Martinez kissed her lips, cold and moist from the chilled cocktail. Whatever Terza might have heard about Sula, he thought, it was forgiven, though possibly not forgotten.

Though he had to admit to himself that he never understood what went on behind the beautiful, placid exterior that Terza showed to the world. Sometimes he suspected she was playing some kind of unfathomably deep game, moving herself and her husband and her family across a board as large as the empire, and in accordance with rules only she fully understood.

Their kiss deepened, and Terza's tranquil, placid exterior began to dissolve under the blazing assault of desire. Bliss descended on Martinez.

He and Terza could start over, living in their palace with their family, and soon they'd both be in the Convocation, a powerful pair acting to reshape the empire, to be succeeded in time by their children.

Their *genius* children. Because, between Terza and Martinez, nothing else was even possible.


MARTINEZ ENJOYED A lengthy breakfast the next morning, with coffee, smoked fish, and rice congee with poached eggs. Terza went to her office at the ministry, but Martinez had arranged a free morning, and he lingered at the table. Benedicta Kelly would visit later in the morning to discuss reviving the Corona Club, rebuilding both the clubhouse and the yachting team in preparation for the next year's season. With Kosch Altasz dead, Kelly—the best pilot—not yet recovered sufficiently to race again, Martinez too busy to participate in a racing season, and, Martinez thought, Severin too busy as well, there was a need for new blood. Too, the yacht carrier *Corona* would require a complete refit after playing host to hundreds of training school graduates on their way to Zanshaa.

Fortunately, the Fleet possessed a large number of talented pinnace pilots, and some of them would be open to recruitment.

It would be another full agenda in a life already packed with full agendas, but Martinez was confident he could manage it.

Mpanza entered and prepared to clear the table. "May I have a word, Lord Divcom?"

Martinez suspected that Mpanza had a reason to butter him up with the flattering title of divcom.

He returned his coffee cup to its saucer. "Yes?"

Mpanza drew himself up formally. "My lord, I should like your permission to marry Warrant Officer Juskiene."

Martinez blinked. "Congratulations," he said. "You have my

permission, provided Warrant Officer Juskiene is willing, along with her captain."

"Perhaps you could speak with Captain Dalkeith, my lord?"

"Certainly."

Mpanza flushed with pleasure. "Of course, Filomena and I would like to share quarters."

The butler, Doshtra, was the only servant who actually lived in the palace, with Mpanza, Mangahas, and Terza's maid, Fran, having apartments nearby. Household servants who didn't live with their employers needed to live close to their work, and there were hostels for servants scattered over the High City, or in the Lower Town by the funicular.

"There should be no problem," said Martinez, "since you're both posted in Zanshaa City."

"But if *Los Angeles* is sent to another station, my lord?" Mpanza said. "We'd be separated. Is there some way Filomena might join your household?"

Martinez considered this. "I'd like to oblige you, but I have no need for a shuttle maintenance specialist."

"She could retrain on automobiles, my lord."

Martinez didn't think he needed a personal mechanic. But then he remembered the purpose of his upcoming meeting with Kelly and grinned. "I have no need for a small spacecraft specialist," he said, "but my *yacht club* does."

A smile rose brilliant on Mpanza's face.

"Excellent, my lord," he said.

# CHAPTER 16

"What I fail to understand is why Ming Lin hasn't gotten her degree," Sula said. She was walking from the Convocation to her car, which was waiting at the curb, while speaking into her hand comm to the principal of the Zanshaa College of Economics, a semi-autonomous division of Zanshaa University. Judging by the melodic quality of his voice, Principal Theel was a Daimong.

"Miss Lin failed to attend her own thesis defense," said the principal. "We could hardly award a degree under those circumstances."

Sula's guards straightened as they saw her coming, their heads swiveling as they scanned all possible avenues of attack. Macnamara stepped out of Sula's car and rolled her door up into the roof.

"She defended her thesis by proving it in the real world. The only reason she missed your little ritual is because Miss Lin fled to avoid assassination," Sula said. "Her book on the financial crisis made too many enemies."

"I know nothing of that," said Principal Theel.

"You know it now," said Sula, "because I'm fucking telling you."

"I hardly think—"

"You hardly think. Sounds about right." Sula slid into her Hunhao, and Macnamara rolled down her door. The flowers in the car's vases sweetly scented the air.

"So what we need," Sula continued, "is for the thesis defense to be rescheduled."

"I'm afraid, Lady Sula, that too much time has passed." An offended note had strained Theel's vocal harmonies.

"It seems to me," Sula said, "that Ming Lin's accomplishments in successfully running the Restoration's wartime economy, and her current positions as adviser to the Imperial Bank and the Lord Senior, might reflect well on your college."

"We might consider an *honorary* degree," said Theel. "I could raise the matter at the next biannual meeting of the Scholastic Review Committee."

Sula's guards piled into the two escort vehicles, and the small convoy set out onto the Boulevard of the Praxis.

"On second thought, I'm beginning to think that Ming Lin's reputation would not be enhanced by an association with your school," Sula said. "Your school graduated Kannitha Seang, did it not?"

"Yes, but—"

"Seang, head of the Imperial Bank, executed for conspiring to sell fraudulent securities created by the investor Cosgrove— Cosgrove, whose bankruptcy signaled the economic collapse which in turn precipitated the war. Cosgrove was executed, too, of course, and of course also attended your school."

"Cosgrove never graduated," Theel said stiffly.

"Seang had an assistant named Fen-lur, graduate of your fine academy, who dealt exclusively with Cosgrove, aided his frauds, and was likewise executed," Sula continued. The statues of *The Great Master Delivering the Praxis to Other Peoples* paraded past her windows.

"And of course," Sula added, "your most celebrated recent graduate was Lord Minno, who specialized in stock fraud schemes before being appointed head of the Treasury in the Gruum administration, where he used his position to enhance his personal portfolio at the expense of the empire." She offered Theel a heavy sigh. "It's a pretty little group of criminals you've produced at your school, Principal Theel."

"I remind your ladyship that Cosgrove never graduated," Theel said. "And that the college has graduated thousands of distinguished candidates who have gone on to eminent careers in finance and government . . ."

"Yet you seem to have gone badly astray in recent years," Sula said. "I'm still on the Committee for Banking and Exchange, and I may have to call you and other members of your faculty and administration before the committee to explain not only why you graduated such an infamous gang of crooks, but why you refuse to give a degree to the woman who *exposed* your fine gang of graduates."

Indignation clashed like steel in Theel's voice. "That is hardly fair!" he said. "You hold up only a handful of cases, and fail to mention the thousands of distinguished—"

"You're hardly one to talk about fairness," Sula said. "What would be most *fair*, I think, would be for Ming Lin to receive her degree in, say, three days' time. What do you think of that?"

"What about—"

"I think we're past that, don't you?"

There was a few seconds' pause. "I will see what I can do," Theel said.

"Right then," Sula said. "I hope we won't have to revisit this issue." She ended the call and barked a laugh. "Now *that*," she said to Macnamara, "is how it's done!"

Macnamara gave her a cynical look over his shoulder. The boulevard was packed, and Sula managed to complete a pair of calls while trapped in traffic.

She was on her way to a long and delightful afternoon and evening of derivoo, as one of the judges in the competition at the Rose and Dagger. She would see Alana Haz at the club and was pleased that Haz's first exposure to derivoo had made her a convert dedicated enough to turn up for a full day of performance by students.

Once it left the government district, the convoy turned off the boulevard and headed north into less crowded residential neighborhoods. They went as far north as they could, then turned west along a road that more or less paralleled the northern edge of the escarpment. The road didn't actually border the precipice, for there was a row of deluxe palaces lining the edge of the High City, each with a glorious—and presumably very expensive—vista of the Lower Town. Fences, trees, and buildings walled Sula from the view beyond, but she knew it well enough, from a time when her fighters had to hold the High City from assaults coming up from below.

The convoy approached an intersection with the only road that connected the High City with the Lower Town, a switchback that zigzagged up the cliff to the Gates of the Exalted. On the far side of that road lay a restaurant and entertainment district, with the Rose and Dagger a few streets beyond. Sula remembered the turrets with antiproton guns that the Naxids had placed to guard the switchback road against assault, turrets that had to be destroyed before Sula's improvised army could storm up the road to occupy the High City.

The lead car, with its bodyguards, was forced to suddenly brake as a truck swung out of an alley and blocked its route. Sula looked up as her own Hunhao braked more gradually and came to a halt two cars' lengths behind the lead car.

Rising caution whispered in Sula's inner ear. She looked at the truck, at the stalled traffic, and turned around to see a gray-painted bus coming up from behind.

The situation had a disturbing familiarity, because when she was the White Ghost she had set a great many ambushes, most successful.

She reached for her sidearm. "Macnamara," she said. "We need to reverse out of here. Tell the other drivers to back up."

Macnamara's head snapped upright, his eyes scanning. He triggered the lapel mic he wore that communicated with the two guard cars.

"Situation maximum. Shift into the oncoming lane and back away at speed. Perform a J-turn when you can."

Macnamara already had the wheels cocked, and as soon as he finished his transmission he made an abrupt acceleration that threaded the big Hunhao between two oncoming Sun Ray sedans. Sula saw the surprised driver of the oncoming car staring at her open-mouthed through his windshield. The Sun Rays were proceeding at moderate speed, and Macnamara had to brake in order not to ram the sedan behind him.

Still in reverse, they passed the third car in the convoy, which likewise backed and slotted itself into the queue behind the second Sun Ray. The lead car had plenty of room to reverse—Sula saw the silhouettes of her guards inside and un barrels protruding from open windows—and the car rocketed rearward on smoking tires, then vanished in an explosion so vast that her own car briefly sprang into the air. Debris spangled the windshield with stars, and Sula's breath was punched out of her as if she'd been hit in the chest by a Torminel heavyweight prizefighter. Her pistol tumbled from nerveless fingers, and she desperately tried to heave air back into her lungs. She thought the stricken car had disintegrated until it tumbled from the sky and crashed on its roof in the front garden of a white marble palace.

*That was supposed to be me,* she thought. If her car had advanced just a little farther, she would have been placed right over the bomb, which was presumably hidden in a utilities conduit or a sewer below the street. The whole plan had been for the truck ahead to slow traffic to the point where the bombers couldn't miss.

The traffic on the road froze in place as terrified, bewildered drivers slammed on the brakes. Sula groped for her pistol below her seat and was unprepared for her car ramming the motionless Sun Ray behind her. She rocked backward on the seat and lost her pistol again.

Sula sat up, staring over her shoulder at the stalled Sun Ray. A growl of rage escaped her throat. A kill zone was being set up, and she had only a few seconds to escape it. Frantically she waved at the Sun Ray's driver, urging him to move on.

Macnamara was more direct. He pulled forward, then reversed and rammed the Sun Ray again at full throttle. He kept the throttle down, and smoke poured from the tires as Macnamara shoved the smaller car down the road, the Hunhao jouncing on its suspension all the while.

The Sun Ray's driver got the right idea and accelerated. Macnamara followed, then found enough space for a J-turn and slid the Hunhao clean around, tires shrieking, then accelerated away from the bombing.

Except they were running out of room to run. The gray-skinned bus that had been coming behind them turned to block both lanes. Sula looked over Macnamara's shoulder to see if it was possible to get around the bus by climbing over the curb and detouring over a palace lawn or two, but the bus driver had chosen his position well, and his bus was protected by stone garden walls fore and aft.

Sula looked for an escape route—they could abandon the car and make a run for it, dashing through the genteel districts of the High City and hoping to lose any pursuit amid the palaces and gardens—but then she glanced to her left and saw a small palace, a near-cube of pale golden marble with green pillars. What attracted her attention was not the pillars but a pair of military constables conspicuous by their red belts, body armor, and rifles. They stood before a pair of imposing double doors and peered in the direction of the explosion.

Sula had no idea who lived in the palace, but it had to be someone ranked high enough to rate guards, and she liked the idea of some well-armored fighters to add to her entourage. She leaned forward over Macnamara's shoulder and pointed.

"There! There! Guards!"

Macnamara leaned on the control wand, and the Hunhao bounded over the curb and bashed through a box hedge onto a green lawn. Macnamara spun the car around again, shouldered an ornamental fountain out of the way, and ended with the car pointed out in the direction of the street and the rear aimed at the front door.

"Weapons and armor in the trunk, my lady," he said, and released the trunk latch.

Sula rolled up the door and lunged from the vehicle, her hands raised in the hope that the constables wouldn't shoot her down. Indeed, they looked ready to do exactly that, their rifles shouldered and bearing on the car that had just barged up to their doorstep.

Fortunately, Sula was not only in the uniform of a convocate, but with her military-cut tunic, shoulder boards, and silver-gilt hair she was one of the most recognizable convocates in the empire. One of the guards could only goggle at her, and the other started to brace at the salute, then went back on guard.

"Ambush!" she said. "Call for backup!"

She hauled armor, weapons, and ammunition out of the trunk. The Hunhao with the surviving bodyguards bounded onto the lawn and came to a stop short of the porch. Three guards jumped out, rifles at the ready, and went to their trunk for helmets and ammunition.

Macnamara joined Sula in dragging gear out of the trunk. He slung a rifle over his shoulder and grabbed a case of ammunition and a holdall with body armor. Sula had already equipped herself and made a sprint onto the porch and to the front door just as the attackers opened fire and sprayed the front of the building with fire.

Sula shouldered open one of the imposing double doors and nearly fell into the foyer. She staggered, the holdall with its armor tumbling to the floor, and then came to a halt in front of a startled Gareth Martinez.

She stared up at him as the fanlight over the door shattered beneath a storm of gunfire.

"Ah. Hah," she said.


THE EXPLOSION CAME in two stages, first the light and noise and blasting wind that shook the windows in the frames and shrieked down the chimneys, followed less than a second later by the ground wave that seemed to pick the house up off its foundation, then drop it down again. Coffee cups and glasses clattered, light fixtures swayed, objects tumbled from shelves and bounded off walls. Martinez, frozen in shock, stared into Kelly's black eyes.

He rose just in time to prevent a rocking vase from toppling off his office shelf. He placed the vase safely on the carpet and looked out the window to see a dark cloud rising just a few hundred paces from where he stood. Kelly was reaching for her canes.

"I'm going to see what . . ." His words trailed away as he left the room and dived for the stairs leading to the ground floor. "Mei-mei!" he called. "Chai-chai! Are you all right?"

Gareth the Younger's high, clear voice called down the stair-well. "Nonii!" he said. "What just happened?"

"Find Mei-mei!" Martinez called. "Then go to a safe place and stay there!"

"Was that an earthquake?"

*"Find Mei-mei!"*

Young Gareth's answer was cheerful. "Message acknowledged, forebear!"

A series of crashes sounded from outside the building—not explosions this time, but noises like a giant blundering around an ironworks. Martinez reached the ground floor and loped toward the front of the building, and as he entered the foyer the front door burst open and Caroline Sula stumbled into the house burdened with weapons. The fanlight above the door exploded to a burst of fire as if it were an overture to a hellish symphony of violence.

*She's here to kill me!* Martinez thought. He thought of him-self lying lifeless on the carpet, staring at the ceiling like Hector Braga.

Sula righted herself and stared at him, her eyes wide, shock showing on her face.

"Ah. Hah," she said. Gunfire smacked into the front of the building.

He found words. "What the hell is . . . ?"

"The Counter-Restoration," Sula said, words that sent searing heat shooting up Martinez's spine. He had been in danger before, he had been in battle, but never had his own children been at risk. For a moment he was nearly paralyzed by a tsunami of adrenaline storming into his veins, and then he and Sula were nearly trampled as Gavin Macnamara and three armed constables stampeded into the foyer. Past them, Martinez could see his own two guards returning fire, rifles leveled at an invisible target.

"Pull back!" Martinez told them. "Get into the house!" The palace, solid masonry faced with marble, was proof against anything but explosives.

Sula had passed into the front parlor and was directing her people to the windows. Martinez's own guards scuttled through the double doors, then pulled them shut.

Doshtra appeared, his gray Daimong face set by nature in a bland expression completely at odds with his arrival on a battlefield. He gazed at the warriors upending furniture, opening cases of ammunition, and crouching behind windows.

"My lord?" he said. As always, he spoke in perfect bell-like tones.

"Find my children," Martinez said. "Take them down to the cellar, and build some kind of shelter to help keep them safe."

"Very good, my lord."

Martinez ducked as a window shattered under fire and tumbling bullets buzzed through the air. Doshtra ignored the gunfire and turned to walk to the elevator. Martinez crouched and shuffled to where Sula was crouched behind an overturned table, dragging body armor out of a holdall.

"Is this happening everywhere?" he asked.

Sula shrugged. "Damned if I know."

"How many of these people are there?"

"A bus full maybe." Sula shrugged. "I really don't know."

Martinez glanced over the busy scene, the guards taking position to cover all possible entrances.

"You know more about this kind of war than I do," he said. "What should I be doing?"

She gave him a feral grin. "Lock all the doors and windows, for a start," she said.

"Right." He opened his sleeve display and told the house to lock all outside doors and windows. He glanced behind him and saw Kelly coming down the stairs, moving slowly and with care, her pistol in one hand and her canes in the other. Bullets buzzed through the air like hornets. Martinez rose from his crouch, dashed up the stairs, picked Kelly up bodily in his arms, and carried her to the ground floor, where he laid her on the floor next to Sula.

"That wasn't necessary!" Kelly said. "I was doing fine!"

"Yes, you were," Martinez agreed. "Back in a minute."

He ran up the stairs and down the hall, where he found Mpanza rushing toward him carrying his pistol in its holster. Martinez strapped on the offered gun belt, noted that Mpanza had already donned his own sidearm, then went to his office and opened his gun safe with his thumbprint. He hesitated between a rifle and a shotgun, then gave the shotgun to Mpanza and took the rifle for himself. He handed Mpanza boxes of shotgun shells and stuffed rifle magazines into his pockets.

His heart leaped with every gunshot. He realized he didn't have body armor—that was in the trunk of the car that had taken Terza to the ministry.

Mpanza looked uncertainly at his shotgun. "I'm a weaponer, my lord," he said, "but I've only trained on missiles."

"You'll be my runner then."

"Yes, my lord. What's a runner?"

"I'll let you know when I need one."

Martinez was uncertain about what to do next. Sula had shown up at his front door and brought a battle with her, and he had no contingency plan for that. He opened his sleeve display and made an emergency call to Lord Chen at the Commandery.

Chen appeared on Martinez's display, half-distracted by something off camera. "Yes Gareth," he said. "What can—"

"My house is being attacked by a pack of armed men," Martinez said. "Your grandchildren are in the building, though fortunately Terza's at the ministry."

He now had Lord Chen's full attention. "That's *you*?" Chen said. "I've had reports of an explosion from Lady Sula's party, and I'm sending constables to the area."

"Send more," Martinez said. "Sula picked my house to hide in, and it's a proper battle here."

"Right away, Gareth. I—"

Martinez twitched aside the window curtains and saw crouched figures in helmets moving along the side of the building.

"They're going for the back door," he said, then looked at his sleeve display and said, "End message." He slapped a magazine into his rifle—it wasn't a military weapon, but an antique hunting rifle with a seven-round magazine, its grip and stock made of arculé wood chased with silver. Martinez went for the back stairway at a run, dashed down three flights of stairs, then went down the fourth and final flight more cautiously.

The rear door, not being intended to impress people, was less sturdy and less imposing than the heavy doors at the front. It featured solid wood paneling set into a steel frame, but it had a large window of strong safety glass designed to withstand hammers or footballs or thrown lawn furniture, but which would probably not stand up to gunfire. Outside the door was a patio suitable for al fresco dining, and inside was a well-lit pantry, refrigeration, and food preparation area that formed the anteroom to the kitchen on the east side of the building.

Martinez nudged open the door at the bottom of the stairs and peered out to see a dark silhouette at the back door. Martinez recognized a Daimong, the lower part of its head muffled, with only the round black eyes visible beneath the brim of a helmet—one that had come from the Urban Patrol, apparently. The Daimong was trying the door, shoving it back and forth in hopes of popping the bolt.

Martinez shouldered the rifle and tried to take careful aim, but to his frustration his charge of adrenaline made his hands shake, and he braced the rifle against the doorjamb in order to keep the sights on the Daimong's center of mass. He was on the verge of squeezing the trigger when he realized that the Daimong seemed to be bulkier than most members of its species, and that he was probably wearing armor. Martinez raised his sights to the Daimong's head and tried to calm himself. The sights jittered. Martinez let his breath out in a long sigh, and when the gun seemed to jitter in the right direction, he squeezed the trigger.

The bullet made a neat hole in the glass and knocked the Daimong backward and out of sight. There was a pause, and then return fire came, the thunderous chatter of automatic weapons fire that shattered the windows at the back of the house and sent pots and pans clattering from shelves in the pantry.

At the torrent of bullets, Martinez's heart leaped into his throat and he ducked his head between his shoulders. Mpanza, crouched behind him, gave a strangled yelp and flopped onto the stairs.

The volley died away. Martinez chanced a look into the pantry and saw nothing. He readied his grip on the rifle.

He gave a spasmodic twitch as another silhouette appeared at a window. This was a female Torminel, the fur on her face erect to form a kind of brown-and-white puffball broken by large dark eyes and a snarling fang-filled mouth. The Torminel stuck the muzzle of a rifle into the window and held the trigger down, sweeping the room with fire. More pans clattered to the dark marble floors. A refrigerator door blew open, spilling liquids and sauces and food-stuffs. Martinez pulled back into the stairway as bullets turned the plaster over his head to dust.

The gunfire died away. Martinez chanced a glance and saw the Torminel standing in the window, her oversize eyes tracking the room for a target. Martinez shouldered his rifle, placed the jittering sights on the Torminel's chest, and fired.

The Torminel gave a shriek and leaped straight up, hanging in midair for a surprising stretch of time before dropping onto her feet. Snarling, she bounded through the window in a single clear leap and raised her rifle, the barrel tracking across the room and moving in Martinez's direction.

Martinez overcame surprise to fire first, and the Torminel sagged, the gun barrel dropping. Martinez shot her again, and the Torminel dropped to the floor amid a clangor of pots and pans.

Apparently this one wasn't wearing armor.

Martinez gasped for breath—a gunfight turned out to be surprisingly physical—and then he saw the Torminel's rifle lying next to her lifeless fingers.

"Mpanza," he said. "Can you crawl out and get that rifle? And as much ammunition as you can find?"

"My lord?" Mpanza lay supine on the stairs, both hands clutching the shotgun.

"I'll cover you," Martinez said.

Mpanza took a breath, picked himself up, and peered out of the stairwell and into the pantry. "Which rifle now?" he asked.

"The one next to the dead Torminel."

"Ah. Right."

"Go."

Mpanza put down the shotgun, took a deep breath, and threw himself onto his belly. He squirmed across the pantry floor, knocking pots out of his way and sweeping away broken glass. Martinez shouldered his weapon, braced it against the doorframe, and tracked the sights from one window to the next. The room smelled of propellant and blood.

Mpanza reached the Torminel and plucked the rifle away with his fingers. Then he began searching the dead body for spare magazines, found three, squirmed back across the floor, then crawled into the stairway. Crimson Torminel blood stained his hands and clothing, and shards of glass spangled his arms and wrists. Mpanza was panting, and Martinez realized that Mpanza had been holding his breath the entire time he'd been on the pantry floor.

"Breathe next time," he advised, and took the Torminel's rifle from Mpanza's fingers. The weapon had a laser sight, which would help with Martinez's jittery hands. The digit counter showed only five rounds remaining in the magazine, and Martinez found the magazine release, dropped the old magazine, and fitted in a new one.

"All right, runner," he said. "Run to the front of the house and tell Lady Sula that the attackers are trying to get in here, and I could use reinforcements."

"Yes, my lord."

Mpanza took another deep breath and readied himself to launch for the corridor.

"Breathe," Martinez told him, and Mpanza launched himself down the corridor. He had been gone only a few seconds when a brilliant light illuminated the hallway and the shattering sound of an explosion hammered Martinez's ears.


SULA THOUGHT THAT the defense was going well. Armed and armored guards at the windows were forcing the attackers to keep their distance, and as yet there seemed no real organized attempt to storm the house. The attackers were hidden behind incidental cover, which provided decent protection, but they were so scattered it was difficult for them to organize anything. None of the defenders had been killed, and wounds were confined to nicks and scratches, mostly from flying glass.

Sula looked for Macnamara and found him at one of the windows, tracking an enemy with his rifle. He fired, then dropped into safety as return fire cracked over his head.

"Macnamara," Sula called. "Take another of the guards and go upstairs. See if you can set up a sniper's nest and push those people away from the house."

"Yes, my lady."

"And see if anything's happening on our flanks and rear. It would be embarrassing if they all just walked in the back door."

Macnamara looked at the other guards, then gestured at a small red-haired woman who had been part of Sula's guard team for three or four weeks. The two paused to resupply with ammunition and crawled out of the room.

The yacht pilot named Kelly, one of Martinez's protégées, was still sprawled near Sula, her pistol trained on the front door. Sula looked down at her.

"Doing all right?" she asked.

There were bright spots of color high on Kelly's cheeks. "If I suddenly go mad and tear out my hair," she said, "it's because I've remembered the siege at the Corona Club. But right now I can't remember anything, so I'm grand."

"Nonii," Sula said. "We'll be all right as long as the ammunition holds out."

And then the double doors at the front of the building blew inward with a flash and a thunderous concussion. Wood splinters as long as Sula's arm hummed through the air. Sula's vision went black as the table behind which she and Kelly sheltered hurtled into her face.

The acid reek of explosive clogged her throat. Sula could hear nothing but the shrieking in her ears. She was stuck under the heavy table and she tried to struggle out, but her movements were strangely uncoordinated; getting free took a lot longer than she intended, and the effort left her exhausted.

Her helmet had been tipped forward over her eyes, and she pushed it back to see a room full of mist or suspended dust. The defenders were sprawled at their posts, making the slow, blundering movements of people fighting their way back to consciousness. The large wooden double doors had been blasted open, and one hung cockeyed, nearly blown from its hinges.

The attackers wouldn't have blown the door if they didn't plan to come in, Sula thought. The idea seemed to float slowly into her head through a sea of golden syrup. It would be desirable, she thought, to prevent enemy ingress. She marveled at the way the term *ingress* had floated to the top of her mind, then reached for her rifle and tried to drag it out from beneath the table. Her fingers lacked the strength.

"Shoot, shoot!" she shouted. "Keep them back!"

She barely heard her own words over the wailing in her ears. Dark figures appeared in the doorway. Again, she tried to seize her rifle and managed to drag it free, but then she flopped onto the floor, lying on her back like a turtle.

Words floated into her mind through the lake of golden syrup. *I am going to die here. And it will be colossally stupid.*

Bullets were flying in the room but she could barely hear them. She tried at least to point her rifle in the right direction.

And then Gareth Martinez appeared in the hall doorway,

walking upside-down into her field of vision with a rifle at his shoulder. Upside-down Martinez was shooting, and she could see bursts of fire spitting from the muzzle. She rolled onto her stomach and thrust out her own rifle and saw dim figures outlined in the arch of the front door, and she saw that they were dropping. She got her gun to her shoulder and began to fire. She didn't think she was managing accurate fire but at least she could add to the volume of bullets flying out the doorway.

Other members of her small army were beginning to react now, either shooting those coming through the door or firing out the windows to keep the attackers pinned down. Martinez dropped the empty magazine from his weapon, put in another, and fired a few more rounds before he could no longer find a target. Then he stepped forward, knelt, and with one hand picked the table off the floor and set it again as a barrier.

"How's Kelly?" he asked.

Kelly lay inert next to her pistol. Sula put out a hand to Kelly's throat and felt a pulse.

"Alive," she said. The word felt like a sponge ball she had to work hard to push out of her mouth.

"They're trying to get in the back," Martinez said. "I was trying to hold them off but this seemed more important."

Sula tried to hear the words over the screaming in her ears. She nodded.

"I need to borrow a guard or two for the back," he said.

Sula nodded again. She was still sprawled on the floor, and she tried to pick herself up, rising to her knees behind the shelter of the table.

"They had one bomb," she tried to say. "I should have guessed they'd have another."

She had the suspicion that the words came out so garbled that no one could possibly understand them, and apparently Martinez didn't.

"Can I have a guard?" he asked.

Sula nodded yet again.

Martinez crawled to one of the guards who seemed not to be shooting at anything, gestured for him to follow, and crawled out of the room with the guard following.

*Fucker*, Sula thought. *He saved the day.*


**MARTINEZ ENCOUNTERED MPANZA** lying propped against the wall in the corridor. A piece of flying debris had knocked him on the head and flattened him, and blood ran freely down his face while he looked at the world through dazed eyes. Martinez touched his leg.

"Agustin," he said. "Try to find some shelter. Bullets are still flying."

Mpanza looked as if he were trying to process the words.

"Do you understand?" Martinez asked. "Find some shelter till you feel better. We want to save you for Miss Juskiene."

Mpanza nodded. Martinez continued his crawl down the corridor. He stationed his new guard behind a sturdy food prep table, then took his own post in the stairway. No one had entered the back of the house since he'd been gone, and the fighting in the front seemed to have died down while the attackers worked up another plan.

He called Lord Chen. "We still need help," he said.

"Has no one arrived?" Chen asked. "I've sent every constable available, and I'm even sending units from the Lower Town. I've called the Motor Patrol, and they said they were responding."

"Can you connect me to whoever's on the scene?"

"That would be Lieutenant-Captain Bhatti."

"Oh. I know him from the warehouse raids. Stand by."

Martinez told his sleeve display to connect him to Bhatti. Bhatti, a young man with a black-eyed, aquiline face, appeared on his display, apparently sitting at ease in his vehicle.

"This is Fleet Commander Martinez," Martinez said, inflating his authorized rank so as to seem more formidable. "My house is still under attack. Where are you and when can we expect your arrival?"

"My lord!" Bhatti straightened in his seat. "We're a short distance away, but we've been stopped at a roadblock by an officer of the Legion. She said there was a Legion action under way and we would only interfere."

"The *Legion*?" Martinez was taken aback, and his mind spun for a few seconds before a response occurred to him. "Lord Elcap, the Legion of Diligence isn't involved here," he said. "That officer is either an imposter or a part of the insurrection. Kill her or arrest her, and bring your constables here at once."

Bhatti's eyes flashed. "Yes, Lord Fleetcom!"

Martinez sat in the stairwell and kept a watch on the rear windows while waiting for the next development. Broken glass, still hanging in the window frames, tinkled in the light breeze. The sense-clogging scents of propellant and explosive slowly cleared from the newly ventilated palace with its walls of shattered windows. Desultory fire sounded from the front of the building. No one seemed interested in charging the house from the rear.

Then a loud electric warning tone came from the street, and there was an increase in shooting. Sula's voice sounded down the corridor. *"They're running for it!"* A series of metallic crashes followed, then another shout from Sula. *"Don't let the bus get away!"*

Martinez left his guard at his post and returned to the front of the building. Mpanza had crawled from the hall and left a bloody trail to a bathroom. All the windows of the front rooms were occupied by defenders maintaining a steady fire on the retreating enemy. Sula knelt behind one of the windows with her rifle shouldered. Through the windows Martinez could see a gray-skinned bus trying to bash its way free of stalled and abandoned vehicles. Surviving attackers were alongside the bus dodging from cover to cover as they took snap shots at the building. The bus wasn't armored, and its windows gaped open and its flanks were riddled with bullet holes.

Kelly still lay on the floor near her canes. Martinez knelt by her side and turned her over. She gave a sigh and her eyes slitted open, then widened as they recognized him.

"What . . . ," she murmured.

"It's nearly over," Martinez said. "Don't worry. Just take it easy."

She made a disgusted face. "I was knocked out *again*?"

"You're getting better at it," Martinez said. "You won't be in a coma this time."

"Nonii." Kelly closed her eyes.

The sounds of combat outside rose to a tremendous volume, and Martinez concluded that Bhatti's constables had finally arrived at the party. He rose and took a careful look through a window in time to see the bus crash into a Sun Ray van and come to a stop. The attackers were in full flight, running from cover to cover while throwing away their weapons and equipment. After them came Bhatti's constables in remorseless pursuit.

Martinez went to his sleeve display to call for as many ambulances as the Glory of Hygiene Hospital could send.

SULA DUMPED HER helmet, body armor, and rifle in the wreck-age of the front parlor, and then paused while she tried to think what to do next. There would be an inquest, she supposed, and she would be required to make a report; but she had a merciless head-ache, her ears were still ringing, and her mouth tasted as if she'd swallowed a handful of propellant—which, she reflected, perhaps she had.

She made a circuit of the room to make certain that her guards were well. There were no major injuries, though some showed signs of concussion. A woman appeared in spotless white with a tray of biscuits, and a weaponer with a bandaged head and a curling mus-tachio brought in a tray with glasses and chilled soft drinks. Sula approached him and took a Citrine Fling.

"Got something stronger?" she asked.

He nodded. "Of course."

Martinez had rescued a chair and sat in it, speaking softly into his sleeve display. He wasn't ignoring Sula, she thought, but he was definitely choosing to engage with something else.

Sula's headache beat at her temples with lead-weighted cudgels. The weaponer returned with another tray, a bottle, and cut-glass tumblers. Sula recognized the bottle as being the Martinez estate's Laredo whisky, which she felt herself obliged to hate on principle. Nevertheless, she poured herself a stiff round and drank it off.

Her sinuses afire, she put the tumbler back on the tray and found Gareth Martinez standing nearby and giving her a specula-tive look.

"That's new," he said, and sipped his fizzy pomegranate drink.

Sula shrugged. "I have decided to fully engage with the grand pageant that is life." Proud that she had managed to articulate an entire sentence, and an ornate one at that, she poured herself an-other round and drank it off.

Perhaps, she thought, one day she and Martinez might meet on an occasion that didn't involve firearms.

"Ambulances are on their way," Martinez said to the room in general. "The injured should be looked at, along with anyone in the sitting room when that bomb went off. You all need to be checked for concussion." His eyes turned to the weaponer with the bandaged head. "Including you, Mpanza."

"These other people first, my lord," Mpanza said. "I'm all right."

The clarion voices of children began to sound from the passage, and a girl and a boy stormed into the room, accompanied by a Daimong butler. Sula had seen pictures of Martinez's offspring on the walls of his sleeping cabin during the period when she spent more time there than in her own quarters, and she recognized young Gareth and Yaling as older versions of the children in the photographs.

Young Gareth took a few steps into the room and stopped, his eyes wide at the wreckage of the room, the guards in their armor, the weapons propped against furniture or shelves.

Fortunately for his tender young mind, the bodies lying in the foyer had been dragged outside onto the lawn. Their blood still smeared the floor.

Yaling marched straight to Sula and looked up at her. "You're Lady Sula!" she proclaimed. "You're *famous*!"

Sula couldn't help but laugh, then winced when the laughter sent another bolt of pain through her head. "That's right," she said.

"I want to be just like you when I grow up!" Yaling said.

Sula thought Martinez might just choke on his fizzy pomegranate drink.

Sula thought she might find herself liking Terza Chen's kid. Her forthrightness, anyway.

"I advise constant target practice," Sula told Yaling. "It may come in handy."

If Martinez was striving to conceal his stormy expression, he failed.

Yaling made pistols of her fingers. "Pssh! Pssh!" Shooting the attackers down.

"The fighting seems to be over," Martinez reported to the room in general. "We took some prisoners, mostly wounded."

"Ambulances are here," reported one of the guards, looking out the window. "And some other people."

Ahead of the medics came another pair of guards, who ventured carefully into the foyer past the broken door and beneath the shattered fanlight. Glass crunched under their boots. Following was Terza Chen, her normally serene expression tautened by anxiety. She walked into the foyer, stopped dead, and slowly surveyed the sitting room, her gaze passing over the wreckage, the bullet holes, the guards, and Sula standing next to her daughter.

*Oh dear,* Sula thought. *How very awkward.*

# CHAPTER 17

"My lord, this is Ethgro Tribe."

Martinez looked at image of the young Daimong officer on his sleeve display, with his fixed expression of polite surprise. Martinez had got Tribe back into staff work on his personal recommendation, and now Tribe was assigned to Junior Fleet Commander Khalil, who was busy assembling files on every available officer of the Fleet and every resource obtainable in order to accelerate Wei Jian's plans for replacing the hundreds of ships lost in the war.

"How may I help you, Lord Ethgro?" Martinez said.

Martinez was walking through the elaborate Nayanid-style corridors of the Chen Palace while on his way to the Commandery for an appointment. His own bullet-riddled home was unlivable, and likely to stay that way for a while, and so he and Terza had moved their family into her childhood home, with its mellow beige stone, its strange, winged gables, its great library, and its paintings and statues of hundreds of generations of Chen ancestors.

Plus Lord Chen, of course, wandering aimlessly about his home in a more or less constant state of inebriation.

"I thought I'd let you know that we've been interrogating the surviving attackers of your home," Tribe said, "as well as tracing messages and money, and we've discovered the person responsible for the attack. It was Lady Distchin."

Martinez was deeply surprised. "Really? That was very good work, finding out in less than a day."

"Apparently Lady Distchin considered the insults offered by Lady Sula at the Court of Honor a mortal offense and decided to kill her."

"She brought enough people," Martinez said. "So many, just to kill one person?"

"Other attacks were contemplated," Tribe said. "Lady Distchin was determined to retain her patronage of Spannan and intended to kill anyone intending to take that privilege away from her. Your brother, Lord Oda Yoshitoshi, Lord Chen, Lord Ngeni."

"They were just going to drive around in that bus killing people?"

"Their plan didn't seem very well thought-out."

*Apparently I wasn't important enough to kill,* Martinez thought with annoyance. *Distchin was just going to murder everyone around me.*

"Thank you, Lord Ethgro," Martinez said. "I appreciate your letting me know."

Martinez walked into the courtyard of the palace and stepped into his Hunhao. His guards entered their own vehicles, and the three-car convoy turned out into the Boulevard of the Praxis.

Martinez felt only relief. The attack on Sula hadn't been the first blow of a new civil war, it had been the spiteful revenge of a Peer so upper-upper-upper that no one had ever said no to her.

He called Roland on his sleeve display and told him about Lady Distchin.

"That's a relief," Roland said. "Now we know how to pitch the story."

It had been impossible to hide a long and noisy firefight in the

High City, but the official news reports had been cautious. They'd been afraid of labeling the attack an act of insurrection and making the government look weak, and instead reported a fight between "two groups of armed individuals."

Roland's tone turned triumphant. "Now we arrest Distchin and make it clear the attack was that of a private individual, not an enemy army."

"Introduce a resolution to take Spannan away from Clan Distchin," Martinez advised. "And take out the other great absentees while we're at it."

"I would be delighted to do exactly that," said Roland. "Though there remains the problem of who will become these worlds' new patrons."

"Do developed worlds even *need* patrons?" Martinez asked.

"The worlds may not," Roland said, "but *we* do. We like having powerful families owing us favors."

"I have an idea for a new patron of Rol-mar," Martinez said.

Rol-mar, a newly discovered world, had under its current patron, Lord Gonihu, fallen into insurrection, and with the rest of the empire busy with a vast civil war, it had managed to retain its precarious independence.

"Rol-mar will require an enormous initial investment," Roland said. "And the previous two patrons failed. Who did you have in mind?"

"Walpurga."

There was a long silence while Roland contemplated the suggestion. "Our father's already patron to three worlds," he said. "The Convocation might be reluctant to give the family a fourth."

"Is there a better candidate?" Martinez asked.

"Another issue is that Walpurga has no children," Roland said. "So there's no one to leave the job of patron to."

"She could adopt. Or get married. Or just appoint someone. In any case, it's a problem for the future."

"I'll talk to her," Roland decided.

"Spannan could go to a Ngeni," Martinez said.

"I've been talking to Lord Ngeni about that," Roland said. "We'll talk some more."

"Be careful," Martinez said. "Lady Distchin might not be the only Peer who wants you dead."


RIVVEN'S HAUGHTY GRAY face hovered over the far end of the table. "I hope we can get through the hearing quickly," he said in his melodious Daimong voice, "while memories of the incident are still fresh."

Sula leaned back in her chair. Headache battered at her temples, and her ears were still singing from the explosion the previous afternoon. When she closed her eyes, she could see the bomb sending the guards' car skyward, smell the combined odors of propellant and blood, hear the thunder of the bomb that blew the doors inward . . . The faint scent of Rivven's rotting flesh did nothing to help her suppress the memories.

"Let's begin," Sula said, "and get this over with."

"I would like to introduce a note of caution," said Serdar Gunaydin. He sat on Sula's right at the Commandery conference table. "I am Lady Sula's personal physician. She has been exhibiting signs of a possible concussion, and if she becomes fatigued, or if her condition worsens in any way, I will bring this hearing to an end."

"Very good, Doctor," the defector said. "Under the circumstances, I do not wish to stress Lady Sula unduly."

The three were alone with a clerk/recorder in the monumental conference room, designed to accommodate the towering Shaa.

Murals of warships and planets filled the walls. Rivven signaled the recorder to trigger his instrument, and turned to Lady Sula and asked his first question.

He led Sula through the ambush, the bomb, the firefight at the Martinez house. He concluded by asking Sula if she had any idea who was responsible for the attack.

When she'd finally had time to think rather than react, Sula had first blamed the manager at the Rose and Dagger Club, who might have invited her to the derivoo competition with the intention of ambushing her, but she'd later reconsidered. The derivoo competition had been widely publicized, and the attackers had enough time to plan the attack once Sula's appearance had been announced.

Sula said that she had no idea who might have been responsible. "But I have made enemies in my career," she added.

"Those who uphold the Praxis," Rivven said, "will naturally make enemies among the weak and disloyal."

With that sententious statement, Rivven signaled the recorder to stop. He turned to Sula and his inner mouth parts writhed prior to speaking again, when he was interrupted by his sleeve display. He answered.

"This is Gareth Martinez, my lord." The name still had enough impact to send a jolt through Sula's nerves. "I've just been informed that the attack on Lady Sula was organized by Lady Distchin."

Another jolt of electric fire crackled up Sula's nerves.

"That is very surprising!" Rivven said.

"The attack was driven by personal animosity," Martinez said, "and apparently had no political dimension."

"To think that such a grand Peer would so lower herself as to plan a sneaking assassination!" Rivven proclaimed.

"The Peer's grandeur came from plundered wealth," Sula said, "and if it weren't for all that grandeur and money, she'd have been tossed in the Blue Hatches Prison long ago."

Rivven's frozen face managed to seem even more indignant than normal, as if he were offended on behalf of the whole Order of Peers. *What?* Sula wondered. *You haven't yet worked out that we're just a bunch of brigands?*

"Ask if Distchin's been arrested," Sula said.

Rivven repeated the question, which Sula was certain Martinez had heard perfectly well. "Not yet," he answered. "The constables are still putting their raiding party together."

"I'll meet them at the Distchin Palace," Sula said.

"Be careful not to warn Distchin and her crew!" Martinez said in sudden urgency.

Sula laughed. "I know how to call the shots on an ambush," she reminded him. She turned to Rivven. "If we're done here . . . ?" she asked.

Rivven's black-on-black eyes turned to her. "Yes, my lady. I think we have everything we need."

Sula turned to Dr. Gunaydin. "Are you coming?"

He gave her a wary look. "It seems I am."

Sula had her guards equip themselves with armor and weapons from their vehicles before setting out, and then approached the Distchin Palace along the Boulevard of the Praxis before turning onto a side street, where it was possible to view the palace from across a park. Even though a cold winter sun shone in a clear sky, white snow from the previous night's fall still crusted windowsills and outlined the dark iron pickets of the palace wall. The palace itself had an imposing façade of red-veined marble in the Devis mode, but Sula could see Tanyl-style windows hidden away beneath gables, and elements of elaborate Nayanid stylings tucked away in obscure corners, and so had the impression the palace was remodeled every generation or so into the most up-to-date and fashionable style. Apparently this was the sort of thing the Distchins spent their stolen money on.

Sula waited on the edge of her seat, her eyes narrowed as she looked into the blank windows of the red-veined palace. Then she straightened as a low burnt-orange limousine drew up to the front of the building. Several people came out the front door, and Sula recognized Lady Distchin less by her appearance—she was swathed up to the neck in an indigo-colored winter coat and had darkened bubbles over her nocturnal eyes—but Sula knew her by her arrogant carriage and the way the others in her party deferred to her.

"Alert!" Sula said. "The target is moving!"

Gunaydin stirred uneasily at her side. "Isn't someone else supposed to deal with this?"

Sula looked at him. "Do you see someone else here?"

Adrenaline sped through her on a river all aflame. She turned to Macnamara in the driver's seat. "Turn around," she said, "and prepare to intercept."

Macnamara spoke on his circuit to the other drivers, and the three vehicles turned in synchrony across the side street toward the Boulevard of the Praxis just as the burnt-orange limousine drew away from the curb.

"First car cut them off," Sula instructed, "third car keep them from reversing. Everyone stay alert."

"I am suddenly aware," said Gunaydin, "that not only do I carry a pistol I'm not trained to use, I'm the only person in this vehicle without armor."

She put her hand on his knee. "Get into cover right away," she said.

Gunaydin barked a laugh. "You promised me your life in Zanshaa would be dull."

The guards remembered that three of their number had died yesterday and were highly motivated to get this right. The lead car slid in front of Distchin and braked, and the rear car cut off her retreat. Macnamara drew to a halt alongside. Doors rolled up and Terrans with guns tumbled out. Sula got her feet onto the pavement, crab-stepped to the rear of the vehicle, and leveled her rifle over the trunk. Astringent winter air chilled her cheeks, her fingers. She was aware of Gunaydin hovering nearby, holding his pistol in an uncertain hand.

"Everyone step out of the car!" she said. "Hands in the air!"

*Please resist.* The voice whispered in a corner of her brain. *Please resist, and then we can riddle you and leave you dying in the gutter.*

No resistance was offered. Lady Distchin stepped out of the vehicle, her proud carriage now slumped, her hands high. Sula grinned at Gunaydin.

"Humiliation now," she said, "flaming fur later."


"I'M SORRY, PRINCESS," said Naveen Patel. "We knew about it, but we didn't think it was political."

"They didn't recruit from any particular unit in the police or the Legion or the Steadfast League," said Julien Bakshi. His pointed face turned wry. "Someone from this group, another from another group. We thought they were going to do some kind of crime, a hijacking or something."

"Also," said Patel, "a couple drawn from the *Legion.* That was interesting."

The commission would demand a share of any big crimes

committed in its territory, Sula knew. And if they discovered any member of the Legion involved in criminal activity, they would certainly take advantage of that, demanding information about Legion operations.

There was potentially a big payday involved. Sula wasn't surprised that they'd seen what they wanted to see.

"We called it wrong," said Julien. "I'm sorry about it."

"Well," said Sula, "I wouldn't have guessed either. Lady Distchin raising a private army as part of a personal vendetta? I suppose it's not something you'd look for."

They were in Julien Bakshi's private office, a place of brass and red leather above the restaurant he owned off Harmony Square in the Lower Town. The air stank of the cigarillo stubs crowding Julien's ashtray. He politely refrained from smoking in Sula's presence, but the reek of tobacco was so strong that it hardly mattered.

The leather-padded door opened, and one of Julien's associates put his head in. "Mr. Sagas is here."

Julien automatically reached for his packet of cigarillos, then withdrew his hand. "Might as well go to dinner," he said.

They rose from their chairs. Julien winced, then pressed a hand above his left hip.

"Shrapnel still bothering you?" Sula asked.

"Shrapnel's taken out," Julien said, "but I have what the doc calls adhesions."

"Good luck with all that," Sula said. "Just keep telling yourself it could have been worse."

They began to descend the narrow back stairs. Cans and boxes of food supplies were neatly stacked on one side of the staircase, and they had to descend in single file as it narrowed.

Cooking smells floated up the stairway. A sudden need for alcohol settled into Sula's bones.

"Let's stop by the bar first," she said.

Julien looked over his shoulder and raised an eyebrow. "Picked up a new vice?" he asked.

"I do, every decade or so," Sula said. "It keeps me young."

MIDWINTER WAS A season, Severin thought, of weddings and executions. Lady Distchin died first, strung up and disemboweled at the Blue Hatches Prison, and then the leaders of the old government were killed on the ring after their lives had been so fully mined for scandal that there was nothing left. Gruum died with dignity, Tu-hon screamed about how she was no worse than anyone else, and Minno looked as if he'd stopped caring long ago.

Lord Pa Do-faq, back on Harzapid, was granted a more merciful death, being merely shot in the head.

As for weddings, a great many had followed the end of the war, and Severin's would take place in a few weeks. Now his future in-laws were hosting a celebration at the Baldpate restaurant in the Petty Mount. The Bellanti family weren't prepared to wait for the wedding before imposing themselves on Zanshaa—they were reviewing every contract the Exploration Service had open, in hopes that Severin would help them win the bids, and because they were using the Martinez family as a model, they were in the process of shifting every young, single member of the family to Zanshaa, in hopes of matching them with High City families. Severin thought they were going about this in completely the wrong way, but they outnumbered him and were very insistent.

They were also vexed with him that he wouldn't let them buy

him a colossal palace in the High City to serve as the headquarters for their operations. Severin was insistent that he wasn't going to be a Peer, and that he would live off the Old Park in a modest part of the Lower Town.

At least his fiancée, Alaya, was in accord with his wishes.

Martinez had described her as a pleasant person, and truly she seemed pleasant enough. That she was a widow made things simple—they could plan their marriage in the same way old veterans might plan a campaign, without illusion or undue sentiment.

He didn't love her, but perhaps some form of love would come in time—though he thought it was fine if it didn't. Lady Starkey had left a hole in his heart so vast that no one else could ever fill it.

The scent of roast Hone-bar phoenix rose from the buffet, a regional treat for the Bellantis, who hailed from the Hone Reach. Severin received congratulations from the premiere lieutenant of the *Expedition*, Chungsun Cleghorne. "She's quite a peach, my lord!" Cleghorne said. "Quite the peach!"

Severin would have described her more as a plum, with her deep brown hair, turned-up nose, and dark complexion, but Cleghorne's compliment was kindly meant, and he thanked his lieutenant, then turned to Martinez, who followed Cleghorne up the buffet line.

"I see you're a fleet commander again," Severin said.

"And about time," Martinez said.

The Convocation had just passed an ordinance stating that any promotions made under the authority of the Restoration government in exile were made permanent, with seniority dating from the day of commission, and now Martinez was again wearing the insignia that Wei Jian had insisted he remove.

Martinez brandished his plate of Hone-bar phoenix and almost shot his breast fillet back onto the buffet. "Do you know what

I'm doing with my advanced rank?" he said. "Planning Wei Jian's parade! That's all my battles and years of service are good for!"

"Come now," Severin said. "You turned the Fourth Fleet into a weapon. That was your real accomplishment—building a machine so perfect that Wei Jian adopted it without making a single change."

Martinez was mollified by Severin's praise. "But still," he muttered, "a *parade*."

"It's a compliment to your planning skills." Severin smiled. "Take comfort from the fact that you predicted Jian would opt for the parade and for the rank of Supreme Commander, and you were right."

Martinez smiled. "And I was right about Alaya, wasn't I?"

Severin looked over his shoulder in the direction of his fiancée, who was chatting with some of her woman friends and a few officers from the Exploration Service. "You *were* right, mostly," he said. "Though her family is a good deal more insistent than you led me to believe."

Martinez gave a wry smile. "That's families for you."

"It turns out that Alaya is a fan of my puppet shows," Severin said. "She wants to see more, so apparently I'm a puppeteer again."

"There's still plenty in our world to satirize."

"I suppose so." Severin looked up as one of his soon-to-be in-laws approached. "Speaking of families . . ."

There were a lot of Bellantis and Severin couldn't quite remember this one's forename. *Bellondo? Benegal?* Something like that, anyway.

The young man didn't wait for Severin to address him by name. "Nikki," he said. "I was wondering if you could introduce me to Lady Atasi Sukhija? Her brother is in charge of procurement for the Second Fleet at Magaria, and . . ."

"Yes, certainly," Severin said. He turned to Martinez. "If you'll forgive me, Gareth?"

"Of course." Martinez seemed amused by the avaricious family he'd unleashed on Zanshaa, and on Severin.

Severin let Bellondo/Benegal take his arm and guide him toward Lady Atasi and the hoped-for contract.


**LIGHT SHONE ON** the party guests from the clerestory above. The tart citrus savor of her brandy sunflower flooded Sula's tongue. She swallowed and felt the alcohol burn its way down her throat.

"Of course I'll recommend you whenever possible," she said. "But I'm not involved with procurement in any way."

"I'm sure your recommendation would be treated with respect," said Sempronia Shankaracharya. Her eyes narrowed as she looked across the room at her brothers, Gareth and Roland.

Sula was amused at how the party was dividing itself into camps. The Martinez family and their friends had claimed a large swath of the dining room. Sula, Sempronia, and Nikkul Shankaracharya were at the center of another grouping. The Bellanti family formed another group centered on Alaya, and they raided other groups in hopes of plunder. Meanwhile, Nikki Severin wandered from one group to another, amiable in his blue uniform tunic and Explorer's Medal.

"We have a new upgrade for our sensor suite," Sempronia said. "Nikki has already placed an order, though the paperwork is caught in the bureaucracy for the present. We'd like to sell it to the Fleet if the Chen-Martinez wall isn't too insurmountable."

"I'll introduce you to Supreme Commander Jian," Sula said with an inward smile. "She decides these things, not your brothers."

"Well in that case," said Sempronia, "we have more things on offer than the sensor suites."

Nikki Severin ambled toward them, a drink in his hand. "May I hide among you?" he said. "I need a refuge from my future in-laws."

"The very last thing an arriviste family should do," Sula said, "is to actually *act like an arriviste family in public*."

"I told them they were doing it wrong," Severin said, "but they wouldn't listen. They're lower-middle-middle, they can't act as if they were home in Hone-bar."

"I expect they'll learn," Sula said.

"Or not," said Sempronia.

Severin turned to Sula. "Is Dr. Gunaydin with you?" he asked. "I haven't seen him."

"He's at his work," Sula said. "He got a job at the Glory of Hygiene Hospital."

"Good for him," said Severin.

Sula had strong-armed the hospital into choosing her candidate. None of the others applying for the position had the recommendation of a prominent convocate, and the hospital directors were only too happy to oblige. Gunaydin had been surprised and delighted to be accepted by the capital's most prestigious hospital, and at a salary that would actually permit him to live in Zanshaa.

He wouldn't have to be anybody's fancy man, not unless he wanted to.

The conversation turned to other topics, and eventually Sula noticed that her glass was empty and went to the bar for a refill. She sipped, and suddenly the whole party was too oppressive: too noisy, too crowded, too hot, too frantic, too full of hustle and business, too full of people surnamed Martinez. She left room and found a quiet courtyard with tables, benches, and a fountain, all protected by a glass lattice overhead.

Sula sighed with relief and sipped her brandy sunflower. She approached the fountain, but the plashing of the water sent a series of small bright shocks to her axons, and she found herself grinding her teeth. Sleet spattered the glass overhead. The relief she thought she'd found dissipated. For some reason the whole afternoon had turned wrong. Undirected anger simmered in her blood.

"No. No. We crushed the enemy's rear division before the eight hundred relativistic missiles hit Do-faq's rear."

At the familiar voice, Sula felt her nerves coil into a furious tangle. Martinez had entered the courtyard, striding in like a conqueror, his attention on his sleeve display.

"The solar missiles were later," Martinez said, "after I turned the division toward the enemy center. The decision was made by that point."

He paused in his march, then looked up at Sula in surprise. Sula gave him a tight-lipped smile and raised her glass in an ironic salute.

"Any more questions, send them later," Martinez said. "I'm still at Severin's party."

Martinez brought the conversation to an end. Sula looked at him and raised an eyebrow.

"Assuring your place in history?" she asked.

"Vipsania's doing another video series," Martinez said. "You'll be contacted if you haven't been already."

"Good," Sula said. "I'll point out how you left my command in the lurch while you charged off to win the war and glory."

His mouth twitched as if she'd slapped him. "You seemed to be doing all right," he said. His tone was resentful. "And you didn't ask for help."

The tinkling of the fountain made Sula want to crawl right out of her skin. "I should have thought the need for help would have been bloody obvious," she said. "You could have detached a squadron; it would have made all the difference."

"You could have asked," Martinez said. "I felt the main body posed the greater threat and wanted to bring my division to bear where it would have the most effect."

Sula drained her glass and balanced it on the edge of the fountain. "We'll let history decide," she said as she walked toward the door. She hesitated. "But then, your sister is the one who gets to *create* the history, isn't she? I wonder how she'll play it?"

Martinez watched as she walked past him, and then spoke before she could make her exit.

"Are you sure this conversation is over, Gredel?" he asked. "Or do you prefer Margaux?"

SULA SPUN TO face him, and a small, mean part of Martinez rejoiced at the terror in her glittering emerald eyes, a terror soon suppressed by a visible act of will. She rubbed the pad of scar tissue on her thumb and regarded him.

"I suppose you think you know something," she said.

He stood over her, close enough to smell the brandy on her breath. It felt good, after all these months, to just let it out, to let the tension and suspense and anger drive the confrontation.

She'd started it, after all.

"I know you're not the real Lady Sula," he said. "I suppose she had an accident or something, and you stepped in."

She gave a snort of derision. "If you think I'm not the real Sula, you can check with the Peers' Gene Bank."

"I imagine you fixed the Gene Bank after you stormed the city in the Naxid War. You had wartime powers then. But I remember once you were more touchy on the subject."

Once, years ago, he had asked her to marry him. She had seemed delighted at the idea, then hesitated, then started an argument and walked away. It had occurred to him recently, with the force of revelation, that at some point he had mentioned the necessity of donating a drop of blood at the Gene Bank before getting married, and that perhaps that had prompted her hesitation and subsequent flight.

"I suppose your friend Lamey helped you adopt your new identity," Martinez said. "And then, on Zarafan, he probably tried to blackmail you. And you . . . dealt with him."

She watched him with narrowed, angry eyes. "How can you have *everything* so wrong?" she asked. Her hands waved. "It's beyond belief." Her lip curled with contempt. "I guess you think this gives you some kind of advantage," she said. "That you can get me to do whatever the fuck you have in mind."

Martinez was genuinely surprised at the accusation. "No," he said. "Not at all. I have no plans to use this information at all."

She gave him a skeptical glance. "Then why bring it up?"

"Because it's been nagging at me ever since Zarafan. I couldn't understand why you did what you did . . . So I started looking into things. It wasn't hard to work out."

Her gaze was flat, angry. "Yet I'm supposed to trust that you'll never use this."

He spread his hands. "Why would I? I can't prove anything— not if you've got the Gene Bank covered. So there's no reason to wrap me in a carpet like Braga and stick my corpse in an abandoned refrigerator."

She snarled. "Other than the sheer pleasure of it?"

Martinez sighed. "We each have a gun at the other's head. You killed Braga, but I helped you hide him—that makes me an accomplice to homicide." He raised a hand. "And another point—should something happen to me, it would be entirely possible for an investigator to follow my tracks. You know what my family is like. Don't give them an excuse to look into my discoveries."

"Your *discoveries*." Contempt oozed from every syllable. One of her hands made a fist. "Here you are congratulating yourself on how clever you've been, and you *still have it all wrong*."

Martinez waved a hand. "You're welcome to correct me."

An angry flush touched Sula's pale cheeks. "Lamey wasn't blackmailing *me*. Lamey was going to blackmail *you*."

Martinez blinked. "Blackmail *me*? But how?"

"He was going to tell Terza about us if you didn't get him money from your family. I couldn't let that happen."

Martinez stared at her. Sula gazed up at him in defiance. "You don't have anything clever to say? Even though it turns out to have been all about *you* the entire time—and damned if I don't know why that wouldn't please you. You have no comment?"

He managed to find words. "Apparently I don't."

"I've silenced the great Gareth Martinez. I should get a prize." Her green eyes flashed. "So *now* is this conversation over?"

"I won't stop you from leaving."

Her lips twisted in anger. "*As if you ever could.*"

She turned and swept to the door. The clicks of her heels on the tiles were an echo of the other times she'd left him, marching away while his heart wept scarlet drops onto the dust.

Martinez realized that there had been a part of him that still treasured a sliver of precious hope, and that the hope had just evaporated, leaving behind a void that he could never fill.

He and Sula hadn't been lovers in months, and yet to Martinez it seemed as if love had just said a last goodbye before striding from the scene, heels rapping on the tiles.

SULA SAT AT her desk in the Convocation and listened to the droning of the members—she couldn't call it a debate, since none of the speakers seemed to have a distinct point of view, let alone a point of view concrete enough to argue with anyone else's equally vague ideas. They just talked around the topic—whatever the current topic was—a witless chatter so disconnected with reality that it managed to be about nothing but itself.

Impatience and anger jabbed at Sula like someone's knuckles grinding into her skin. She was going to spend the rest of her life listening to this sort of drivel. She was going to be trapped in the vast Convocation hall while one Martinez or another told her what to do.

*You know what my family is like,* Martinez had said. And alas, she did.

She looked toward the podium, where Lord Saïd drowsed in his red cloak, his fingers idly dancing along his copper wand of office as if he were silently playing a flute. Saïd, who would soon leave office, and who had perhaps hinted he would prefer that he not be succeeded by a proxy for Roland Martinez.

*Well,* Sula thought, *if not Roland, why not me?*

She knew the answer well enough: she was too young, too inexperienced, and far too tactless.

On the other hand, the Sula name placed her at the highest levels of society, and she had talent and boundless energy. She had important friends—Lady Koridun, for one—and her work with the Secret Army had given her contacts all over Zanshaa, including members of the underworld, who in the past had proved useful for one thing or another.

If she couldn't become Lady Senior herself, she might be able to form a faction large enough to tip the balance in any election.

Perhaps it was time to see what she could manage.

"A careful Caroline," Gunaydin had said, "is someone new to me."

She waited for the discussion to trail away to its end, then voted on the measure convinced that neither the measure nor her vote mattered a damn. Some departments in the Ministry of Public Health were to be reorganized, and in the end be as useless as they were before.

As soon as the measure passed, she was on her feet asking to be recognized.

Lord Saïd looked up at her with his sharp eyes. "I am pleased to recognize Lady Sula," he said.

"Thank you, Lord Senior," Sula said. "I would like to introduce a resolution thanking members of the Naxid community, and particularly Lord Nishkad, for the aid given to the Restoration by those Naxids involved in logistics, ship construction, and in crewing vessels of the Fleet."

Members stared. She sat down and waited while chaos boiled up around her.

Most members of the Convocation were unaware that Naxids had been employed during the war, and they were reacting with anger or alarm or both. They demanded answers to their questions, which Sula was pleased to provide.

"Is it not illegal to employ Naxids on warships?" one demanded.

"There was no Judge Martial to whom I could refer the matter," Sula said. "The fact is that we had simply run out of trained Terrans. The need was great, and I decided that the benefits exceeded any possible risk. After all, I earned my reputation killing Naxid rebels, and no one can say I was ever in sympathy with the Naxid cause. In the event, the Naxids proved both loyal and capable and were instrumental to the decisive battle at Toley."

Other members wanted assurances that Naxids were no longer employed on warships, and Sula was able to tell them that the Naxids had been returned to their home worlds and mustered out of the service.

The matter degenerated into a good deal of pointless, angry declarations by one indignant Peer after another. None of them, Sula observed, had taken part in any fighting—unlike Nikki Severin, who very kindly supported her resolution.

In the end, Roland Martinez rose and smoothly suggested that the matter be tabled until the Convocation could be better informed about what Sula and the Naxids had done, and when.

She was drinking tea in her office with its view of the Boulevard of the Praxis when Roland arrived. "What the hell was that about?" he demanded. "I'm going to have to spend precious hours calming down the members before we can get on with our agenda." He ground his right fist into the palm of his left hand. "At least Oda Yoshitoshi is in charge of the censorship. None of this will escape into the media."

Sula took a deliberate whiff of her tea's smoky bouquet. "The Convocation passes such resolutions every day," she said. "Why can't we say thanks to the folk who helped us win? Who put *you* in a position to say who gets thanks and who doesn't?"

"Because to half the population of the empire, the Naxids are a pack of murdering rebels!" Roland said.

"Well," Sula said, "they're not, as we both know. I think the rest of the empire should know too."

Roland loomed over her desk, big hands, angry eyes. "I don't want any more such resolutions introduced in the Convocation," he said. "We've got an agenda, and we need to get it passed. Understand?"

Sula took a deliberate drink of her tea. "I hear you," she said. Which, as they both knew, did *not* mean *I hear and will obey*. He stared at her for a long, angry moment, but she just stared back, as if to remind him that he wasn't Lord Senior nor one of Severin's upper-upper-uppers, and she wasn't subordinate to him.

If he took the message, he didn't show it.

Behind her opaque expression, Sula quietly rejoiced. Roland had just made a mistake.

Naxid convocates formed something like 8 percent of the voting members of the Convocation. Roland had just thrown them away and given them every reason to offer their votes to Sula.

After Roland left, Sula sent a message to Lord Nishkad telling him that she had introduced her resolution of thanks, and that it hadn't gone well, but that she hoped to reintroduce the resolution later.

Which was an unsubtle way of asking Lord Nishkad for his help without actually asking for it. He could form a Naxid faction faster than she could—and would, because she had made herself a powerful voice for his species—and could not be blamed for placing it at her service.

Then she gazed out the window at the Boulevard of the Praxis and considered her situation.

The Naxids were a start, she thought. Roland had just passed on his chance to be patron to the entire Naxid species, and she wasn't going to make that mistake.

But still. The Naxids weren't enough.

If her plans for the civil service examinations passed the Convocation, she'd have the support of every junior civil servant in the empire. They weren't votes in the Convocation, exactly, but as the junior civil servants rose to become middle managers, then seniors, they would have a great deal of influence in how legislation was interpreted and put into practice.

She'd have the numbers in terms of population, then. But Sula knew that she lacked the kind of fortune that would enable her to expand her power base in the Convocation. Lady Koridun would support her, and Koridun had buckets of money, but if Koridun was paying for everything, then it would become Koridun's faction, not Sula's. Even if Lady Koridun considered herself a loyal subordinate, ultimately it was the money that mattered, and the power would inevitably shift to her.

She finished her tea, then put the cup down, triggered her comms display, and asked to be connected to the Lord Senior.

Saïd answered quickly. "Yes, Lady Sula? How may I be of assistance?"

Sula heard a hum in her nerves, a knowledge that things were about to change irrevocably. *Why not?* she thought. *Love hasn't worked out. Might as well go for power.*

She gathered her thoughts and spoke. "I wonder, Lord Senior, if you can tell me a little more about your grandnephew Eveleth."

There was a pause, and then Saïd responded. "With pleasure, Lady Sula."

Sula sighed. In the near future, there would have to be a very awkward conversation with Gunaydin. She imagined that he would be *reasonable.*

And then, she supposed, she would have to get a dog.


"**THE MOST IMPORTANT** thing that can happen to a person is love," Martinez said. "Love with the right person is delightful and fulfilling, and always surprising."

He looked out over those attending, most glittering in their dress uniforms, and before him the two people at the center of attention.

"I have no doubt," he said, "that Agustin Mpanza and Filomena Juskiene have found in each other the right person, and I would like to celebrate their love by asking all present to raise a glass to their continued happiness."

There was a growl of assent from the crowd, and a general raising of glasses. Neither Juskiene nor Mpanza were from Zanshaa, and so the celebration was attended chiefly by friends drawn from the Fleet, mostly warrant and petty officers given leave from their ships to attend. Santana and Banerjee were the only two commissioned officers other than Martinez.

Mpanza and Juskiene had just returned from the registrar, where the actual wedding had taken place, and now it was time for the celebration. Martinez's gift to the couple had been this party in a rented room at the Fleet Club, with a buffet dinner and an open bar. After Severin's, it was the second such party he'd been to in four days, and he hoped to hell it would be the last for a long, long time.

His head swam with the effort of making his speech, and the glittering company was lost in dazzle. He kissed Juskiene's cheek and thumped Mpanza on the shoulder, and then slipped out of the room to draw a breath in the corridor.

*The most important thing that can happen to you is love.*

True, but the phrase would mean a different thing to Mpanza and Juskiene than it meant to Martinez. For him, love had been not only the most important thing but also the most devastating thing. The most soul-crushing thing. The thing that exalted him and stirred him and left him wretched and stumbling half-broken into the light of day.

Tears sprang to his eyes and he wiped them away with the back of his hand.

Mpanza and Juskiene deserved their happiness, and he told himself that he was glad that someone at least had won love's lottery.

And what, he thought, had he really to complain about? He had delightful children, a beautiful and accomplished wife, and a place in both the Fleet and the Convocation—even though Wei Jian was firmly in charge of the Fleet, and in the Convocation, Martinez was a mere auxiliary to his brother.

Perhaps he should simply devote himself to his family and to his yacht club. It was hardly the life he had envisioned for himself after defeating the empire's largest fleet in battle, but it was the life that Wei Jian had confined him to. It would last until Jian made a mistake, and Martinez had to admit that Wei Jian made very few mistakes.

At least, he thought, he was not sharing his bed with a murderer. Even if Sula had killed Braga to protect Martinez, it had been a singularly cold act, and Sula hadn't bothered to offer an explanation until a year later, and then only to flaunt it in anger.

If he could reason his way around the gaping hole in his heart, he could almost convince himself he was happy.

He returned to the party only to say goodbye, claiming that he was needed at the Convocation, and then he got in his car and went to the Chen Palace and his family.

*AFTER TEN YEARS*, thought Terza Chen, *I'm finally rid of the bitch.*

She sat in the music room of the Chen Palace, a spacious room that smelled of rare woods and rosin. Her harp stood gleaming in the corner like a golden statue in the Devis mode.

She had just learned of the engagement of Caroline, Lady Sula, to Lord Eveleth Saïd. She wanted to laugh aloud.

She turned to look out the window at the garden, sere and brown in the midst of winter. It was in that garden, here in her father's house, that Terza had first met Gareth Martinez. He had attended a meeting with her father, and had then spent a pleasant half hour drinking tea in the garden with Terza and chatting about nothing at all.

By the end of the conversation, Terza knew she wanted this decorated war hero more than she had ever wanted anything in her life, and being a rich and privileged woman who generally got what she wanted, she set herself to working out how she could make Martinez her own.

She saw Martinez again, a few nights later, at the lower terminal of the High City funicular railway. The chill night was aromatic with the scent of chestnuts roasting over charcoal fires. Martinez was with Sula, watching acrobats perform on the apron in front of the terminal, a dangerous dance with knives and elastic. Neither of them saw Terza watching them from across the apron.

Martinez had his arms around Sula from behind, and from the way the night lights glowed on their faces, and from the glances they gave each other, Terza knew they were very much in love.

Terza wished that Martinez was looking at *her* in that way, but she wasted little time on jealousy. Time was of too great an importance—the war was on, and Martinez might be posted away at any time.

Terza had been raised in a world frozen in amber, with the Great Masters on top and families like the Chens just below. The highest level of the Zanshaa Peers, secure in their station and in themselves, enacted the stately rituals that marked their lives. Terza had grown up closely supervised by her parents. She'd had a superb education in the best academies of the High City, where she learned not only to rule an empire, but to dance, to play the harp, to participate in sport, to dress superbly in every climate and situation, to walk with poise and distinction, and to dictate the menu for a dinner party involving five different species. She became engaged to Captain Lord Richard Li, a childhood friend, not coincidentally the man deemed most suitable by her mother.

But then the last of the Great Masters died, and within months the Naxid War began. Richard died at Magaria along with most of the Home Fleet, and Terza began to suspect that her old world was disappearing and might never return. The amber in which she'd been raised had melted in nuclear fire, and she and everyone else must learn to survive in this uncertain, newly revealed world.

Or die.

She suspected that if anyone could teach her to navigate this perilous new world, it would be the ambitious officer who had ridden to fame on the back of the empire's only victories over the Naxids. It would be Gareth Martinez.

The afternoon following her encounter with Martinez at the funicular terminal, she paid a visit to Roland Martinez in his office in the shambling old Shelley Palace that hosted the Martinez family. She found Roland formally dressed, as he was later in the day attending the wedding of his sister to Oda Yoshitoshi.

"Lord Roland," she said, "I want to marry your brother."

Roland looked at her in grave surprise, and his eyes went to the white mourning ribbons in her hair, worn for Terza's fiancé who had died at First Magaria, the battle that made Caroline Sula famous.

"Very interesting," Roland said. "I wish you every possible success."

"You're going to have to make my father do it," Terza said. "He'll never allow it unless he's forced, and you're the only person who can force him."

"That . . . will be delicate," Roland said.

Roland had loaned Lord Chen the fortune that he needed, after the devastation of war, to keep himself and his shipping empire afloat. Adding Terza as a new condition to the loan was dangerous, but she thought Roland, if he were anything like his brother, had the steel to do it.

"Another thing," Terza said. "No one can know this is my idea."

Roland was happy to concede that, and happier still to move fast. Within days, Terza was married to Gareth Martinez and spending blissful days and nights in a suite at the Hotel Boniface with her new husband. He had been stunned by the speed of the engagement, but he wasn't blind to its advantages: a link with one of the great High City families, a father-in-law on the Fleet Control Board, and Terza's aunt Michi, who would take him aboard her flagship as her tactical officer. The marriage had assured his professional future.

He didn't know Terza's part in the marriage plot, and he viewed her as a victim of his brother's scheming. He was solicitude itself. A thoughtful partner, a caring lover who could set her nerves aflame with a mere stroke of his hand.

She never bothered to inquire what had become of Sula.

In marrying Gareth Martinez she found a freedom she'd never expected. Her friends looked at her with mixed compassion and regret—the Chen heir forced into marriage with a provincial half-barbarian. But being with Gareth gave her permission to do any number of things: to invent a life independent of the Chen family, to occupy herself with work and politics, and—when threatened—to fight for her life and those of her children.

Martinez had told her before the marriage that he wanted a child as soon as possible. Possibly this was at Roland's urging, to make sure that a Martinez fathered the next Chen heir, but it fit in smoothly with Terza's own plans. Any child would be, in effect, a hostage for Martinez's good behavior.

After the final battle of the war, at Naxas, Martinez and Sula were sent back to Zanshaa, each in command of a warship. Their proximity set alarm bells ringing in Terza's skull. She readied herself to counter any backsliding on Martinez's part—she met him on the very day he landed, young Gareth in her arms, and as he gazed in rapture at their son, Terza glanced over his shoulder to see Sula's devastated expression—after which Caroline Sula got into her car and sped away. Terza had made her masterstroke and won the game.

Yaling was born during the peace, another hostage.

Before Second Shulduc, Terza had been appalled when her aunt Michi appointed Sula as Martinez's tactical officer. Not only were they in the same fleet, they were in the same ship, a dangerous proximity with barely a bulkhead separating their sleeping cabins. Her friends—their schadenfreude undisguised—warned her that the two were growing far too intimate.

Terza gathered her two hostages and planned for the battle of her life, but all her worry and all her preparation turned out to be unnecessary—Martinez himself dismissed Sula, sent her off on an errand in command of a miscellaneous collection of ships, and then he'd told Terza that he would like them to have another child.

Another hostage. Relieved, Terza was only too ready to comply.

Sula had no business interfering with Terza's marriage, which—without Sula—would have been perfect. Terza still wanted Martinez as much as she had the day she met him. He was a devoted father, a considerate and thoughtful partner, and a lover who could turn her insides to molten lava with a mere touch.

And now, with the marriage to Eveleth Saïd, Sula was conceding defeat. Terza wanted to dance and kick up her heels.

She rose from her chair and gazed out into the brown, withered garden where, years ago, she had met the man she wanted and now so thoroughly possessed.

Everything in her life, she thought, was as perfect as perfect could be.

# APPENDIX

## DRINK LIKE A PEER

My friend, the author and mixologist Terry Boren, has created two original cocktails based on my characters, the Blue Gredel and the Lady Sula. It seems only fair that I share these with my readers.

(There already exists a nineteenth-century cocktail called the Martinez. For the sake of completeness, I include the recipe below.)

### The Blue Gredel

This refreshing cocktail features a transformation that emulates that of Gredel herself.

2 ounces gin, either Empress 1908 or any gin colored with B'Lure Flower Extract
basil leaf
¾ ounce limoncello mixed with lemon juice
2 dashes orange bitters

1.  Measure the gin into a rocks glass, then add ice to taste.

2.  In a separate glass, muddle the basil leaf, then add the limoncello mixture and the orange bitters.

3.  Add the limoncello mixture to the gin and stir. Watch Gredel transform into someone new, someone born to the purple!

### The Lady Sula

In my opinion, this complex and luxurious cocktail is a master-piece. It even gets me to drink rye whiskey, which I normally don't care for.

Luxardo cherries, with their juice
2 ounces rye whiskey
½ ounce Averna
½ ounce cold press coffee
½ ounce dry sherry
Black walnut bitters

Rim a coupe or martini glass with Luxardo cherry juice. To an ice-filled shaker, add the whiskey, ½ oz. each Averna, coffee, sherry, and one or two drops black walnut bitters. Shake, then strain into the prepared glass. Garnish with a Luxardo cherry.

### The Martinez

This cocktail is first recorded in an 1884 bartending manual and is the direct ancestor of both the martini and the Manhattan.

1½ ounces gin (for true nineteenth-century flavor, use Old Tom gin)
1½ ounces sweet vermouth
¼ oz Luxardo cherry juice
2 dashes Angostura bitters
Orange or lemon twist, for garnish

Pour the gin, vermouth, cherry juice, and bitters into a mixing glass with ice. Stir. Strain into a martini glass or coupe and add garnish.

Cheers!

—wjw

ABOUT THE AUTHOR

*New York Times* bestselling author Walter Jon Williams has been
nominated repeatedly for every major science fiction award. He
lives near Albuquerque with his wife.

# ALSO BY WALTER JON WILLIAMS

**A Novel of the Praxis, Volume 2**
## Fleet Elements

Following *The Accidental War*, the second book of a brand-new series set in the Praxis—an epic mix of space opera and military science fiction, from a grand master of science fiction.

**A Novel of the Praxis: Volume 1**
## THE ACCIDENTAL WAR

Set in the universe of his popular and critically acclaimed Dread Empire's Fall series—a tale of blood, courage, adventure, and battle in which the fate of an empire rests in the hands of a cadre of desperate exiles.

**DREAD EMPIRE'S FALL:**
## CONVENTIONS OF WAR

Now in trade paperback, the climactic final episode of the Dread Empire's Fall trilogy—what started with *The Praxis* and *The Sundering* comes to the brilliant conclusion in Walter Jon Williams's epic space adventure.

**DREAD EMPIRE'S FALL:**
## THE SUNDERING

Following *The Praxis*, Walter Jon Williams's critically acclaimed mix of space opera and military science fiction, the conflict grows for the fate of humanity...and the universe.

**DREAD EMPIRE'S FALL:**
## THE PRAXIS

A young Terran naval officer, Lt. Gareth Martinez is the first to recognize the insidious plot of the Naxid—the powerful, warlike insectoid society that was enslaved before all others—as the interstellar battle begins against a merciless foe whose only perfect truth is annihilation.